Hidden Realities

T. B. Prowting

Hidden Realities
T.B. Prowting

ISBN 9781914615634

A CIP catalogue record for this book
is available from the British Library.

Published 2023 Tricorn Books,
Treadgolds
1 Bishop Street,
Portsmouth PO1 3DA

Hidden Realities

Acknowledgements

Hidden Realities published by Tricorn Books in association with the author, Mr T. B. Prowting. Book cover design by Mr Dan Bernard, Creative Director at Tricorn books. Book marketing by Gail Baird, Marketing Director at Tricorn Books; editor and proof reader Liz Bourne.

Historical research and book cover photographs by Mr and Mrs Adrian and Shannon Abbott in association with the author Mr T. B. Prowting.

Contents

Chapter 1
Letter to my Father

It all began on 24th January 1971 to be exact, when my father received a letter from a gentleman who wanted to know if the two of them could be related in some way. Back then it was harder to trace family links, with no internet to look back into the history of your ancestors. More leg work was required then, so it could be quite a shock to receive a letter out of the blue from someone you didn't know, but who held the same surname as yourself.

It is also true that tracing relations in family trees is very time consuming and tended to be carried out by, may I say, the more mature person. Those, who in their golden years were able to afford themselves more time and money to the project; and have already over the years gathered titbits of information regarding their ancestors that fit into the historic puzzle. With visits to libraries, churches, churchyards, record offices as starting points, searches delved deeper with the likes of the Kelly's and telephone directories to name just a few resources. Then there were the oral histories recorded by family elders who will often open up to the mature student of ancestry, who has placed them at ease in what could be considered by some to be an invasion of their privacy.

Even in today's standards, it was better to receive a letter from a stranger than have one turn up on your doorstep. So, to write first showed that this gentleman was genuine and would leave the recipient of the communication – in this case, my father – in the driving seat as what to do next.

When the letter arrived, I was in my early twenties, newly married and working for myself as a plastering contractor. While it was a hectic time for me, I knew that Dad would tell me all about the letter when he was ready. He did not rush headlong into things; patience, he said, was a virtue and would often remind me when I was keen to go like a bull at a gate into things. He would often ask me what's the rush and that thing would still be there tomorrow.

My mother, on the other hand, was a bit of a sceptic and looked upon the arrival of the letter as some form of scam which must have a catch to it. She told my father he should leave well alone and forget it. That was a natural reaction Mum had to things she was not sure about and she was not a person to push the boundaries of her comfort zone. Mum also worried if any of our family attempted to exceed beyond the social norm, until that is the new project or interest proved to be a success and was nothing to worry about after all. As it is often said, sometimes taking the first step is the hardest!

However, regarding the mysterious letter, I got the impression that deep down she wanted to know what may unfold if Dad just threw caution to the wind and wrote back to the gentleman. But with the uncertainty of opening a can of worms for the family, the letter became the topic of conversation for a few months. We all had an opinion – my sister wanted Dad to write back and find out more about the person, whereas my brother was not as interested. The final decision was Dad's to make, and we told him that when he was ready to do something about the letter, we would be happy to help.

Chapter 2
Fighting Asthma

I had a very good relationship with Dad. Not only was he good father to my siblings and I, but he was also a devoted husband who worked hard to make sure our family had all we needed. In my early life, I needed more of his attention than my siblings because I suffered with asthma, a horrid disease that made breathing so difficult, often striking without warning. The need to stay as calm as possible when each debilitating attack started was paramount. My dad's calm disposition was so important during these horrendous episodes and was critical for keeping me calm as each attack took hold.

I would try not to panic as my eyes felt like they would explode from their sockets, as I gasped for breath thinking the next could be my last, my chest becoming so tight to the point of almost passing out. Each attack was the same and had to take its course with the constant coughing up of what lay on my chest. The driving force for needing to spit out the blockage in my airways and trying not swallow which could result in choking. As it was, I felt I was suffocating and could not inhale properly, even through my nose. Often, I became speechless throughout the whole attack, unable to communicate my fear as my body was burning and soaked in perspiration; worn out by this emotional repetitive horror that left me so frightened and totally reliant on the people around to help save me from these frightening and unpredictable attacks. Episodes that became too regular and would take you almost to the jaws of death and back. Then as my misty eyes began to clear somehow, I connected to my dad's kind brown eyes as I began to come round and the realisation that he had been with me throughout was such a safe feeling. Once again, Dad had helped me into recovery, something I will be forever grateful to him for.

Each attack seemed to last longer than the one before and always followed the same pattern. Developments in the research of asthma and its triggers were personal but all linked to an allergic reaction to something like a food product. Reaction to pollens or just the lack of good fresh air, whatever it was that you were sensitive, to needed to be identified. However, if you had an allergy to more than one thing, tests would have to be done. In my case I was injected over time with 52 possible substances I could be allergic to. Five small needles on the end of a round syringe, each needle with a different substance was injected into my arm. If any of them swelled up then I was allergic to it, and of the 52 things that I had been injected with, 48 had been identified as a problem for me.

They ranged from all sorts of things including dust, the fur from cats, dogs, rabbits and mice, as well as lipstick, hair spray and perfume – all things you would encounter on a day-to-day basis. With the development of testing came the education from doctors to asthmatics and family members as to what to do when an attack began. For instance, trying to keep a record of the events leading up to the attack and what triggered it if that was possible. But recording events was the last thing on everyone's mind when dealing with an asthma attack, as dying was a distinct possibility if you couldn't draw breath. The stress for everyone watching at that moment was unbearable. All remained at the mercy of circumstance, unable to help or do anything until breathing in and breathing out returned to normal and became the most wonderful thing to witness.

To see someone in that state renders you helpless and angry that you have no control over the situation unfolding in front of you. After each attack, Mum would place a cold compress around me to bring my body down to its normal temperature; she then gave me warm, freshly squeezed orange juice to sip. She would be in and out of the room when the attacks started and comfort my brother and sister. They did not like to see me in that state, nor did they fully understand what was happening. Mum, like my siblings, could not witness it all because it was too upsetting for her. After each attack, I was worn out and needed to sit and rest, Dad would sit with me and keep me calm as I could not sleep. I was too frightened that I may not wake up again, a thought that always made me shiver; but being sat with my Dad, knowing I was safe, meant everything to me. They were long nights for the two of us and during these times Dad told me tales about his grandfather and the farms he had worked on.

The stories my father told were from no particular timeline, just events that took place way back about my ancestors and the county events. Dad told the stories in the same passionate way they had been told to him by his grandfather, about the characters who all lived in the small Hampshire village of Durley, just a few miles from our home on the outskirts of Southampton. I had in fact been there before, so I was aware of the village even though I didn't know how to get there, given my age, and I think that's what made it so interesting when Dad told me the tales. So, with the seed having been sown as I eventually fell asleep from the exertions of the night, it was with the romantic thoughts of life on the village farms and my relations who worked on them tending the land and animals alike.

But the reality was that asthma would control my early life, and once a month I had to attend the local clinic. One appointment I had coincided with an attack I had a few days before a meeting with Doctor Stowell, the man that looked after my case. He had been concerned about my condition worsening but having seen the way I looked after the latest attack suggested to Mum that the best option for me would be to send me away to a place where he had sent other asthma sufferers, resulting in positive outcomes for most of the children.

He went on to explain that many asthmatic children may eventually grow out of the condition if they could live in an environment with plenty of fresh clean air. He also explained, looking mainly at me, that If I went away my health would improve and would hopefully help me get better as I grew much stronger. He said it would be strange in the beginning, but it was much needed.

Doctor Stowell asked me If I understood, and it was only for health reasons that would take me away from my family. This was the first time anyone had talked to me about my condition. I usually had to earwig in on what was being discussed by my mother and the doctor because I didn't want to miss anything that was said. I confirmed to the doctor that I understood what he was saying, but I was only just six years old, and I had never been away before except staying with my godparents with my siblings who did not live very far away. The doctor, after writing notes, told Mum the place he had in mind for me was in West Sussex – they called the homes Open Air Schools, situated either near the sea or in the heart of the countryside, and that the fresh air did wonders for children like myself. The place that I would go to was called Dedisham Farm. As soon as the doctor said the word 'farm' I began to relax about having to go away, as to live on a farm would be, I thought, wonderful and I could not wait to get home and tell my dad.

The doctor told Mum it would take about six to eight weeks to set up; he also told Mum he could hold off with the paperwork until she had a chance to talk things over with Dad. Mum said she could speak for them both and for the doctor to proceed with things as she and my father wanted what was best for me. On our way home, Mum said I should not worry; she and Dad would talk about things with me when he came home. Our conversation about my move did not last long as Dad asked me if I understood what was going to happen. Dad calmly told me it was in the best interest for my health and that was the only reason he would ever let me go. I told my father that I understood why I would have to go away, however, after the joy of being told by the doctor that I was to go to a farm a few hours had past and I was beginning to worry about what it would be like.

I told myself if I wanted to get better then I had to go, but I did ask Dad if I didn't like it could I come home, which rather put him on the spot. I was not sure why I even asked him, I suppose it was some sort of safety thing if it was not for me.

Of course, I was scared inside about going away but I was more scared of the asthma, so I would have to be brave and face the unknown. All Dad said was for me to try it, and that the family would visit whenever they were allowed and for me to trust everyone who was doing what was best for me. Of course, I trusted my parents completely and the doctor so eventually I became comfortable with the knowledge that very soon I would go to the Open Air School when the date was set.

Chapter 3
Marking Time

Until that time, I continued my schooling if I was able. My sister and I attended the local Church of England school. It was the last term before the summer holidays. We would walk each day with Mum and my brother from our prefabricated bungalow in Barnes Road. The walk took us past the green pasture fields where large cows grazed up close to hedgerow that ran parallel with the path. One of them would often put its head over the hedge that was higher than the pathway. I tried many times to jump up on the bank so I could touch one of the cows, but they were just out of reach and never phased by my attempts of affection.

It would not be long before the open fields would become land for new homes on estates that began to emerge and made each village closer to each other; also, our old prefab was no longer good enough for a dwelling anymore. I loved the old place it was very cosy; its big garden was secluded and where I always felt safe. However, you cannot stand in the way of progress, and, like many of the families in Barnes Road, our family were to move to a brand-new Rema home, a state-of-the-art concrete building put together like a kit, all set in place by big cranes. Progress indeed.

At the weekends in the summer, we would spend time with one of Mum's sisters and her husband, my Aunt Alva and Uncle George Wilber Sims. Uncle George would pick us up in his black Austin 7 car, Dad would sit in the front with my brother on his lap, my sister, Mum and I would sit in the back. Mum sat forward on the edge of the narrow back seat and my sister and I would sit back each side of her so we could all fit in. We would set off slowly in the car and would sing as we went along. 'My old mans a dustman' and 'Does your chewing gum lose its flavour on the bedpost overnight' were popular classics.

Our Aunt and Uncle lived in a wonderful old farmhouse in a place called West End about two miles from our home in Barnes Road. Uncle George Wilber's family had farmed much of the land surrounding the farmhouse for many years; in fields that rolled away into the distance where grazing animals could only be identified by their dark shapes silhouetted on the horizon where the land meets the skyline.

But now as more land was set aside for much needed housing, the farm was reduced in size. Fortunately, the farmhouse could never be sold for development because it had a preservation order placed upon it. For the time being, the farm buildings and orchard that were still intact would be the place where on Sundays at least, my brother and I would become farmers and play in the old redundant stables and pig sties that housed our imaginary horses and pigs. We would spend time in the massive barn that was full of tools and an old tractor that had seen better days. The barn also housed a small cart from another era, no longer useful as its wooden wheels stuck fast from inaction, and old chickens, who were no longer laying that would have been as tough as old boots to eat, were reprieved to live among the dust and grime, scratching about waiting to meet their end as old age crept up on them. Uncle George Wilber let them roam freely, the last remaining stock in what was once a crowded muddy farmyard where many cows moved slowly to the milking shed to be relieved of their daily contribution to the community, provided by the lush grasses they fed on, in what was part of the daily repetition that would keep the farm in business until the lands they fed upon became the primary source of income. But for two enthusiastic children it represented contentment to see this vision of the past and on a Sunday at least the old farm became alive again if only in our heads.

The farmhouse itself was beautiful. The oldest part was at the back just three rooms under a thatched roof. On entering through the back door into the very low-ceiling dining room, its thick old beams looked very sturdy, and their shape not uniformed, looking as if they had been cut and used straight from the tree.

A small window overlooked the cottage garden to the north and the external thatch overhang at the head of the window formed a soffit that ran around the outside of the old part of the cottage. To the left of the back door was a tiny kitchen that you would step up into, to access the sink and cooking area and to the right of the entrance one of two latched oak doors in the room, one on the west wall, opened into the bedroom of our cousin Michael.

Michael was someone we looked up to as he was a teenager, he was also very clever, and his hobby was woodwork. He could make anything and in his room was a white six-stringed guitar that he had made; and as he was older than my brother and me, he would often be out when we visited so we did not see a lot of him. Aunt Alva would let us have a go on the white guitar but told us to be sure we placed it back exactly in its place or Michael would know we had been trying to play with what was his pride and joy. But the urge to let loose and make a real noise on the guitar was too great and made us laugh as we each tried to strum it quietly. But that was impossible so reluctantly we put it back in its place and hoped that Cousin Mike never found out.

Back in the small dining room the latched door on the south wall took you to the front of the property. This was a two-storey newer addition and from a small hallway through a third latched door you would enter an inviting comfortable lounge. Its low ceiling was again exposing large oak beams that ran north to south; this time more uniformed in appearance indicating a more professional approach in the construction of the new addition. Proof indeed that regular profits from the farm enabled the family's rise in becoming a well-respected dynasty within the community. These sturdy beams were black in colour, painted to complement the cream decorated ceiling between them and blended in well with the white walls. This mixture of emulsions made the room look bright and homely.

A dark oak sideboard sat under one of two south-facing windows displaying photographs of winning animals sporting rosettes and badges, prizes of successful entries at county shows from yesteryear. A matching oak table and chairs were placed under the other window, both overlooking the neatly kept garden and lawn. Family photos adorned the walls and two-winged backed chairs, each with a small side table and footstool, were beside an open brick fireplace that indicated this was the place to relax. Against the west wall, a flight of open tread stairs leading up to a pair of double bedrooms and a small bathroom, neatly decorated. It was a delightful place, but sadly today it now sits hidden, surrounded by 19th-century homes built with no respect or any attempt to match the new with the old. Instead, just a narrow path separates the farmhouse from the intrusive newer homes that now stand where the orchards and outbuildings once were. High bushes and fencing hide this beautiful old building, only the upstairs windows can be seen from the road when I drive by; and like eyes, they look out, longingly following my gaze as if to recognise an old friend and beg me to come back and rescue it from its cramped existence and give it back its dignity.

The farmhouse was subject to a preservation order, but the developers made sure every inch legally available to them was taken from the farmhouse.

All houses have spirits that make you feel relaxed, and once connected the feeling never fades. Something you were once part of stays with you in your heart and mind as do the echoes of the people who made the moments there special. For us, we enjoyed afternoon teas on the lawn eating Aunt Alva's wonderful homemade cakes and sandwiches. Those halcyon days are gone but not forgotten.

Once a month on a Sunday my brother and I went with Uncle George to collect rents from people who lived in two properties owned by his family. Uncle George always looked very smart in his brown pinstripe suit, white shirt, red tie and shiny brown shoes. The look was finished with a dark brown trilby hat with a black band around it and he looked every inch the country gent. The first property we went to was not far from the farmhouse in West End. The man living there had worked at the farm, and although retired he remained in the house that was too big for one person. Still, after years of service, he would live out his days in the property that once housed him and his family. With his wife long since passed and his children moved on to pastures new, the man would mend bicycles for people as a sideline. He used the front room of the house as a workshop, a grubby curtain covering the whole of the front bay window, to hide the fact that a small business was carrying on there. Uncle George said the man worried that the tax man may find out what he was doing but from the road outside you could see a dim light behind the curtain that made it obvious work was carried out there. Surrounding the outside of the house many bikes were evidence that some form of business was going on. Also on the driveway was an old two-wheeled trundle cart, its shafts that once harnessed a pony leant forward, resting in the long grass now hosting summer weeds that crept up them. Two of the four shell boards where still in place on each side of the cart, the other two missing from the back and front like they would when the cart was in use holding more 'up muck'.

'Up muck' was good-quality manure and 'down muck' was not so good. By leaving off the shell boards, the trundle would move slowly, pulled by the pony around the lanes, and the rhythm of the pony's trotting would lose some of the unwanted down muck onto the road. Uncle George told us he would drive the trundle for miles and the fresh air would have been good for me – if such carts were still in use the smell of the dung combined with the fresh country air would do my condition the power of good. So, the trundle, redundant tractor and hay cart in the old barn at the farmhouse would be added to my imaginary farm where I had already imaginary chickens, pigs, cows and horses, of course all part of a young boy's dream.

From the house at West End, we would travel to the second property in the nearby village of Botley. We didn't stay long. Uncle George would pick up the rent, and we would be off to Durley where Uncle George's mother and sister had a smallholding. On the way, we stopped off at the Robin Hood public house, where Uncle George would have his lunchtime pint and bring my brother and me a glass of lemonade and a packet of Smiths crisps each. I remember each bag had a small blue bag of salt to shake onto the crisps that sometimes seemed soggy, but we soon polished them off anyway.

From the Robin Hood, we would drive down the hill to Ashton to the smallholding. After saying hello to Uncle George's mother and sister, my brother and I would have a good look around. At the back of the smallholding were badger sets; it was interesting to see the area. We had never seen a badger; however, you could see the marks in the sandy soil where they had been. Further on, at the foot of a hill, we could often see some large hares. They had big floppy ears and very long back legs that looked strange compared to their smaller front legs. According to our uncle, to catch one we should do what he did and chase the hare down the hill till it fell over its long back legs, then dive on it with a sack. However, if we got anywhere near them, they would all take off in different directions as they were so fast. I could not see how anyone could catch one. Uncle George was built for comfort and not speed, but all his yarns had an air of disbelief about them. The way he spoke in his soft Hampshire accent sounded so convincing to us back then; he could hold an audience telling his yarns, and I would not want the stories to end.

When Uncle George was ready to leave, he would call us to the cottage to say goodbye to his family. His mother always gave my brother and me a few sweets and commented on how well behaved we had been. She was a nice lady and very much a country person. I think that is why I liked her; she had worked hard all her life and was a fountain of knowledge regarding farming and the countryside. It was no wonder Uncle George knew so much about everything in the country. I regarded it my duty to remember all I learnt from him, and along with my father's stories handed down father to son, I would always be rich in knowledge that would stand me in good stead when my time came to work on the farm.

On leaving the smallholding, we drove back through Durley on the long winding road, taking us past fields on either side of the road, and I always wondered if these were any of the areas where my ancestors worked. On the route we travelled, Uncle George said he once found a sack of rope that had fallen off a tractor-trailer, and he opened the door of his car and scooped it up with his foot. Back then, car doors opened outward, front to back, apparently the rope came in very handy as did the sack. Each time we travelled along that long winding road through Durley, I would look ahead in the hope of spotting something so uncle could demonstrate his skills. But I never saw anything, and Uncle George somehow knew I was looking and would sit back in the driver's seat and laugh as we drove homeward. I knew it must be another yarn, but I would look anyway, just in case.

In early September 1956, at my monthly meeting with Doctor Stowell, he told us he had arranged for me to go away in October that year. Mum had the paperwork with her that she and Dad had signed agreeing to the terms. I remember feeling uneasy at the realisation that this was it, I was going away. I momentarily went through all sorts of emotions of wanting to go and not wanting to go, it was a strange feeling. I was too young to realise that my parents must have been going through the same emotions. If we all said what we felt right, then we all would have said, 'Don't go.'

Doctor Stowell handed Mother a list of things to take and told us that all new pupils were accepted at weekends. Visiting was every other Sunday, letters and parcels could be received, but phone calls were not encouraged. All parents would be contacted by the school if there was a problem with any of the children.

Despite an offer of a chaperone to escort the new intake with no charges involved to the parents, Mum told the doctor she had prearranged with my godparents to take us. I was glad Mother told him because the doctor spoke so very quickly. It was all repetition to him, I am sure. Still, for me hearing all this for the first time, I found it hard to take it all in. I didn't know how to feel about things and felt nothing no matter how hard I tried, I just felt an emptiness. The fact was I had to go. I would have no choice or say in the issue; I was only a child after all.

Before we had finished at the clinic, the doctor told my mother he thought it would be helpful if he made an appointment at the ear, nose and throat clinic at the South Hants Hospital in Southampton before I went away. He wanted me to have a procedure done to clear my nasal passages again; it was just one of many things I had to have done in my short life. None of them were comfortable and they all hurt me in some way. This procedure involved placing two thin metal tubes up my nostrils. They were connected to a machine. The nurse held me down in the chair from behind, pushing me downward, her hands one on each of my shoulders, which seemed a bit excessive the first time I had it done; but she had to hold me as still as possible because when a doctor started the machine, it started to pump out the mucus from my nose.

It was the most excruciating pain. The thin metal pins up my nose would get hot and scratched against bone. The whole procedure took about a minute but felt like much longer than that and the pain in my forehead was like eating ice cream too quickly and would last for quite a while afterwards. The nurse's firm robust actions were indeed necessary because your first thought when the machine started was to get the hell out of there as soon as possible. Also having it done a second time and knowing what they did was stressful to say the least; there was no easy way to do what they had to do, so you would just have to take what was coming and get over it.

When I had it done the first time, I was given a lead spitfire aeroplane with only one wing by the nurse. Mum was so upset having to watch me have that done, when we got outside, she snatched the plane from me in disgust and threw it hard down into the gutter and down the drain. She pulled me into her side as we walked to get the bus home. Her warm hands stroked my head to relieve the pain for me. The procedure made little difference to my breathing through my nose. It took away my ability to smell certain things and was a complete waste of time, but it could have helped. I needed all the help I could get at the time, so I went along with anything and would be used as a guinea pig, if you like, to try any new system that could have had positive results for all sufferers, so it was worth the effort I suppose.

Mum received a letter soon after I had it done with the date. I was to go to Sussex the second weekend in October 1956, so now I could count the days down for the impending move.

In September 1956 we moved with other families from the prefabs to the brand-new houses on the Thornhill Estate, situated on the east side of Southampton. The roads were named after famous poets, in keeping with the streets on the old estate that abutted the new one, joined by a main road that ran through the two estates. As it turned out, our new house was less than a mile from the prefab as the crow flies on a road called Byron Road, a continuation of Byron Road on the old estate where Mum was brought up.

She lived in Spencer Road just off Byron Road, where our grandfather, Charles William, still lived alone after the death of our grandmother, Lucy Jane. My grandmother had passed away before I was born, but Mum would often talk about her when recalling her early years at Spencer Road. Mother told us Lucy Jane had died of cancer and had suffered much at the end. Mum was one of four daughters and had one brother. Lucy Jane was born on the Isle of Wight in Freshwater, her family moved to the mainland when she was a girl, and her father was a lifelong seaman and her mother fostered children in Southampton as well as having a boarding house that was run by Lucy Jane's sister, our Aunt Florrie.

Grandfather Charles William was born in Kent. His family were confectioners and master bakers and he and his brother followed in their father's footsteps. Both brothers, when qualified, went to sea working on the big liners. They would make fabulous wedding cakes for people on board as well as creating delicate dishes for the rich and famous to mark special occasions. Charles William also served on the Olympic, the Titanic's sister ship. In World War One, the Olympic was used as a troop ship and Charles William, along with other crew members, received the defence medal for their contribution to the war effort. Charles William's sea life could never be classed as your average seaman, bringing both the danger and excitement you only hear about in stories. His brother moved to America and owned a restaurant in New York. Mum often talked about him with her father, and I would constantly earwig in on grown-up's exchanges. If something was not for my ears, Mother just mouthed the words to whoever she was talking to. But having so much time off school, earwigging became an exciting pastime. I would hear some big words even though I had no idea what they meant; it relived the monotony of endless days at home not able to go out.

Before his retirement, our grandfather ran a small café within the Southampton Docks called the Provadore. It catered for people working in the Docks and visitors who came to meet passengers back from holiday cruises.

The Docks was a hive of industry. I remember how everything looked so big back then as children. We were taken to Mayflower Park next to the dockside, a popular place for people to watch the big liners come in and depart to far-off seas. The long loading shed next to Mayflower Park, known as dock 101, was where Dad worked. From 1946, aged 26, he worked as a checker, but before that he had been at sea from the age of 13. Dad would share stories of sea life, and how he had been around the world three times before the age of 16. Working first as a laundry boy, then working his way up to other jobs that paid well.

The extensive loading sheds stretched the whole width of Mayflower Park; the road that ran beside the loading sheds had railway lines inserted into it that went all the way to the dockside. Great cranes, grey in colour, lowered jigs down into the cargo holds and then emerged with all manner of things, to be distributed onto waiting lorries and long wooden goods trucks pulled by impressive steam train engines that shunted along pulling its load on rails. The steam engines would cross the main road after large white gates had been opened across the main street, holding up the traffic to enable the long line of rattling rail trucks to be pulled onward to distant towns on the mainland. Other large steam engines pulled posh railway carriages bringing people from the cruise ships to the mainland rail station at Terminus terrace. At the terrace, people either met their connection home or stayed in the world-famous Great Western Hotel where many films and singing stars stayed, such as Laurel and Hardy. Their visits were well documented and shown on television newsreels and enhancing the hotel's already famous reputation.

It didn't take long for us to settle into our new home. It was interesting to see who our new neighbours would be; many moving from the old prefabs and of course some had chosen to move to other estates. But many of the people we were familiar with moved to Byron Road, and it was not long before a new community began to emerge. As one by one sheds went up if not all at once. Soon after, paths were put down, lawns laid, and plants and shrubs placed next to the low chain-link fence that separated each garden that would in time give each home more privacy while still being part of what turned out to be a genuinely caring community for many years.

Chapter 4
Pastures New

The date was set for me to go away. With the paperwork done and bags packed, on the second Sunday morning in October 1956 my parents and I set off with my godparents and drove to the Open Air School in West Sussex. I sat quietly as the car pulled away from Byron Road past my grandfather's home on Spencer Road that looked different from inside the vehicle. It was not long before we reached the countryside, passing open fields to our left that seemed to stretch for miles; the empty spaces to our right began to decrease as the road took us closer to the coastline where trees leaned inland, bent by the prevailing strong winds. Then as the road worked its way back inland, the coastline became more distant to us.

We reached our destination around lunchtime and left the main highway driving onto a long gravel road; between fenced-in fields on the right, sheep grazed uninterested by our passing car and to the left two horses looked over and began walking to the fence. One of them, a grey, seemed to make eye contact with me as we passed while still chewing grass. As I looked back at the horses, they dropped their heads once more and continued to feed and maybe made a note of the new arrival. The gravel road and the sight of the sheep and horses made my arrival at the school more relaxed for me because, the longer we had driven the more apprehensive I became, wondering at each bend in the road how much further away from home we would be going. I thought to myself how I would ever get home if I had to, it was a daunting feeling but seeing the animals and knowing I would see them again helped put a new prospective on things. This comfort made me braver if you like, and ready to face the unknown because as a six-year-old being so far away from home, anything that would make the churning in my stomach disappear I would latch onto. It helped me through the loneliness I encountered and educated me in the art of coping with solitude that would eventually become commonplace. It was solitude and isolation that taught me that I need never do anything or go anywhere if I did not choose to. It could to some be considered reclusive, but it is never that, it's a safety device and means you choose When, Where and How you do something and that it is safe to trust.

The gravel road led to a wide gateless entrance into a car park in front of a big house that looked very impressive. We all got out of the car, my uncle took my things from the boot, whilst Mum held my hand and Dad placed a hand on my shoulder, both to reassure me. They knew I would be looking for reasons not to stay, and that fear sometimes got the better of me. They had to be firm and act as if everything was fine while thinking they didn't want to leave me. It was difficult for all of us, we had to pretend that all was well when it was not; we had this thing called asthma, that would rule the roost whenever it chose to. So, we hid our fear and made our primary focus on how to defeat it.

We all walked into the reception area of the house and were greeted by a slim dark-haired lady who introduced herself as the manager and welcomed us all to Dedisham Farm. Then we were taken to a large room at the back of the house where we sat at a long table while another lady brought us all a welcome cup of tea after our trip. After which my parents and I went with the manager to meet Matron who took us on to the bedroom that would become part of my home for the foreseeable future.

The bedroom housed four beds, one in each corner of the room with a matching wardrobe. I was given the bed that ran against the north wall under a window that was partly open. The head of the bed was against the west wall. An open fireplace in the middle of the west wall was lit, surrounded by a large fire guard. In the centre of the room stood a table with plenty of books, pens, pencils and drawing material placed upon it and four chairs were tucked neatly underneath. My mother helped me unpack while my father talked with the matron. When we were ready, we all walked back to the big room and joined my godparents.

The matron showed us out into the garden where many other children sat around with parents and friends; it was difficult for me to look around as I felt so out of place not knowing anyone. So, I did what I always did, and blocked everyone out. It's easy to do if you look long enough at one thing and focus on just that, then your eyes water and become misty, not with tears just a moistness to hide behind, until you felt settled and hoped no one would approach you until you felt confident enough in the new surroundings. Shyness gets you that way when you're a child and a long way from home where living in your head becomes a way of life.

At 3pm people started to move out of the garden and made their way to the car park. Matron told me that when I had said goodbye to my family, I was to meet her back in the reception hall. My parents shook hands with Matron, and we walked outside to where the car was parked; my godparents said their goodbyes to me, and my mum and dad knelt and embraced me. There were no tears just a warm embrace that was enough, any words and I would not want them to go. We all knew if there were tears it would have ruined the progress we had all made in excepting that being separated from each other was the only way I would get well and I understood that even at my tender age. My parents had to be brave as well, all the problems I had healthwise was a worry for them.

I found out when I was much older that I had an older brother, who unfortunately had died one week after he was born, Melvin was his name. He was a full-term birth but was taken from Mum as soon as he was born, and she never saw him again. This was a tragedy for my parents, and that is why I am proud of myself for not making a fuss when things were hard. I was also proud of them for going through everything with me after what they went through with Melvin. He was referred to by my mother as her beautiful boy and Mum marked his birthdate in her diary every year.

My parents got into the car, and I watched as they drove away. Each member of my family waved a hand out of the car window till the car was out of sight and I returned to the reception as instructed by Matron. She told me as we walked to my room that I must rest on my bed for one hour, then when a bell rang, I should assemble with the other children to have our tea. Rest time was usually after lunch but on a Sunday, because of the visitors, rest time was taken later.

When we reached my room, the three other boys were resting on their beds. Matron informed them of my name and collectively they all raised a hand and smiled. I returned the compliment and climbed upon to my bed to rest. One end of the bed was raised up on blocks to help keep your air passages open at night, and the bed, while not being a cot, did have sides, one of which was pulled up every night to stop you falling out. Given the angle of the bed, my bed sheets were on top of an orange rubber TB sheet, the smell of which I have never forgotten and often can somehow still smell it. The clean white sheets would often slip because of the TB sheets, and you would often wake up in the morning crumpled in a ball having dropped to the lower end of the bed in your sleep. The windows were kept slightly open all night in all weathers to maintain the flow of air; the fire in our room was kept going all the time and at night some sort of herb was rubbed into a brick that was placed on the fire. The aroma was very helpful if you felt chesty or had difficulty breathing, which I am glad to say was not that often.

But while I still had attacks, they were never as bad as when I was at home. It was Matron and her staff who educated us all in the ways to counteract an attack, what to do and what not to do and never to panic or worry if an attack started if one did; then you had it right where you were not rushing for help as help was always on hand and in time you could recognise the events that would lead up to an attack. And I soon became more confident at handling my condition. Matron, and her staff did everything to help us all.

Our days were structured in such a way that we were always doing something positive. Everyone had to join in. If there were any weaker children then the others would help them. We did everything as quickly as the slowest person among us, we learnt to look out for each other even though most of us didn't know each other's names. That didn't matter because there was not that much communication between six-year-old children and under; it was a question of following the matron's instructions and her helpers. We followed them like sheep and felt safe in doing so because we needed them. They had a great responsibility for our well-being, and every child was grateful to them, and that's why the people at the farm would remain in our minds as we grew up, thankful for the confidence they instilled in us all.

Each day at the farm began with us being ushered by the helpers while still in our night clothes and dressing gowns to the bathrooms. There was nothing private about this and if you had regarded your ablutions to be something sacred then that belief would soon be shattered. The boy's bathroom had a row of urinals on the left side of the room; a long double line of sinks down the centre and eight low-standing toilet cubicles with half doors on the right-hand wall. At the back of the room, double doors led to a big communal shower room. On entering the bathroom you were asked if you wanted a number one and told to line up on the left if that was your chosen relief before showering. However, if you were unfortunate enough to want what I always knew as 'number twos' you were in for a shock. Number twos at the farm were referred to by a large lady who would look down the line of children and ask at the top of her voice if there was anyone for "Big jobs". If there was anyone for big jobs she would lead them to one of the available cubicles on the right of the room. I have always taken my time to reflect when carrying out that particular relief and ponder on what the day ahead may hold; but at the farm that was not possible because the lady in charge of 'Big jobs' would walk up and down the row of cubicles, sticking her head over the door like a large dray horse peering over its stable door and scrutinising as to how much longer you would be. So, if you wanted to go when you went in the cubicle, you didn't once you sat down and were disturbed before you could muster a motion. You may have succeeded in having a number one while in the cubicle, but it was not really worth the embarrassment.

After washing our hands, we went into the shower room where two helpers took our night clothes and sent us through the showers after which they would help you to dry yourself. Everyone was issued with fresh underwear and clothes for the day, none of the clothes were your own, they were all items that had been collected from the local community for the home. The clothes were not brand new but in very good condition and the only things you kept of your own were your shoes and slippers; your own clothes were kept in your wardrobe and used when you had visitors. Everything was well organised by the matron's nurses and helpers. After the early morning experience of the bathroom it was time for breakfast. This was taken in the first room I had been to where my family and I had been given cups of tea on our arrival.

At breakfast time the room was set out with both long and round tables that seated six children around each one, and behind two big shutters at the back of the room was a well-equipped kitchen where all the food was freshly cooked. The only noise in the room were the sounds of the helpers moving about the room bringing food and hot beverages to each table. We had a choice of cereals or porridge to begin with, followed by our main breakfast that consisted of eggs on toast – either scrambled or poached. Toast was readily available from a toast rack that was in the middle of the table, accompanied by fresh juices in beakers that the helpers would top up for us. Twice a week grilled sardines on toast was served, but other breakfasts, including beans on toast with a sausage, or probably my favourite of all omelettes, were available. The meals were very filling so there were never any complaints about the food.

After breakfast we had the opportunity to use the toilets again and the children who had to have medical attention would go with one of the nurses to Matron's room. The rest of the children remained in the breakfast room and waited till everyone came back ready to go on our morning walk.

As the days went by, I began to feel more at home and confident that I would settle in. I made a mental note of who was who and what they were responsible for; it was clear that Matron oversaw the nurses and that the manager sorted out the helpers. There were also two teachers and two assistants that took lessons every afternoon, they were the main people I would meet, and I knew that if I was happy with who was looking after me it would enhance my state of well-being.

So it was from an early age that I learnt to read people and their body language; eyes can tell you everything about if you should trust someone or not. It is said by some that we should trust till we are betrayed, this is all very well in an adult's world, but not in the world of children who are told not to talk to strangers. It's the first thing a responsible parent teaches their children so just because you are in an institution, does not mean the rules should be any different. Adults have to earn the respect of children, and children have to earn the respect of adults – it's a two-way thing.

Mid-morning, we had to have cod liver oil from a spoon or capsule form and were encouraged to drink milk. I always had the small red capsule. I was not fond of milk or having a spoonful of cod liver oil – it was horrible stuff!

When everyone was ready, we put on outdoor shoes and coats and went for a long walk. This was a daily event. The walk started at the back of the house – its garden backed onto the farmyard and two large barns, one containing straw and the other hay, could be accessed via doors from the farmhouse garden.

When I had been at the home for a few weeks and got my bearings, during the free time in the afternoon I liked to sit up in the straw barn and watch what went on at the farm. The dust from the straw never affected me at all as it did not linger in the air, but the dust from the hay would start me wheezing so I kept out of the hay barn.

Our morning walk began from the straw barn, and we walked down a rough track at the side of a massive field where the straw was grown. When we reached the end of that area we had to cross over a river. Two large railway sleepers formed a bridge at the narrowest point between the banks and we would take care as we walked across the bridge. At that point, the water was very shallow but to us children we looked upon it as a daring event. The pathway continued from the bridge and went into the woods. From the low-hanging tree branches, bunches of dead jet-black crows tied with string hung upside down. I had never seen anything like this before, the birds just looked as if they were asleep. Their beaks were big and their feathers looked oily, and you could see different colours when the sunlight was shining on them. We were told that the dead crows were warnings to others and would stop them nesting close to the field. It did not prevent them from going on the restricted areas; they would swoop down from the high treetops and make a screeching sound as they landed like small planes onto the field. I am not sure they would ever be defeated no matter how many dead ones the farmer hung from the low branches.

The pathway through the wood was interesting, and we all made our way back over the small bridge into the big field, this time walking back up the other side that took us past the field I had seen the horses in when I arrived. The two horses I had seen were standing at the gate, both moving their heads from side to side as we approached them. One of the helpers stopped and told us that we should never go near the horses, and we should stay behind a smaller fence that was about 15 feet from the main fence that kept the horses in. She explained that the dust from the horses' coats could affect us, and that even the wind blowing against the horses caused the dust to circle around them. We could of course look at the horses and enjoy talking to them, but we should never go near them.

The wind did blow strongly in West Sussex, but it was good to be breathing in the fresh Sussex air that was so good for your state of mind. The only thing I had to get used to was being away from home, I embraced everything we did with vigour and followed each instruction I received to the letter. Such was my determination to adjust to my new way of life; however, I did sometimes have pangs of home sickness. My stomach ached when anxiety set in, mainly at night when darkness fell and I thought about home. I felt weak and would turn my face to the wall and began to cry; it was a horrible feeling and only sleep could make it eventually go away. As much as I loved the things we did, the fact I was feeling stronger meant I missed my family so much that I just wanted to go home. The staff knew the children suffered with homesickness and there was not a lot you can do because, when it creeps upon you just a passing thought of home or of something someone once said brings forward this overpowering feeling of being lost, rootless in fact. You find yourself trying to remember the faces of the ones you love but they will not come into your head, a head that is aching at that point in time.

Momentarily you belong to no one, you are in an empty room; your mind has nothing to remember, and memories of past events abandon you leaving you in a wilderness that only sleep can banish. Yet when morning comes, and you emerge from under the sheets all seems well again. It's as if the spirit of the Lord who surrounds us all has protected another sacred child. From the allied combination of symptoms that come attached to the primary sickness, there seems to be no escaping its accompanying black cloud that shadows you 24/7.

After our daily walk we returned to the dining room where we had sandwiches for our lunch. Nothing too grand as our main meal was in the evening. After lunch we had to lie down on our beds till the bell went, I didn't think sleeping at that time of day was that easy, however when you get used to a regular rest period you look forward to it. After our rest we would have afternoon class, nothing too difficult, there were no budding academics among us, and the teachers identified that early on. So many of us had either missed lots of school or had not even started because of our delicate condition, so we would learn to read and carry out simple arithmetic. We were asked to draw and paint with water colours and display our artistic skills; to be artistic would in the future cover the fact you had been so poorly educated because of the lack of schooling and when you did attend school trying to catch up with the whizz kids was impossible.

Modern education would not wait for the slow learners and preferred for you to be placed in classes a year behind that of your age group. So, if you were artistic or good with your hands then you could concentrate on the skills you had and bluff your way through the rest to cover up your lack of education that actually became an art in itself. The education we would have was to learn about Mother Nature, the animals and the changing seasons; we would go walking in all weathers to get stronger and took care of other people. We would get to what was mapped out for us in this world at our own pace but first we needed to be well enough to do it. People who ran homes like the one in Sussex along with the NHS would make sure that we did.

At 5.30 pm each evening we had to wash our hands and faces, change any dirty clothing, and have our evening meal. Dinner was always something nice like cottage pie with a crispy potato topping and a crusty base, it was piping hot and all homemade that afternoon. We often had fish of some sort in lots of oil – someone must have said they liked oil at some time, we had been told it was good for our bones so we soaked it up with bread that would fill us up. Puddings were just as good and were a nice finish to the meal. At 7 pm each evening we had to get ready for bed. This involved another collective visit to the bathroom, this time not so frantic. We had to shower and wash our hair properly and make ready for bed. We could sit on our beds for half an hour and then before it was lights out, we were encouraged to thank the Lord for our day – I always did anyway. At home my siblings and I went to morning Sunday school and while I was not into God, I have always believed in a greater power spiritually wise and liked the stories we had on a Sunday and, given my condition, I needed all the help I could possibly get Godly or otherwise.

At the end of October, I had my first fortnightly visit from home. Mum and Dad came with my godparents and brought my brother with them. It was good to see them all, I had missed my brother terribly, and after showing everyone around I was taken out to an old cottage tearoom where Mum took my photo.

She and Dad said I was looking well, we all had sandwiches with cream cakes from a special glass stand, it was a lovely afternoon. Still, soon over when we went back to the farm, I had butterflies in my stomach at the thought that they would soon be going home without me. It seemed that the first two weeks at the farm that I had worked so hard to try and fit in should have culminated in me going home with them. I felt better and may have looked well, but inside I begged them to get me out of the place. But the reality was that I was not well enough, and I knew the home was second best!

Right then second best was best for my health, if not necessarily for me, and to see everyone go again and again was never easy. I never said anything but if they had not come to visit, I could have coped better with being away. It meant I had to start all over again after each visit and suffer this repetitive anxiety and not tell anyone how it made me feel, and by appearing to take everything in my stride did me no favours at all. I was never as strong as everyone thought I was, I hid behind a mask to please others. But I wore it well, and in time I began to lose the feeling of being wanted anyway; it was much easier to be detached.

I still loved everyone the same as I had always done, but when I was away in the end, I was someone else, numbed with an ability to not feel anything. I hated asthma and being homesick and so did many other boys. Our battle was with our sickness. It could make us small boys cry and debilitate us, it could take us to the jaws of death and back, but it would never defeat us. We all had our own way of dealing with it the best way we could, and it hardened us. Asthma, they say, never leaves you nor does homesickness. You may wear the armour against them for all time, but you are never free, even with modern-day medication. It's still loitering in some dark corner; it is just a question of how strong you can get as quickly as you can to counteract its effect on you. You may outgrow it, as the doctors say, but it will be lurking when you reach old age and you begin to lose your energy. So, you must live your life with vigour and try and achieve as much as you can. The home installed in me at the tenderest of age to take each day as it comes and thank the Lord at the end of each one.

Christmas 1956 and we were allowed to go home for the holiday. I was looking forward to seeing all my family members again, I had missed them all, but I had become accustomed to life in the home and in a strange way I felt nervous about going. It was a funny situation to be in when I wanted desperately to go home because I was homesick when I could not, and now when I would rather stay where the better air was, I had to go home. It was very confusing because I would have preferred to stay at the farm till I was well, Christmas really did not mean that much to me, particularly if I could not breathe properly back in Southampton. However, I would have to do as I was told. If I told my father what I wanted to do he would have let me I was sure of it, he would understand, but I could not upset my Mum by saying I did not want to come home until I was well enough. She and Dad had done everything for me so I could not, nor would I ever upset them by telling them how I really felt. If I had to breathe in the bad air of Southampton that was vastly different to that in West Sussex then I had to go along with it. I had learnt in the short time I had been away how to cope with my condition and knew not to panic if an attack began.

I arrived home two days before Christmas having been picked up by my godparents. The nine weeks I had been away I noticed a vast difference in our new home. My father had been busy in the garden; he had planted small privet bushes around the garden that in time would make a nice hedge. Mum said that her brother and his wife, my Aunt Estella and Uncle Ramon, had rode their bikes, with the small cuttings in sacks tied on their backs. Dad had made an area to grow vegetables at the end of the garden, and to the right had planted flowerbeds ready for the spring.

Inside the house, Mum had been busy too. She made new curtains and nets for the windows in each room, new linen and blankets had been brought for all the beds, and we had a new table and chairs in the well-equipped kitchen. The house looked really nice, it was brand new, and my parents deserved it. They had started off living in two rooms in a bungalow next door to the Salvation Army church in Northeast Road in the Sholing area of Southampton. Mum said she wanted a nice place for Dad when he was on leave from the Army. Mum and her sisters worked in the aeroplane factory at Hamble Le Rice, making parts for the spitfires by day and at night she was the air raid warden for the Sholing area of Southampton. She made sure everyone had observed the blackout rules and helped people after the air raids. Mum received the defence medal for the work she did in the war effort, so my parents had worked hard to achieve what they had, along with the new home that they would eventually take up the offer from the council to buy as did many other families that made a move to the new estate.

Christmas of 1956, the first in the house. We had lots of family coming, which would become the norm for years to come. The family parties became legendary, everyone did their party piece, and my mother was the catalyst in all family events organising everything and making sure everyone was catered for. While I was home, my dad talked about how I was getting on at the home, and of the good report by the matron as to my progress. He said he was pleased things had been going well and how it was a big thing that someone so young had to be away from home. I told him I liked it at the farm and would stay as long as I had to. It was good to talk to him about my progress, he understood fully that even at my young age I had to grow up quickly because of my condition, and not having a normal childhood made me appear to be older than my years. My father was a wise man and listened to everything I said about how I felt about the home and how much better I felt being there, and how breathing in the fresh country air made me feel safe. I told him I did get homesick, and he told me he knew what that was like because he had suffered with it when he first went away to sea when leaving school at 13. He understood it could be frightening for someone of my age. Our conversation helped me a lot, I had been worried about telling him how I felt as I didn't want him to think I was ungrateful for thinking that way.

To be able to tell Dad everything meant so much to me he said we should not say anything to my mother who would surely not understand and take it to heart. Being able to tell my father everything stopped me having to bottle things up, so my coming home that Christmas ended up being helpful and I could clear my mind of worry and return to the home with a fresh mindset. I would encounter more stress and concern, that was for sure, but knowing I had someone to talk about it made all the difference.

That Christmas I managed to see all the people who were important to me, and I would take back new things to think about when times became difficult for me. My parents continued to visit me every two weeks without fail, the farm and the people there became a big part of my life and the reason I was becoming stronger as well as the fantastic fresh air of west Sussex. Then after 11 months it was considered I was well enough to go home and, while I was very pleased to be going home, I was also naturally a bit concerned as well, but I was told that was only natural. So in September 1957 I returned to Southampton.

Chapter 5
Home Again

It was good to be back with my family and I soon picked up where I had left off. I looked forward to the weekends when we would go with Uncle George Wilber to the farmhouse. Some Sundays my brother and I spent a lot of time there with our family and it never seemed to matter if it rained, as we would just play in the barn and of course enjoy Aunt Alva's wonderful Sunday teas.

My brother and I still went to Durley, to Uncle George Wilber's mother's cottage and that place also still had the same draw for me as of course did Durley itself. I had thought a lot about Durley when I was in West Sussex, but now I was back I seemed to notice more things when driving through the village. Before I had not really taken any notice of the church, for instance. It sat surrounded by trees at the top of the hill, and now it seemed to stand out more as we passed by. I had always noticed the animals grazing in fields in front of the church before but now I noticed a lovely red brick barn with three arched openings where the animals would seek shelter in wet weather. So, I was noticing more. I knew my mind was always occupied looking for things in the road ahead for my uncle to scoop up with his foot which could be the reason I had not noticed these things before. Or maybe because I had been away for so long and missed my trips to Durley, I realised just how important the village was to me. I had been rather preoccupied in just getting by at the home so my focus when I did think of Durley and the stories of my ancestors was when I was trying to counteract the homesickness and I could not always bring the stories to the forefront of my mind.

It could be that the times thinking about Durley when I was homesick helped get me off to sleep and made the village even more important to me unconsciously or spiritually. It was difficult to know the only difference was being one year older, but my intention was still to work on a farm no matter what; and now I was back in recognisable surroundings I was even more determined. It was my uncle's farmhouse and stories of Durley that had kept the dream alive whilst I was away, and I thanked the Lord for the gift of remembering the important things to me that would help aid my recovery. These things may have been out of sight to me but never out of my mind.

I could not start school till the following term in January 1958, at the brand-new school just around the corner from our house that had been completed while I was away. My brother already attended the school and liked it so I was looking forward to going when the new term started, even though I would have to catch up and I hoped the teachers would make allowances for time I had missed. In the meantime, my mother would set me work to do at home each day. She was very pushy and would lean over me telling me what I had done wrong before I had finished. Mum was not a good teacher, and I was on edge most of the time doing the work she set me. Mum worked three days a week with Uncle George Wilber on the family fish round that covered the local villages and between terms and school holidays my brother would go with them on the rounds. I would stay with my grandfather Charles William at his bungalow in Spencer Road and that was better than any lessons set out by Mum. She still put work in my bag, but I forgot to do it most of the time, Charles William would teach me interesting things that were more practical, he would tell me about his sea life and the places he had been.

His bungalow was small but compact; he spent most of his time in the kitchen at the back of the property, which looked out onto the garden to the south through large windows. Against the north wall was a large kitchen table and to the right was a door that led to the rest of the bungalow. On the left of the table, Grandad had a comfortable chair placed between one end of the table to his left and the kitchen facilities to his right, that all sat beneath a long kitchen window on the west wall. Above the big kitchen table was a shelf that had an old valve radio this was on most of the time during the day and would sometimes fade in and out due to poor reception.

Under the shelf, Charles William kept a pipe rack with a selection of pipes. He would take his time to fill one of them and then sit back and tell me interesting things about nature and the garden birds he fed every afternoon. He taught me how to keep milk cool when the weather was hot and demonstrated the method by placing a steel bucket in his shed half full of water and placed two lumps of black coal in the bottom. The milk stayed very cool, I was not sure how. The water had to be changed each day because the bottle would become slimy if the water was too old. He also had on the wall outside a wooden box covered in thin mesh that he kept meat, eggs and cheese and other things you would normally keep in a fridge and somehow it never went off or let any insects get in the box.

My grandfather was also a fantastic cook. His hot cheese scones with butter were something else, and he made his own bread and butterfly cakes with thick butter icing that he made by the doze. The combination of the smell of fresh baking and pipe tobacco did somehow complement each other. Grandfather's days were structured and, now in his retirement, he enjoyed the simple practical life. As with my Uncle George Wilber, I could not have asked to be related to two men that, while completely different, both had a great influence on me. Teaching me so much about things that you would not find in books and may never use in daily life, but the knowledge gained made you the richer for it.

One of Charles William's specialities was the lunchtime fry-ups we often had when I stayed with him. They were not your run-of-the-mill greasy spoon type offerings; Charles William was a trained chef and confectioner so everything he cooked and baked was of the highest standard. Before he started, my job was to fetch the milk from the bucket in the shed for our cup of tea and he got everything he needed ready to start the frying process. He would cut two thick slices of bread from the home-made loaf and cut off the crusts and diced them into small pieces, they would be part of the fry-up too. The crusts would be in the pan from the start to crisp up like fried bread, along with mashed potatoes and vegetables left over from the day before which was made into bubble and squeak and cooked halfway through the process.

He would keep the gas flame low and let the whole thing simmer whilst he got on with spreading our bread with dripping and sprinkled salt sparingly over the bread. Then when the fry-up was nearly ready, he placed the kettle on the stove and lit the gas; he could time the kettle to boil perfectly. The last thing Grandad did before serving was to pick up the frying pan and shake the contents. He sometimes hummed as he did so and then without warning would toss the contents of the frying pan into the air and catch it on its way down, shaking it all the time from side to side, making the fry-up roll over in the frying pan.

I was tasked with placing two plates on the table and as the kettle's whistle sounded, he tipped the contents of the frying pan equally on to the two plates before making the tea. He would tidy up and wipe a damp cloth around the frying pan before sitting down for food. It was the most fantastic fry-up; it was crispy on the outside and inside it melted in your mouth. Once we finished, Grandad would often ask me to pour him another cup which I always did with pride, ensuring I did not spill anything. We then began the tidy up and I took the milk back to the shed and together we washed up. Grandad always left the things to dry on the draining board; he would say that washing up the crockery and utensils properly was very important. After all, they were the tools of his trade, and when you used them, they should look like new to achieve the best results when cooking and who was I to question, he was a master chef after all.

When lunch was over, Charles William would light one of his pipes and we would tune into The Archers (both of us liked the stories told on the show). When the programme had finished, we took out the bread from the larder previously baked and leftover just for the birds. Grandad would soak the bread in water before placing it on a bird table in the garden and sitting back and watching the birds feed. It was wonderful to see so many birds feeding together. I learnt so much from my days with Charles William and will always cherish them.

I may have had a condition that ruled me out of playing sport with other healthy children, but I was so lucky I had so many fascinating grown-ups around me and that I learned so much about the simple things in life and what we need to get by.

One other important person in my formative years was my mother's Aunt Florrie. Aunt Florrie was my grandmother Lucy Jane's sister, who lived at a big, impressive house on the main Archers Road in Southampton, right opposite the Dell home of Southampton Football Club. On match days, the area was packed with enthusiastic football fans who would line up at the turn stiles right opposite Auntie Florrie's house, which became a hub for my godparents and other family members, also Saints' fans, on match days. Using Aunt Florrie's car park, they could walk over the road to join the ever-growing crowds to watch the match. Aunt Florrie ran the boarding house that was started by my great-grandmother Cynthia Mary Draper, who was also responsible for fostering many orphaned children, some of whom would be brought up as cousins to my mother and her siblings and of course would be referred to by my siblings and me as aunts and uncles.

We would often visit Auntie Florrie at the great house at Archers Road that had a vast garden. She kept chickens at the top of the garden next to some massive greenhouses full of fruit and vegetables that her gardener would look after. He was responsible for the upkeep of the beautiful gardens. At the back of the house, where on a raised lawn lots of wicker chairs were set out around several tables for paying guests, we would have drinks or just sit and enjoy the surroundings. It was very peaceful in the gardens, and you would not think you were in the middle of the city.

At the front of the house the ambiance was quite different. The sound of passing traffic reflected the vibrant life of the city. The front garden included a well-manicured sunken lawn that looked wonderful from the house. It had neatly mown lines that the gardener made when riding on the big Dennis motor mower, which had a large roller that the seat was placed on to give the lawn the best affect.

One of my great-aunt's hobbies was breeding French poodles – strange-looking things in my opinion. One of them called Mitze had deformed back legs that were crossed permanently but she was quite happy with life and when Aunt Florrie called the bitch to the room, she would come bounding in on her front legs. It was a very strange thing to see.

The big house was always full of people, some paying guests but mostly family members. Aunt Florrie Hill was a successful business lady. As well as the guest house she had a fish and chip shop, and her son Stanley James Hill had several ladies' hairdressers shops in and around Southampton called Marcia and Anton's. Stanley also had a construction firm and owned many properties too, but his policy was never to employ family members which put him at odds with some of the family. Stanley had been in aviation to begin with and then took on some of Auntie Florrie's business interests. He later became a local Conservative MP, and he dropped the name Stanley from his title and became just James Hill and went on to become Sir James Hill. He served in the Conservative government for many years working for the government at Brussels on common market business.

Also living in the house was great-grandmother Draper, her husband great-grandfather Draper was a lifelong seaman. I have seen photos of them both taken at Spencer Road at one of Mum's sister's weddings. Grandmother Draper survived her husband by many years and lived in a room on the ground floor of the big house and she was by this time bedbound. My brother and I would look around the door at her. She just laid there, and it was spooky for two young boys, I recall on one occasion I found myself looking at her to see if she was still breathing. Creeping ever closer to her bed to look for signs of her bed clothes moving, her eyes were closed tight as I got closer to her. If she had opened her eyes at that point, I probably would have filled my pants, and more than likely so would she with the shock of being woken up with a boy staring at her.

I remember being scolded one time, when I was almost next to the bed and became convinced she was not breathing. Slowly I traced my steps backwards out of the room and went and told my mother that I thought grandmother Draper was dead. I was told off after Mum and Aunt Florrie went rushing to the room and coming back to tell me to keep out of the room as she was not dead, but just sleeping very deeply. I remembered thinking to myself, not being medically trained, how they knew because I thought everyone moved when you breathed but I based that on my own situation.

Sometimes, when I was asleep, my dad said I moved around as if I was kicking a ball but then my breathing patterns were irregular anyway. Grandmother Draper did eventually die but not for another ten years. By that time, she had been moved first to Moorgreen hospital at West End, which was originally the old workhouse. I went with Mum and my sister to visit her several times. She was still bedbound and she still said nothing, and eventually she went to a rest home in the New Forest where she finally passed away in 1966 aged 94 years. In her long life, she helped many children make their way in life. Grandmother Draper's last wish was to have her ashes scattered at sea between Southampton and the Isle of Wight.

This task was left to Aunt Florrie's brother who took the ashes back to the island. He worked on one of the pleasure cruisers that took holiday makers around the island and was supposed to scatter Grandmother Draper's ashes on one of his lunch breaks. Unfortunately, he had kept the ashes in a box under his bed unbeknown to his wife, who was mortified when she found that she had been sleeping with her mother-in-law's ashes under the bed for over 12 months. She angrily ordered that the ashes should go the very next day. Her husband obeyed, taking the ashes to work again intending to scatter them on his lunchbreak.

This time, however, when he took the plastic bag to the side of the boat, as he attempted to pull the bag open it slipped from his grasp and fell into the water. The bag of ashes just bobbed up and down on the waves and was noticed by some of the passengers trying to identify what was in the strange bobbing plastic bag on the water. So, Grandmother Draper did get her wish but not in the way she wanted, and who knows where the bobbling bag ended up, maybe going in and out on each tide between the island and the mainland.

I was lucky that I had the company of so many nice people. But, if I had to choose where I could visit, it would be Uncle George Wilber's farm and Charles William's bungalow. At the same time, Auntie Florrie made everyone welcome, and it was great if you could talk to her one to one; she was a very busy lady and time spent with her was limited. With her living in the city where the air was not good for me, I often got very wheezy after travelling by bus to Southampton, and while I enjoyed walking it was quite a walk from the bus station at Bedford Place to Archers Road. So much traffic would mean more lousy air to cope with, so it would be the rustic surroundings where the air was fresh and clean.

Things changed for me when I started the new term at the local school. I was still prone to the asthma attacks, but they were never as violent as they had been, mainly because of what I had been taught at the home. However, the problem I had if I felt unwell at school, was that I could not just leave the class and carry out what I had been taught regarding my breathing. The teachers did not understand. The school did have a matron who was fine if you had cut your finger, but her knowledge of dealing with an asthma sufferer was nil and in any case the school made it clear they would rather anyone with a problem like mine would not be on the premises. So, I was having more and more time off school. This did mean I had more time with Charles William whilst Mum worked which was all well and good but I was ill so I could not enjoy my time with him as usual. I worried that all the work that had been put in at West Sussex was gradually becoming useless to me; I needed fresh air and no stress. I was not growing and remained so thin you could have played a tune on my rib cage; my weight was not what it should have been either. I still went to the clinic once a month and both my parents, who attended the meetings with me, wanted to know what could be done as my condition began to worsen.

Things came to a head when one Saturday in the summer holidays. Mum was at work and my brother and I stayed with Dad who had told me I could not go out of the garden. But when my brother went with two of his friends to the school to play football, I sneaked out without Dad knowing and went to find my brother. When I got to the end of the path and went down the small bank, I could not see my brother. There was no one around at all and I began to panic. Then as I turned to go back up the bank, I began to lose my breath. With my father not knowing I was out, I realised I was going to have an attack and really should get back to the garden where he would see me and help. But I could not move, my chest tightened and the pains in my back as I tried to breathe in felt like I had been punched. The pain lingered as I could neither breathe in nor out properly. At the home we had been trained to relax and not panic, but I was on my own and everything I had been taught seemed to have deserted me at that moment. My only wish was I did not want to die, not there with no one with me. I managed to crawl to the concrete path and tried to get my face on the cold surface to somehow help stop the burning sensation. It was the worst attack I had ever had, and I was only saved when the lady who lived on the end of our block heard me struggling and alerted her family to get my father. Dad came running down the path and lifted me up and ran back home with me under his arm, with my head low to the ground in the hope I would be sick and clear the stuff that had built up in my gullet. I struggled to bring it up and as we got to our garden Dad held me over the flowerbed and put his finger down my throat and I was sick but still reaching and gasping for breath. Some of our neighbours by this time had gathered and offered help to Dad who was naturally upset himself. We had been through a lot before, but this was the worst we had experienced together.

It took some time for me to breathe normally again. The neighbours stood around in our garden. They had been shocked at what they had seen as they knew I had attacks, but this was the first time they had ever witnessed one taking place. Dad had called Doctor Stowell and, while we waited, he brought me a chair out to the garden. I always wanted to be able to breathe fresh air after an attack, if it was cold outside it did not matter to feel air go up your nostrils, cold air preferably is a great feeling. You may need a coat or blanket around you to keep warm but fresh air is what I always needed when recovering. Our neighbours eventually left the garden after Dad thanked them for being there for us and he sat on the step beside me and began to come around himself. As I looked down at him from the chair he looked as if he needed an arm around him, we both did but we were too weary from the shock of what happened. Dad said nothing to me about going out on my own, there was no point, that attack would have happened sooner or later, and I was glad it was over but knew it would come again one day. That was the worst thing about having asthma.

After Doctor Stowell finished looking me over and asking about the chain of events leading up to this attack, he gave me an injection. I had not had one before, however, from then on, I was to have one every Monday evening at the doctors surgery, administered by the nurse. The doctor wanted to see me the following Wednesday and expressed his disappointment as to how far my health had begun to deteriorate after the positive results from my stay in West Sussex. It was clear he thought things had to change and told Father I may need to go away again and because I was now eight and a half, he wanted more medics involved in my case. The visits I had been having at the clinic once a month were just check-ups regarding my height and weight. I had to have respiratory tests as well and they had not shown anything untoward with my lungs, so we needed to find out what was going on.

When Mum came home, I was sat in a chair by the open kitchen door. She knew straight away that something had happened and was upset that no one went to get her. My father explained to her that there was no time. Mum never knew how bad that attack was which was just as well. Dad had to repeat what Doctor Stowell had said and told Mum that I might have to go away again. We had to attend the clinic the following Wednesday indicating to Mum there would be no debating on the matter and that as a family, we had done all we could. And now it was time for me to receive more severe medical attention. Mum said nothing but nodded in agreement and, looking at me, smiled and said for me not to worry about anything. It was that day the three of us became aware of just how bad things could get. The house was tranquil that weekend, my siblings had no idea what happened that Saturday afternoon to change our family's way of life once more in another attempt to make me better by sending me away again. It would affect us all, but as before, we would cope.

When we arrived at the clinic on the Wednesday, we were sent straight in to see Doctor Stowell and a person from the health authority who would be setting up my move to another home. It was taken as read that I would be going and after a brief discussion with my parents, we were told that places would soon become available for me at two homes. One was in Switzerland, somewhere I had never heard of, and the other in Ventnor on the Isle of Wight at a home called St Catherine's. It was made clear that both places had very good reputations and that St Catherine's was both a home and a school, while the place in Switzerland was more of a clinic. It was also overseas and was in reality not the best option for my needs. St Catherine's had strict rules – visiting was only once a month, given the travelling needed from the mainland for some families who would need to make a weekend of it. They would have to think about the cost of it all and where to stay, St Catherine's did however have resident rooms that could be booked in advance and were cheaper than a hotel, but many families found it difficult both time-wise and financially. Also, another rule was that no boys would be allowed home until they reached the right weight thought necessary by the medical people and that would mean no holidays including Christmas or otherwise until the medics were satisfied that the child's health had improved enough to let them go home. I was not really bothered where I went as long as I could breathe properly, nothing else mattered that much but I knew it would be difficult. I had experienced being homesick and the loneliness of being away from my family, but the isolation that I was having to endure being off school and not able to do anything strenuous whilst waiting for the next asthma attack had a profound effect on me. Looking back, the thoughts I had as an eight-and-a-half-year-old worrying if I would ever breathe properly again was difficult to endure.

I had seen first-hand at the home in West Sussex, children that had to breathe with a mask attached to a big air bottle. The boundaries of their existence depended on how long the tube was that helped them breathe; I did not want that to happen to me. But I was not able to convey that message to anyone other than my father, who was the only one I could trust and who understood my anxieties. So, I was not bothered where the health authorities wanted to send me or if I had to stay there till I was fit, that did make perfect sense to me, and now we were at the clinic I hoped things would be sorted quickly.

My parents and Doctor Stowell agreed that St Catherine's on the Isle of Wight was the best option for me. Our family had relations still living on the Island, my mother said she would feel more comfortable if I went to the Island because it would be easier to visit me and stay overnight with her cousin. The health authorities set things up; it still took around six weeks for everything to be finalised. In that time, I was able to see the people that were important to me before I went away again, all of whom wished me well. I also went with my father to see his mother; he regularly went every Saturday morning. It was the first time he took my brother and me with him. We were visiting the house Dad was raised in and where all the stories of farming at Durley had been told to him. I had been there before when I was younger, but it was only at that point in my life did I appreciate the connection between the stories and the house where they had been told when my dad was growing up. The more I thought about my father's side of the family the more I wondered why my siblings and me had not seen any of them as often as my mother's side of the family. When we had family gatherings, for instance, none of Dad's close family attended. When we lived in the prefab, I did see one of his brothers and his wife who came on our birthdays. We did stay with our Nan once or twice for the day. Dad had always talked about his grandfather, but I could never recall him say anything about his own father. It was only then I began to think about it. I knew that our Grandmother Lucy Jane had died before I was born so it could have been that our grandfather, whoever he was, had also died. It was indeed food for thought and I would soon have plenty of time on my hands to do so because eventually at the beginning of September 1959 I was given the all-clear to go to the Island.

St Catherine's Home was for the Delicate and Asthmatic at Ventnor. It had been there in one form or another since 1879. Back then, people with advanced tuberculosis were sent there and nursed by the nursing sisters of St Margret's from East Grinsted in Sussex.

In 1908, Sister Kathleen arrived at St Catherine's, and within two years she became the sister in overall charge. She was the person who would make provision for the care of delicate and asthmatic children. She reorganised St Catherine's Home to make it a nursing home, as well as a school and her word was said to be law. So, everything I was about to learn and gain from my new experience at St Catherine's would be from the vision of Sister Kathleen. I would, as I had done in West Sussex, do everything in my power to make my stay a success both for myself and in appreciation to someone like Sister Kathleen; she had the vision to try and help people like me.

Chapter 6
St Catherine's

In early September 1959 my mother and father took me to the Southampton Central train station and handed me over to a Mr Butterworth, who would take me to Ventnor from Southampton to Portsmouth on the train and then by ferry to the Island. We would then catch a final train that would take us on to Ventnor.

After saying goodbye to my parents, I walked with Mr Butterworth up over the covered bridge from platform four to the main line on platform one to catch the train to Portsmouth. Mr Butterworth was a very tall man, immaculately dressed but said very little to me for the whole of the journey; he would point and indicate where we should walk. He had probably done the trip many times to Ventnor with other children, however it was like travelling alone, everyone on the trains and ferry were strangers to me. I had my small brown case with all my personal things with me, as my main luggage had been sent ahead, and I held onto my little familiar case firmly for the duration of the journey. I remember as the ferry crossed the Solent in the dim-light, the lights inside the craft made the windows become mirrors and I could see myself sat next to this very tall man and thought it all an adventure and wondered how much longer it would take to reach St Catherine's.

When we arrived on the Island, the trip's final stage was to catch the Ventnor train. By the time we reached our destination, it was dark, and as we walked down a very steep hill from the train station, I had to hurry along to try and keep up with Mr Butterworth whose long stride was like three of mine. I remember it was cold. And for the first time, I breathed in the fresh air of Ventnor, it felt like I had been born again into a world with no contaminated air – could there be such a place!

I was still a little chesty sometimes, but I felt comfortable with my lot which is the best way to describe how I felt right then. When we reached St Catherine's, we went in through a high set of double doors and into an office. There was a nun dressed in black from head to toe, with only her face peering out through what looked to me like a white hood. She moved across the room as if on castors, her legs hidden by the heavy-looking attire that she wore. After a few words with the nun, Mr Butterworth left without saying anything to me at all, and the nun said little more only to tell me I was to have my weight and height measured. She was quick and efficient before leading me into another room, gave me a uniform wrapped in noisy brown paper, then told me to sit at one of the small tables, and said she would fetch me some food. I was hungry after the rigours of travelling and when she returned with a selection of sandwiches, biscuits and a warm drink I tucked into my first food at the home.

As I did so I could hear the sound of other children from down the long corridor and I began to feel settled. However, when I had finished my food, another older boy came into the room with the nun and I was informed I had to go with this boy. I thought he was going to take me to my room or a dormitory, but I was shocked when he took my uniform and walked out through a back door into a dark courtyard and looked back signalling for me to follow.

I was confused because although I had only just arrived at the home, I was starting to think of the room I was in as part of my new boundaries; but having to leave it had thrown me. I said nothing to the older boy who broke the silence and said I would be staying at the big house called Elm Grove at the top of the hill. We began to ascend. I could see the lights of the building from the bottom of the hill as we began to walk towards it. The boy said if I wanted to cry it would be OK because most of the young ones did when they first arrived and everything would be all right once I had settled in. I told him I had been away before so knew what it was like to be away from my family, and as I said it I felt tears run down my cold face and made no attempt to wipe them away. The salty tears ran down and reached the corner of my mouth, I moved my tongue to each side to gather in the evidence of my sadness; if I could have gone home right then I would have if I knew where the hell I was, that is.

By the time we reached Elm Grove, I had composed myself. These pangs of emotion got to me sometimes and went as quickly as they arrived. It only takes a word to start them off when you are not on your guard because when you are away, you're not yourself. Just a version in a get-by mode of survival, so it would not be the last time. They were, for most of the young boys, par for the course.

On entering Elm Grove through an impressive wide front door, the older boy handed me over to a man who introduced himself as Mr Busbridge. He was a master at St Catherine's, and I would be under his stewardship. As soon as I meet him I liked how he spoke and he made me feel at ease. Mr Busbridge, as it turned out, would become a father figure and mentor to all the boys in his care and had a great reputation within the home. He made us feel relaxed and gave us great encouragement in all that we did. Mr Busbridge showed me to a dormitory on the ground floor of the house. He told me to unpack my small case, and that my other luggage was in his office that he would fetch for me. He also told me the other boys would be back after they had finished preparing for bed in the washroom supervised by a nurse and a helper.

As I walked into the dormitory, I noticed to my left against the south wall were two beds, the foot of each bed facing to the middle of the room then on the long west wall four more beds were set out, two each side of a wide bay window that had thick black bars on the inside. On the north wall a long table was set in front of an even wider bay window, this two had bars on the inside. The darkness outside made the room and its contents look bigger, reflected by the lights within the room. Then on the east wall that stretched back to the middle of the room before becoming L-shaped, this had two more beds against it. The wall then stretched from the middle of the room continuing along the north wall past a locked half-glazed external door into the corner meeting the east wall. There was one bed in the corner, its head set against the wall next to the external door. This bed faced the door I had just walked through into the dormitory; it was to be my bed and was well positioned. I would know who would be coming in and out of the room. I could also see out into the hallway and the entrances into two other dormitories.

As I was unpacking my case, eight other boys returned walking in single file led by a nurse and another person following behind them into the dormitory. The nurse introduced herself and the helper, followed by each boy one by one. The boys went to their respective beds, six of the boys looked about the same age as me, the two other boys were older and looked fitter than the rest of us who looked as if we would collectively have a job to blow the skin off a rice pudding.

Mr Busbridge returned with my luggage and told me that after breakfast the following day I would go with a staff member for an induction morning. I was then told to get my wash things and nightclothes and went with the helper to shower, after which we had a hot drink before bed. It had been a long day; I was tired and had no trouble getting off to sleep that night.

The following morning, we were up at 7 am and went with the helpers to the washroom; boys from the other two dormitories joined us on the ground floor. I was given clean pants and a vest. I unpacked my school uniform of a grey shirt and long-sleeved jumper, short grey trousers and a pair of long grey socks that complemented my highly polished black shoes. Each boy always had to have clean shoes; it was a well-organised system. Unlike the chaos I encountered on my first morning at the farm in West Sussex, the helpers were not that old, about 15 or 16 years old, who would today be called childminders. After brushing our teeth and showering, we dressed and assembled at the door.

From the washroom we went back to our dorm. We had to wait for other boys to come down from dormitories on the first floor of the house to go for breakfast. While I was waiting, I looked around my dorm for the first time in daylight, and as I walked from my bed into the middle of the room and looked out of the big bay window at the front of the room, I was amazed to see the most fantastic sight. From our lofty position at the top of the hill we looked out over the town of Ventnor and yonder to the wonderful panoramic view of the English Channel. It was an intoxicating image and would become for me a source of comfort whenever I felt down in the dumps. The overpowering sight of the sea that sometimes looked still and calm and on other occasions looked so wild and rough that the trawlers that regularly fished the area would disappear out of sight hidden by great waves and I would count the seconds before the boats came back into my vision, and I breathed a sigh of relief when they did. My love of Ventnor and that view began that very day and its power and the desire to reconnect with it has never deserted me, whether it's to go back to see it again or just recall it in my head; it gave me peace and sometimes a sanctuary to hide from the world's worries and the sea's spiritual calming has never let me down.

When all of the boys, nurses and helpers had assembled ready to go for breakfast we would walk military-style back down to the buildings at the bottom of the hill that I had arrived at. All our meals would be taken there, and I always looked forward to my breakfast. It was a noisy atmosphere of boys chattering and the sound of cutlery against ceramic plates. It was both vibrant and, in a way, relaxing because there was no rush placed upon us, we could take our time over breakfast. The only concern we had was if we left anything on our plates the nuns would glide across the floor and look down on us after we had thanked the Lord for what we were about to receive before starting. The nuns looked upon the leaving of food as disrespectful and would lean over you looking through cold eyes. They also smelt strange and had tight wrinkled lips that never smiled and resembled my mother's leather purse that she kept shillings in for the gas meter. Sometimes boys even licked the plates clean so as not to displease them because they looked so scary. We were also able to, on occasions when the nuns were not looking, hide the thick bacon or tough meats into our pockets to dispose of on the way back to Elm Grove, and many a fat cat would line the pathway upward in anticipation of receiving the welcome scraps.

After breakfast, I went back to Elm Grove with the helper to meet the matron. I had a basic medical and Matron made sure that all medications were recorded to be administered on the right date and time if, as in my case, injections were required then the matron would need to see you as soon as possible. Matron would turn out to be, for all the boys, a person we relied on, and her medical room was mostly full at various times of the day. Matron was a tall lady, firmly built and she spoke with an accent that I had not heard before. Her dedication to the job made her popular with both the boys and their parents who would meet her. She spoke in a loud voice and could be heard sometimes reprimanding a boy for having dirty hands and knees; saying that cleanliness was next to Godliness, and no one should turn up at her medical room with dirty hands and knees and she often threatened to "Spit in yer eye" if anyone did.

Matron used many nautical terms if when you knocked on her door she would say "come aboard" dragging aboard out to a whisper, and she wanted everything "shipshape" in the medical room, no clothes left on the floor when having a medical, we had to fold everything neatly. Some boys had to often strip naked because of their eczema, a horrid itching condition that came with asthma. Matron's remedy for that was lots of calamine lotion that was put on and around the affected areas, applied gently with cotton wool. The lotion would turn chalky when dry and relieve the itching. Matron had a long table in front of a window, the bottom half of which was frosted glass and the top fanlight was clear glass you could see through. She would ask you to stand upon the table while she proceeded to gently dab on the calamine lotion, then while it dried, we would look out embarrassingly through the top fanlight window until the lotion became chalky. We then looked like floor graders but the relief from the itching was unbelievable. It was a process that would for some be a daily routine. Some of Matron's methods could be far from the norm, but she cared very much for us; we were grateful to her for helping us cope with our condition.

After my first meeting with Matron, a lady member of staff took me around the rest of the house and as we were on the first floor, showed me the other dormitories. They were set out the same as the one I was in at the front of the building. The washrooms were at the back of the house along with the resident nurses' rooms, next to them was the sick room for boys who had chronic asthma. These boys would not be going home, their asthma was just part of their problem combined with something else that made life difficult for them all. If you were lucky and never confined to that room, you could thank the Lord for that.

When the first-floor tour was over, I was taken back downstairs, this time via a back staircase used by servants in days gone by. At its peak, St Catherine's would have over 150 children in its care. Elm Grove was just part of a portfolio of properties in Ventnor and around other parts of the Island, all of them dedicated venues for the sick.

Back on the ground floor at the back of the house, there were several storerooms. One room for the boys to clean their boots and shoes, a small kitchen was the last room at the end of a long passage at the back of the house. From its back door, you would walk out into a large courtyard. It was here the scout group assembled and practised their marching under the guidance of Mr Whittington, I think his name was. He lived up in the hills above Ventnor. From the courtyard through a double gate, a path led you to two small staff cottages.

The last room I was shown in the Grove was a great hall with a stage at the back of this massive room that ran the length of the house north to south. It was two and half times the width of our dormitory east to west and was used for recreation by all the boys at the home. We had four houses – Oak, Ash, Elm and Maple. Each house had jobs assigned for boys to do both inside and out through the week, for which we received either 16 Quality Street sweets each per week or we could have two bars of chocolate instead. The sweets became our currency to barter with. Every Saturday in the big hall we had a film screening. My favourite films were the Marx Brothers – they were so funny, more so than the Three Stooges that were often shown as well. The great hall was the hub of the house, and many games were played by the boys. In one corner there may be a cigarette card game going on for instance. Each boy who wished to play placed one of his own collection of cigarette cards against the skirting board. So if there were six boys playing each had a turn to flick one of his own collection of cards to try and knock the six standing cards over; and whoever knocked the last card over would win all the cigarette cards gathered on the floor. It was a very popular game and some of the games took ages to finish and commanded a big crowd watching on to see who would win the big pot.

We also had a blow football table that was most amusing, as you could imagine with two players on each side of the table and one boy at each end acting as the goal keepers, all blowing through a plastic straw to move the ball in the direction each team wanted it to go. The games were often held up because another boy had to take over from someone who had run out of puff, so we needed plenty of boys standing by. However, most of the games had to be stopped to wipe the pitch dry from the spittle deposited through the straws by half a dozen wheezing asthmatic boys. All of them had a highly competitive winning nature but just lacked the energy and puff needed to succeed in that pursuit of getting the small red football to go where you wanted it to go. Mostly it just wobbled round the pitch unless someone succeeded in mustering up a good puff of air to get it up the other end of the pitch away from your goal. The problem with the game was if two boys found the energy for a big blow then the ball would fly up into the air and onto the floor. It was the most frustrating game to play and a waste of valuable air for some with all the blowing required. But sometimes winning was not everything; the camaraderie between the boys, who knew their limitations and may never be winners, but were happy to be part of a team who always tried and the fun we had in the search of success formed many a bond between us all.

The big hall at the house was also the venue for a show we put on that many people from Ventnor came to see. I was asked to sing with another boy called Charles Enticknapp, and we sang 'Catch a Falling Star'. Neither of us could sing well but did our best. The only problem was that we had to do all the hand movements as we sang, like catching the falling star from the sky and then putting it in our pocket to save for the rainy day. We had to wiggle our fingers above our heads to indicate the falling rain drops, however things started to go wrong when we had to sing 'For love may come and tap you on the shoulder one starlet night'. The routine only grew more complex when we sang 'And just in case you feel you want to hold her we would have a pocket full of starlight' and as we pulled make-believe starlight from our pockets some of the audience began to laugh. The song was clearly meant for a boy and a girl to sing to each other, and it was embarrassing to have two shy boys sing it to each other. It was not meant to be a comic performance, but it was viewed in that way and we took some ribbing for our performance from other boys afterwards.

Everyone however was required to do something, that was the whole point of it all and looking back it was very funny, Charles Enticknapp was the only boy I knew the name of. I didn't know where he came from but soon afterwards, he was sent back home, probably having reached the right weight and other criteria necessary to be released. I often think about our one and only performance that did not lead to stardom and wonder if he remembers singing it. So many boys came and went, it was hard to keep track of who was who.

After my tour of the big house, I was reunited with the helper and as it was almost lunchtime we walked back down the slope to the canteen. On our left outside of the grounds, many nice houses stood, all built with fine stone. One had a thick wisteria growing all the way across the front elevation of the house above a glass-covered veranda that was supported by impressive ironwork pillars. The wisteria's purple flowers hung down like bunches of grapes, complementing the richness of the stone, indicating it was a residence of someone that had made it in life. It was something else that stayed in my mind through the years. Halfway down the slope was a red-bricked hotel that was the width of three properties. Its rooms overlooked the school and the sea beyond and I often thought what a lovely place it would be to live there as well. At the bottom of the slope, the ground levelled out and we walked by another fine house, this time within the grounds of the home and was Sister Kathleen's residence, and we would walk by quietly because she was in advanced years and had not been well. Sometimes she could be seen standing at the window looking out over the home that she had helped create. I always looked up and she was the only one of the nuns I ever saw smile.

When we reached the canteen at midday, the other children had finished the morning classes, and everyone assembled at 12.15 for lunch. Unlike breakfast's relaxed mood at St Catherine's, lunchtime was run like clockwork, finishing at 12.45 on the dot, after which everyone would have a rest hour, something I had done at the farm in West Sussex. When rest was over, we had another two-hour class in the schoolhouse. My teacher was Mrs Vine she was a very interesting teacher, encouraging children in her class to try and work hard with what she taught them. Morning classes included subjects like maths, English and history and in the afternoons allowed class members to work on individual projects ranging from painting, craftwork and group reading. Mrs Vine allowed me to work on a farming project that I enjoyed. We also had access to the impressive library next to the homes chapel. Mrs Vine's class was for boys up to the age of ten years old and with many changes due to children that went home and new ones arriving halfway through a term, she coped very well and did her best not to cover the same subject twice. The older boys were in Mr Johnson's class (Josh as he was affectionally called), although he was not as approachable or as lenient as Mrs Vine according to the older boys who said his lessons were boring. However, school was fine as far as I was concerned. I was not quick on the uptake with all things relating to maths and a few subjects I thought I would never need to learn. I managed to make my projects interesting enough that Mrs Vine was suitable impressed and left me to my own devices, as long as I kept handing work in and looked interested in the morning class it was easy to get by and, because of that trust placed in us all, there were no classroom troublemakers.

After each school day, everyone returned to their place of residence, this time not as one group. If you wished to mix with other boys or you may want to catch up on things with home then between the hour from 4 to 5 pm, when dinner was served, was free time. You would be expected to be on time for dinner in the canteen and not many missed it because dinner was always welcome after our busy day. So, settling in at St Catherine's was quite easy. I liked my surroundings and each positive thing I experienced helped me.

I had regular visits once a month from my family who always filled up our day doing interesting things, but when they came it was sometimes difficult when they went home because, for the few hours I spent with them, I felt my age and could relax in their company. It was very normal and when they went I would switch back to the 'get by' mode which after many months was easy to do. There was a good attitude among the boys my age. Some never had visits, and for those of us that did, we would not talk about where we had been or what we had done when we got back. My parents even offered to take another boy with us, but were told by the nuns it was not a good idea and when boys came back with gifts we usually placed them on the table for everyone to use. I felt guilty sometimes being taken out when other boys had no one visit them, we were more associates than friends joined in a fellowship organised by a body of people. Nuns, nurses, masters and teachers alike, all with different reasons for helping us, each with a limited liability towards us and even if unwittingly were collectively responsible for us becoming institutionalised. For some of the boys it was confusing and so difficult to adjust to being away from their home environment, it took a long time to come to terms with the new surroundings and for the boys that had never been away before homesickness could hit them for six.

What was so difficult for everyone was the fact the nuns showed no compassion and looked upon it as a weakness of character. The house masters and teachers tended to leave it to the nurses to offer some form of comfort, but they were governed by rules laid down by the nuns that they should not show any love to any one individual, believing they would make a rod for their own backs if they did so. Only Matron broke that rule; if she thought a child needed to be shown love and compassion she did so. She said tough love helped some individuals as did tenderness towards the ones that needed it; she was the only one who could distinguish between the two sets of needs. So, the boys learnt early on that sometimes strides made towards becoming more confident and feeling wanted could be destroyed by showing any form of weakness. It would be left to the boys themselves who would notice someone move away from the group when feeling desperately unhappy and would just gather around and walk with the individual until their melancholic mood had passed, because we all knew what it was like. The last thing you would want to hear was cruel words from a nun as to your personality and no one wanted notes made to go on their records indicating they were of weak character. So not only did we have to cope with our condition, but watch how we acted when close to an attack or feelings of despair. We learnt to look out for each other, something that would stay in your character for always.

Despite some rules that we thought unfair, I liked it at the home and enjoyed what we did at weekends. There were lots of long walks in all weathers, it was healthy and kept us fit it even if it was all done at a slow pace of course. We all had to keep up with each other and we walked in pairs so we would notice if anyone became detached from the group, especially when we climbed up St Boniface Downs. St Boniface towered over the houses that nestled beneath it and from the grounds of St Catherine's you could see the white chalk pathway leading up, with small figures climbing its well-worn path to the top. It was an incredible gift of nature, the sheer size of the Downs; to look up at it was breathtaking, as were the panoramic views from the top of it – you could see to all points of the compass, way across the English Channel and the rest of the Island.

Wildflowers flourished despite the prevailing winds and weather-hardened animals roamed the Downs used by farmers to fatten stock. It was amazing how sheep grazed on the side of the steep hill. Our time spent on St Boniface was never dull and Mr Busbridge would monitor each boy's ability as to how high he would let them climb in one go. Several benches placed at various stages going up were welcome targets to reach. If you had to sit for a while to catch your breath, you could feast your eyes on the intoxicating view. In time, after a few months everyone would be able to reach the top; the strength gained at St Catherine's both mentally and physically was, for me, down to Mr Busbridge. He said we could do anything in time if we took things easy.

At the foot of St Boniface was an old disused railway tunnel that we would walk through behind Mr Busbridge and his helpers. Torches carried by helpers led the way as it was so dark. It took a long time for your eyes to become accustomed to the darkness; you could still not see your hand in front of your face but we followed the light of the torches that lit up the width of the tunnel before us and we also had sight of the daylight at the end of the tunnel we were heading towards. Halfway through the tunnels the natural construction went to the right and for a minute or so we could not see the daylight at either end of the long tunnel. We all gave the impression of being brave walking through that part, keeping quiet because someone said the tunnel would fall in if we made too much sound. We were always a little cocky when we eventually saw the light at the other end of the tunnel. It was a great experience, not many people can say they have done it and it ranks as one of the best things I did at the home.

We all loved sport but could not always play, so Mr Busbridge devised the games so we could even play football if we did not go like a bull at a gate. He made the pitch smaller and had more players on each side, so we didn't need to run so much but instead pass the ball more. Eventually when we became fitter, we could do a little more making sure we did not exceed our personal limits.

At the beginning of December 1959, the local school challenged the boys of St Catherine's to a football match at their school. Of course, when Mr Busbridge told us about the challenge we were all up for it. We took around 25 boys between the ages of eight to ten years old, the same age as the opposition's team members. We had to take that many because most of us could only last for around ten minutes at any one time. We walked in pairs all the way to the local school and were very excited at the prospect of playing in a real game. Our kit was borrowed and much too big for most of us and we had to tie the elastic around the waist in a knot to stop the shorts falling down around our ankles. Each shirt came down well over our backsides, and the socks would have come up to our groin if we pulled them right up. And we played in our shoes. The home team's master refereed the game and when he blew the whistle to begin, even though we had the advantage of the kick off, we lost the ball immediately and the home team began to run rings around us. Mr Busbridge sent on more boys but did not take anyone off; he did not have to because we were dropping like flies. Still, we kept going as each boy regained enough puff to have another go. We sometimes had around 16 players on the field, with a few flaked out on the touchline, who if the ball came in their direction made an effort to get up and join in again as another boy sloped off for a breather. Needless to say, we lost by a cricket score even though we had two supposedly rotating goalkeepers. Most of the time the two of them were in goal at the same time but still managed to concede a hat full of goals, and on two occasions both tried to make a save at the same time and still managed to let the ball in before arguing whose fault it was.

After the final whistle, we received a round of applause from the home team followed by three cheers which we of course returned in the time-honoured way in boys' football back then. We had been chasing shadows for most of the afternoon, but it was great fun and we even had tea and sandwiches supplied by our hosts to round of our afternoon of sport. Walking back slowly afterwards, we all talked about how we were stuffed, but we all gained a great deal that day because we never gave up. To top it off, Mr Busbridge said he was proud of us all and that meant so much to us and we gave him three cheers for taking us. We all slept so well that night, nodding off with a smile on our face for a change.

Christmas that year was a strange affair; not being allowed home for a holiday seemed unfair. Still, we knew the rules before accepting the placement offer, so we could not complain. On Christmas Eve, the morning went slowly. After our breakfast we went walking along the seafront. Many people were out and about to soak up the atmosphere of the accelerating winds that blew salty beads against their windswept red faces that looked like tears of joy upon their cheeks for being close to one of nature's wonders.

When our walk was over, we went back for lunch. It was early on Christmas Eve because at 4 pm we had been invited to the town's Church of the Holy Trinity for their carol service. Some of us would be singing a carol as part of the service; the home made a choir up of whoever was not flaked out at the time and, like the football team, we had a lot of singers. Also, just like the football team, we were not that good, but we could belt a carol out as good as any run-of-the-mill group of singers. So, after lunch and our rest period, we got ourselves ready for the walk down to the church that was situated just down the hill at the bottom of Grove Road. It was an impressive building and rather unusual, I thought, to have a church right in the town graveyard and all. It was one of three churches at Ventnor; one was close to the local school called St Catherine's church on the outskirts of Ventnor and another further up in the hills above Elm Grove. We attended them all, rotating each Sunday evening's compulsory church. We also had our own Anglican chapel at the home that was used on special occasions.

The carol service went really well. The church's own choir sang beautifully, as did the congregation joining in with renditions of regular Christmas carols. It had been a wonderful service. When we left to walk back up to St Catherine's, it was dark and even though we were in a group I felt a bit lonely, in fact no one said much on the way back. We seemed to know how each one of us felt. We had a nice time and were made very welcome, but there was still that feeling of not belonging. Something we would of course shake off after a while, but the feeling was always at the back of your mind no matter what you did, because to the people of Ventnor we had come from the home and many locals thought we were there because we had done something wrong. When in reality all we wanted was to get well, so being in a home and saying you have been in a home can give a false impression if not explained it was for your health. From the church, we quickly went to our dorms and assembled again to walk down for our tea. The canteen looked rather dull because most of the areas at the main building had been decked out for Christmas. However, after we all finished tea and went back to Elm Grove, we could do what we liked till lights, so the evening was nothing special, even being Christmas Eve.

Christmas day 1959 arrived and we were up at our usual time. After washing, we went down for breakfast before going on to the Christmas morning service in the home's own chapel. Following the service, we walked back to Elm Grove and assembled in the hall. It began to buzz with enthusiasm as we lined up around the perimeter of the big hall that had long trestle tables down the centre of the room. The tables were laden with drinks and sweets that were gifts to the children from the staff of Elm Grove. We also heard the sound of bells, and music began to play as Santa came into the room being pulled on a sleigh loaded with presents that he handed out to each of us wishing us a merry Christmas. As soon as he was pulled out of the room to rapturous cheering, we were invited into the middle of the room to help ourselves to sweets and drinks. I have always remembered that Christmas morning. It was such a surprise, we may have been away from home but that day we were all made to feel so at home because in reality Elm Grove was now home. It was at times like that when everything felt so normal and I could breathe in the fresh air which made me not want to leave the Island. It also made me feel guilty thinking it, remembering my family at home. It was so confusing and very emotional, but I will never forget that morning.

After the excitement of the morning and the receiving of gifts, it was time to go down for Christmas lunch. The walk down was relaxing in the chilly winter air and the sea seemed calm. As we walked down the slope, I watched it till I could see it no more until I went inside the main building and from the long windows in the corridor became reunited with the sea's majesty and its ability to please the naked eye with just a glance never failed. As we reached the canteen, the sound of the younger children from the main building woke me from my daydreaming, and as we walked in the dining room it had been transformed into a Christmas grotto. We took our places at the tables that had thick white tablecloths, turning the usual ordinary-looking tables in to classy-looking ones.

Jugs of water were placed in the middle of the table with Christmas crackers for each person and one card to wish whoever was seated at the table a merry Christmas. Before the lunch was served, one of the nuns gave a short speech and said grace, and as the echoes of our collective "Amen" faded, the food was served. It was a wonderful lunch that was followed be mince pies and Christmas pudding, with lots of talking among ourselves as we pulled the crackers and put on our paper hats. We swapped the gifts from inside the crackers if someone wanted a particular item. We all had plenty to eat and had a wonderful time. Mr Busbridge then stood and asked us all to stand with him and give the people who had worked so hard with cooking the wonderful lunch a round of applause and we all did so willingly, along with a few hearty cheers to boot.

January 1960, the start of a new year and new beginnings for everyone and we all looked forward to a visit from home. I was never disappointed; my parents never missed the opportunity, and I had lots to say about the events at Christmas. Both my parents noticed I talked a lot and was more confident from not having to worry so much about having attacks which of course my parents were pleased about. Before we all went down to Ventnor for lunch, we walked around the grounds of Elm Grove. I showed them St Boniface from the lawn and how we went up from time to time. As we walked back into my dorm to get a jumper, we bumped into Matron. Mum and Dad had not met her before and Matron said hello and hoped that we had a good visit, smiling in her usual way. Mum stated she hoped I had been behaving myself, to which Matron replied in the way only Matron could. She told my parents that I was a pleasure to look after, and said I always had clean hands and knees, and patted me on the head before saying if they were not "I'll spit in his eye" and walked off laughing.

My dad didn't know what to say and looked at me. I told him Matron was very strict and always said that to everyone but was a very nice person. Mum saw the funny side of it and said she would try it when I came home. We all had a nice day out, and when it was time to go, they left me in the nun's office. Boys were never allowed outside to see visitors off because it was too upsetting for some of them. Sometimes parents got upset as well. I had seen that happen at West Sussex on the farm. It was not very nice when a visit was over, some boys were pulled kicking and screaming by angry nuns who would lock the door as the boy tried unsuccessfully to pull it off its hinges. If the nuns had been more caring that situation would have been easier; unfortunately, some of the nuns could only offer tough love and hated weakness in boys and let them know it as well.

At the end of January 1960, I had my first weighing session. All boys that had been at St Catherine's for three months would have to be weighed every month. It always turned out to be manic – some boys, keen to reach the required weight, would fill pockets with stones, toy cars and tuck books into their pants, some even put on more than one jumper. However, the nuns made everyone strip down to their underpants before they weighed them, they also told you to remove your shoes and stand flatfooted on the floor while the measuring stick was lowered firmly down on top of your head. Any attempt to try and stretch yourself upwards to gain more height was impossible once the bar was in place and with your shoulders back firmly against the wall you became locked in. Your natural measurement could be taken, and you would always be shorter than you thought yourself to be when released from the measuring apparatus. They were as reliable as the old-fashioned scales you stood on while the nuns operated the machine by moving a weight across the long arm until it reached the point where it would slowly drop indicating an exact weight. For some boys, they had the disappointment of what they considered at the time to be scales of injustice, indicating another month to be added to the very necessary incarceration regarded by the medical staff to be essential in the pursuit of healthiness. Every inch and ounce would be scrutinised by po-faced nuns who could never be fooled, no matter how hard you tried.

This happened every month and some boys had been so fed up with being at the home, they decided to run away but this too would be foiled because we were on an island. By the time the runaway had got to the ferry, the port had been notified that St Catherine's had a runaway. The port staff could spot the deserter a mile off, usually a skinny wheezing specimen of a boy, hungry and poorly clothed against the elements he encountered. When darkness fell, this poor wretch found himself between the devil and the deep blue sea.

The only thing he would gain from his efforts would be to learn something about himself, a strength of character he didn't know he had before running away. He may have led everyone a merry dance in their attempts to track him down, well so what, unhappiness makes you do all sorts of things considered wrong by others. We all at times in our lives want to run away from something but not everyone has the guts to do so. But for a fresh-faced boy with no commitments other than to look out for himself, it was the best thing to find out he had the guts and that strength of character, maybe not right then but later on in life. And for those of us who hoped he made it, he was a hero in our book, although there was no escape off the Island from 'El St Catherine's'.

As my health progressed, I was more at ease with my situation and felt fitter from lots of walking, and my confidence was on a high which was all down to the positive attitude instilled in us by Mr Busbridge. St Catherine's also put on lots of trips away from Ventnor. We took a coach to Newport on the Island one evening to watch a travelling gang show. That was so funny and when we got back we had hot drinks and toast before turning in. We visited the local cinema to see Tommy the Toreador staring Tommy Steel, and the song 'Little White Bull' became a popular song among the boys. Everything we did was interesting by design to help us all become more robust in mind and body.

At St Catherine's we were almost on automatic pilot because we had nothing to set us back, nothing to cause us to worry and hinder our recovery. We accepted that the nuns had little or no compassion, indeed looking after children seemed a strange occupation for them. They had chosen to take up a calling that would have no need of motherly instincts, that component had been locked away with all that was worldly when they took up their vows.

We also knew we could trust Mr Busbridge, Matron, as well as most of the helpers and nurses and, with the comradeship of fellow inmates, we dealt with everything that came our way. However, in all good stories there is always a villain, an anti-hero, someone who would be an obstacle to overcome, and St Catherine's had one such obstacle in the shape of one of the masters who mainly looked after the older boys. A 'dark tall figure' who was regarded by some of the older boys as a Rambo-type character, Superman without the cape, Batman with Robin in the shape of half a dozen gullible asthmatics who hung on his every word. This man loved himself and used the older boys as informants. If any of the younger boys did anything wrong, they reported them straight to him and he would then carry out a beating with a size 12 plimsole on the backside of the boy in question. Most of the younger boys kept in groups anyway, so we did not come across him that often, and we had safety in numbers. He sometimes was on the walking party if all the boys went together but was all sweetness and light when around other staff.

It was one Sunday evening when we attended the service at Holy Trinity Church in the town. As the service progressed, we would as usual be up and down on our knees to pray. Each time the five boys I was sat with got down to pray, the old bench we were sat on squeaked and did so again when we got up. This went on right through the service. When church was over and we lined up to walk back to St Catherine's, the master in question singled me out and told me to report to him when we got back to the home. As we walked back into Elm Grove I was almost at my dorm when I was grabbed by the scruff of my neck and marched into the toilet and was accused of making the church benches squeak deliberately, to which I replied that we could not help it because the bench was so old. But he would have none of my reasoning. He was determined to beat me and beat me he did. He made me pull my pants down and leaned me across the sinks and hit me with his plimsole six times as hard as he possibly could. It hurt so much I could not stand up. He then pulled me up and pushed me against the wall, his red face was right in mine and his breath stank. Shaking from his exertions, he had saliva that stuck to his lips as he said I should watch my step in future if I knew what was good for me and walked out leaving me on my own, trembling and stunned by this man's actions.

I pulled my pants up and staggered slowly back to my dorm, relieved my bed was next to the door as I tried to walk in without being noticed but I could not hide my pain as I crawled onto my bed. Keeping my head to the wall, I wept. I could feel the welp marks on my backside and the sting lasted for some time. I was not sure what to do and could not sleep that night worried he would return. The whole episode had knocked me back; the strength and confidence I had acquired over the months at St Catherine's so easily shattered in that one moment of cruelty by someone who was in a position of trust.

But I would have to start again. The confidence I had already obtained would stand me in good stead I was sure, and I had to outwardly show or pretend that my beating had not fazed me in any way because who could I tell who would believe me over a master, was what I thought. I knew I had done nothing wrong, but I could not risk telling anyone, even when I had a visit from home that same month. My mother said I was quiet so I had to pretend to them. My father, if I had told him, would have taken me out of the home and I could not have that happen, the air was so clean on the Island and I needed it. Dad would have wanted to kill the master for hurting me, I knew that but the stress of not knowing what to do for the best was horrid. Somehow, I managed to put on a front and look and behave as I had previously done, but inwardly I was a wreck and worried most of the time.

I started to think of ways to kill the master myself. Not literally, you understand, but, in my mind, I thought up ways of getting rid of this bastard of a man who I hated with a passion. It also dawned on me that he had taken a risk beating me because I had visits once a month. If he had beaten boys who had no visits, and he did by the way, he was safe in the knowledge he would not be found out. But he could never be sure that I would not tell and that in a way saved me from more beatings. Sometimes when my parents came and the master was around, I would look towards him, pointing to something else, telling Mum and Dad something about the sea or something over in his direction so he could never be certain I was not informing my parents of his fetish for beating young boys in his care. I never told anyone because I thought no one would believe me and I thought at the time that was not a true reflection of St Catherine's and the home in general or most of the people who worked honestly to carry on Sister Kathleen's work. They would have no idea they had been infiltrated by people whose main agenda was their own perverted wish to satisfy a fetish, for beating and abusing sick young children supposed to be in their care. Those actions were not that of the collective responsible body of people who had in affect been fooled by a certain individual. Groomed, if you like, into believing the abusers in their midst are genuine people with only good intentions, so I kept quiet about what happened to me, and it stayed with me for over 45 years in fact.

With the invention of the internet, people who had been in institutions began to have forums. Old boys' and girls' networks groups set up to discuss stories and share information about the places they went to for all sorts of ailments, the master was named and shamed in the posts online with no alleged included in the post of the cold-hearted treatment he dished out that still affected the people he hurt. At last, we could feel somehow vindicated that we had done nothing wrong. It may have been a long time ago, and some people may say we should forgive and forget. All very well if it had not happened to people with those thoughts, but for the victims of that abuse while we did not fill every waking hour remembering what happened to us, it was something that you could not forget and certainly not forgive in any way, shape or form. Other cases online told of a man who in 1954 was a house master at St Catherine's who also had his favoured boys who he sexually abused, one of whom told another boy at the time that the man abused him at bath time and was frightened to tell the people in charge. So, the boy he told went to see the person in charge and within 24 hours the boy that informed on the house master was sent home, and nothing changed because the person in charge did not believe the boy over the master. The story was just one of many reported online, and the abusers would of course be dead by the time the stories went online and the abuser's family may be shocked to learn of their people's involvement but that would not stop me and others I am sure from dancing on the graves of the perverts whose dark cloud hung over everyone at the home for so long.

My time at St Catherine's coincided with the end of Sister Kathleen's era. Reluctantly she had to relinquish her position as Sister in charge and, while she was ill, still watched from the window whenever I walked by. Sister Kathleen also made her last appearances while I was there at her birthday which was celebrated each August by holding a garden party in the grounds. She also came to Harvest Festival that year, an event I have always liked, when the fruits of the summer seasons produced by farmers throughout the countryside are celebrated. At St Catherine's, the festival was the best I had ever witnessed. We had two donkeys that we all followed, walking over real palm leaves. The procession moved all around the grounds and under two big archways leading to the chapel to thank the Lord for the harvest. It was times like this, celebrating events from past religious happenings, that I remember most.

Church was a big part of our education if we wanted it to be, but it was never thrust upon me by my parents or at St Catherine's. We would be invited to get more involved if we wanted to. Other than the Sunday evening compulsory attendance at church, I have always enjoyed the stories from the Bible like the story of Moses, and I have always tried to live by the words of the Lord's Prayer even though I do not regard myself as religious, but think a greater power exists who created us all. It is that greater power I have a spiritual relationship with; I don't worship religion that is preached but thank the Lord for each day for my energy, animals and all things that grow and are nourished by the earth in Mother Nature's great plan for the benefit of all. It is, I believe, each person's own choice when it comes to religion and to respect the choice of others accordingly.

As the days became weeks, and the weeks turned to months, I got stronger, and I had grown steadily. My asthma became more controlled, but I still needed injections and to see Matron or the doctor for check-ups. At the beginning of September 1960, the medics considered I was fit enough to go home, and once they had decided I could, things happened very quickly. Everything had been arranged with my parents regarding the date. I would be travelling back and the first I knew of the decision was when I was called from class and told to go with a helper to pack my things. I had no time to say thank you to Mr Busbridge or Matron, the two people I had the most respect for. My departure was swift. The helper travelled back with me by the same reverse route that Mr Butterworth and I had taken originally. By the end of that day, I found myself back with my family who all knew my travel arrangements and were at the station to greet me when I arrived. The months I had been at St Catherine's had been harder than my time at the farm in West Sussex. So much more than I actually realised, because when I was told, I was allowed to go home, I felt several emotions. I was pleased that I would be back with my family, I also relaxed and felt so at ease that I could try and find myself again after months of having to live on my wits.

I realised as soon as I walked out of the gate that I was free from having to pretend in order to survive. As I was walking up Grove Road on the other side of the wall next to the grounds of the home, the place that had been home for just over a year, that all of a sudden felt like it had been forever, I found myself hurrying up the hill as if I wanted to get as far away as possible from the place, and with each step I cast off a layer of protection I had wrapped myself in to keep me from the real fear that had made me unable to feel real feelings. The suppression during incarceration did affect my ability to trust and have real feelings again for anything. St Catherine's had helped boys with their asthma but taken away part of who they were. We became clinical, serious, suspicious and altogether different people and only realised this when we were allowed to leave. The component within us that made one love, want, desire and trust had been filed away, not having those emotions helped us through our time there because in reality we were just unhappy boys trying to get by the best way we could.

But outside away from the place we would need to find them to function properly back in the normal world. We would find it hard to shake off the shackles that locked us into the people we had become by the institution's tough rules and lack of compassion. We were only children after all, but the innocents and our individuality had been knocked out of us in an attempt to turn us into one of the same, and you would only realise this when you left the people that had been nice to you is what you held onto. We would find compliments hard to accept and found it hard to react to kind words spoken by genuine people whose only wish was to get to know us. Delay and reaction before replying, people found off-putting as it was a struggle to try interpreting their every word to be positive ones and not detrimental to us before replying. Many boys could not risk being damaged anymore because there was no energy left for that, so for me communication with people would be brief and they became associates the same as in the homes. I found it easier that way. I would be a good friend and my friendships lasted years. I was reliable and a good organiser however, I did not find it easy to do anything I had not arranged, preferring to miss out altogether on things set up by others who of course did not understand my reluctance to join in and eventually had me down as not being a party animal but shy and reserved, and I did nothing to discourage their opinion of me.

The disease that had controlled my early life and the time away from home at such a young age all culminated in me having to build myself up again to lead a normal life. My family helped but had no idea about my inner fears; I compartmentalised the bad things while I was at St Catherine's and referred only to good things but only when asked. I followed everyone's lead at home, who unknowingly led me back slowly into the person I was before I went away and considered my time away to be lost years.

Chapter 7
Back Home Again

A lot had happened while I was away, and when I returned to school, I did my best to catch up. I had plenty of help from my teacher Mr Court, who was also the school football team manager; he was pleased I participated in sport. He was surprised how good a footballer I was and selected me for the school team. I still had to take it easy and pace myself through games and my position in the team, right-back, was perfect for me. I learnt to read the game well from that position. I also played cricket for the school and took part in athletics, but only the long jump as sprinting and distance events were still closed for me, but I enjoyed watching our team against other schools. While I worked hard to catch up with lessons, I was well behind the other children; however, I was never at the bottom of the class, which was a positive for me.

Projects were high on the school's list of finding out about a child's ability to study and convert to written work and of course, my choice was farming. The work I did with that subject for the eleven-plus exams earned me a place at a farming and gardening secondary school that I would attend the following year when I became 11.

I also enjoyed time with family members again. Uncle George Wilber and Aunt Alva had moved from the farmhouse while I was away and lived opposite Grandfather Charles William at Spencer Road. Uncle George's family still owned the farmhouse that was rented out, so my brother and me could still go and visit with our uncle but we could not go in as before. It was nice to see the old place anyway. Uncle George told me he got the new bungalow at Spencer Road at a knock-down price because it had a World War Two unexploded bomb underneath it. He said it came down in the road outside and went right under the front garden and ended up roughly under the front room. Well, I was speechless and had to shake my head at this story to envisage such a thing happening. The road outside was not that wide and it must have just missed Charles William's bungalow by a whisker. As was his way, he said it was true, keeping a straight face as always, and began to talk about something else regarding the Second World War. Uncle then took a photo out of his wallet that he had taken when in Italy fighting in the war. It was of a man hanging on what looked like a lamp post.

He told me it was a picture he had taken with an old box camera and the man in the photo was Benito Mussolini, the Italian dictator who the British were at war with. Well, I had no idea who Benito Mussolini was at all and if my Aunt Alva knew I had seen a picture of a man hanging, Uncle George would have been told off. But all I could think of was the unexploded bomb. What about the neighbours, I thought to myself, did they not worry? I found it difficult to believe that my aunt and uncle lived with an unexploded German bomb under the bungalow.

I did ask Mum about what Uncle George had told me. Mum said the road was like a track with long sunken channels caused by the rain that ran down the hill. The bomb caused a shower of stones that landed everywhere, breaking some windows in the process. I further enquired how we knew it would not go off, and Mum just said, “If it was supposed to go off, it would have done so by now, surely!” and changed the subject. Of course, Mum had been around when bombs were dropping in Southampton because she had been an air raid warden so was used to talking about such things in a matter of fact way. I was going to tell her about the picture of the man hanging but I couldn’t remember the man’s name and it was probably just as well as it may have got Uncle George into trouble with Mother too.

On a Saturday, my brother and me would visit our Grandfather Charles William. He gave us both ten pence pocket money every week and was always pleased to see us and was particularly pleased that I was fitter after my time away at the home. I had missed the times we had together when he looked after me and I learnt many things from him and thought about him often when I was away and struggling to cope with everything that was going on. He had always been special to me, and now I learnt that he was struggling himself made me appreciate what he had done for me even more. My Aunt Alva and Uncle George looked in on him every day and made sure he ate well, and Mum would go in every day with shopping and sit with him for a while after work. Grandfather looked forward to my brother and I going to see him every weekend, but from week to week I could see he was a little slower. He had been a very independent man so having people fussing after him was difficult for him. But he did not complain, he knew his limitations and got used to people popping in to see him to help with simple tasks he could no longer do.

Then one day when we arrived home from school, Mum told us that Charles William had died. She had gone in as usual with shopping and found him in his chair, his head resting on his chest as if asleep, his favourite pipe on the table next to him, and the radio on as usual. Mum said the doctor confirmed he had died peacefully in his sleep, and I hoped that he suffered no pain. He had been an important person in all our lives and we all had nice memories of him. Grandfather Charles William was laid to rest with Grandmother Lucy Jane at the local churchyard. These days I often pass by and think of him. I have at times gone in and tended their grave and would find myself talking to them. Talking to dead people is not so strange, they are in your heart and mind and who knows their spirit my hear you. I like to think so anyway and once I had got over the sadness, when he did pass away, I would think about all of his teachings and have many fond memories of him.

When Christmas 1960 came it was rather downbeaten having lost Grandfather, however we still had a houseful for Christmas Day lunch but not like the party atmosphere we had in the past. Most of the people that came were from my mother's side of the family. I had thought about this many times in the past at quiet moments as to why. I knew Dad had brothers because one had attended a birthday party with his wife previously. Dad also had sisters as well, I had heard Mum and Dad talking about them at mealtimes. We had all been to his mother's who lived quite a distance away. So maybe it would have been too far for Nan and the other family members to come on Christmas Day, was the usual conclusion I came up with each time I thought about it.

However, I was determined to ask my father at some stage because I had all the information in my head regarding the farms at Durley and the stories that his grandfather had told him. But when Dad told them to me, he never included anything about who his father was. I would also think that our Grandmother Lucy Jane had died before I was born so it could be that Dad's father may have also passed away before I was born too so there would be a simple explanation, I was sure. I would not like to upset Dad by asking questions but hoped that there would be a time when I could ask.

On Boxing Day that year, after lunch our family walked up to Uncle George and Aunt Alva's home to join other relations for the afternoon and have tea. It was rather strange walking on the other side of Spencer Road and going into number 25 rather than number 20, Grandad's old bungalow. Other people now occupied the bungalow and it no longer looked familiar to me as the place that my grandfather had lived. I was also told that he had rented the bungalow from a local family who owned other properties in Thornhill. Well-known family builders, the Kendals, lived at a large estate at the back of a row of shops, one of which Uncle George's family rented from them and was where Mum worked. Colonel Kendal lived on the estate and had a reputation for being very protective of his land. There was many a story told about him patrolling his grounds with a blunderbuss and he would fire a buckshot into the backside of anyone he caught trespassing on his land. Uncle George said he had seen the blunderbuss and it was a long thing with an end like a trumpet, that was all pitted and black from firing buckshot at people and sometimes when Uncle George was in the shop, he said he would hear the sound echo from the woods as Colonel Kendal discharged more buckshot at an unexpecting intruder. No one ever knew if the Colonel hit anyone, not even Uncle George. The only problem believing the story of Colonel Kendal and his blunderbuss, was because Uncle George always seemed to add a bit more on to the legend every time and I never knew, like all of his stories, if they were true, because he was so convincing.

Even that afternoon while family gathered, he convinced my brother and I that we should try a drink that had a special secret ingredient only known to a few gypsy ladies. People handed down from mothers to daughters who once were regarded as white witches, they travelled from county to county in fine horse-drawn caravans. They would stop off each year at familiar places and read fortunes; the men folk would set up a grinding wheel to sharpen the knives and tools blunted from seasonal use in the fields and farmyards. Their way of life was rustic and would rely on the good nature of village farmers who allowed them to stop on their land for a few days and work in the fields in return. The white witches kept the secret well and if discovered would be placed on a ducking stool, like one in the village of Swanmore in Hampshire and dropped into the river until they admitted they had magical powers. Uncle George said such travellers would stay at the old farm and that was how he knew about the potion. Everyone watched as Uncle George poured this scarlet-coloured liquid gently into two small glasses, careful not to exceed the required amount that would help. He told us it would put hairs on our chest and keep a glint in our eyes and told us to drink it down in one. The secret potion he said was mixed with oxen blood. The travelling ladies swore by its power to keep you healthy; no one disputed what he told us, and we drank it down in one. It was thick and creamy and actually it tasted quite nice. We never did find out what it was, as Uncle George had moved on to another story. I eventually had quite a hairy chest, but I doubt it was down to Uncle George's secret potion, and my brother's chest was almost hairless. Uncle George Wilber will always be the great orator in our family!

New Year's day, Mum and Dad took us to Southampton to shop and after looking around lots of shops that were quite boring, we actually went to see Dads' mother, much to my surprise. We had been there before in the past. Our Nan lived in one of the long rows of rented houses that were identical and situated in the Shirley area of Southampton. The house was old, and the area was rather untidy looking. Once inside the house you would walk straight into a long hallway. Its carpet was well-worn, showing signs of much traffic, and its once colourful patterned weave was faded by the years. The carpeted hallway ran some 13 feet and stopped at the foot of a steep flight of stairs and continued up the middle of each stair tread. Each side of the tread was painted white and stood out in a uniformed manner, giving the stairs a wider appearance. To the left of the hallway a white-painted panelled door opened inward to a small front room. This room was immaculately kept and obviously reserved for guests. The furniture included two chairs and a matching sofa that looked like they had never been sat on and they complemented the wall-to-wall light-coloured fitted carpet on which stood against the main wall an oak glass-fronted cabinet full of Nan's keepsakes and photos from a time gone by. This whole room was clearly her pride and joy, its statement proof of her determination to have one room that identified who she was and what was important to her, in the hard life that people lived back in times of war and poverty. It was poverty that mirrored the rest of the downstairs of the house, walking from the front room turning left, back onto the hallway a few more strides took you past another smaller room. From its open door, it looked rather sparse in its furnishing and the floor was just polished floorboards. Once passed that room, was the hub of Nan's existence, the kitchen, and like my Grandfather Charles William had done, she spent most of her time in this well-used room that had seen better days.

The ceiling was cracked and yellow rings were evident around damp patches from the room's leaking lean-to roof. Nan had two large biscuit tins and a bucket placed about the room to catch the water that dripped, each one filling at different times depending on which way the wind blew or how hard it rained, and how big the hole in the roof was above each container. The dripping was accompanied by the radio, just loud enough to stop you going bonkers, with the sound of each repetitive drip. Nan also had a big table in the middle of the room and on it were a few empty stout bottles and a large ashtray with lots of roll-your-own cigarette ends in it.

Half a dozen different style chairs leaned against the table, and before my mother sat down, Dad placed a large brown paper bag for her to sit on because of the state of the chair. But Mum was a bit of a snob anyway when it came to cleanliness and Nan's kitchen was not high on the list of perfect hygienic places you could visit. There was also a wooden washing line with three slats held together with string, that was pulled up and down by a thin rope hanging from the ceiling. Nan ducked underneath the washing to fill the kettle from the sink, before ducking back under again. Some of her washing stayed on her head as she walked to the corner of the room, placing the kettle on the stove to boil. Whilst the kettle boiled, Nan talked to my siblings and me. She spoke with a genuine polite voice as she lit a roll-up. She took one drag and, coughing quickly, put it out apologising to me, because she said she had forgot about my asthma. I wasn't concerned as my Nan was a very nice person, and she had a very hard life so whatever gave her pleasure was fine with me. I only wished she lived closer to us as I would have liked to have seen her more. When the kettle boiled, Nan made tea and brought out the most beautiful set of bone china crockery that she placed on an equally impressive silver tray along with the tea pot, milk and sugar.

Picking up her treasured possession, she walked majestically to the front room, the scarf on her head her crown and housecoat represented that of ermine. We all followed her into the lovely front room that she proudly kept for special occasions, and for a short time she was in her best room away from the poverty that surrounded her. She was queen of all she surveyed, and my father looked at her with a pride brought on by her obvious devotion to him and his siblings born into the poverty of the early 1900s.

This was the room that Dad's grandfather had told him all the stories of Durley and why he talked of their importance; because back then they had given him his rich history and taken his mind off the difficult world he had been born into. In the same way that the stories of Durley helped me cope with all the problems I had, being in this room helped me realise that both my father and I used the stories to escape from bad things, and that's what bonded us together. This room had been where Nan's father had been laid out when he passed away when Dad was a boy. This old tradition went way back when the deceased person would be brought back home, for one night and a day so relatives could come and sit and pay their respects and talk to each other about times gone by. My father said he watched as his grandfather laid in his coffin with two pennies, one covering each eye. Dad said he kept looking around the door to see if the pennies had moved because his grandfather just looked as if he was asleep.

My great-grandfather George John, along with his own father, my two times great-grandfather William Henry, had brought their two families and all their history to live in the town where more jobs became available. They still lived as they had in Durley all under the same roof, and Nan had to share a bed with her sisters and an older cousin. They were still hard times both in the town and the country, and it felt good sitting there watching the grown-ups talking. When it was time to go, Nan asked us to come over again whenever we wanted to. I knew Dad visited her some Saturday mornings so it was possible that I may be able to go with him one day. My Nan lived a simple life. I was not sure who else lived at home with her, if indeed anyone did, so I asked my sister (she was older than me and had been to Nan's more than my brother and me). She said that Mother did not like Nan because she smoked, drank stout and the house was not very clean. My sister also said that one of Dad's brothers lived in the house when he was home from sea. He worked on the big ships as a waiter, and according to my sister he was strange. She did not give a reason why, and I listened intently to what she said but had not seen any friction between Mum and Nan, but in fact they talked and laughed together like old friends.

Mum would not have said anything in front of Nan but if she had an opinion about anyone or anything she would voice it, not always to the person in question but to our family sometimes. Mother drew conclusions about people without knowing all the facts; she would want you to see the person or thing in the same light and if you did not agree with her opinion she tended to sulk. Then if she heard something else that put the person or thing in a better light, then they or it would become flavour of the month. But regarding Nan, as it turned out she just didn't like the fact she drank, smoked and didn't keep the house clean. She would say that her mother, Lucy Jane, did not drink or smoke and looked after her home but died very young and while she thought it unfair knew that was life and no one could do anything about it. It just annoyed her and wasn't about not liking Nan. Mum could be a bit of a snob and did not like how my father had been brought up in "that house" as she referred to it.

However, because Dad lived in grubby surroundings it made him very conscious that he wanted his own home to be clean and considered our hygiene should be as high as his. Dad set the standards, as he always looked smart, and he would be clean-shaven every day. If we had visitors come unexpectedly, he would go and shave again and put on a clean shirt. He also did most of the housework and would polish you if you stood still long enough. He cleaned the windows inside and out every month and even took the glass screen out of the television and polished that. He put Mum to shame in the cleaning stakes. He was all round a gentleman.

Looking back, that Christmas signalled the end of my childhood and as the new year of 1961 began, so did my education at the farming and gardening school, and with that came more responsibility. I had to be up early each day, leaving home at 7.30 am to travel on two buses to my new school, so needed to be disciplined to be on time for each connection. It was a long way to go to school by bus, with a brisk walk to complete the journey each day, come rain or shine, but I wanted the opportunity to work on a farm so however difficult it was sometimes to make that journey each day I had to do it. I was not hundred per cent fit and still had the occasional bad night, also I still needed to have injections every Monday evening. The travel arrangements for this meant I had to be home and changed ready to catch the bus to the doctors surgery. So as soon as the school bell went at 3.55 pm on a Monday, I would have to get to the bus stop to catch the 4.05 pm bus to meet each connection home. I didn't have to rush because I paced myself in everything I did and became well organised, a good thing for the career I hoped to have.

I settled in quickly at the new school, all the work I did regarding gardening and farm management was taught by a wonderful teacher, Mr Weston. He was getting on a bit and was referred to by pupils as Pop Weston. His mind was full of information and if you were interested, working with him was very rewarding. He was aware that many of his class wanted to go and work on the farms in some capacity, so made sure as the terms progressed that we kept a record of everything we had learnt about the gardening side of things. For example, what we had planted, when and where, checking first it would flourish in the place selected or if it needed more light than shade. We would have to be able to recite to him the plant's particular cultivation details and whether the plant was a bulb, tuber or seed.

Once it was in the ground it was our responsibility to look after and nurture. Every plant had a use – it may be a legend in history, fabled for its beauty or smell with mythical stories attached to its name. We had to remember everything about the plants we grew and their role in Mother Nature's vast tapestry. If it was a flower that was easy on the eye. Or a vegetable to feed the hungry once we released its energy to grow, we had to see it through to its conclusion. Mr Weston said a bulb was just a bulb and a seed just a seed until it was fertilised by God's earth. Then it would become something else "weather providing" of course, he would always say that before a sentence or at the end of one. Statements like "Now weather providing" we will plant this or having planted something he would say "Now that should flourish weather providing". Pop Weston would place his clenched fists on the table when talking; his two thumbs would be outstretched to give him balance as he leaned forward, and when relaying information to us he would close his eyes as if he was actually carrying out the task in his head, recalling every part of the procedure. He was not like a real teacher but unique, a man that had seen it, done it and got the farming and gardening t-shirt, truly a man for all seasons and well respected by his students.

Regarding the farm management exams that were mainly written work, he insisted we researched all we could because working with animals and planning in advance work that needed to be done throughout the year was so important. Mr Weston explained that the seasons' work was repetitive on a farm, so the initial learning should not be missed or guessed at. You would need to show one hundred per cent commitment to the workings of the farm and care of animals in your charge. There was much to learn and the responsibilities relating to farming and indeed the gardening side of things meant you had to be reliable first and foremost then make sure you listened and took notes. Pop Weston would prefer to stop a lesson and make sure we all had understood what he was talking about. He encouraged everyone to ask if you were not sure and that often would lead to debating the subject. These impromptu debates sometimes took up half the lesson but if we were wiser afterwards then Pop Western had done his job.

In one lesson, someone noticed from the window that the hens and cockerels we kept in large free-range pens, seemed to have blood on their necks. The class was stopped and we all went out to discover that the young cockerels that were hatched from incubators had reached the stage where they had begun to fight in order to establish seniority within the group. The problem with hatching eggs in the incubator is that you don't know what you will get from the fertile eggs – more cockerels or hens. Again, if we placed the eggs into the incubator, then we were responsible for what was hatched. Cockerels for meat and hens to lay more eggs. But like the plants, they needed looking after. Mr Weston told us to take the birds into the class and we each took turns if we wanted to assist with cutting the birds' beaks, cutting their claws and clipping their wings. Some of the beaks looked rather strange when we had finished, and it would be a while before they would think about fighting again. Their claws too looked uneven but passed Mr Weston's inspection, and having their wings clipped stopped them trying to fly and instead would make them go round in a circle from a lack of balance. So things like that spur-of-the-moment lesson happened often; we learnt so much about interesting methods that if you only read about them it would still be interesting, however hands-on impromptu problem-solving was more rewarding. Handling live birds and animals was a good experience for everyone.

The school also organised field trips. We attended the farming trade shows at Earls Court in London, and the New Forest Show which I had been to many times with Aunt Alva and Uncle George, as they went every year We also went to working farms in Hampshire, and were shown how to work with sheep dogs, the workings of the milking sheds and at one pig farm we had a hands-on lesson on how to move pigs around the yard into deep litter housing sheds. Most of the pigs reacted well and cooperated with us when we took turns using boards and a stick to encourage them into the shed. It was all very interesting.

By the time my second year came around I had learnt a lot, and Mr Weston said I should, if possible, try and find work on a farm at weekends and in the summer holidays. My weekends were full as it was. Saturdays I had a job helping the milkman and also played football for the local scout team. Some of my old school team played and we made a decent team I would meet our milkman, Brian Laws, early on his round and help till we got to the school, then I would go and play in the match and finally catch up with Brian further on his round. I was often asked to play for my school but travelling by bus six days a week to school did not appeal to me. At Millbrook we had two wonderful sports masters, one Mr Don Cartridge, a fine cricketer, table tennis player and all-round good sportsman, lived not far from me and could not understand why I would turn down the chance of playing football for my school. Nor did Mr Sam Stevens. He was a fine football coach and he too lived on my side of the water. When I said I could play, it was a requirement someone had to give me a lift to the game on a Saturday . But they had other commitments at the weekend and realised it was not an attitude problem on my part. If I was picked, I always played for my house team, St Georges, in matches in school time. As long as I got a game for the scouts and later the youth club at the weekend, I was happy with that. It was never the case of not wanting to represent my school but more about other commitments I had on a Saturday and the travelling was the main issue. Neither of my parents could drive so playing locally satisfied my footballing interest, and the level I was playing was enough for me because I never had to push myself. The higher the level of football, the quicker the pace of the game, and I knew my limitations. I got through games easily at the lower level and just wanted to enjoy it.

In one match for the scouts at our old school that was at our home ground, I played upfront for the scout team and, back then, the goal nets were never up for some reason. After I scored a goal, I watched as the ball went near the fence surrounding the ground and saw my dad watching from the other side of the fence. Mum had often watched me play for my old school, but my father never had, given that all school matches kicked off at 4 pm when school finished, too early for Dad to attend. So, when I got home after helping the milkman, I told Dad I had seen him watching the game. He told me he watched me play from time to time and was just happy I could after all I had been through with my illness. It was good to know he watched me play and that meant a lot to me.

In the summer of 1962, my mother had been waiting to see a specialist doctor about a problem she had with a hernia. It had been troubling her for some years. She was told it was necessary for her to have an operation and it was considered a big operation and a last resort when the condition got worse. Mum was also diagnosed with having angina, a heart condition that would be controlled by placing a small tablet under her tongue whenever she felt the need. The hernia operation took place at the chest hospital in Southampton, however there were a lot of complications, and Mum ended up staying in the hospital for over three months. Blood clots became a problem, and it was a worry for us all at home. Dad went every night to see Mum and for two weeks no one else was allowed to go and see her. My siblings and I looked after ourselves, my sister would cook for Dad but most of the time he had food at his mum's, going straight from work and then going on to the chest hospital. He had very long days and by the time he got back home was tired, but we all mucked in and after te three months, Mother came home. She had to take things easy for a long time; it was well over a year before she could lift anything at all, and my father did not want her to work again until she was fit enough to do so.

Mum would not work with Uncle George again, the job involved too much heavy lifting for her, even with the new walk-in van that even Uncle George had problems getting used to. Three steps had been cut out at the centre of the back of the van. A pair of doors were fitted that would each open, concertina-like, whenever someone pushed a large red button on the back of the van if they wished to come into the mobile shop, and walk up a centre aisle that had floor-to-ceiling shelving each side of it, stocked with all manner of produce.

Uncle George could gain entry to the back of the van from his driver's seat by ducking down under the bulkhead of the van, to serve and collect people's money. However, each time he made this simple manoeuvre, more often than not he would hit his head on the low bulkhead. He did not have much luck either when exiting from the back of the van, again catching his head as he negotiated his way down the top step. Uncle George had a permanent cut on his head that, even when covered with medical dressing and a flat cap, still regularly managed to take the scab off. Sometimes he thought he had ducked down enough but came up too soon and just caught the back of his head, this time causing the skin jst to fold without drawing blood. Uncle George would end up walking around with his head cocked to one side if he was in the van or not and it became common practice in the end for us to look first at any new scarring before saying hello to him. He developed a habit of bending forward when meeting anyone, displaying any new cuts so we could examine the latest gash without having to debate how he got it. Aunt Alva said she thought his eyes must be going because he could not negotiate his way past anything low these days.

Even bending to get things from the fridge or a cupboard he had a problem negotiating the distance, and she would wait for the sound of a yowch from the kitchen whenever he went to perform the simplest of tasks, like making tea or having a sandwich. She would end up attending to another scrape, scratch or scuff that added to Uncle George's list of abrasions. Eventually, Mother took a job at the local factory making electrical components. It was easy work and she could sit down to do it. Many ladies from the estate worked in the factory, and Mum settled in well. So as a family we all had important things going on and only Sundays did we manage to all be together, and it was the best day of the week for me. I always went to church first thing because the scouts' leaders insisted we did if we wanted to play football for them. When I returned home, the smell of many households cooking roast dinners gave off a nice aroma, Mum always had British Forces Network on the radio. The programme was for people with family members in the forces. They had a record played for them as well as having messages passed on to loved ones. My father enjoyed a brown ale with his Sunday lunch and would send one of us up to the local British Legion to collect a bottle he had arranged with the steward, and we never had a problem with people saying we were underage.

Dad was also responsible for making the Yorkshire pudding and his was something else – very crispy and not dry; it was also very thin and tasted lovely. He would turn the oven off, leaving some in there while we ate our roast dinner and afterwards, when our dinner had gone down a bit, he would take the warm Yorkshire pudding and spread jam on it and it was wonderful. On one occasion, however, Mum had the table ready and Dad quickly took the top off the brown ale and dropped the bottle. He stood and watched open-mouthed as the frothy contents of the bottle ran around the skirting board and disappeared under the kitchen lino. Mum joked that she thought he was going to get down on all fours and catch the fluid as it ran along the floor. Dad managed to throw a towel over the residue and mop it up. He picked the bottle up and stood it upside down in a glass. Whilst we all ate lunch, we breathed in the lovely smell of brown ale, while Dad kept one eye on how much beer was dripping from the bottle into the glass. As the bubbles settled, eventually the bottle was empty and the beer was as flat as a witch's tit! Dad picked up the glass, put his head back, placed the glass to his lips and waited for what was left of his lunchtime drink to run slowly over his tongue and down the back of his throat, smacking his lips to savour the taste, much to the amusement of the rest of us. Dad did see the funny side of it eventually. Our family enjoyed a simple life, it was full of comical events from time to time. We put on no airs and graces or pretended to be anything other than the working-class people we were. Like many of our neighbours, we all looked out for each other and helped one another whenever we could.

Chapter 8
Working Life Begins

In 1964 I set out to find myself a weekend and holiday job working on a farm. I rode my bike from farm to farm offering my services and willingness to work at anything, explaining that I attended a farming and gardening school and wanted to get some hands-on experience that could potentially lead to a job when I left school. The first place I tried was a large farm about half a mile from my house, on the main road north out of Southampton. It was a very large dairy farm that we always passed when we went with Uncle George to his old farm about a mile away. The farm was owned and run by a Polish couple, all the milking sheds where close to the road and I had in the past watched from there at all the activities going on in the busy yard. The farmer was very happy to talk to me but said he had four sons of working age, and it would be difficult for him to find work for another person even at weekends. He wished me luck with finding work and said I would be welcome to come back anytime just to watch his operation in action if I wanted to. I thanked him and went onto the next farm thinking it would have been the perfect place to work, not being far from home. The next farm I enquired at was more of a small holding, but they had no jobs for me. Eventually, I reached the village of Botley. This was about two and a half miles away from home but by taking short cuts through the lanes and woods I could ride there in half an hour.

The farm was on the outskirts of the village at Brook Lane; it was a poultry and pig farm, and this time I was offered a job working on a Sunday, assisting with looking after the pigs and keeping the yard clean. Mr Wiltshire, the owner, told me if I shaped up, he might be able to offer me a job when I left school. I left the farm and was delighted to have been taken on because it was something I had always wanted to do, and now it was a reality. I considered myself lucky, and if I worked hard, I might hopefully be taken on when I did leave school. When I arrived home, my parents were pleased. They thought it was a bit far to ride my bike but agreed it was a start and wished me well.

I had to report to the farm at 7 am the following Sunday morning and the first job was to help clean the pig sties out. I was given blue overalls to put on and a pair of wellingtons, there was a shower room and a locker to keep my clothes in; I had taken a change of clothes in anticipation that I would be getting dirty. The pigs could be let out of the back of the sties into a large area to spend the day on a deep litter bed of straw. It was a nice way to treat them, they had plenty of room to move about and enough food and water that had to be checked on through the day. The sties were a real mess and the runs at the front of the sties were ankle deep in pig manure, and like pea soup to try and move. I was given a shovel that had sides to it and had to scoop liquid manure into a barrow, and some of each shovelful ran up the handle and on up the sleeves of my overalls, with some dripping into my boots. It was not long before I was covered in pig muck and stank to high heaven.

However, while it was rather uncomfortable to begin with, I soon got used to it. The best method of moving the manure was by scooping and pouring it quickly into a high-sided wheelbarrow then, when that was half full, I slowly pushed the runny contents to a pit at the end of the yard. It was slow work but very enjoyable. You could say I was as happy as a pig in you know what!

After cleaning the sties, the foreman showed how to place the pigs' straw bedding around the sties' perimeter walls; each housed four medium-sized pigs. I then had to wash down the yard, clean the wheelbarrow and shovel and put them in a large tool shed. It had been an interesting morning's work and looking after pigs was very rewarding. The pigs all looked in excellent condition and the batch I was looking after were to go to market when they reached a certain age.

While the pigs all looked the same, after working with them for a few weeks, it was quite easy to identify one or two by their personality. My Uncle George would say pigs were ignorant, but they were also very intelligent creatures and watching them was a fascinating pastime. I worked for six months with the pigs on Sundays, and in the school holidays, I worked three days a week. I learnt so much about pigs – the management of the sows and the preparation of the impressive boar that would not only cover the farm's own sows, but other local pig owners would bring sows to be covered by this massive specimen of a pig that was the champion of all Mr Wiltshire's stock at Brook Farm.

At the end of the six-month period at Brook Farm, Mr Wiltshire offered me a full-time job when I left school, I had one more term to do and gladly took the job. However, it was not the job I had been covering for every Sunday. The job that I accepted was that of poultry boy. Brook Farm had massive battery houses; the hens had light 24 hours a day. Their food and water were on a timer, and at a specific time pellets dropped into feeding trays at the front of the cage and each bird in the cage was eager to be fed, which caused fights for supremacy. The cages each held several birds, with hardly any room to move and it would be the survival of the strongest. Many smaller birds died and were eaten by the other birds; cannibalism was a regular occurrence and almost impossible to prevent. Brook Farm also had several long deep litter hen houses, the birds in them never saw the light of day either, only artificial light. The birds reacted aggressively towards anyone that entered into the houses to collect their eggs; they would fly at you to prevent their eggs being removed. Sometimes you would have to pick the bird up off its nest and throw it far enough away and quickly take the eggs before they came back at you. It was a fight each time I went in. The birds were brainwashed by the conditions they lived in, and cannibalism also took place in the deep litter pens. This time they would eat birds that were weaker.

It was not really what I wanted to do; the job changed hands regularly because boys couldn't handle the conditions. It was a terrible job to do and the conditions I faced, both in the deep litter and the battery houses, made me ill even though I had a mask on. The dusty conditions were not good for my asthma, it affected my breathing and I had to go outside for fresh air. But I did stick to the job and said nothing to anyone at home, even though it took me longer to ride home each night, and that was commented on by my mother. I got round that by saying that I worked on at the farm.

As the months went by, I worked out how to help the weaker smaller birds in the cages; I could push a switch and the system became manual. I would take out several small birds and put them in a box, then after switching the system back on collected all the eggs and placed them on large egg trays and took them to the counting room. I then filled in the egg chart. I also wrote in the relevant box that the cage I took the birds from had fatalities. No new birds would be put back in till the dropping trays had been emptied. This we did once a week. Two flaps, one each side of the cages, would be opened, and a large trailer was pulled to the side of the cages by a tractor. We then pushed the birds' droppings with long-handled scrapers into the trailer. This was when the full horror of the cannibalism among the birds was revealed; some of the birds were just carcases, every bit of meat had been eaten by other birds. It was a terrible way to keep poultry.

That's why I took some of the smaller birds out in boxes and sectioned off an area in the deep litter. If they stayed together, they were accepted by other birds; they were fine and had a better chance of surviving. Chickens are also very intelligent. Again, it was my Uncle George who told me that they could count, and if you put six birds in with six birds already housed, they would size each other up and because their number was the same the chickens just went about their business. But if you placed four hens in a pen of six, the six would attack the four. If one was singled out, they would in effect worry it to death. The smaller hens had a better chance in the deep litter of surviving and after a while one area of one of the deep litter houses had about 30 hens. I took them from the cages and as I saw it, if they laid eggs, it would not matter where they laid them profit-wise. I could justify the low egg count from the cages by saying we had more deaths and of course adjust the egg charts, and say eggs laid in the deep litter were laid in the cages so it was easy. I also just let some birds go and they ran off into the woods like an escaped prisoner.

They stood a better chance of having some sort of short life because their natural instinct to forage would take them deep into bushes and bracken. A clever chicken could survive for quite a while by keeping on the move by day, and at night they would roost in trees. If they stayed healthy, they could still lay eggs and if they kept moving and did not change the landscape, they could remain undetected. It is only when chickens stay in one place and, if you see the pens of free-range hens, it is completely barren of vegetation, with no place to hide from a fox. But if you went into any pen and stood near a bird and placed your hand over it, then it would freeze, just hunch its back and hope it would not be taken. Some would probably end up being taken by a fox if they stayed too long in one place, but to me it was better than being eaten by one of your own and not being able to do anything about it.

The farm foreman worked out what I was doing and said sooner or later I would be found out. He told me this while hitting one of the runt pigs over the head with a small lump hammer and throwing it up on the compost heap. I asked him why he killed them when they may pull through. He answered that if they were runts now, they always would be so and could get sick and pass on the sickness to the other pigs. He did have a point and, eventually, the litter's runts were cremated – burying them was not an option for contamination reasons – and Mr Wiltshire to have great-looking pigs to go to market, then there had to be casualties, it was part of Mother Nature's great plan or the survival of the fittest. I could move birds and alter the egg charts for a while, eventually things would return to how they were and the only way to have great eggs and healthy chickens was to go free-range, and I have always thought that. Still, if they are not free-range, you can minimally help them. It is only a token, but the lucky ones have a little longer on God's earth.

At the end of 1965, my health deteriorated further from working in the farm's terrible conditions. I was fit but I had problems breathing. It took me from the time I left work till the time I got near to home to recover from working in the disturbing conditions. I hid well the state I was in from my family; my method was to push my bike all the way home some nights, stopping to rest against it to get my breath. I suppose deep down I always knew something like this would happen. I could pace myself in my sporting life, take my time riding to and from work, but at work I would have to pull my weight and keep up with everyone else; no one would cover for me. So, I had to tell Mr Wiltshire I would have to leave, unless it was possible to change jobs by working with the pigs again. But then it may not be acceptable to Mr Wiltshire, he was running a business and could not let people pick and choose what they wanted to do. The reality was I was not cut out for farming healthwise and would have to face it. So, I went to see Mr Wiltshire and gave in my notice. I told him that I suffered with asthma and was finding working with poultry impossible given the conditions they were being kept in. Mr Wiltshire didn't like me criticising the way his poultry were kept. I told him I understood it was the modern way but for health reasons, both for myself and the birds, it was not for me. I offered to work the week's notice because I didn't want to let him down.

We agreed I would leave the following week, and when I got home, I told my parents I had decided to leave the farm because I was having trouble breathing while working in the dusty conditions. Dad said he had been worried because my breathing at night was erratic and had looked in on me a few times and was going to talk to me anyway about the job. Mum said she was worried as well and glad I was leaving; she thought something would go wrong, and I should not have started the job in the first place. Mum had a way of making you feel like shit when you already felt that way. She didn't mean any harm, and I took her usual stock well-rehearsed remarks for such occasions with a pinch of salt. We had become immune to such comments and why we ever told her anything in the first place was a mystery to me, we knew what the reaction would be. But we all fell into the trap probably because we respected her, and if we didn't tell her anything and she found out then we got the same tactless reaction so we couldn't win.

So, our family sayings were "Don't tell Mum because" or "Shall we tell Mother because". Mum would rather no one did anything that might fail. It was not her fault, the Victorian values she encountered when growing up had left their mark. She looked upon any failure by the family as a direct reflection on her, and that weakness to fail could never be attributed to her lineage. It must have been her scholarly teachings from teachers who knew nothing about life and encouraged young girls never to take chances regarding anything. None of her family members I had encountered would say or think that one should not try, it was quite the opposite. My dad would say nothing, he would close his eyes and pause a while until the negative energy in the room dispersed. His silence made Mum sit up and look around as if woken from a trance and wondered why it was we looked so confused. She didn't know what she said, it was a well-rehearsed comment made each time she thought someone messed up and would possibly embarrass the family in the process.

My father followed the enforced silence and continued the conversation by saying to me I needn't worry about rushing into something else right away. He asked me if another job allied to farming would be of interest to me, say in an office somewhere. I thanked Dad for saying I had time to look around and whatever I did end up doing would have to be hands-on. The whole thing about farming was just that and the freedom. The animals could not do without you, and to an extent, I could not do without them – pigs, cows, horses and properly-kept chickens, would all make for a happy working life if you were fit enough. So, whatever it was I would end up doing would have to give me the same buzz.

I worked my notice for Mr Wiltshire, who had been fair with me all along. I had served him well too and left on good terms with him. I was not out of work for long having seen a job advertised for someone to work in the warehouse of a local furniture store. I called them up and went to see the manager who gave me the job. It was a dead-end job, I knew that, but I wanted to be independent, and it was just a stopgap until I found what I was looking for. At that moment in time, I had no idea what that would be, but the job would do for now, is what I thought. Mum just tutted and smiled when I said what I would be doing next and told me I had no training for moving furniture about. And she was right, I didn't, but I had to start somewhere. So, I had to catch the bus into town each day, a journey I was familiar with from my school days. The 9 am start meant there was more traffic on the road, and the bus took an age to get to town and sometimes I got off early and walked briskly through the parks once the bus got to town because I had to be first at the shop to sweep the shopfront down before we put furniture out on display.

Wynton's was the shop's name, owned by a wealthy Jewish family, and only had the best furniture in the store. Bernard Wynton was my boss, his father called him Bur and he was a class act, always immaculately dressed. After working on the farm with men with their arses hanging out of their pants, working for Bur was a bit of a culture shock. Another one of my jobs was to go out with the delivery driver and help take furniture to really smart houses. The driver used to work in the shop as a salesman but had enough of the 'bullshit' is how he put it. He asked me what the hell I was doing working in a dead-end job, suggesting I would soon get fed up with it and I had to laugh because I knew that before I started. The driver, whose name escapes me, was easy to work with and shared his tips with me. He was a dab hand at touching furniture up if something in the back of the lorry took a tumble if he hit the brakes hard. He also drank six pints of something every night and with the smell of the lorry engine and his flatulence, I had to travel with the window down, but it was fun.

The only thing that kept me working for them was because on a Thursday halfway to work a rather nice-looking girl got on the bus. She always went inside the bus but before getting on looked up at me. At first, I thought she was looking at someone else but after a month realised it was me. Not only that, when we got off the bus at the last stop, we walked with other people up to London Road. She would not pass me, nor would I overtake her, it was bizarre. Sometimes when people pushed by, we almost touched shoulders but still we said nothing, not even good morning. Then when I got to the shop she would walk on up to where she worked, and I watched till she turned the corner and she always looked back. I told my friends at the youth club about it, and they all said I should say something, and I should have and regretted that I had not when after six months at the furniture shop, I left to work on the railways as a junior porter.

Another dead-end job but better paid, I had to work shifts 7 am till 2 pm, then 2 pm till 9 pm. It was interesting, I got to see lots of people, some of whom were famous, but the job was not for me, and after another six months I left to work this time as a plasterers' labourer/improver. The advert said I was to work for a gang of plasterers, the boss was a workaholic and wanted someone with the same work ethic and he would teach the person the art of plastering. Two members of staff worked for him on other jobs, so we had two gangs. My boss, whose name was Ronald Appsie Bray, was a giant of a man, a former southern area heavyweight boxing champion for the Army. He came from a travelling background and would often talk about the hard life he had growing up, having to break the ice on the water butt in the mornings to wash. I had been working for him about a month when I realised that plastering was just the job for me. I had no issues with the materials we used, which was unexpected; the only thing was the lime we used that made me sneeze. Apart from that, it was only the hours I had to work that made the job hard, Dad said Appsie was a slave driver and he was right. But I was learning the trade and I enjoyed it, the only thing I would not have was a day release at college every week.

Mum said I could not be a proper plasterer, if I did not have papers to prove I could do the job and she was right. However, I probably learnt more than the average apprentice plasterer, I worked more hours than they did, that's for sure. I had worked for about four months without going out, I was either too late home or too tired. But one evening I did go to the youth club and talked with friends about our various jobs which were mainly in the construction industry.

One of my friend's said he had paperwork about the college exams, that covered the day-release papers that you could do without attending college, rather like an evening class. So, when we walked home and I went in to collect them, when we got there his mum was in the kitchen. I knew her from junior school when she came to the football matches; she knew I had been away for health reasons and was pleased I had found a job I liked. She told us to go into the front room because they had visitors, and she would bring drinks in for us.

When I walked in behind my friend, to the right of me was the girl from the Thursday bus ride. I was closer to her now than I ever was, and we still said nothing. It was so obvious to the other people in the room that we had seen each other before. I was introduced to the rest of the people then my friend took me into the kitchen. I told him the girl in the front room was the same girl I had told him about from the bus stop when I worked at the furniture shop. The girl turned out to be a relation of his, and as we talked, she came into the kitchen and my friend saw that as his cue to leave us together. We talked about the time walking to our respective places of work, and how we both wanted to say something but didn't and agreed that it must have been written in the stars we would meet again.

That evening I took her home, and from that day forward we were inseparable. I had never liked anyone as much as I did her and felt confident, about seven feet tall, whenever we were together. My parents liked her, in fact Dad adored her, Mum said she hoped I was treating her with respect, and I knew what she meant by that. My only problem with having a girlfriend at 16, was I didn't earn a lot working for Ron Bray, even with long hours. But I still tried to see her most nights, even if it was for an hour. She lived on an estate not far from my house and to get there I had to walk down Barnes Road where we once had our old prefab. It was now an area for parking but the shortcut onto Barnes Road went right through where our garden once was.

I had not been back that way before, but it became a well-trodden pathway for us both. My working life went from strength to strength and when I was 17 and passed my driving test, Dad helped my buy my first van by standing as guarantor, and by the time I was 19 I had learnt a lot and became confident enough to begin working for myself. I left Ron Bray's employment and the hours I had put in with him, and the high standards he demanded regarding all jobs stood me in good stead. Ron was not too pleased when I left but understood and knew that one day, I would want to work for myself.

At first, finding work was difficult and something I had not factored in when setting out on my own, but once word got around I was working for myself, then a steady run of work came in. I advertised in the local paper twice a week and found, while work was not that quick to come in, people would keep the advert for when they needed the services of a plasterer. I had to get used to the paperwork, tax was stopped by the main contractors at 35% so, the first year I just broke even. However, after that any overpayment to the taxman was paid back, so it was a bit like saving money. When I got to know how to work the system and had cash customers as well as paying tax on work that went through the books, I found that working for myself at the job I loved was very rewarding. I would meet so many people from different walks of life. It may not have been farming that I made my way in life but it was the next best thing.

Chapter 9
Marriage and Life

In 1970 with work going well, my girlfriend and I married, and with the help from our respective parents, purchased an old house. It needed rather a lot of work done, but I had the know-how, energy, and an understanding bank manager who, while considering me to be an optimist, provided me with funds. Back then you could sit in a room with the 'top man' and lay out what you intended to do, with no computer saying yes or no to requests. Mind you, if you told the manager funds would be back in the time agreed, you would have to make sure they were or he would have you in for a grilling. It was very much a question of trust.

My parents also purchased the family home, and with a very generous discount from the council could plan for the future. They had things worked out in that respect and intended to work till the age of 60 and then retire to the Isle of Wight. Mums' family had originated from there, and with visits to me while I was at St Catherine's, as well as family holidays, the Island gave them an insight into what to expect and look forward to in the future. Also, that year my parents decided that they would have a holiday in California and stay with Mum's youngest sister and her husband. They had been talking about it for some time, and now it was the right time for them. Mum was in constant contact with her sister by letter and sometimes phone calls, and they even kept in touch with tapes recorded and sent back and forward to each other. We all had the microphone placed under our noses from time to time to say hello to our aunt and uncle, and to give them news of how things were going on this side of the pond.

My aunt was the youngest of the four sisters. She and her husband were both ambitious and thought America would give them a better life. So, in the summer of 1970, Mum and Dad travelled to California. They had a wonderful month's holiday. My aunt and uncle had a big plush bungalow with a swimming pool and all the trappings, and really made my parents' holiday one they would never forget. They took them to film sets and they watched how the stunt men worked in the cowboy films and meet the actors from Bonanza a popular cowboy programme in this country at the time. They also went to the best restaurants and had a great time at the casinos and watching shows at the Desert hotels. My aunt and uncle had no children and worked long hours to have the lifestyle they wanted and did my parents proud while they were there. Other members of our family also went over for holidays; my brother had been and had a great time, he was my uncle's favourite nephew. When they lived in England, they both liked cars and my brother, being around nine years old when they left this country, looked upon our uncle as his hero. He always had a smart car and would tell my brother about all types of fast cars that he had driven each week at the Southampton car auction rooms. Many of the dealers who took cars to auction wanted our uncle to drive them through. He could make the roughest of engines sound good and when the auctioneer shouted "Rev it up, I have the logbook", Uncle Stan Wade would make the car purr and the bidding began.

Also, that year my brother married his girlfriend, and my sister – who was also married – lived near to the family home and had a young son that Mum and Dad doted on. Things changed rapidly in all our lives and all through 1970 I worked hard with my contracts and on our house. I also helped my Aunt Alva and Uncle George doing small jobs to their home. It was good to help them because they had been so good to me over the years. Uncle George had now retired after working hard in his family's firm that was run by Uncle George's brother Owen Sims. Apparently, he had been asked by their father to make sure that George was always looked after with work and receive help with a home and money if needed.

Mum had told me my uncle had to leave the Army after discovering he had a defective heart, and the condition could minimise his longevity of life so he could only work for the family part time. His father made sure he was looked after, and for me, that was wonderful because he deserved it.

I also spent time with my dad, just talking about things in general and on occasions, about the stories of Durley. He enjoyed reminiscing about them and was glad I remembered them, telling me that our Durley history was important and that back in time, our ancestors had a tough time of it. How long you stayed working on the land depended on your energy. His grandfather, George John's great-grandfather, David had been famous for making sure fellow farm workers received a fair day's money for what was a very long day's work. Dad had talked about this man before when I was a boy, and how he was in some way either connected to the church or lived in a property owned by the church.

In our talks, Dad said more about individual people, specific grandfathers and certain dates in the timeline. He was keen for me to know about Durley and the life there. However, with all the talk of grandfathers, there was never any mention of who his father was. Sometimes I was tempted to ask who his father was but I could never bring myself to. I don't know why. Whatever I was to learn about that part of our history would have to be from my mother, and the love she had for my father meant if there were some big secret connected to it she would have made sure it was well hidden!

I didn't know why, I felt there was something, call it intuition or maybe something in my subconscious. A subliminal message I picked up on occasionally, indicating there was something else about which I should know. It was when I was concentrating on work it came on sporadically and when the concentration was broken all thoughts of there being something else vanished like being woken from a dream. I didn't discuss this with anyone else or try and find out if it was a natural thing, that other people felt in a spiritual way a gift if you like. But something you would not talk about for fear of not being taken seriously. There were groups of spiritual people who debated such issues and who would respect the fact that others felt this unusual feeling. I just didn't have the time to spend finding out, and all the time I was busy, my thoughts were focused on the job in hand and that was making money. I wasn't greedy but I soon found that being married and having a house was expensive, as well as the cost of living and had no time to go in search of some romantic notion of lost history, one day maybe but not right then.

And so, 1970 had been an interesting year. At Christmas, the family got together as usual but not like the past, no singing and dancing now we were older. It was more talking about events, funny stories and risky jokes no longer frowned on by Mother. We talked about lots of things and how everyone's year had gone, what was in store, if anything, in the new year. I remember that Christmas as being very relaxing.

When the new year began, I was swamped with work and, now fully established, I could budget for the year. In time I was turning jobs away and could cherry-pick the best of them. But it would always be the most taxing of jobs with a rich history connected to them I would always try to get. If the owner had the same vision and commitment to restore the relevant work, then I always did those and the first five months of 1971 I was nonstop. Then in June I had a call from a Mr Fry, a builder from Durley. He had two cottages that had been made into one dwelling situated on the main street that ran through Durley. I had passed the cottages many times over the years on my way to work, and in the past with my brother and Uncle George Wilber on our way to his sisters. While that was so long ago, it felt like yesterday as I pulled onto the driveway of the cottage; something I had seen from a far and now close up to was much bigger than I envisaged.

Mr Fry greeted me and showed me round. He wanted me to render the outside of the building and re-plaster the internal walls. I had been recommended to Mr Fry and I had heard of him, he was a very meticulous person, very quiet but a brilliant tradesman, so it was a pleasure to work for him. He gave me a free rein and trusted that I would make the place look how I thought it should look with some of the historic features that lesser builder would not have allowed me to do. For example, keeping the red-brick feature around the head of the windows and along the front of the building that would protrude from the external render, forming a frieze that would allow you to render the top half of the front elevation of the cottage in one go and would have no joins in the work, and internally particular beams would be left exposed that would indicate the building's age.

Because the job was situated on Durley Street, the main street through the village, I was often asked for my card by people who in the future would use my services. The name on my van was commented on by older people who recognised it as being a local village name and asked me about its origins. Unfortunately, I could not tell them because I didn't know all the details. I confirmed the family had connections with Durley and after talking with people about Durley's past made me even more interested in whatever the connection was I would in time need to find out. Spending two months working on the new cottage and talking to many people who were all very interesting, each of them knew something about the old cottages, like who had occupied them in the past and telling me that the cottages once had thatched roofs until damaged by fire and replaced by a slate roof.

The cottages had four big chimney stacks and Mr Fry had done well to incorporate the four into the new layout of the new cottage. At one time, the old cottages had been part of a farm called Oaklands, situated across the street, and knowing something about the properties I worked on always gave me great pride. I enjoyed knowing that the work I had carried out would become part of its history and add something that would be talked about in years to come. I liked working on such rustic properties that were like rural statues, reminders of times gone by and each one having the feeling of warmth about it that could only have been acquired by close families inhabiting such properties down the years. Each leaving their stamp of togetherness from hard work and commitment to each other as well as the village they loved.

Having been busy, I had not seen my parents as often as I normally would have, so that weekend I dropped my wife off at her parents and went to see mine. When I arrived, my dad was busy in the garden, Mum was in the kitchen. She made tea and I sat with her before going out into the garden. She asked how we were and about work, I told her we were fine and about the work on the cottage and that people had come in to look at the work and asked about the name on my van and having said they thought it was a local name. Then my mother, thinking I was going to start asking about Dad's family again stopped me in my tracks and said that she wished I would forget it and that my father respected his mother but was dragged up in that dirty house. He had scurvy as a boy and as the oldest child would sit on the stairs while another one of his five siblings was born. I thought to myself, well where did that come from, and told her I had no intention of asking anything of the kind. It was as if Mum had rehearsed this moment in her head for whenever she thought I would bring the subject up, but she had jumped the gun this time. She then finished by saying Dad's father died when he was a baby so leave things as they are. It was not a telling off, she did not raise her voice, but she just repeated words that sounded as if she had rehearsed and prepared them to be spoken when a certain utterance from me was brought into a conversation. Just like the scene in the film The Thirty-nine Steps when the memory man is asked by Richard Hanny in the audience at the music hall "What are the thirty-nine steps" and the memory man repeats in a trance-like manner the information about some impending crime that would take down the government. It was extraordinary! There was enough information in Mum's short statement to keep a shrink in work for a month of Sundays, and for me to digest when I had time to do so. After Mum made Dad a drink, we joined him in the garden. Dad asked me how Kath and I were, and as Mum walked back into the house, she looked down her nose in my direction and gave a stern look she kept just for me.

Dad asked if Mum told me about Uncle George, who had been having problems with tiredness and that doctors had increased his medication. I could see now why Mum was not her usual self and, when I left, asked Mum to tell Aunt Alva if I could do anything to let me know. She agreed and apologised, stating she should have said something earlier about George and that it would not be a good idea to go up to see him just yet.

When I drove away, I thought about my strange conversation with Mother and the first thing that dawned on me was if, as Mum said, that my father had to sit on the stairs while new siblings arrived, who was the father of the newborn? It could not be my father's father if he died when Dad was a baby as I was being led to believe. Mum had let something slip there and it needed further investigation. Still, who to ask would be something else that would have to be placed on the now overcrowded backburner. My only motivation for wanting to know anything was purely for historical reasons. I did not want to stir up ancient misdemeanours by long-lost relatives that would upset present-day relations or hurt anyone connected to our lineage. But I could not tell Mother that I would not get past go! if I said anything she thought would lead to asking questions she disapproved of, for reasons best known to her, then the subject would be changed or would receive the type of interruption I had encountered earlier. For heaven's sake, we are talking about my father's side of the family. Mum's side of the family was as pure as the driven snow, or so we were led to believe. I could, after all, if I had the time – and did not – spend it looking into Dad's side of the family. I knew about Nan and George John, Dad's grandfather, but who was Dad's father and what dark secret surrounded his existence?

I had to respect the fact that my parents had been born in an age when history would only get to relations by word of mouth. There would be records of immediate family, the ones closest to you; it could be you had a cousin living streets away and not know about them, unlike today – with a flick of a switch, the world is at your fingertips. And so, while it was frustrating, I had to respect the fact we lived in another age and that I should accept the old methods and assume the position of burying one's head in the sand and forget anything ever really happened before I arrived on this wonderful planet.

As the weeks passed, my wife and I had time to see my Aunt Alva and Uncle George. He slept a lot of the time as the drugs given to him made him drowsy. He could talk to us slowly but was very frail, and his same lovely smile would greet us. It was clear to me I would lose my dear uncle and my aunt was very brave. They were so right for each other and together had looked after my brother and I so well, and my uncle's legendary stories that even then at the age of 21 I still had no idea if they had been true or not.

My mother called me on the 23rd of September 1971 to tell me my dearest Uncle George Wilber had died. He had a fall, and my aunt managed to get him onto his bed and went for help. But when she and the help returned, he had passed on. My cousin Michael sorted everything out with his mum; my uncle had a nice send-off. Like my grandfather, Charles William, my wonderful Uncle George Wilber had been such a big part of my early life, and while I was sad my uncle had passed away, I was glad he would no longer suffer. He was a legend; someone I would never forget.

My Aunt Alva spent time with my parents as well as with her son and family at his home, and we all helped her through her sorrow. In November of that year, she was invited by her sister to travel to America and stay for as long as she wanted. Aunt Alva had never flown before, but she took up the invitation and stayed for two months enjoying Christmas with her sister and brother-in-law. Mum and Dad talked with them on Christmas Day on the phone and our family did things differently that Christmas. We still went to Mum and Dad's but not collectively. My wife and I had lunch at her parents and then went on to mine in the evening. Now everyone was married, things changed. Gone were the days of our youth, people moved and had others to consider. To get everyone together again as before would never happen again. The parties that had been so funny in the past when everyone let themselves go, and relations who were normally reserved would join in the embarrassing songs. Dancing took place with the conga being a favourite through the lounge into the kitchen and dining room, then back into the lounge where everyone sat back down laughing. They had been fantastic times but never to be repeated.

It was my mother who was the catalyst in the organisation of it all, making sure everyone was catered for, and that is why I could never get angry with her. She was there for everyone it was just sometimes she could be so rigid, and almost afraid of things she did not understand and thought wrongly that we as a family could be hurt and looked down on if there was a skeleton lurking in a cupboard somewhere. That's why she was so keen that my father did nothing about the letter he received regarding his ancestors. I would wait until my father asked me for help in the matter. I also had to respect Mother's feelings. I had never fallen out with anyone so far in my life back then! I always tried to see everyone's perspective, even to my own detriment on occasions, and I could wait; the truth would out when the time was right, as Dad always said, and I learnt to appreciate patience was a virtue.

While I may have been persistent, I had to display a certain tolerance and hide my tenacious attitude and use a reverse psychology that would indicate that things relating to my ancestors were not that important to me. But I was ready to hoover up any information that had any relevance to my pet subject.

1972 started off as busy as the preceding year. Auntie Alva returned from America in early January and Mum had everyone over for tea to welcome her back. She looked well, the holiday had certainly done her good, she brought back small gifts for us all and it was so good to see her again. I always miss people when they are away and seem not to be able to settle until they have returned. I don't worry about them, I suppose, if they are very special you just miss them. My cousin Michael wanted my aunt to move in with him and his family; he had a new annex added to his home that he had built himself some years ago. Michael had always been a fantastic tradesman, someone I had always admired from the days my brother and I tried to play his white homemade guitar. Throughout his working career he worked his way up and became one of the top men in the National Federation of House Builders. Michael was indeed a very special person.

My aunt was not sure if she was ready to move from Spencer Road. She had lived there at number 20 with her parents, William and Lucy, and her siblings and then at number 25 with Uncle George, 'bomb' and all, so she had an attachment to the area. But eventually she decided to make the move and it was the right one as far as I was concerned. We still would see her, and she would get on a bus and come and see Mum and Dad or at the weekend my parents would visit. She had her grandchildren living in the main house so she could be independent or spend time with her family.

My parents also had a nice summer holiday on the Isle of Wight staying with Mum's Uncle Albert. He was Mother's uncle and had a house in Chile on the Island. We had been there when I was a child, I remember Albert would cut the hedge on the narrow road outside his house and place two red flags one each end of his property warning drivers that work was in progress. He also had in the garden an amazing model village made out seashells that he picked up from the beach; it must have taken ages to build. My parents enjoyed a relaxing week on the Island, and I was glad they enjoyed it.

1972 also brought good news as my brother and his wife told my parents they would be grandparents again and would have another grandchild to dote on. In September of that year, my wife and I informed them that we too would be having a child. My parents were so pleased that the family was increasing, also they were getting plenty of practice at having a house full of family.

At the weekends, my sister, her husband and son would visit as well as my brother and his wife. Dad loved it, he was very good with children and glowed with pride, and he told me when we were on our own that he was looking forward to me being a father, saying I would make a good one. This meant a lot to me. After all, we had spent some dark times together when I was a child, and I suppose surviving all that somehow formed a bond between us. We had never talked about that sort of thing, and he showed me no more love than he did to my brother and sister, but sometimes he treated me in a way that made me feel just a little bit more connected with him; a mutual pride in each other born from a will never to give in.

My mother was pleased she could tell the ladies at the factory of the impending births and had all her knitting things out making things for the babies. At work, the women had a chart for who could predict the weight of a newborn baby, and with the factory so full of ladies from the estate when each child was born, the grandmother or mother had plenty of cards.

Workwise, things were still going well, and in November, I took on a contract to plaster eight new houses, which would keep me busy until after the upcoming Christmas. It was the first big contract I had taken on. While I would always prefer working on restoration jobs, this was work that, while being repetitive, was near to home with good money, with each unit set to show a good profit on completion. The new contract started very well; each unit took about two weeks to complete. I kept well in front of following trades and had time to fit smaller cash jobs in as it was getting near Christmas; more money came in very handy at that time of the year. I worked right up to Christmas Eve, the weather had been fine, so the site was not affected by frost as sometimes is the case in the winter months.

Christmas Day that year was to be spent with my wife's family, and on Boxing Day, we were going to my parents. But, on Christmas Eve, Dad called me to say that Mum had picked up a flu bug from work and that he thought he was going down with it as well. Mother thought that everyone should stay away so as not to give the bug to anyone. I agreed with Dad. I told him to let me know if they needed anything; he said that he and Mum would look after each other and have Christmas Day later in the week if they felt better. However, the flu virus hung around for the rest of the Christmas week leading up to New Year's Eve and my parents saw in the new year by watching the fireworks with neighbours who gathered outside their houses.

On the 2nd of January I had a small job to sort out and went in and took a list of things Mum and Dad wanted dropped off. The two of them had improved, saying they felt better but Mum looked ill and on the 3rd of January, when I went in, Mum was still upstairs feeling unwell. I did not go up but called out hello to her and she replied, sounding very bunged up. My dad was in the front room and we talked for a short time and I took another list of things he had asked for. As I was going, my Dad said he had a strange pain in his stomach that made him keep belching. It had come on over night and said it was painful to begin with but had eased off with him moving around. I told him that the two of them had been very poorly with the bug and should call the doctor if either of them felt any worse and that I would be back at around 5 pm because I had agreed that I would go with friends to play football and catch up. I got to the ground at around 2 pm and after about half an hour my brother turned up to say that Dad had been taken to the hospital, so I immediately left and picked up my wife and we went to my parents' house.

My mother was distressed as she told me that Dad was in a lot of pain to begin with but by the time the doctor came the pain had eased. Still, the doctor wanted him in hospital because he had been ill. Anyway, the doctor also said it could be an appendix problem and he went with Dad. Our neighbour stayed with Mum until my brother turned up and was sent for me. My brother wanted to go and stay at the hospital, but they would not allow him to, saying we should call every hour for an update. The first call I made I was told that Dad was down in the theatre. The second call an hour later I was told that he had an operation to clear up some mess, as they called it, in his gut and that everything had gone well, and the surgeon was pleased. My dad was now in the recovery room. We had to call every hour on the hour for an update, we did that till midnight and then at 6 am in the morning. I was told Dad had a comfortable night and we were allowed to visit the hospital. We could go at 9 am but not too many people and not for long. So, I was able to tell Mum everything they had told me and she began to relax, but she was still very poorly herself. I was not happy for her to go at 9 am because she had been up most of the night and looked terrible. I wanted her to go later in the day after resting properly. But she would not hear of it, so she was to go with my brother and my wife, while I stayed and manned the phone to tell family members what the latest news was.

At 8 am my brother first took his wife home and then went with Mum and my wife to the hospital. The first person to call was my sister and I told her what was happening and that I would call her when I knew more.

At 9.15 am the phone rang and when I answered it was a lady from the hospital asking if anyone was coming to see my father. I told her that family members had left over one hour ago. As I said it, I began to worry as to where they had got to, thinking something had happened to my mother. All these thoughts rushed through my head in seconds. Then I told the lady that I could be over in 20 minutes. She told me that if I wanted to come over that I could and paused for a second then said she was very sorry to have to tell me that my father had died.

I could not take in what she was telling me and wanted to say that they had said that my dad was doing well but the words would not come out. I could not string two words together, she must have got it wrong, or I must have misheard what she said. I was devastated. The lady said she was so sorry and put the phone down. I didn't know what to do, my whole world had collapsed. I walked from one side of the room to the other. I could hardly stand and in the end sank to my knees and just wept uncontrollably. The man that had looked after me and saved me so often was dead, this beautiful person who had never hurt anyone and was only 52 had been taken from us. And, as I sat on the floor, the phone rang again. I hardly had the energy to pick it up. I eventually picked it up, not knowing what to say. I just stood there. It was my godmother, my Aunt Una. She asked how things were, and I tried to talk but could only cry. She said she would be straight over. She worked some miles away but the next thing I remember was she and my godfather, my Uncle Bernard, were walking up the path to the door. When I opened it, I could not say anything to them. My uncle called the hospital and my aunt just held me. I was like a child in her embrace, I could feel nothing nor could I move, I did not want Dad to be gone.

I was getting to know him more than just a father but as a man, together we had moved closer from me needing him to a mutual companionship that was blossoming every day, like new love. The chance to do things with him had been stripped from me, I felt all emotions, especially anger, and that I had been robbed of someone who could never be replaced. My Uncle Bernard confirmed to Aunt Una that what I had been told was all true and I began to try work out how to find out where my mother was, and I wanted my wife with me more than anything right then. I also had to tell my sister. I told my aunt and uncle that I must go and tell my sister and asked them to stay at the house because I had no idea what had happened to mother, wherever she was she would be in a state of shock, that was for sure.

When I got to my sisters, she knew as soon as I got out of the van that something terrible had happened and we just sat, not really knowing what to say to each other. I left her and she said she would make her way to the house later. I am not sure how long I drove around for but ended up in Durley churchyard, a place I always seemed to retreat to and think, but I could think of nothing and left. When I arrived back, my mother was home and when she saw me, it broke my heart to see her like that, having lost her one and only love. She could not control her emotions and screamed at me, wanting to know why but I had no answers for her. I felt useless as her heart broke.

By this time our house was full of people saying nothing but each helping each other through the tears and when Aunt Alva arrived, she and Mum leaned on each other. Mum pushed her head deep into Aunt Alva's chest and her loud cries became muffled from the pressure of their embrace. My brother had gone to the docks to tell our father's best friend and the people at the docks gave my brother brandy because he was in shock when he got there, and several men brought him back home to the house that was in mourning for my dad. The doctor came and had given Mum a sedative to take when everyone had gone and one by one each person left until it was just Mum, Kath and me. We stayed with her for a few nights, my brother and sister shared the duties of looking after her.

The first night was the most difficult for me. She wept aloud, and it sounded so painful but when I went into her room she was weeping in her sleep. Kath and I sat up most of the night, we did not say a lot, but we needed each other. It was like we had been before in our courting days. Whatever the Lord thought I had done wrong in my life or had too much too soon and had to pay a price for, then he took the only thing I would never have given up at any price.

That awful day changed our lives. Mine seemed to be like when the electricity has a surge, and the lights first dim and then brighten again but mine stayed dim. And I thought they would forever, and they did and, in a way, I never recovered from the time the lady at the hospital told me Dad had died, right up to the present day. I do not dwell on what I missed out on with my father, that would be stupid. I feel his warmth about me all the time and I use it as a motivation, because I want him to be proud of me and what I do. But you know what, you never get over that first kick in the balls, and as for my mother, well when Dad passed away part of her went with him, she was never the same and it was left to my brother, sister and I to try and help her pick up the bits of her broken life. She lost about four stone in weight but was determined to move on and to her credit she tried but it was to be hard. The well-worn ancient road to healing is indeed a long one, with its highs and lows and many willing to assist you on your way. But you have to want to travel down its ancient twists and turns leading to something new, taking steps forward then back. Grief and sorrow are something you have to get through, you do not get over them and you have to do it on your own at your own pace. There are many who offer advice, who say what you should do most of the time to make themselves feel better thinking they can only feel better if they know you are!

Then you find yourself saying you are fine when you are not, just to please others. That is why grief is so lonely, it isolates you from all others, keeps you in safe solitary confinement until you can move forward on your own. I recall the passing of the days, lots of things needed to be done the Dock board and Dad's union sorted out everything for my mother. The man that took Dad to work each day as well as being his best friend, was the person who dealt with the families at times like this for the Dock union. He was wonderful, Bert Trigs was his name and he was a credit to his position. He helped Mum sort out all my father's pensions from the Docks and legal probate papers, something that would have caused Mum stress if she had to do it all herself. So, Bert and everyone at the Docks who helped did my father proud.

On the day of Dad's funeral, we had a service at the church first and then on to the crematorium, both well attended. I didn't notice anyone; all I could do, with my brother on each side of our mother, was to make sure she stayed upright and got through the day. As we walked from the house to the waiting funeral cars, lots of our neighbours lined the path in disbelief that one of the families who had all moved together onto the estate and become mutual friends had lost one so respected and so young.

As the funeral procession pulled away, one man walked to the top of the road in front of the cars. I never took my eyes off my father's coffin from the time we left home till it passed through the curtains for the cremation. Many people kissed me and shook my hand, but I remember none of them, and so many flowers lined the path outside the chapel. I will never forget the sound of cremation fires starting up and the black smoke that bellowed from the tall chimney stack. That was just another thing to endure, something I think they could have spared us, or it could have been just me that noticed it. I remembered that sound each time I took flowers with Mum to the garden of remembrance on Dad's birth and death dates, and to look at the book of remembrance that's open on the same date and records that dreadful day when we lost my father.

When I recall the church service before going to the crematorium, nothing that the holy man said was any comfort to me, about going to a better place and the Lord wanting my dad. Well excuse me, he was not done on this earth yet and I had always believed in a greater power. I didn't know what that was. I hoped it was the Lord and that to follow the Lord's Prayer is how I always tried to live my life. But he would have to forgive me at that moment, when his holy man said what he said that took the sting out of the loss for some on the day but when reflected upon was bullshit as far as I was concerned right then. The Lord would need to forgive me until I could recover from the beating he had just imposed on me, before I could think of him again as the greater power. My only consolation was that I believed that the spirits of our loved ones remain near to us and are kept alive within our hearts and minds. I have always taken comfort from that my father will always be 52 and life's troubles will never harm him. I may see him in the eyes of my children and remember how close we had always been, and I would have to accept and come to terms with the fact we would never see each other again, not in this life anyway and that was the hardest thing to endure.

My mother faced life without Father and was, to her credit, positive about her future without him; no one could ever take his place. No one did, she worshipped him from then on, but the experience changed her. She was still very popular at work, and with neighbours, everyone got on with her. She was still the go-to person for all the family when they had a problem, but my mother became very bitter. It wasn't easy to know how to please her. If she had to unload on someone, then it was usually me. If someone said anything she didn't like, I got it in the neck on behalf of whoever had upset her. I made a rod for my own back by not taking her side but giving my opinion on what I thought about the thing that got her back up. So, I became over time her own personal battering ram, but I did not care, it was such an interesting scenario. I would go and see her; we would have a cup of tea and talk about family things and then she would put on the verbal boxing gloves and try and beat me into submission about what someone had said or done was wrong.

I would try and make her see both sides of the argument much to her dislike, but it was good exercise for her. A good verbal workout once a week did her the power of good, and it usually ended up with her saying that I made her sick for not agreeing with her. We always finished on good terms, it was a weekly thing, and I did the rest of the family a favour. They were lucky my situation would never become vacant, and I knew just how to handle Mother's moods. She was still my wonderful Mum and I always told myself not to push her too far, and that my dad would probably think it was funny but would want me to look after her.

Mum sometimes tried it on with my brother but he was not as good as I was when she started one of her rants. He agreed with her and as the story would usually be the same and when she came up for breath in that pause he would know when to say yes and when to say no. But Mother would catch him out and my brother would say yes when it should have been no and vice versa, which resulted in Mum telling him that he made her sick for not listening. He would end up well and truly in her bad books, for whatever period of time Mum would decide not to talk to him. It would usually be until she wanted something done, so never that long. My brother and I would ring each other if we had been confined to the doghouse so we knew what to expect when we went in to see Mum. Sometimes, it was embarrassing for us if someone told us that they thought they had upset Mum and wanted to apologise, but we would put them at ease and explain that Mum had become difficult and hard to please and they should not worry. And that is how things continued. Our mother had changed, that was it and all about it.

Chapter 10
New Life

In May of that year, my wife gave birth to our first child, a daughter. It was a great experience for us to start our family, and everyone was pleased for us. Within 18 months, we had our second daughter, and it would be the start of what I would say was the best time of my life. We went on to have two more children, this time boys, so by the time we were 30 our family was complete. It was hard work but we had plenty of support. My wife's mother was a brilliant lady and helped us so much; without her, it would have been a struggle. My father-in-law was very good to me and loved the fact he had grandchildren. Mum too was pleased we had a family. Still, she was more reserved about everything by the time the children came along and would worry she could not help as much as my in-laws money-wise, with buying things for the children, but she gave nice gifts on birthdays as well as Christmas.

In 1978 my sister and her husband moved to Cornwall. After two years they asked Mum if she would like to go and live with them. It would mean she would have to put the house up for sale, something I was not pleased about and asked her to think about such a big decision. But, because I was the only person against it on the grounds Dad had worked his socks off to buy it – they both had – Mum went against my wish for her to keep the house. Her going to Cornwall was fine, it would make my life a little less stressful and not have to have regular conflicts with Mum which was beginning to get me in the doghouse at home. So, I should have been happy about it, but I was not. Mum said she knew what she was doing and everyone else thought it was a good idea, so that was it. The house was sold, Mum first went back to California to stay with her sister for one month before going to Cornwall. However, while she was there, she and her sister fell out. My aunt could not have known how Mum had changed and was so easily hurt if anyone said something out of turn. People would not get to finish their sentence when in conversation with Mum; if a word was used Mother didn't think was right or it was in some way critical of her, that was it, she would go into her shell and not come out. Mum's emotional wounds had not mended and maybe they never would. My uncle begged the two of them to make up. But the sisters had the same DNA and were as stubborn as a pair of old mules, and Mother came home of course. I tried to see both sides of the problem and would not take her side, which made her mad and so off to Cornwall she went with a flea in her ear.

I am sure many people have difficult parents – it can be a right muck and fuddle sometimes, can't it, having to watch what you say and how you say it can be so stressful. So, when Mother went to Cornwall, it was a great relief and gave me a bit of respite, and not having to walk on eggshells made things easier at home. I was busy with work and enjoyed my family, my wife worked very hard with the children, and they were all fun to be around. I was still interested in football and took on the role of manager for a side I played for. This would lead me into non-league semi pro-management that lasted 20 years and I was successful.

My teams meant everything to me. I was very protective of them all. The teams I managed had a wonderful dressing-room atmosphere, our teams won titles and cups and I always liked the fact my players enjoyed playing for the clubs I managed. They would bring their fathers to watch the teams, and I always wished that my father could have watched one of my teams. He would have been proud, I am sure. The history books show what I won, I never bothered with medals and have none for the things I won. Doing it was good enough for me and I made many friends from my time in football.

Five years after Mum moved to Cornwall, my sister and her family had a chance to move to Australia. So, Mother came home to Southampton, and for a while lived with my brother till she moved into a nice warden-call flat complex. Mum settled in well and joined in with all the events and outings etc. and was well liked by all. However, her attitude toward me was still the same and it was not long before she was sick of me. Once more my wife and I did everything to make her feel welcome. I would go and bring her down for Sunday lunch which she loved and could be with the children, but it was hard work, there was no happy medium for me.

I was glad I had the football and work. I took my daughters horse riding; one liked it and one did not. The one that did has had horses all her life, and my eldest son always came to football with me. The youngest son was not really interested in football and was happy doing other things with his friends. So, I had a busy life and as time passed by and my children grew up and started to do their own thing so did my wife and I. She had friends and would do things with our daughters, and I still found my work interesting as well as my now long-established football management career.

One thing I picked up again was my connection with Durley. The little information I had put together so far gave me something to work on now and then. I would go to the churchyard at Durley when I took my daughter to attend to her horse and passed the time looking around the yard while she did so. However, I was determined not to let Mum know she had touched on the subject a few times after Dad died, but I was not going to give her the satisfaction of repeating another reprimand. I had long passed that mistake, and what little I had on my ancestors from Durley was something I held dear and was not to be frowned upon or belittled in any way. Mum sometimes mentioned the letter Dad had received, but only in passing, and I did often wonder what did happen to it. But all I did was wonder because so many years had passed between, and Mother had moved twice.

I was approaching 50 by this time and had reached another bullet point in my life – after over 30 years with my wife we got divorced. My daughters had already moved out of the family home to be with their respective partners, something I found difficult. They were all grown up and I missed them. It wasn't long before my boys moved out to make their way in life. I soon got used to being on my own, and my children were regular visitors, something I enjoyed. After my divorce, I built five more rooms on the house. It all went well. I finished with football and I thought I would miss it. However, I did not and I still had Mum to look out for and she had been very supportive of me when my wife and I split up. Mum always liked her and thought I should have tried to mend things, and of course, I made her sick for not trying to. I finished the work on the house, and my sons had been helpful in doing it, and when I took more work on the two of them wanted to work with me.

We had a good team and took on some interesting renovation work. My eldest son had worked with me before. My youngest son was a jack of all trades, not interested in one trade in particular, he had worked in many. It was handy him knowing something about most trades. We worked together well. It's not easy for sons to work with fathers, but I told them when at work it was the job that was the most important thing. After work we were family, it was not all plain sailing, and sometimes we all had an opinion on how a job should proceed, but we got there in the end, and I enjoyed that time of my working life.

Chapter 11
The Truth Will Out

With work steady and the house finished, I found myself with more time on my hands. The boys had made my working life so much easier. My eldest son was a meticulous worker and turned out good work; my youngest son stayed with us till he had a chance to go and work in Spain, leaving his brother and I working together. I would give him work to do on a price and it worked out well. My eldest daughter and her son had a small farm and worked hard to maintain it, and my youngest daughter and her partner lived near the New Forest with their three sons. So, with four children all doing well enough, and having four grandsons I was a happy man. My dad would have loved them all, the fact he never got to see them was such a shame for everyone. So, you see the history that was being created in our family, the moving on of generations with information added to the mix, something I encouraged my family to do. I encouraged recording and talking about the family's history, for future generations and they could ask me anything. If I knew the answer, I would pass it on and not hold things back as my mother had done with me.

There was one such conversation one afternoon, with my mother talking about my children and how I was making sure my history would be passed down. If they would be interested it would be there for them to see, I wouldn't force it on them but in time everyone wants to know something about the past. Mum looked over her glasses at me, and said I was just a "clever clogs" and picked up her paper to read. Mum was now 80, but still as feisty as ever and as I sat there, I felt a change in attitude. She said I was a "clever clogs" in an almost complementary way and not in a damming 'you make me sick' way. So, I just sat and looked out of the window, and began to start talking about how people talked about each other in the past and it was not very nice having everyone knowing your business or looking down on you. Then she said that Nan, my dad's mother, did not care what people said about her and went on again about how Dad was brought up in a dirty house. I still didn't say anything but felt the hair on the back of my neck stand up, thinking she was going to tell me something and the longer I sat not saying anything she would I was sure be wondering why I had not jumped in and asked about my father's father.

She then said that the trouble with me, was I don't care who I upset asking questions. At this point I visualised her putting on her 'poor me' hat, sometimes she would act like a fully paid-up member of that club. But I still said nothing, I just sat still and looked at her. Then she took off her glasses and leaned out of her chair and said, "Anyway, there is no one left to ask now so why drag up the past?" So I said, "Mother, I was talking about what history I was going to hand down to my children. I have not said anything about what you have not told me, but if you know anything that would be relevant to me and my history, I would like to know. It is my right to know, in my opinion." Mum said, "Well, I do not, so there" to which I said, "What is wrong with you? Was my father illegitimate or something?" and I sat back in silence.

There was the usual silence and I thought, well, here we go again Trev, you have done it now, it's sulk time. But it was not. Mum leaned over and said in her posh voice that she kept for when she was really pissed off with someone, that was usually me in particular, "Well yes he was if you want to know." I thought, my God after all this time she was about to open up and she did but what she was about to tell me was going to blow me right out of the water. I said to her, "Before you start, Mum, I don't care if dad was illegitimate, he was my father, that is all I care about" and she started to weep. I was ready to say 'don't worry about it now, Mum', but before I could she began to talk She first said what she was about to tell me I had to promise that I would do nothing about it. I told her that I could not make that promise until she told me what it was and that even then I didn't think I would be able to give that assurance if I was honest. Mum just sat and looked at me like a card shark with the cards close to her chest and holding all the aces. She knew I wanted to know what she had kept a secret for so long.

But she also knew that I wouldn't want to know if I couldn't have all the facts, and that if I did, I would leave no stone unturned in pursuit of something so important to me. So, then she said that if she did tell me and I did try and find out anything, that I should not talk to my father's sisters and bother them. And whatever I did find out, that she did not want to be told or shown anything. In fact, not to ever talk about the subject again. I felt like I was being cast out, banished from the fold like some black sheep of the family and that I was committing a crime by wanting to know what was so fundamentally my right to know.

It was standoff time; she was not going to change the rules of this game and I could take comfort in that fact at least. She was an honest enough person who would not move the goal post as we went along, and what she would tell me would come warts and all and be God's honest truth as she knew it. So, I said yes, that I would agree to her revised offer and so my mother began to tell me the most amazing story, as far as I was concerned anyway.

The reasons she did not want Dad's sisters bothered was because they were his stepsisters and not real sisters, nor were his brothers. They had a different father and had been born the first of them some seven years after my father. Mum went on to say that the father of the stepchildren was not a very nice person, who had in effect, according to some people, ruined Nan's life. Mum said that the stepchildren and the father were nothing to do with Dad's Durley connections, and that his father was not linked to George John Prowting, Dad's grandfather. Our family name and links with Durley were not paternal but maternal through Nan who, when Dad was born, kept her maiden name.

So, everything that Dad had told me about the stories of Durley had all been genuine. I was linked to them all by my maternal links through Nan. So, in effect the surname we went by was not our real surname. I asked Mum if she realised this, and she looked over at me and asked if I thought she was stupid and of course she did. She then also declared, "To be honest with you, I have always had a problem with your father's illegitimacy. It did not make me love him any less, but it did bother me and every time you kept on asking questions, because you think you are entitled to know everything about everyone, it hurt me."

Mum's bottom lip began to tremble then, recovering her composure, said, "There are some things that are difficult to deal with, but you have never thought twice about other people's feelings, have you?" She continued by saying they both decided if I or my siblings ever asked, we would say your father's dad had died when Dad was a baby. "Also, something had to be put on our wedding certificate regarding the groom's father and his occupation so we said his name was the same as your father's and that he was deceased. But I always thought one day the truth would need to come out, and it had to be you that would poke your big nose into something that did not concern you."

I said to Mother that illegitimacy did not make people any different, or the way people should think about someone that was. They are who they are, and if some people didn't like the fact someone was illegitimate before dealing with them then one would be better off not knowing a person like that.

However, for information regarding family trees it is right that the truth is known, if you leave a blank box on a birth certificate regarding the father of a child for instance. When you know who the father is then you're changing history and by the same token if you put something that is not correct that too changes history.

I told Mum I understood why she would have wanted things looking right on a certificate, just for cosmetic reasons and it could have stayed that way as far as non-family members were concerned. But where blood relations are concerned, they have a right to know if they ever ask; if they don't ask then the story remains until someone does and in my opinion, someone will always ask, as I did. It bothered me that Mum would not answer questions as much as it bothered her, because I knew inside there was something else. I should know. It is a spiritual thing, instinct, call it what you like but if a person is in touch feeling wise, they can feel something's wrong if they are told a lie. The fact that Mum never said anything but just shut me up with a peer power attitude did not help and I had too much respect for my parents to stamp and shout, the odds made it even more frustrating.

Mum said nothing but nodded indicating she understood. I then told her that all she had told me so far seemed straightforward enough to me and not worthy of all the cloak and dagger stuff surrounding it. Mum sat back and laughed before saying, "You've heard nothing yet mate!"

She began by telling me that she would take my sister every week to see Nan and pick up Nan's sister's granddaughter Marg on the way. Marg was my sister's age and the daughter of one of Dad's cousins. Mum would take the two of them out shopping in the pushchair. One day when she was taking the girls back to Nan's, the lady that lived next door to Nan stopped and talked to Mum and after some minutes asked how my dad was. Mum said he was well and working hard, the usual chit-chat as you do, and then the neighbour said Dad was such a lovely boy growing up and should never have been brought up in that place, pointing to Nan's house.

She then told Mum that Dad's father was a fine upstanding Italian Naval Officer, who had been Nan's boyfriend in World War One. Nan was broken-hearted after the war when her boyfriend had to continue his naval career back in Italy and did not know that she was pregnant with my father. So, Dad and Nan lived in the house with her parents and some of Nan's siblings until her parents died and siblings moved on. Nan took on the house, or rather was taken over by the father of Dad's step-siblings, who was the son of a wealthy lady and would not marry Nan but just used her.

Mum said she was flabbergasted, and she didn't know if she should tell my father about the Italian links, or if he knew or not. I asked her, did she not notice if he looked different, and she said no she loved him and she didn't care about anything else. Mum said when she went into the house, Nan asked her what the old busybody from next door was talking about. Mum just said she wanted to know how everyone was and had asked after Dad. Nan's response was "Yes, I am sure she did", and gave Mum a strange look and that was about all Mum could tell me. The lady didn't say what the Italian's name was, and Mum said she was too shocked to ask anyway.

I asked Mum if my father's letter in 1971 was anything to do with all she had just told me. She gave me a direct answer that she had no idea and thought at the time it may have been, that's why she wanted Dad to do nothing with it. Dad was also reluctant to show her the letter till such time he had time to investigate the details, and she had no idea if he did anything about the letter before he passed away, none of us did.

But I had enough to be getting on with. I had no leads whatsoever to go on and not sure how I would start or if it were worth trying; it would be something to think about. Mother said, "Well you wanted to know so now you do, good luck to you" and that I would be mad if I wasted time trying to work that one out. I asked her if she felt better for telling me, which she did and seemed relieved. We had been talking for over two hours and were both hungry, so I suggested we had fish and chips for tea which Mum was up for, so I went to get them. We enjoyed them together; it had been an interesting afternoon.

When I got home, my head was spinning from all the concentration, so I decided to leave things until the next day regarding what to do first in my attempts to discover my Italian links. It sounded so strange to say or even think that somewhere I could have Italian relations. As I began to think more, I was delighted that it could be a reality. Still, I knew it could also result in finding nothing because it had been so long. I also had to think what my father would say to me if he knew. I was about to start a journey into the past to find out who his father was. Would he approve or not? I couldn't answer my own question, but I was the only one that could.

So, I decided that when I did start, I would go with the flow. If one bit of information, i.e. a birth certificate took me to another record that fitted, complemented, and enhanced the search giving it credibility, then I would carry on. I would need the full version of each record hoping something in them would give me a lead.

I also decided that although I had given my word I wouldn't talk to Dad's sisters about the Italian link, I didn't see why I shouldn't try and find them, after all they were my step aunties. It was a bit of a feeble reason, so I decided to wait and see if something led me in that direction. At that time, I was doing small jobs so could sort things out around my work, at the weekends now I would go and see Mum. I would take out the week's papers and rubbish, run the hoover round the flat for her and turn her mattress. She could still do all her washing and cooking but lifting things was too much for her. Every other Sunday, I would cook her a roast dinner at my home; she liked the house and all the work I had done to it. I had kept it up, together with the idea of one day moving on. It was too big for just me and was after all a good family home.

It would be three weeks before Mum said anything to me about things relating to the Italian situation. I made sure I said nothing when I was in her company. I wanted her to come around and become involved in what I was doing, but knew it would upset her and to have that worry that each move would have to be done considering someone's feelings was a nonstarter. This had to be done from start to finish as a project. It would I was sure be emotional at times, but I was ready for that and the setbacks that would surely come with it.

I could not tell her about ordering certificates or anything personal regarding my father, she would not like that. So, if she did ask, I would just say that it would be difficult, and I was not sure how it would turn out. She would be happy with that, not because she did not want me to find anything but that I may give up if things got too difficult, so we didn't talk about it. Mum was just concerned for Dad's sake and that was fine, but I knew deep down that nothing in my father's history would show him in a bad light; and that's what kept me going. If I looked at his photo I would know if he would not approve of what I was attempting to do so I pushed on.

Dad's birth certificate was the first record to arrive, so I took it to the city library, along with notepad and pencil, items that you cannot be without when starting investigative work in the library's archives. There were strict rules – no pens, phones, drinks or lunch, and if you wanted a copy, they would do that for you. I found them most helpful and the first thing I looked up in the street directory was the address where Dad was born on the 18th of September 1919, at 1A Chilworth Road, an urban district of Southampton. This was the hospital, but when I looked at information regarding where it was situated, it was built on lands set aside for Southampton's new workhouse. The next box on the certificate was that the child was a boy, then a box with who the father was. As I expected, the box was empty except for a long-perforated line across it "- - - - - - - -". As I looked at the line of dots they seemed to get longer and move about in an otherwise perfect empty box. I wondered if I counted the dots that would be how many letters the father's name would contain, but it was what it was, just a dotted line and that's all.

Then we came to Nan's information – her name – but I still had one eye on the perforated line. Why would she not put the father's name? According to the lady next door to Nan, he was a smart Italian naval officer. This was the first real thing I didn't understand, but I hoped somewhere down the line I would find out why and carried on looking at Nan's information. The certificate said she was a domestic servant at 10 Cross Street, Kingsland, another urban district of Southampton. So, this supposedly was her place of work and where she lived, something to check on the census forms. Another thing to go on my list of things to find out.

I looked up in the street directory number – 10 Cross Street Kingsland, Southampton – and it turned out to be a cottage called Hope Lodge. The cottage was run by the church in connection with the Diocesan Union of Preventive and Rescue Work and was part of the Southampton refuge for the friendless and fallen. That was a bit of a shock, more so than finding out where Dad was born as it looked to have been the workhouse and to read these things so early in my investigations would have been, I have to say, a good enough reason to put it all away. But what I needed to find out was, did my Nan work there or was she a fallen woman?

At this point, I was glad I did not persuade Mother to get involved in the research; she would be in orbit by now if she thought Nan was a fallen woman. After all, Mum would say that Nan drank, smoked and lived in a dirty house so one would follow the other and Mum would have Nan down as a card-carrying scarlet woman. She would be seeking sympathy for being related to such a person. At the same time, I understood how it would be easy to conclude if that were all the facts we would be getting. But I had only scratched at the surface, and you cannot make such judgements at this early stage, and I preferred the calmer approach.

If Nan was a fallen woman, then so be it. There would have to be a reason for it but given everything Dad had said about how close Grandfather George

John's family was, I could not see how Nan could be when Dad was born. She was 27 years old. I could not see why her family would turn her out, after all, the Italian naval officer was said to be a smart upstanding man so he must have been known to the family. In World War One, the Italians had been on our side, but I was sure when I found more evidence, one way or the other, we would know. So, until then I would keep an open mind and anyway, we are talking about over 80 years ago, attitudes were different then, even a defiant female would have been punished and marginalised by society's judgemental culture obsessed with tight morality. If you had a sexual stigma attached to you then you would become an outsider; if a woman was seduced and betrayed by a man then she would also become the victim of other hypocritical men and treated unjustly even by the law, such was the culture back then.

I asked a member of staff at the library if they had any records relating to the Southampton Refuge for the friendless and fallen. The person then disappeared into the inner sanctum and after about ten minutes returned with a small box that was placed on the desk in front of me. I was told to go through the contents and if I wanted anything copying to ask at the main desk. In the box I found report books for the Southampton Refuge at Hope Lodge that was number 10 Cross Street, and the refuge was run in connection with St Thomas Home in Basingstoke.

Hope Lodge turned out to be a training home for young domestics who, after falling on hard times or rescued from bad homes, were placed at St Thomas's to be re-trained and work their way back into society. If young mothers found themselves with nowhere to go, having been turned out because of their condition or just lost souls, then they could stay for one month. There was no limit on the age of the fallen person, so my Nan could have been turned out and Hope Lodge would have taken her, but I preferred to think that at 27 she was living at home and worked at Hope Lodge. Her mother was still alive at that time, as was her father, but the census forms would confirm, and I would search the records from 1900 to see what happened to my Nan.

So, my first venture had been very informative. I asked the lady on desk duty at the archives if I could have five of the small report books copied off. They were just folded paper stapled together to form a book. But I hoped to find plenty of information to help me, each of the books cost one pound. Much of what people wanted copied did not cost that much at all. I had spent the whole of the afternoon at the archives on my first visit.

When I got home, I made a list of things I needed, facts on census forms that may reveal the staff at Hope Lodge at that time and further on. And as I looked through the interesting report books, I found that Hope Lodge had six places for women, with no limit on age, but no girl or woman would remain at the lodge for more than one month. Once they had been admitted into the lodge, the report book had records of a few cases, and the girls and women would only be referred to by initials, for instance A.V., a girl of 15 who lived with her mother in a single room, the mother was a bad woman and a drunkard and shamefully neglected her daughter. She would go to bed early and lock the girl out and she, after staying out till midnight, would sleep in a sort of cellar. The girl had been rescued from a bad life and placed in a home where her conduct was so exemplary that it was difficult to realise the state in which she had lived. Some reports like that were very painful and pitiful, all reported by sub warden H. M. Ellis.

One thing about the report books, they left nothing to the imagination. Whatever the girls and women suffered, was all there in black and white for all to see. The fact each case was only referred to by the person's initials was their saving grace, as far as I was concerned. It was the right way to go and let society know just how bad life was for some, who had become helpless individuals with nowhere to go or know which way to turn. If my Nan turned out to be a fallen woman, it would have been only one part of her life, when she had made maybe the wrong decision and I would not blame her for that, in fact the more I found out about the friendless and fallen of Hope Lodge, the more I was sad that my siblings and I had been kept from my Nan, indeed it seemed that punishment came to her in many ways.

If I had known her when I was a child, as I knew my Uncle George, Aunt Alva, Grandfather William and other family members, then I was sure I would have been the richer for it and loved my Nan as much as all the others. So, we had both missed out because of people's bias towards my Nan. I did not blame my mother for one minute because Nan's way of life or the way it had been portrayed was completely different to Mum's. I had to commend Mum for not judging my dad on inuendoes that may have surrounded his mother.

I understand why she would close her mind whenever the subject of my father's family was mentioned, and so finding what I was uncovering was helping me indirectly to understand my mother more. She was still difficult and moody sometimes and would unload on me at the drop of a hat, but that was her make-up. Sure, many people who had the same attitude as Mum would indeed give members of their family's a hard time. But those attitudes were not considered by society to be alien in Victorian values, and therefore not condemned, but someone whose unfortunate circumstances led them to become fallen, maybe from seduction under the promise of marriage. But little distinction in some quarters of society was made between single mothers and prostitutes that had been betrayed by men. The loss of character stigmatised them; they were made to carry their guilt and be grateful that they had been rescued.

In one of the books, the Bishop of Guildford wrote, "When a woman stoops to folly, learns too late those men betray; what art can soothe their melancholy what gift can take her guilt away; There is nothing sadder than a fallen women she cannot rely on her ready wit and hope to survive, Yet man evil as he may be can move from place to place untouched by evil ways." The Bishop waffled on about how God was the woman's only saviour if she repented her sinful ways. The Bishop's comments were so out of touch with life, a time in the stocks may have been the best place for him and let the fallen women or otherwise sort him out. Poverty with the help of organisations like the one he represented that stand by and watch people fall and fail before lending a helping hand and expect the fallen and failed people to be ever thankful was quite typical of the clergy.

After reading the five small books that I had picked out by selecting random dates from 1906 through to 1920, to give me the chance to look at how things changed before and after the great war, it was interesting that in all the report books, war was not mentioned at all. I could see that cases reported from the 1906 book were nearly all of young girls whose ages ranged from ten years old to 19, only one woman of 30 was reported in the book of 1906. It seemed that young girls, if thought to be with bad parents, had been reported to the refuge who would then seek to prevent the girls from further danger. They would try and work with the parents to begin with but, in a lot of cases I looked at, it was poverty that was the greatest cause of families breaking up or finding that they could not cope with such a hard life.

It was just a matter of time before the father deserted his family or one of the parents took to drink, or in some cases both. Parents would also, if a young child displayed behaviour that would lead to the possibility that they may stray, were taken to the refuge by concerned parents who asked the refuge to help prevent them from falling. And from what I had seen so far reported in year books, of the refuge the many prevention workers did their best to cope, with limited funds coming from donations collected by thrift and boot clubs from each church in the urban districts of Southampton. All connected with the Diocesan Union of Preventive and Rescue Work, indeed the trustees seemed to make ends meet and from the accounts shown in the report books all the receipts went out in covering the expenditure, so whatever funds had been collected in a fiscal year were all used in keeping the refuge in business. To be solvent was the reward, it seems, and to prevent someone from becoming friendless and fallen, there was unfortunately some that could not be saved but it was not from the lack of trying.

It took me about two months to research everything I wanted to find out about the Southampton Refuge, and it would have been easy to become too involved researching into things for the sake of knowing more about the movement. But all I wanted was to find records of people who worked for the refuge and if my Nan had worked there. I was sure it would be recorded somewhere, however one of the archivists suggested to me that further records other than the basic ones like the annual report books I had and those promoting the work the refuge did could all be subject to a no-admission access for 100 years. This would be to protect everyone connected to the refuge in all capacities.

I could see his point. It was something I had not heard of before, but once it was explained it did make perfect sense. If someone had been in the refuge and then made good, they would not want their past life dragged up. But that rule also protected the people that had caused abuse, because in some cases if a domestic servant had been violated and worked her way back into society by retraining at Basingstoke and was put back in service, the chances of it happening again must have been high. The wealthy house owners would not want history of servants being used as playthings by the great and the good to be banded around, so the girls were in a very dangerous position. I would find out about the no-admission access; however, it was time for me to move on to the next thing in my quest. First, I had to catch up on some work, my son had been keeping things going, and I had to help him with the workload. While he did not complain, it was important to get clear of some of the work If I had to have any more time off, I would not be leaving him with too much to do.

Also, while I had still helped Mother at her flat, she had not been to my house for Sunday lunch for a while, so I invited her down. She asked if I was busy with work. Of course, I said I was. Had she known I had been in the bowels of the civic centre archives most of the time and not working then she would think that was a waste of time, and I did not want a lecture, so it was easier to tell her a white lie and avoid any form of stress.

I had cooked Mum a lovely lunch and afterwards she liked to sit in one of the rooms I had added on that looked out over the valley, with a large ceiling to floor window that spanned the width of the room at the back of my home. I would make her tea and sometimes she would nod off to sleep for a while. I didn't disturb her in her rest, she was getting on in years now and had been without Dad for nearly as long as the two of them had been together, in fact. But she adored him still and quietly mourned him if truth be told, and as I watched her rest and breathe gently, and gazed at her wrinkled face that showed her scars of sacrifice, I realised how lucky I had been to have her as a mother. She was difficult and could be all so bitter and cutting in her comments, but they all manifested post my father's death and so when we argued, both of us as stubborn as each other, neither of us would give in. But we both knew if one of us needed the other we would be there one hundred per cent. Sometimes when she was very difficult and spiteful it wasn't nice, and I found myself thinking what it may have been like if my dad had survived her.

Chapter 12
The Italian Links

The next plan was to find records of Italian navy ships in Southampton waters during World War One. So, on 18th January 2005 I sent a letter to the Italian Embassy at Hobart Place, Eaton Square in London, asking for information about Italian navy ships in British ports during the years 1917–1919, along with personnel records for the same period. I didn't hold out much hope of hearing back from them, still it was worth a try because what did I have to lose, I had nothing to go on anyway.

But to my surprise, in the February of 2005, I received a letter back from Capt Guido Saltini, the Italian naval representative in London, thanking me for my letter and that he had forwarded it to the Italian Navy Historical Branch in Rome, and that he would contact me when he had received a reply. Well, I was pleased that I had got a reply and that things had begun to move, if only slowly and that someone was taking me seriously.

I also decided that now was the time to go and see my aunt, one of Dad's sisters. Her name was Winifred and my parents referred to her as Winn in conversations. I could remember when I was a child her family lived on the east side of Southampton. So, the following week when I was working in the town of Romsey, near Southampton, on a small job, I decided that at lunchtime when the job was finished, I would call the number I had found in the directory that I thought was Dad's sister. I could have got the number from Mum, but I would have got the third degree, and I was not revealing anything to anyone in case it all led to nothing. As planned, I called the number and as it rang wondered what I would say, but while I was thinking a lady picked up the phone and said the number. I said, "Hello, is that Aunt Winn?" and the lady said, "Yes it is, who is calling?" I told her who I was and that I would like to talk to her.

She asked if anyone had died and I assured her that no one had died, and she said they only ever heard from our side of the family if someone had died. I began to think I had done the wrong thing by calling her, after all I had never seen her. She then said, "Are you Mick's eldest son?" and I said "Yes I am." Now Mick was my dad's nickname, his Grandfather George John called him that because Dad would take messages to people and would run fast like Mick the miller, a famous greyhound of that time. Aunt Winn then asked me where I was, and after confirming I was in Romsey, she told me they were in Millbrook so please come on over.

So I did and as I made my way there, all I could think of as I travelled was what would I say when I arrived. But I need not have worried. When I got there and approached the door it was opened by my aunt, who looked like my Nan as I remembered her all those years ago. When I walked in, she gave me the most wonderful welcoming embrace and held on to me as we walked into her lounge. She introduced her husband to me who seemed a bit uneasy to begin with but soon settled as we began to talk. Aunt Winn said I was the image of my father and how he had always looked after his siblings and that every year she never forgot his death date and got flowers. She told me that Nan said she could never understand why my siblings and I had been kept from her, and she asked me if I thought it was because of my mum. I didn't know what to say, clearly Aunt Winn knew something about Mother not liking to go to Nan's, so I just said I didn't know but my aunt was very pleased to see me and told me I should stay in touch.

She got up to make a cup of tea and left me with her husband Phil, and before he had a chance to say anything I told him not to worry, I would not be asking any questions about Aunt Winn's father. I could see he was relieved as I said it and I was glad I did; we had a really nice chat, and I was invited back any time, all I had to do was call. I told my aunt that I would like to know more about my Nan and if she had photos I may be able to look at. Of course, she had lots and would sort them out and call me when she had. It was so refreshing to see them both and it was a contact I wished I had made before.

It was not long before Aunt Winn got back to me and invited me over again, and I was pleased to go and see them. This time I felt at ease with them and felt if I did approach the subject of who Dad's father was that I would not be put off in any way, but I had to remember that Aunt Winn was much younger than my dad so would not know a lot about the Italian link.

My aunt showed me some very interesting photos of my dad as a young boy, photos I had never seen before of him with his siblings and other relations taken at a wedding. He was all dressed up and looked very smart as they all did. I was also shown a picture of George John, my great-grandfather. He was standing with one of Nan's sisters at a wedding. He too was dressed to the nines, with a bowler hat and was smoking a pipe. It was nice to see what he looked like after all the stories I had been told about him. My aunt gave me the photos and said I could keep them. One of them was of Nan with Dad's stepbrothers and sisters all sat on a bench. Aunt Winn said they had all gone to see Dad where he was stationed in the Army and they all looked very smart.

I was told that Nan used to do a milk round with a horse and cart around the Shirley area as well as working in a hotel to make ends meet. Aunt Winn said Nan worked hard and indicated to me that she got little help from the children's father. She also told me that when she and Phil married, it was my dad who gave her away at her wedding and not her father. It was clear all was not well with the subject of her father, and in all the photos I was shown he was in none of them, but there were lots taken of Aunt Winn and Nan.

In another photo, there were four very young girls at the same wedding. Aunt Winn ran through who was who, from left to right. The first was Betty her sister. Then Winn herself, Marg as a child, a cousin of Dad's and the mother of the child also called Marg that Mum would take out with my sister. Then another child called Malena, the daughter of Doff who was also a cousin of Dad's, who was about eight years older than him. Aunt Winn said that Doff had married an Italian man called Alasandro Amadeus Mahona and went to live in Florence, Italy, where Malena was born but Doff could not settle and came back to England. Alasandro worked on the ships and would spend half the year in England and the other half in Italy, but the interesting thing was that, according to Aunt Winn, Malena lived in Southampton and she and Phil would see her now and again when out shopping.

I asked Aunt Winn if she had an address for Malena, my thinking was that if Malena's mother Doff was close to my dad, then Doff may have spoken about Nan's Italian boyfriend. Malena's grandmother was my Nan's sister, and the two of them forged Doff's age when she went to Italy to marry Alasandro Amadeus Mahona. Aunt Winn told me that when Doff came home with baby Malena, they lived with Doff's mother and father, so Malena may have heard conversations about all sorts of things. I was thinking on my feet really but it was worth a shot.

Aunt Winn said she did have her address and gave it to me. I asked if she minded me asking questions and she said if she could help me, she would, then she asked me if I had been looking into who my father's dad was. I told her I was and had only just found out about him and had nothing to go on. I told her what Mum had told me about the Italian, I also said that Mum did not want me to bother her. To which she told me not to be so silly, and that I could ask anything. But I had to remember she was much younger than Dad, and he was more like a father to her than a brother. She had no idea who the Italian would have been, and that Nan did not talk much about her early life. I told my aunt that I was so grateful for what she had told me and that I had been worried about pressing her for information.

She said if I did find anything out, she would like to know and said that her best friend growing up who lived next door was the daughter of the lady that knew everyone's business in their road. Aunt Winn said that she and Phil had coffee with her best friend when they went on the bus once a week to the market and that she would ask if she ever heard anything. I could not believe how helpful my aunt had been, she was a breath of fresh air. I had got so much to go on now, and from thinking she would have closed me out. I was overwhelmed with how she had greeted me, at last things began fitting in like a puzzle. It was just a question of time as to when the next bit of information would turn up.

I thanked my aunt and uncle for their help and left. When I got home I filed everything away and thought about my next move. For some time, I had thought about having a DNA test, having read information about how it's handed down father to son. If my dad's father was Italian, then my DNA would show that I had Italian links. Furthermore, if other people decided to have their DNA taken and matched up with yours then you would have shared a common ancestor. I didn't understand it but thought I should order the kit and send it off once completed to see what happens. It was said to be simple and easy to understand and even more simple if you got a match, but I did not want to look that far ahead.

The kit arrived within a week, so I followed instructions to the letter, packed it all up and sent it to America. If it were a scam, well, we would soon find out. It did seem to be too good to be true and too easy if you were a sceptic like Mum. I also sent a letter to Malena telling her who I was and that I would like to meet her as my father was her mother's cousin. And that I had been given her address by my Aunt Winn, my father's sister, and I was working on my family tree and interested in her Italian links and hoped she would be interested in helping me.

On 21st April 2005, I had a nice surprise from all my endeavours. I had a reply from Captain Guido Saltini, the representative for the Italian Navy at the Embassy of Italy in London. It said, "Dear Sir. Further to my letter dated 10th February 2005, I have just received some information from my Authorities. After a thorough search through our archives, we managed to locate the Italian Navy Ship Libia in the English harbours during November 1918. Regretfully we have no details of Italian military personnel based in Southampton or Portsmouth between the years 1917–1918, I hope that you will appreciate Records tend to fade over the years; however, I am sure that this will not spoil your interest in them," signed Capt. Guido Saltini Italian Navy.

This was great news I wanted to find out as much as I could about the Libia and started by sending a fax to the naval archives in Portsmouth to ask if they had any information regarding the Libia because Portsmouth was, after all, a naval base. Hence, it followed that Portsmouth might have catered for the Italian naval ships there in World War One. Plymouth naval dockyard could also be an option for me to find records if the Libia was in that port at any time, so I faxed them as well. Everything at this stage was a shot in the dark so the more places I thought may have information regarding the Libia the better. It was not long before my fishing for information paid off. I had a letter back from the archives at Portsmouth Dockyard that said while there was no record of the Libia ever having been in Portsmouth harbour they did find a record of a news in brief from The Times from 13th March 1919 that said, "Captain C, Villarey, C.B, M.V.O, and the Officers of the Italian cruiser Libia which is lying in the Thames held a reception onboard on Tuesday afternoon. The Italian Ambassador and the Mayor and Mayoress of Gravesend were present."

So, I was slowly getting information coming in to work on and it was all very interesting, given I had nothing to go on to start with. I needed to find information of the Libia having been in the port of Southampton. I had two dates that confirmed it was in English waters, from two different people – Captain Guido Saltini said the Libia was in English harbours during the month of November 1918. And from the Portsmouth archives that it was lying in the Thames on the 13th of March 1919, but for this to be connected to the Italian officer that the lady had told mother about then the Libia needed to have been in the port of Southampton sometime in both 1918 and 1919, before the war finished and the Italian was returned to Italy, or I could forget it.

The Libia was not in Portsmouth and it would not have been feasible for Nan to have had a relationship with anyone in faraway Plymouth, given the fact that the Italian was known to people in her community. So, all I could really do was to keep researching and it was not long before I found the best place to ask for information. I was told that the Department of the Navy in the United States Department of Defence in Washington DC had the best, easy-to-access information at the Naval Historical Centre and Early History Branch. Given that the American navy would have surely been in English waters it was worth a shot at asking them for this. I decided I would call them. After introducing myself and explaining what I hoped to get help with, I was put through to Christine F. Hughes, Assistant Head of the Early History Branch at Washington DC. She could not have been more helpful and said that she would fax me information on the Italian Cruiser Libia; she also said that Italy's Defence Ministry, called Ufficio Storico Della Marina Militere, would be able to help. But it took time to get naval records from Italy regarding Navy personnel but what she was sending would tell me everything I need to know about the Libia.

I would still need to access the ship's deployments from the Italian authorities. The conversation with Christine F. Hughes was very interesting and informative and I thanked her for the help. I felt that I was really getting somewhere but couldn't rush into things; I had to wait as my father did when he received the letter. Mum would ask sometimes if we remembered it, in fact I often wondered what did happen to it, but it was too close to the time of our family's melancholy occasion when wrapped up in sorrowful thoughts from the loss of Father.

So, as a source of information to what I was doing now, the letter was irrelevant unless it could be found and there was not much chance of that anyway. If my father had done any research on the matter and found it not to be of interest to him then it could have been confined to the bin. What I was doing now, looking for some clue regarding this Italian person after all this time, if I did find anything it would be difficult I am sure to announce yourself as the long-lost grandson as in my case to an unprepared family and expect them to welcome you with open arms and in the process, maybe ruin a man's reputation, you would not be thanked for that in my opinion.

So, for me the research and finding my history is important to me, and I will leave no stone unturned in finding information but given the time lapse would it be right to make yourself known and ask a stranger if they would maybe have a DNA test to satisfy a curiosity! I do not think I can do that. More importantly, no one knows what was in that letter, and only my father had access to that. If it had been about Durley, I know he would have eventually told me and if it was about Italian links and he did know anything about it from the past via his mother's words to him, I do not think he would have told me then. Maybe further down the line. From the two possibilities, the Italian link would have been the harder for him to deal with after so many years.

Two days after my conversation with Christine F. Hughes from the Early History Department at Washington DC, several faxes arrived with plenty of information regarding the R.N. Libia. She had started life as a Turkish ship named Drama and was taken by the Italians when they had been at war with Turkey; and during World War One carried out special missions in Greece in 1917 and in the April of 1918 joined the Naval Chief Command of Albania.

The Libia served as an Italian Protected Cruiser, that acted as the escort to the United States troop ships when President Woodrow Wilson ordered the deployment of the American Navy ships that carried US troops across the Atlantic to France, and assembled in the French harbour of Brest. I was sent a photo of the Libia in Brest Harbour with The U.S.S. Bridport, The Prometheus, and two Destroyers along with other smaller vessels, all in full dress, awaiting the arrival of President Wilson for the Versailles conference in 1919.

So, things started to take shape. It seemed that the R.N. Libia was an important part of the great war of the sea. Then in part of the fax I found reference of the Libia along with troop ships in the port of Plymouth being used as a stop-off, on route to the port of Southampton for maintenance and refits. To my surprise and to cap it all, an A4 photo of the Libia in Southampton docks, lying next to one of the massive dock sheds that looked so familiar to me, like the sheds I had seen as a child from Mayflower Park next to the 101 berth where my dad had worked.

I knew the photo was of Southampton docks as soon as I set eyes on it, and immediately consulted people who I knew who worked in the docks. They confirmed to me that it was 22 berth as soon as they looked at it. So, the Libia had been in Southampton waters. Was Nan's boyfriend on board? I still had no name to go on and no idea how I was going to find out. In another document, it was reported that the captain of the Libia was C Villarey and was in the news briefing of The Times in 1919, information that I already had. But then I found another document that referred to the captain being an Ernesto Burzagli in 1921, who turned out to be a prominent figure in the kingdom of Italy during the early 20th century and had a lifelong career in the Italian navy and rose to the rank of Admiral and Chief of Staff in 1933 and was appointed as a Senator in Rome by King Victor Emmanuel III.

So given that the Libia had such a high-profile captain, maybe there would be more information somewhere regarding him and his crew that numbered 14 officers and 300 crew. So, I sent a fax to Captain Guido Saltini at the Embassy of Italy in London, asking him if I could access the muster list of officers and crew of the Libia and while I did not have a name I felt it would be good to have that information if I could get it.

Captain Guido Saltini had already told me that they had no records of personnel based in Southampton and Portsmouth in the years 1917–1919, however a ship's muster list is different, it's an actual list of personnel who served on board. It was another long shot, but they had been paying off so far.

Of course, writing about this makes it seem like it all happened so quickly, however all this research into the Italy links was to take me some eight years. It was like a part-time job. It was frustrating at times, and I was 58 by the time it concluded, and Mother was in her 80s when she told me the story about the Italian links. So, I was on a hiding to nothing. Still, I pushed on, and between work and family activities, looking after Mum etc., it did not seem that long.

I had also joined a badminton club. I was fit enough and played with a nice bunch of people so not all my time was spent researching family history – I did have a life. But every time something came up regarding my research, I got back to it and I think it must have been about five months after I had written to Malena Mahona when she rang me to say she had got my letter and that she had been rather dubious about contacting me until she had seen my Aunt Winn and her husband Phil when out shopping.

They told her they had seen me and if you like gave me their seal of approval and she was happy for me to go and see her. We arranged a date and time for the following week, and I went to meet her. She was in fact a second or third cousin to me so that made things a little easier for the two of us meeting for the first time. Malena must have been in her 70s so it would be, I thought, interesting what, if anything, she could remember from way back.

The following week I went to meet her at her home. I arrived at 11 am and again, as with my visit to Aunt Winn, I was rather nervous, but I need not have been. All nerves disappeared when Malena opened the door. She was a tall lady and very smartly dressed. She invited me in, and it was so nice to meet her. It was not emotional as it was when I first went to Aunt Winn's; this felt more like an interview. Malena said I was the image of my dad, and that I looked more Italian than him which I was pleased with. I was also pleased that she must have known Dad was Italian, because I had not mentioned that in my letter to her, only that she had Italian links, so this was a good start as far as I was concerned.

I stood with her in her kitchen while she made us tea and then went and sat in her front room. She had got several large envelopes on the table in anticipation of my visit and we began to talk about her life. She was born in Florence, Italy, when her Mother Doff married her Italian sweetheart, Alasandro Amadeus. But only stayed in Italy for the first few years of her life before coming back and living with her grandparents who lived opposite my Nan. Also, Malena's grandmother was my Nan's sister, so Malena spent lots of time in each house growing up. She then showed me lots of photos, some going way back and some more recent of her family. I found everything she had told me about her Mother Doff fascinating, the photos of Doff showed her in a good light. She was indeed very beautiful and Malena said that was one of the reasons for returning to England because her father worked on the ships and while he was away, one of his brothers feel hopelessly in love with Doff and while the whole of the Mahona family lived together, Doff's mother-in-law had a devil's own job keeping order in the household.

Doff wanted nothing to do with the brother but he would not take no for an answer. Malena said that her father decided to bring her and her mother back to England. Malena had regular visits back to Italy to stay with her Italian grandparents as she grew up. Malena said she and her mother made the best of things, also Malena was the envy of school friends because of her regular visits to Italy in the school holidays. We talked for two hours about her history; we did not touch on the subject of my Nan's Italian boyfriend because I didn't lead the conversation in that direction. I asked Malena if it would be possible to come back the following week and talk some more, and she was happy to do that and said herself that all the talking had worn her out. It is true, concentrating to get things right when telling the tales and when listening saps your mental energy.

I thanked Malena for her help, and we agreed to meet again the same time the following week. As I drove home, I thought to myself that meeting Malena could be my best lead because while Mum had told me what Nan's neighbour had said, Mum would have not pushed things further to find out more. Also, while I enjoyed my conversations with my Aunt Winn, she didn't know enough to ask anything too detailed and I had to consider her and husband Phil because I didn't want to risk upsetting them. When you get involved with talking about someone's life it is easy to say something out of turn, like referring to the facts about my Nan's early life. These are things that my Aunt Winn would not have known about, and it would have been so cruel to drop it into a conversation, even unwittingly. We are dealing with people's emotions, and the perception each of us holds of our nearest and dearest is mostly of all the good things. To have someone give you information you had no idea of could be crushing to them, so you need to proceed with caution and respect the fact that if a question cannot be asked then you do not ask it. Even if you are at ease with the person, my Aunt Winn said she would be interested and would help all she could, but I knew in my heart she would not want to know what was alleged regarding her mother.

So, Malena I was sure would be of help to me and that I could ask her anything and the following week when I went back to see her, I was not disappointed. I arrived around the same time and again we had tea, but this time she wanted to know about me. She knew I had been in homes and asked me what it was like, so I gave her a rough overview of life with the nuns. I told her about my wife, children and my work and then told her what Mother had told me about the time she had been stopped by Nan's neighbour and told that Dad's father was Italian.

Malena said she knew the neighbour that Mum had talked about, and that she knew everyone's secrets and that she could be trusted to keep them most of the time. She said that she had known my dad was Italian, because as a child she asked her grandmother why he looked so different and that she was told because he is Italian. So, this was the first bit of what I would call validation. Malena had confirmed to me that what Mother had been told was true. I then told Malena what I had done so far by writing to the Italian Embassy in London for information as well as to Washington DC and that I had positive responses from them both.

I told Malena about the DNA testing, and those results could pinpoint where in Italy people's ancestors came from, if you had Italian relations, and could also match you with other people that had tested who could well be related to you by a series of 12 tests taken. If you had someone match all 12, then they would be direct ancestors from another timeline. If people matched eight or nine, they would be close relations, again from timelines that can go way back. Malena thought this was amazing. I told her I did not understand it fully and that it was a shot in the dark but if it helped it was worth it. I told her that while she had confirmed that Dad's father was Italian, If the test comes back and is positive that I have Italian links, I was still hamstrung with not having a name to go on, to which Malena replied, "Well I know what his name was."

I could not believe what I was hearing and asked her to repeat what she had just said. And she said again that she could tell me what my grandfather's name was. I laughed with joy at this news, so I asked her to wait while I got paper and pen and sat there hanging on her every word. She began to tell me that my dad would often come over to their house, either on his own or with his mother and sometimes picked up things from the shop for his grandfather and would come and ask if anyone in our house wanted anything. When he was seen coming over the road or going somewhere, Malena's grandmother would say, "Look, here comes 'Mick', Miceli's boy." And that's how she knew the Italian's name was Miceli. We talked about how it would be pronounced in Italian. Malena said it would be pronounced Miceli and the c would be the same sound of ch so its spelling would be Micheli if spelt by English people. The C in Italian would be pronounced as a k. It was all interesting and now that I had something to work with, I hoped that the day would come when I was able to undo this tangled hidden reality and find out who my Italian grandfather was, both for me and my father.

I would need Melena's help with all things Italian, and she said she would be happy to assist me if required. I thanked her for seeing me again and we agreed to stay in touch. After finding out so much, it was time for me to pick up on the work front, so I filed everything away and had a rest from researching. I found all the concentrating very draining so getting back to work and being on what I called automatic pilot I did not have to think too much while working and I found it relaxing. I also played badminton twice a week and that required a different type of concentration and I enjoyed the company of the club members.

One of the ladies that played the same nights as I did was a good player and the people who ran the club often matched us up for doubles games. Everyone that played had a tremendous competitive nature so there were no easy games. My doubles partner and I became good friends, she was a property lawyer and like me she lived alone. We got to know each other well but there was no chance of romance; neither of us wanted anything like that but as friends we began to go out for meals. We each had things we wanted to do and see. So, we made a list and in time began to do something from the lists. We travelled together, spent Christmas and new year in special places, going Dutch on the cost. Our mutual friendship was something that became important to both of us, and the fact we both lived alone worked so well; we were both very independent. Still very driven in our respective working lives and each with children that we always put first.

I was happy with my life at that time. I still did my bit for my mother, and she came for Sunday lunch most weeks. We did talk at times about my project and while Mum said she did not want to know anything, she always asked what I had found. But if I began to tell her, she covered her ears, frightened almost about what she would hear. It was a strange situation – she wanted to know but did not want to hear it from me. So I told her I would write everything down for her and if she wanted to look at it in her own time that would be fine, but I never asked if she did. What Mum did say was that she wished I had not started it but complimented me on my tenacity and determination to solve something important to me.

For my mother to say that, then it was indeed a bonus. It didn't take long for the results of the DNA tests to come back and after picking them up off the doormat I couldn't open them straight away in case it had all been a waste of time. However, after my evening meal I sat and read the results slowly and I was not disappointed with them. They confirmed to me that I was definitely of Italian origin and matched strongly with people from Italy places such as Molise, Campania, Apulia, Basilicata, Calabria, Sicilia and some parts of Venice.

I was given my PIN and account number and was told to expect matches if there was any that would go online within two weeks. I was advised that if I had someone contact me and matched nine or ten of the 12 tests taken, then they would be the people to concentrate on. There would be plenty of people who would match four or five, but the distance would not be close between us. I have to say it took some understanding. They offered other tests as well that would be more exact but for now, I was content just to know if I had any that matched nine or ten.

There was also a service that provided people to trace things for you. It was big business indeed. Within two weeks I had two good matches, one person who matched ten of my tests and the other matched 11. I contacted the project manager for the testing regarding test results who explained if my results had a link with an ancestor, if I wanted I could contact them by our PINs and then it was up to each individual to swap emails. To start with, I contacted the two people and was pleased when they got back to me. We agreed to keep the contact by email to begin with and see where we went from there. For me, I was very interested in who they were but not that interested in talking with them at that time.

The two people lived in America, one a lady from California, let's call her K.F. Her great-grandfather had migrated from southern Italy at the time of the Silver Rush and made boots for the miners. He made a good living and sent for more of his family from Italy to join him and created a family link in the United States. K.F. had a nice family and lots of friends and while we never talked, we did keep in touch on Facebook at Christmas and on birthdays or if one of us posted something the other liked the post. K.F. referred to me as cousin T. and I called her cousin K. and to be honest the fact we had even found out about each other in such a way meant that K.F. was very important to me.

My other match, J. M., a man from New York, was really into this DNA thing and had a man in Florence who seemed to be quite knowledgeable on mutations within the Italian population who said that J. M. and I were closely related and that we were all Italians.

He also said if my grandfather's name was Miceli then it was likely he came from southern Italy, from Calabria if the original spelling was Miceli. J. M. had employed this man several times and each time he found something new would share it with K. F. and myself. J. M. was a fascinating man. He had worked for the American government and was at one time the American Envoy to the Vatican in Rome. Now retired, he worked for a voluntary organisation involved with world peace, clearing mines etc. around the world. I followed his progress on the internet. We did not contact each other very often but, like K. F., J. M. was important to me. Two DNA cousins I was proud to have and so with the DNA confirming my lineage and identifying Italian cousins, I had come a long way in my search for the truth. But it was time to close the file on the DNA thing because as with my research into the Southampton Refuge, I could well get tied up in it forever. The DNA had served its purpose. Dad, my siblings and I had Italian links as well as two living cousins.

No one could take that away from us because, as the world now knows, the DNA does not lie. My next job was to look for information regarding the Libia's captain; he was a famous man. So, I sent a fax to Captain Guido Saltini and the Embassy of Italy in London, asking if when Ernesto Burzagli was captain of the Libia, did any of the officers have the name Miceli. It looked like a daft question on paper. Still, I sent it anyway. If I had been bothered about what was daft about any of this according to 'you know who' then I would have given up long ago and I wondered what 'you know who' would say when she read that one of my DNA cousins was the American Envoy to the Vatican in Rome. That would be something to brag about in the common room over coffee! The day after I had sent the fax to Captain Saltini, I had one back telling me that he had received more information from his authorities regarding the Libia. When he had everything in order, he would send it on to me and would ask one of his colleagues to look for officers with the name Miceli. In the meantime, if I wanted to know more about Captain Ernesto Burzagli, then I should look at the private archives of the said captain that automatically become public knowledge after 70 years. This was indeed more good news.

Again, I was not disappointed when on the 19th of October 2005, I had the letter from Captain Saltini and he could not have known how important the information within the letter would be to me. The letter said: "With reference to the Italian Navy Ship R.N. Libia I have just received from my Authorities some more information that on the 1st of December 1918 the ship left the port of Cagliari and during its cruise called at the following ports Gibraltar, Brest, Plymouth, Southampton, Harwich, Gravesend, Chatham, Copenhagen, Stockholm, Saltsjobaden, Helsinki, Lisbon, and Barcelona. The ship entered the port of La Spezia on the 10th of September 1919." Well this was amazing, and I set out to find how long it would take for the Libia to reach each port, knowing full well that the ship was at Gravesend on the 13th of March 1919. That information was set in stone from the article in the news in brief in The Times newspaper.

If the Italian boyfriend of my Nan's had been on the Libia and the fact that my father was born on the 18th of September 1919, then the Libia would need to have been in the port of Southampton sometime in December 1918. Everything pointed to the fact that it was because I was able, with some hard researching, find all the port codes. The first one was when the ship left Cagliari, port code I.T. CAG, and travelled 724 nautical miles to Gibraltar taking around three days. If you allowed another three days for the ship to stock up etc. before travelling from Gibraltar, port code G.I.G.1.B., to Brest France, port code F.R.B.E.S., the 946 nautical miles that would have taken around four days. And again, allowing for another four days to carry out important maintenance before going onto Plymouth, port code G.B.P.L.Y., another 159 nautical miles, that would take less than a day. Then add on another four days, before leaving for Southampton, port code G.B.S.O.U., and travelling the 132 nautical miles, the Libia would have been in the port of Southampton well before the Christmas of 1918.

If that was the last time my Nan would see her boyfriend and had just a few more days together before the Libia carried on its cruise that finished back in La Spezia Italy on the 10th of September 1919, just eight days before the birth of my father back in England, that would lead to my dear Nan to be vilified for her association with the man she had loved and would not see again for if he was to spend his life in the Italian navy, he would have to go where he was posted. I think if he was the fine upstanding naval officer that Mother was told about by Nan's neighbour, and he had known about the birth of my father, then I think he would have done something about it. Because of all I had found out about him, it was clear his association with my Nan was not a one-night stand because, as Malena had said, he was known to people in the neighbourhood.

So did my father know about him? The fact that the emphasis on everything regarding our ancestry linked to Durley and the telling of the stories by my father that dated way back and all about the farming community which was a far cry from anything connected to the Italian navy or otherwise, it seems the secret was well kept by all who had known the truth.

Except by one person who told my Mum that secret and way back then no one would have thought that in years to come we would be able to pull our history right into the 21st century with modern-day technology. That we would be able to access records digitally enhanced and placed on a disc, it was a marvel to me but then I am as rustic as you could get. The modern world is not really for the likes of people like me; I made things and mended what was broken. My art was in the skills I had learnt, I am old school and proud of it but have had to learn the new ways to uncover the past that otherwise would be lost, and history, proper history, will die.

So, I took Captain Saltini's advice and looked up the private archives of the Burzagli family and in particular Ernesto, who I had already found information on in some of the documents sent to me. But the archives had things about his family, his many medals and positions held over the years, that he served the Italian Navy with distinction and was a prominent figure in the Kingdom of Italy. Despite his life service to the state, Ernesto Burzagli was arrested in 1944 for his opposition to Italy's entrance into the alliances which led to war and clashed head on with the Italian dictator Benito Mussolini. who misjudged public opinion of Burzagli and, although released a short time after his arrest, he was forced to withdraw from public life and retired to his estate of Moncioni near Montevarchi until his death, and buried in a monumental tomb in the cemetery of Montevarchi.

So, he was indeed a great man, and I recalled the story my Uncle George had told me all those years ago how he took a picture of Benito Mussolini when he was hung in the public square. Strange how the stories of life connect. Also in the Burzagli archives, photos of him as a young cadet on entering the Navy and lots more as his life in the Navy progressed, through the years there were more pictures of the Libia and a record of a silent film made by Frank Capra when the Libia, captained by Ernesto Burzagli, circumnavigated the world in 1921–1923 to thank all the countries for what they did in the great war. The film was in the Library of Congress in America and so I ordered a copy and, as I did with the DNA, just filled out the order form, paid for it and sent it off knowing it would take some time to be shipped to me. And as I browsed the last of the photos, one hit me right between the eyes. It was of Ernesto Burzagli centre stage, flanked on each side by two officers, all dressed in wonderful white uniforms, and in the background was another officer also dressed in a smart white uniform who was younger than the others. But I went cold because he was the image of my father.

Photos of my dad and me at about the age of the officer in the picture, who would have been about 30, were so similar it was uncanny. Then, further on another photo of Ernesto Burzagli inspecting his men on board ship, this time much older, in his 60s and with him was the young officer himself, much older. This would confirm him as a career officer in both photos. The officer both young and much older, he still resembled my father. In photos I had of him it was a fact that this man looked like Dad, an image that I was drawn to more than any other photo I had seen in the archives. So why was I sure it was connected to my story!

I had told myself early on that it would be easy to try and make something fit and should not entertain such foolish thoughts, but the photos just stood out and the resemblance was so obvious. It seemed so right to entertain the notion that this could be my Nan's boyfriend, all the other things I had found out and had been told fitted in perfectly and would have been impossible to invent. But I wanted to go against my own judgement regarding the photographs, I was not sure why. Was it because it would be too easy to except that it could be the man I was searching for? And as I have said about the DNA not lying, could I not apply the same logic that the camera never lies? I decided to hold judgement on the discovery until I had certain information and number one was the officer known as Miceli – was he on the Libia – and two, did he serve under Ernesto Burzagli? Number three, what port had the photos been taken at? I had set myself a task because I would only accept that this man in the photos was Nan's boyfriend if I found the answers to the three questions. There was no rush, the answers would turn up as everything else had and I had come too far to finalise the project on something that needed final confirmation, i.e. the three questions would need to be answered then I would be sure in my own mind.

I felt I was nearing the end of gathering information and it was time to start thinking what I would do when everything came together. I would want to travel to Italy, that was certain, to where the Miceli name was most prominent. I also wanted to learn Italian, so I had one-t- one lessons in Italian with a French language teacher twice a week and it was interesting speaking in another language and how easy it was to get used to talking in another tongue. My problem was it was fine when I was with the teacher but when I went back into everyday life, I tended to forget what I had learnt and really annoyed my son at work by practising on him while we worked, translating each thing we did into Italian. So much so, he went and worked in another room from where I was reciting my newly acquired Italian tongue. It was all basic stuff. But it wouldn't be long before I could practise my newfound skills on the people of Italy because my badminton partner Mary and I decided to take a four-day break and travel to Venice.

We took an early morning flight and on landing at Marco Polo Airport and clearing customs, walked down to the water taxi rank. You can go by ferry across to Venice but the water taxi, while being more costly, takes you fast across the choppy waters of the lagoon to your destination on Venice, that from a distance looks like you are heading for the Isle of Wight. As you speed onward and pass the wonderful small islands of Murano and Burano that should be on your list of things not to be missed, the water taxi also takes you past the island of Torcello, home to the Basilica di Santa Maria Assunta cathedral. With its wonderful Byzantine mosaics and fantastic illustrated painted domed ceilings, it is a magical place. Also, on Torcello the historic Ponte Del Diavolo Bridge, famous for having no sides to it, stretches over the river that surrounds the cathedral.

After your visit to the cathedral, you can eat at the small café on the island and listen to the impromptu singing in celebration of some event or other. In all, it is all worth seeing. After Torcello, you will pass San Michele Cemetery Island, with its wonderful monumental tombs and headstones dating back to bygone days, and when we visited San Michele, I looked among the old stones for Miceli graves as my DNA test had indicated that Venice and the island around it was the home of early Miceli families.

Indeed, some Miceli families dated back to AD 697, and several occupiers of the Doges Palace on Venice had been members of the Miceli lineage. While on San Michele we walked around the more recent graves and there were tall, monumental tombs, each small tomb on top of the other like a small block of flats. Each tomb housed the ashes of people who had passed on, and at one end of the structure we came across an elderly lady at the top of a tall pair of steps that were on wheels. People would push the steps along to get to a particular tomb and as the lady made her way down the steps, we held them for her. The tomb she had been tending was decorated in bright ribbons and when she came off the steps, she talked with us and said that her husband had been colourful in life and now he was colourful in death. She told us that she got the ferry over from Venice each week, rain or shine, to worship the man she had loved and lost. It was a fine moment. Mary and I each embraced the old lady and left her to walk to the ferry.

I remember all my travels with Mary. We visited Venice many times and had seen so much together in Italy. We danced in Saint Mark's Square to orchestras that played each side of the square – when one orchestra stopped the other would strike up and people waltzed to the music. Ladies would walk around with baskets full of red roses and sing out "Roses for the fine lady!" and give them to the ladies as they danced. We visited many places in France, the Moulin Rouge, Montmartre. We walked right through Paris, stopping off at cafés where local people drank coffee and chain-smoked, all willing to talk to us. We climbed to the top of the Arc de Triomphe and looked over the city of Paris, all wonderful times and I write about them now because after suffering for some time, my dearest friend Mary has passed away this very week on 18th November 2018.

I am left with sadness upon losing Mary. We had made our list of things to do and we fulfilled what we could, and I am left with many memories and photos of our travels together, both home and abroad. So, travel if you can, when you're young and don't worry about tomorrow because it may never come. Talk to people, tell them how you feel about them, if only friends they are a treasure.

Chapter 13
Enforced Retirement

I didn't travel for a few years, because of an accident in 2008 which meant I could no longer go out or work. I had been to see a job and decided to have my lunch on the seafront at Lee-on-the-Solent. It was a bright day and I parked in a parking space off the main one-way road that ran around the village green in a horseshoe shape. I had picked up my lunch and a paper and walked back to my car. As I got in, placed my right leg into the car and closed my door, I was hit by another car that had gone out of control and came over into the parking space that my car occupied.

The impact sent me up and across the front passenger seat of my car, damaging my head, neck and shoulders. The pain was instant and I felt the joint in my left shoulder move and my neck crack. I could not turn to see the car that hit me but could hear its engine still running, and then as I heard its gears click, I felt safe that it would soon pull off my car. But as it did, I could hear the gears click again and the sound of the engine revving as the driver began to speed away from the accident.

I managed to sit upright and watch as the car approached the right-hand bend, its engine revved louder and all the shoppers stood still and watched. The car failed to negotiate the bend and drove into the large car park, smashing into two more cars before hitting a brick wall at the end of the car park. The silence of the crowd was broken as people ran to the car park, some 200 yards from where I had been hit. People also came to help me get out of my car; I was in shock, but the people were so kind. One of the shop people got me a drink and all the people that helped me at our end of the road all agreed it was lucky no one was killed.

To make things worse, when the law turned up, they went right past me to the top of the road. So too did the medics; one ambulance with two medics and two nice new Volvo cars each with a medic on board. They too ignored me and went to the top of the road. I phoned my son to come and help me; my car could not be used, and he would have to take me home.

Eventually, one of the policemen came and asked to see my insurance. He didn't ask if I was all right. He just said, "Well it will not be a problem identifying who was in the wrong with this one", and told me I should call my insurance company to report that I had been in an accident, and told me it was not my fault and I would have no problem with a claim for my car. I asked if I could see a medic, he said they had to deal with the person in the car park who, as it turned out, was an 87 deaf lady. She claimed she was not trying to drive off but had hit her accelerator instead of her brake as she approached the bend.

I was not seen by the medics from start to finish and after all four cars had been taken away on breakdown trucks and the medics driven off in single file down the road, I was left with the people from the shops who like me thought the whole thing a joke. I was still left waiting when my son turned up and took me home. He made calls for me to try and sort things out. He had to return to finish his work that he had left.

The following day he took me to my doctor who identified things I would need to have looked at by physios, and for over six months I walked the two miles, three days a week for treatment at the clinic. My friend Mary worked on the same site as a property manager for the NHS, and I would call in at her office and have a coffee whilst we would catch up on things, or sometimes we had lunch and she would take me home afterwards, saving me the walk.

I found walking on pavements next to the main road difficult; the sound of cars and the draught from them overtaking me at speed was scary. So, I would keep to the side roads that, while taking me the long way round to the clinic, made me feel safer. Also, being a passenger in a car was a problem to begin with – I had to get used to the cars moving fast.

Before the accident, you could travel to work and be surprised how quickly you reached your destination, because we tend to drive on automatic pilot and we know the roads so well. But after being hit, you are aware of other traffic and the noise of the overtaking vehicles seem to be much too close to your car and oncoming traffic too are more noticeable. There were so many things I had to get used to again that one takes for granted in life, after six months I was told they could do no more. My neck, shoulder and back would not heal fully and the residue of each injury would become a problem that would restrict my movement. I could not turn my head round to the left, I also suffered from slight cognisant deficit that was to get better over time but to start with was a worry. I could not remember which hand to hold my knife and fork in, I would sit and swap them from one hand to the other. Eventually that problem resolved itself as the medics I was seeing said it would, but I would forget to turn taps off, lock doors, and even forget if I had put aftershave on. Sometimes I put so much on I smelt like Boots' sample counter; the whole situation had set me right back.

I could not work and, if it was not for my family, I would have gone broke. I still had bills to pay. I had become a non-person. The medical people would ask me to fill a form out with questions to mark 1 to 10 saying how often I wanted to end it all, and did I cry a lot and become angry for no reason. I had to be careful because if you answered the questions wrong and indicated that life was a struggle, then you would become a guinea pig. I may have had a bang on the head and for a while forgot things, but there was no way that the powers that be were going to indicate I was something I was not. I was the same person with injuries, and I was dealing with them the best way I could. Also part of the stress I was under was caused by the legal team I had working on a compensation claim on the instruction of my insurance company. It did not take long to figure out they wanted the best deal for them and not me; the two sets of lawyers and insurance companies worked hand in glove to hammer out the best deal for each other and my team was less than useless. It took over three years for my case to come to court, even though I was fully in the right.

What they do is try and drag it out until you are skint and you will settle. The head medics wanted to prove I was 'gaga' because I had a bang on the head – something you have to come to terms with yourself first, before being fast-tracked to sit in a circle and talk about the negative side of the problem, rather than finding a different way to cope with what once came easy but now took a little more time to adjust to. I found being pushed around very difficult to deal with, and observed and listened like I have always done when I am not sure of people's motives. So, life was a drag but they misjudged me and in particular my biggest supporter my mother.

She was by the time all this would be resolved almost 91 years old, she read every solicitor and lawyer's letter and she did not trust any of them. She was not prepared to take any crap from any of them and kept me going with funds and a fighting spirit until I got my just deserves. The price I had to pay was I became her child again; she would cook for me, come down in a taxi to make sure I was all right and that too was stressful. What with the lawyers, medics and being in grip of a parent again, as well as being a non-person, I felt all my rights had been taken away. I had nothing but my home and if I did not get a settlement soon that could be in jeopardy.

I was asked to go to London to talk about an out-of-court settlement with the other side's lawyers. Mum did not want me to, she said that right was on my side and go to court. She was right, that law was on my side and if the firm of lawyers had got the CCTV footage of the accident it would have not taken this long. I had in fact contacted the council at the time of the accident to get a copy. They told me they could see what had happened but could not release the footage to members of the public. Only the lawyers would be able to request a copy and pay £30, and to top it off also had 30 days to do so before all film footage is destroyed. That was the first time I smelt a rat when I told the law firm to get the footage, because it was not in their best interest. They want work from all insurance firms and are not about to hammer one of them with a big claim for one individual who would only ever put work their way maybe once in their life if that. I tried to tell Mum that the longer it went on, the less chance I had of moving on, and this was a problem she did not want me to be independent again. She worried about my injuries and how I would cope and I had to admit I had gone downhill confidence-wise.

My lack of self-esteem brought on by all this stress made the option of being tied to Mother's apron strings a feasible option an easy way out, but it was not me. As much as I was grateful for all she was doing for me, I had to break loose. I was just about in control in the respect that the lawyers still took instructions from me, if it was proved remotely that I was any way restricted by my accident. Whatever money I was due would be sorted out by the courts and trustees would be appointed to run my fiscal life and I would have no control. I could be placed in and looked after by the court of protection, so it took a great effort from me to try and always second guess what people's motives were. Lawyers I knew were out to shaft me, actual doctors at my surgery I could trust. But medics appointed by lawyers for reports who charged large amounts of money had to be watched.

I made several trips to London's Harley Street, where a very good doctor I did trust gave reports that my injuries would not get worse or better so I would be as I was right then. On the strength of that report, I went to London to talk about a settlement. My lawyers said we only had to listen if we did not like what we heard we could just walk away but I knew that was rubbish.

I was going because they were putting on a show – two sets of barristers and their teams each in different rooms, one lot with me who would go from room to room with my answer to what offer they made. My barrister asked me what my instruction was for today, and I told him to get in that room and get what he told me I would get in previous meetings. He said, "Did you watch Deal or no Deal on the television?" and I could not believe what I had heard. It was rather like that he would start with the bar raised high and work from there. I wanted to walk out. If I had it could take some time to get the other side back around the table. It was clear to me at this point that today had to be the day to get this done.

I thought I was the one calling the shots when all along they held all the aces. They knew before we got there what I would get. Still, they had to make it look good to play out this pathetic game till the end.

I was offered 75% of what was on the table and was asked by my lawyers how much of my 75% did I want to risk on trying to get the other 25%. They argued if I did go to court a judge may think my claim was too high, and he would say what it should be. I had already agreed an amount for loss of earnings and an amount for injuries, so if I did not settle it could mean everything would take longer. My legal team left me in a room to think about it and by that time, I just wanted to draw a line in the sand and just get out of the whole situation. I was being well shafted, and we all knew it.

I had to call Mother, she insisted I did. She wanted to come with me but she would have put a spanner in the works for sure. I would have gone home with sod all; she could not understand how powerful the lawyers are in cases like this. They know that sooner or later clients would give in, it was all a game, played out by two sets of lawyers with you in the middle.

I told Mum what had been said and what was on the table. She said don't take it and that she had plenty of money and to fight on if I wanted to. I told her I was going to settle because I wanted it all to end and have my life back and that I thought we had taken things as far as we could but it was over. Mum said she understood and to do what I thought was best. That was the first real decision I had made for myself in three years.

When my lawyers came back in, I told them I would settle. They said that was fine and the right thing to do. But did I realise that benefits I had received from the government over three years amounted to £20,000, and even though I was entitled to benefits because that's what I needed to live on like everyone else, because I was getting compensation then I would have to pay back the £20,000 to the Benefit Agency. And for the first time I let my lawyers have it right between the eyes. I told them exactly what I thought of them and the methods they used and why did they not tell me this before I agreed to the settlement and that I would appeal against the decision to take back what was rightly mine.

It was all part of the game played out around you; it did not matter what any client, said the lawyers would get their way and the client would be well and truly shafted. So, I came away £20,000 short of what was agreed. I felt let down and it was one of the worst times of my life. I never told Mum about the £20,000. She had been great for me, and I decided to appeal the £20,000 and represent myself. I had to do so by a certain date, or the other side would just settle on what was agreed less the £20,000.

I also discovered that any moneys I did get could be paid into a trust fund, that could be set up and run by two trustee family members and that I could be one of them. It would mean that I would have to clear with the co-trustees, if I wanted any money or wanted to buy something so I paid £500 to set up the trust, making my youngest daughter the other trust member. It would mean that when the compensation was paid it would have to go directly into the trust from the compensator, and that the money could never be considered as capital or earnings, thereby allowing the compensated person to in the future. If they so needed, they could claim any benefit going if you qualified for it and the trust money could never be taken into consideration. The fact that my lawyers did not tell me about this did not surprise me; they and some medics had tried to present me as a possible basketcase when it suited them. No one could say I was not competent enough to run my own trust, I had on record all my injuries and in statements signed by a Harley Street doctor who stated my condition would stay as it was then and that I was a capable person and able to function properly to handle my affairs, all be it a little slower than before. In his opinion, I did not differ from other people who were approaching senior years so the legal team would not go against reports that they had asked for. You see if a court decided that a trust was needed to run someone's affairs, because they are not capable of doing so then who do you think gets to run it? Lawyers. They can invest money as they please, they charge vast amounts in hourly rates, set the clock ticking if they write to you or phone. It is a gravy train for the ambulance chasers of this world, who do whatever they wish with your money and say it is in your best interest!

Once a firm of lawyers is assigned to run someone's affairs you will have a devil's own job to get rid of them, they stick like leaches, and it is all legal. Also, if I did in the future go gaga, none of the trust money could be grabbed by the government for care costs, as so often is the case and so the pendulum began to swing back in my favour. A date for my appeal was set and I represented myself. I gave myself no chance of winning. I was entering the world of the wigs and black-suited con merchants. I was ushered into a room with the biggest table I had ever seen, probably used by lawyers to count their ill-gotten gains on. The table was so well polished the reflection of the judge made it look like it was two against one, but then being two-faced was how that particular profession operated. It is no coincidence that lawyers and magicians both have black capes. They both try and create an illusion fooling the public into wondering how what they thought they had disappeared before their very eyes. I told the judge why I wanted to appeal, and that I considered it to be morally wrong to take back what I was entitled to by law and that the government said that is what a single person needs to live on. Then, the judge told me that I had put forward a good case and it could be considered that taking the money from me was morally wrong but unfortunately it was legally right.

I replied by telling him about the trust fund etc. and did he realise I could claim all sorts of benefits until the cows came home, and it would be cheaper to give me my £20,000 back. Could he not use his unfettered discretion in this case?

The judge picked up his paperwork and tapped it on the table and said that he understood that benefits could indeed, if I so claimed, eventually amount to more than was taken from me, and if I did go down that road, he would not blame me for doing so. He also said it was not always wise to leave your lawyer to tell you about the reclaiming of benefits and he said he was sorry, but he would be rejecting my appeal, so we shook hands and that was it and all about it.

In time the money arrived, and I had to realise that what money I had then would have to last me, because I could no longer carry out my trade and at 61 was on the scrapheap. That was the reality of the situation. I transferred the money back to my family members who had been so helpful. My mother, who had no time for banks, wanted hers in cash so I filled four jiffy bags with cash and gave them to her. She had a secret stash at her flat somewhere, the only money she had in the bank was what she called her demise money for when the time came to meet her maker. I wanted to forget about what had happened and move on. I was in no rush, but I was contemplating moving to the Isle of Wight.

I had seen one or two auction properties on the internet and looked into the viability of such a move. I didn't tell anyone there would probably be opposition from the family, not because they didn't want me to go but because of my medical situation. While I felt all right, I knew I had become slower and had to pace myself. If you can imagine after working hard all day and you feel tired after your day's efforts, but in the morning, you feel revitalised and ready for another day. Well the way I felt all the time was the tired bit. I did everything at a slower pace, it took me longer to come round in the mornings. I did fret at times, I had in the last few years become reclusive, but I had always been able to cope with the isolation from my time in the homes.

It was second nature to me so now that I had my compensation, I did not have to rush into anything and my wish to move became a project more in my head for a long time before I felt able to go forward with it. For six months, I did nothing. I was recharging my batteries and it was nice doing what I wanted again.

My son had been doing the work that came in but as people realised I would not be working again the work became less and less. There would be enough for Kevin to make a go of things himself, he had built up some of his own clients as well. We had the vans, scaffold towers, mixer, and other tools necessary to run a small firm. However, he was not keen on running everything, pricing the work and sorting out materials, as well as doing the work and that was fine. I realised after pricing up two bungalows with him that I would have been able to skip through in no time before the accident. But now as I looked at the walls, it hit home that I was finished with plastering; even if I just priced work and got people to do it on a price that would not give me the same satisfaction as I had when we turned out work that gave me pride. So, I decided that if Kev didn't want to take things forward, I would de-register the firm with the tax man and that would be it. When the last of the work ran out, my son took up the opportunity to go and work in Spain with his brother and their uncle, so that's what he did.

It took some getting used to having them both away, but when he settled in and began to work over there I would, with the wonders of the internet, receive photos of work he was doing. Even suggesting to him methods to use on work, you have to make allowances for the heat in Spain, when deciding on what method to use. But he had a chance to work and live in a lovely country and he took it.

I hadn't done much work on my history project, mainly because I was out of circulation. After all, I had trouble concentrating with everything that was going on, I only went over things I had already done to double-check, if you like. It was a worthwhile thing to do because it looked even more interesting when I looked at everything again. As one thing followed another and fitted into the jigsaw perfectly, it proved that all I had found out and information gained from many sources was leading me in the right direction. And it would not be long before I would be back into the project with a renewed vigour that became, in fact, a therapy for me when I accessed all things pre-accident. I could almost feel the same feeling I had back then when I had full control over everything I did and the people who assisted me were wide-eyed supporters who believed in me without question. It was only my mother who feared what I may find out, and that was allowed because I think deep down she believed in what was happening and how everything that was falling into place was meant to be, and in some spiritual way I was being led to the conclusion of it all.

On the 2nd of February 2011, I received another letter from the Embassy of Italy, this time from Rear Admiral Francesco Maria de Biase Italian Defence and Navy Attaché. He had been asked to look for information regarding officers who served on the Libia from 1917 till 1920 by Captain Guido Saltini, who had been so helpful to me previously. The Rear Admiral's letter said that he had received from his authority's information written in Italian, about officers connected with the R. N. Libia in the timescale. I had asked about one officer, Ernesto Burzagli, who I had already got chapter and verse on, and a great man as Ernesto was, I had read all I wanted to about him.

But as I read on, two more names of officers who served under Ernesto Burzagli on the Libia were just what I had hoped for. There were two, both with the name Miceli, one spelt the same as Malena had told me i.e. Miceli and the other spelt De Micheli. Both variations of the same name. Also officer De Micheli was a sub-Lt on a training ship called the Castor for the navy in 1914–1915, and he was from Venice in the north and as I had found out the name had strong links with Venice. His ship was assigned to various purposes for the Navy so what link he had with the Libia in 1917–1919 was not clear, so I was prepared to hold fire with officer De Micheli because not much information was available i.e. his birth etc.

So, I focused on the other officer linked with the Libia and all the history of his life in the Italian navy, from the time he signed on as a young cadet right through till his retirement from the navy. It was all in this communication. He was from southern Italy. My DNA was highlighted more in the south than the north. The records that had been sent were all written in Italian. Thinking I could translate it by just looking at it was harder than I thought; while I could read some of it, I found I could not translate it all. I then thought about using my Italian dictionary, but that would take ages. In the end it was easier to use the Italian translator on the internet. All I had to do was copy the Italian text and click the button to translate into English.

I was cheating, I admit. If I had learnt Italian as I had I should have been able to read it, but a lot of water had passed under the bridge since then. I had also had a bang on the head to contend with. If I had problems remembering if I had turned the tap off or not, and what hand to hold my cutlery in, then remembering a language I had started learning pre the accident, I had no hope of being able to do such a task.

So, I translated the text of what I hoped would be of the Italian naval officer who could be my grandfather. He was born in southern Italy on the

1st of January 1883, he joined the Italian cadet school at the age of 14, then entered into what the Italians called the Marina on the 20th of October 1904 at the age of 23. Then in 1906 was promoted to Lieutenant and by 1911 became a captain until on the 28th of December 1924 when he was promoted to Lieutenant Colonel. Again, he was promoted in 1930 to the rank of Greater Colonel, and when he retired at the age of 63 in 1946 after years of service, he held the title of Greater General. So, he was a career navy man and was decorated with many medals for his work in the Austrian war; these included gold medals for 25 and 40 years of service and a medal souvenir for the unification of Italy, Commander of the Order of the Crown, and one for Commander of the Order Colonel of the Star of Italy.

Quite a lot to be proud of and now that I had this information, I also had his first name. Until I could link him to the Libia and more importantly to the photos in Ernesto Burzagli's family archives, all I needed to find out was what port the photo was taken in. If I could get that and connect it to one of the dates that the Libia had made stops at, when it made the journey from Cagliari on the 1st December 1918 calling at 14 ports including Southampton before completing its cruise at La Specia back in Italy in the September of 1919.

Until then I would refer to him as just Officer Miceli, because I wanted the replies to my enquires to include a possible Christian name. If I got that and it matched the name I had I was almost certain that this Officer Miceli could be my grandfather. I also was concerned of what I should do if this man did turn out to be my Nan's boyfriend, because it was so long ago – 92 years in fact. If he had a family in Italy and had children, there would be a good chance that they would be long gone. His grandchildren, if he had any, would be around my age and so I didn't know what to do for the best, so I looked at the facts I had.

First Mum had told me what Nan's next-door neighbour had said, then Malena Mahona confirmed that by telling me what her grandmother had told her. Also, I found out about the Libia and its links to the port of Southampton at around the right time for the officer to have known my Nan. The photographs of Officer Miceli and the uncanny likeness to my father, not in just one photo but two from different times and, of course, the service record of Officer Miceli's life in the Italian navy. I just needed one more bit of information to confirm what I set out to do was complete; and if the name came back as Officer G. Miceli in the photo of the four officers who served on the R. N. Libia I had done it.

I decided that it would have to take something very important for me to try and find the family of Officer G. Miceli, if it was him, and so I was going to file everything away and call it a day. I did not think I would get the names of the officers in the photos, the best I could hope for would be the name of the port where the photos had been taken. That would be good enough for me and, as I have said before, I could not ruin a man's reputation by stirring up the past. I felt the richer for what I had found out about my Italian links, I had come a long way, both for myself and my father. It felt right to let it go now and move on to the next thing. So, I shelved the project until I had positive proof that Officer G. Miceli was both the man in the photos and the records that I had received.

Chapter 14
Auction

Throughout the summer of 2013, I looked at several old houses at auctions with the view of making a bid. The auctions were held on a regular basis at the home of the Hampshire Cricket Club, and if you are thinking of buying at auction there are a few things to bear in mind when doing so. Commission is added to the hammer down price, so the auctioneer's percentage needs to be added to your budget. You will need to provide bank information and be able to pay the deposit on the day with a banker's draft and be able to complete in 30 days. Also, your solicitor information will need to be registered. It is possible to use one of the companies that handle conveyancing, who attend all auctions; you may find them a little cheaper and they deal with auction property all the time.

You should arrive in good time to register and take a look at the information regarding the lot number you intend to make a bid for, and it is advisable to have already visited the site of the auction lot advertised. It is not advisable to bid on a whim, you will be disappointed if you do as all auction properties are there because they have something wrong with them or cannot make the asking price with estate agents.

So, auction rooms are the last chance saloon for some people who, for one reason or another, find themselves lumbered with a money pit they cannot get rid of. You will find that the owners of such properties will be at the auction and get involved in the early biding of the property until the room becomes interested, and the natural competitive nature of the public kicks in. So, when mock bidding begins that's when you should always pull out, because the lot in question no longer is the bargain you envisaged it would be. It is easy to get carried away and if you are bidding against someone with no limits you may find they pull out before you do, thereby leaving you with a headache and on a loser before you start.

This had been the problem with the property I was after. It had been in the auction house more than once and was the Cinderella of the auction market and stank like rotten fish. It had been hanging around for so long with several interested parties, all of whom had been seduced by its location way up in the hills above Ventnor on the Isle of Wight. Its panoramic sea views were breathtaking, and people were drawn in to purchase what looked to be a snip at first sight. However, when the realisation kicked in that all that glitters is not gold, most people walk away. Some still see the property through rose-tinted glasses and ignore the reality that water cannot be turned into wine, however hard one dreams at the end of the day, a dog is what it is – a dog.

This poor unfortunate house on the hill was much loved in the past but no longer the attractive proposition it once was. Its very soul had been destroyed, its spirit gone and all that was left was a ruined shell of a building that had been ravaged by mysterious underground happenings. Way beneath the earth's crust a landslide to end all had pushed down from the hills at upper Ventnor above the picturesque Victorian town. It caused havoc among the small community that lived to tell the tale, of the Lowtherville Graben that took away the homes of many and for others who were left with a place to live but worth nothing in monetary terms, they lived in a dwelling that could at any time be struck by the same fate.

It was in the winter of 1960 following a very wet period between August and November when the winter rainfall totalled 713 mm, the worst recorded since records began in 1839. The widespread damage to property and services throughout Ventnor involved the evacuation of over 30 residents, large cracks appeared which became impassable by traffic and mounds of earth that had been pushed upward remained as a reminder of verbosity that had struck. Large sink holes were caused by the volume of water that turned the sand rock into rushing sand, the gault layer above was disturbed as were the other types of layered deposits that made up this vulnerable landscape. That had progressively failed from high volumes of rainfall that while seem to not immediately affect the ground, make up until some ten days after when the damage going on beneath the earth manifests itself. Demonstrating its powerful display of destruction in a landslide that could not be held back, but only monitored and watched as the new land lay-out established itself.

The old property that had been so affected still stood but had a steel belt around the middle of the building to stop it moving or collapsing altogether. Its roof had large purlins sat between and fixed horizontally into the gable ends. The roof joist timbers constructed one by one and fixed to the purlins from timber plates on the north and south walls and joined at the ridge of the roof. When the building moved, the roof dropped causing the north wall to be pushed out and change the shape of the building, rendering it dangerous to be occupied. But occupied it was by an old gentleman who inherited the home from his family, and it was now worthless, and he had gone into a home and funds had to be found for his continued occupation of a single room and his three meals a day.

So, the Lowtherville Graben was responsible for not just the disruption of the earth but to many people's lives as well. For someone with limited funds, who needed to be independent and was not afraid of hard work, this plot was the ideal house. It would have to be demolished, the site levelled leaving the original footprint to repair by underpinning the footings and having just a small dwelling on the same footprint. Something that was big enough for a kitchen diner, lounge, two bedrooms with bathrooms and a study. The site was worth no more than £30,000, and I made such a bid for it pre-auction that would have kept the old gentleman safe and comfortable in the knowledge that he was to be looked after for the remainder of his days or until the funds ran out.

The perfect scenario for him and for myself but unfortunately family members had power of attorney over him, and they chose not to play ball and take the risk in the auction room to get more. The problem for the family members was that people bidding knew about the Lowtherville Graben; it was legendary and so none of the bids reached the asking price of £50,000. A sum they had no chance of getting, given the state of the building, and there was the planning department to contend with. They would not let anything be built on the site that would be bigger than the footprint already in place. The council wanted all properties affected by the Graben to be pulled down and the site left to return to its once natural state of downland.

But the council would not buy it to do that, so the only person to suffer was the old gentleman and the eyesore that the derelict property had become was to stay on the auction books for the rest of that year. By that time the old gentleman had passed away. He died not having the benefits of what was rightly his. It was such a shame. So then at the end of 2013 the property was put back in the auction room, this time with a reserve price of £40,000, still too much for me. But I still went to the auction, and it went for £44,000 to a person from the other side of London, who it was clear had done no homework on the area or knew anything about the problems of the Graben in the area.

It was like lambs to the slaughter. Needless to say, after starting work on the site they soon fell out with the planners for not getting permission to take off the roof and not submitting relevant paperwork to the council. All work on the plot stopped and low and behold, the property found itself in the auction room for the third time. The owner must have spent all sorts of money – just travelling from London must have been costly, as well as the labour cost incurred.

The next auction would not be till March 2014, and I continued looking round but was not in any particular hurry so spent my time helping my daughter and grandson at the farm a few days each week. I found it relaxing working with the tractor to level out the sandy outdoor school each day before the horses practised their jumping skills. There was always something to do at the farm and I found it very therapeutic. Christmas came and my brother and I would each year be asked to help put up the decorations with other relations of the residents at the warden call flats where Mum lived. She herself had so much Christmas things she put out in her flat each year the place looked like Santa's grotto. All the old people came to life at Christmas, they all enjoyed a Christmas lunch, paid for by the rotary, and entertainment was also laid on. The New Year's Eve parties always went with a bang, and it was nice to know that they enjoyed themselves.

Mum spent Christmas Day with my brother each year and I now went to one of my daughters for Christmas lunch and visited my other daughter on Boxing Day. Then on New Year's Eve I had Mum come down for lunch and have a relaxing afternoon before taking her back for her party with all the other people at the warden call complex. After the Christmas of 2013, I wanted to draw a line under my interest in the auction property at Ventnor on the Isle of Wight. March's upcoming auction would be my final interest in the house and plot and while I really wanted it, I was not going to go broke in the process of obtaining it. So, when the day came, I made sure I had all my relevant information and bank details to hand. I had decided that my final bid would be £35,000 and not a penny more. The property was a viable proposition at that price if I got it; I would not have to rush to get the work done. I would have to remember I was a lot slower now, but I had worked out how I would tackle each stage and the help I would need to have.

I had already drawn up plans for what I intended to do and had one meeting at the planning office to show them what I proposed. I had good feedback from the planning officer I had seen, I also had a telephone conversation with one of the directors of the company who had been responsible for the construction of the sea wall defence at Ventnor. He was the son of the owner of the firm. We talked about the sea wall defence and could it be seen as while holding back the tides and preserving the coastline from erosion, would it also be right to think that it acted as a buttress, to hold back the movement of land on the town side of the sea defence; and all the properties and roads that were positioned on the slopes that made up the town of Ventnor would each become a buttress to each other.

You would still have some movement from underground activity and sink holes may still be a problem, but they would be easier to deal with if the earth as it moved down to the coast could not go any further than the sea wall defence. We had an interesting conversation, and he was able to tell me, in his opinion, what I had said could be feasible because any ground movement on the public roads and paths or council-owned land would be dealt with straight away. The problem you would have if ground movement and sink holes appeared on private land was that not everyone would carry out necessary repairs to rectify the problem for cost reasons for a start. So, in theory it was possible but in practice you would need the cooperation of all residents to buy into it.

The other thing one would have to remember was that properties in Ventnor that are at risk or near to a high-risk site would not be insured, only the contents insurance. Companies ran a mile if you even mentioned land slips and that was par for the course with all insurance companies. It had been very interesting talking about the problems of Ventnor, and we agreed to talk again if I was successful in obtaining the property.

On the day of the auction, I arrived on time and registered. One of the people also interested in the property was a man from Middlesex. We had looked at a video showing all the lots; it ran continually before the auction started. His name was Ian Lush and he had a construction firm and thought the site may be able to have two small houses built on it. I did not ask him if he had researched the site, it was pretty obvious that he had not. It would not be a good idea to tell him because he may have thought I was trying to put him off bidding for the property. The best way to lose a property at auction is to tell someone who wants to bid that what they want is no good since they will usually go the extra mile to beat you.

It is human nature to want to win, that is why you should keep your cards close to your chest and show no real interest. While inside knowing your price limit was not going to be enough to win the bid was almost heart-breaking. All the work you had put in and built the site in your head over and over again.

When the lot came up and the bidding started, only three of us in the room made bids, someone on the phone was bidding but pulled out after two bids. The lot started at an amazing £15,000 and only went up £500 at a time. Apart from Ian Lush and myself, the third person bidding I took to be the owner who was keen to keep the bidding going. He was very impatient and was determined to get the price up and was first in each time. Then someone else joined in and took the price to £25,000, and each bid was then raised by £1,000 each time. The owner dropped out at £33,000 and I only had two more bids, and the other two were, I could tell, not going to give in, they both wanted it as much as I did. But I took the bid to my limit of £35,000 and felt crushed as the other two quickly took it past my affordability, so for me that was it.

Chapter 15
Durley Churchyard

It had been a disappointing morning at the property auction, and not being far from Durley churchyard decided to go and have a walk round, as I had done so many times in the past when I wanted to clear my head, When I got there, I was shocked to see the churchyard in such a mess. The grass was nearly up to my waist and in places even higher. I made my way down the old path through the long grass to the west end area of the yard because this was the location of a family headstone, the daughter of great-grandfather David.

My father would talk about him when I was a child. David was a person of few words. Dad said he would tell the rector if it was dry, "Youm Recter Pray for Rain" and if it was too wet would say, "Youm Recter Pray for Sun". David's daughter, Susan Matilda, married the local cobbler, a man known as shoemaker Bob Houghton. Susan Matilda had died in her early 40s and her grave was at the end of the churchyard close to the woods. As I walked round trying to keep to the overgrown path, I could see a man trying to cut the grass with an electric mower. He was not having much luck as the grass was so thick and he could only go as far as the cable reached.

It looked a bit ridiculous to be perfectly honest, and from the state of the place I was not sure anyone ever cut the grass on a regular basis. I asked him why the place was so poorly kept and that it had always been so clean and tidy. But that was many years ago when I thought about it, when villagers took pride in keeping the churchyard up together. The man said they only had volunteers who did the best they could, and as I walked away, he said sarcastically that I was always welcome to help if I had any tools. But I didn't answer and carried on walking to my car. I was not in that good a mood anyway, having just lost out on the house at Ventnor. In fact, the closer I got to my car, the more I thought I should have told the man what I thought of his offer. But I just got in my car and drove off thinking if I did get involved with clearing the churchyard up it would be a huge task, given I was a lot slower now, but at the same time I thought there would be no need to push myself. I could start when I was ready and finish when I had enough, and when I was almost home, I made up my mind to go back the following day and start sorting the churchyard out.

So, the following morning I took the tools I needed and turned up at the churchyard. On entering through the south gate and turning left to the west, I had to hack my way through giant hogweed, stinging nettles, shrubs and grass that was very long and as tough as old boots. The hogweed, when I cut into its stem, was like the stem of rhubarb and just as thick and when cut into squirted out an acid-type liquid that burnt if it got on your skin or in your eyes. So, it was important to have your arms covered and safety glasses on to protect from getting burnt.

At around lunchtime on my first day as a volunteer, the man who I had seen the day before came in and was surprised to see me there. He was grateful for the help; he was in fact the churchwarden and he asked me what I intended to do in the churchyard. So, I told him I was going to clear around the grave of my great-aunt and clear the pathway from the gate down to the edge of the woods. The churchwarden said that before I did too much of what I intended, it would have to be talked over by the church PCC at their next meeting. I asked when that was and was told in three weeks' time and that the church council had wanted to keep the west end of the churchyard for the wildlife. I had to laugh and told him that I could not see any signs that resembled anything remotely like a wildflower growing and with no wildflowers you had no hope of wildlife. Not much would grow anywhere near giant hogweed, that grew at the expense of everything else; in fact if you wanted to attract wildlife then whatever wildflowers had been dormant under all the rubbish, they would need the light of day to enhance their chances of regenerating. I also said I didn't want to tread on anyone's toes, but in three weeks I could have a lot of the unwanted growth out of the way. Adding that if any of his PCC members liked the hogweed so much I could save it for them, and they could have a fine display in their own garden and not in a place of rest.

I asked him to trust me not to mess the churchyard up, and that I had seen it in its pomp when I was a boy and had a mind's eye of how it once looked. If I decided to stay around I would try to return the churchyard to its former glory. I also said that I would not do anything drastic without first consulting him. If he would give me licence to make decisions that were in the best interest of the churchyard, rather than wait while committees gathered, who in reality, along with previous groups of people, had set the standard for the present state of neglect.

It was clear that the subject of what was best for the churchyard had not been on the top of anyone's list of priorities for some time. While you could not apportion blame to any one person, the collective complacency through the generations was there for all to see. It may have seemed to the churchwarden that I was laying down the law, but I was not, I was establishing some ground rules – that the only thing that mattered was the churchyard and all who rest within its boundaries. If I was going to get involved and do it for history's sake and not be financial rewarded, then it would be on my terms.

It was like taking over a football club that was down on its uppers – there was only one way to go and that was forward with someone who would lead from the front and I am glad to say that the churchwarden agreed to trust my judgement. So the beginning of this mammoth task began in earnest. My mother wanted to know when I would stop chasing rainbows and lost causes, but the answer was simple – never. If something was wrong then it had to be put right and that applied to most things in which you could make a difference.

The first area I started to clear was from the gate situated at the south boundary hedge, running north across the churchyard till it reached a path that ran all the way through the middle of the churchyard east to west. On the other side of the path were more overgrown graves, but this time kerbstone graves with a headstone at the head of the grave and then the kerbstone was set around the actual perimeter of each grave. They had all been packed into a confined space and it was difficult walking around them because over the years the moles had made big molehills in between them, almost joining them all. The grass then took over and hid most of the kerbstones that surrounded the individual graves. It was an area that would require serious attention at some stage but for the time being my task was to start in the area the other side of the path to the south.

When I began to clear the area, my efforts eventually revealed some 30 old headstones that had been hidden by the long grass and hogweed. One or two of the headstones did have people tend them but they had to negotiate their way through the overgrown area. The headstones were in nine different rows of graves, each with around 19 graves per row. The graves with no headstone were just slight bumps in the ground but it was obvious they were graves, and all from the middle of the 18th century. Back then, not everyone was able to afford to have a headstone; most people would have been agricultural workers so money for headstones wasn't readily available.

The main thing they had to barter with was the value of their personal energy and skills; that was their stock in trade and once unable to work and no help was afforded them, then the workhouse became the reality they all feared. So, it was even more important to me to try and find out who occupied the graves with no headstone. I was not sure how but knew something would turn up through some form of record. Because this was all new to me, each day gave me more to think about and make notes of how to solve each question. I was asking myself while still carrying out the main task of clearing the churchyard of the intrusive growth that had taken over and changed completely the landscape into an unrecognisable once-loved historic churchyard.

After one month working every day except Sundays, for six hours each day, I had cleared an area that contained over 30 old headstones and another 160 possible unmarked graves. As for the headstones, it would be possible to identify who the people were who rested within each grave. But first I would need to consult a stonemason as to the best way of cleaning the historic stone. I could not risk any damage to them – they are a work of art – and the inscriptions, while being hard to make out completely, contained lots of information about the people who had been buried at Durley. So, there was no rush to clean them, and it would have taken time to do, so I needed to first concentrate on clearing the areas.

When all the bracken and weeds had been gathered up and placed in large one tonne bags to be taken to the east end of the churchyard for burning, the first area looked so much better. The headstones stood proud as they once did many years ago and it gave me great pride in what I had started. Also, people from the village started to come in and enquire about what I was doing, and I had some interesting conversations. I was honest with all of them, telling them I was no expert in historic grave searches but was finding out as I went along how things had been done in the past and it was a slow process discovering all that had been lost. Some of the older people when they knew who I was and recognised my surname told me that they knew it to be an old Durley name and some even remembered when they had been children their parents did business with my ancestors.

It was fascinating to meet so many people. I would never have thought that a churchyard had so many visitors each week, some just visiting churchyards or walkers who took in churchyards as part of their ramble. Of course, the regular people who tended their relatives' graves all were interested in what I was doing and as the weeks passed, I became more connected to the area, and with the people who gave me so much encouragement.

So, with that first area done it was time to tackle the area where my great-aunt Susan Matilda's grave was, on the edge of the woods. The bracken was so thick and overhung her grave. As I cut it back, I was shocked that beyond the row her grave was in I could see deep in the woods. More headstones were situated there, and it was sad to see, so I stopped working. No one who had come in while I was clearing the first area had said anything about there being more graves beyond the woodland boundary. I had not been close enough to the edge of the wooded area before to notice, but I could just make out the headstones that were well hidden. It was only the light that came through the trees and made them visible and even then you had to look hard to recognise what they were.

It was difficult to understand how this could have happened, that a village churchyard could be lost with in its own boundary, to become so overgrown that it became something else entirely. A dense woodland that had been untouched for what must have been many years. How many, I could not imagine, but the headstones were there. They may have been surrounded by trees and almost hidden, but they had stood the test of time, waiting for someone to come along and release them from the trees and bracken that pushed against them. An unsuccessful attempt to dislodge them, such was the strength of the stone, that was the only thing to indicate more people had been buried within what had now become a woodland area that once must have been part of the churchyard itself.

So, I decided to leave Susan Matilda's grave that was at the northwest of the row and start working from the southwest left to right. The ground that I had already cleared began to run uphill and continued into the wooded area.

The ground within the woods was much higher and as I began to clear the bracken and overgrowth, I found that it was not the natural ground that had continued into the woods. But instead, it was piles of spoil that had been put there, and within the spoil, I found lots of bricks and broken slate that had been covered with thick ivy and weeds. Mother Nature's way of hiding her embarrassment. The rubbish covered the natural soil with bricks and slate, stopping halfway across the line I was working across. The debris indicated to me that some sort of building had stood on that spot at one time, and the roof and walls had fallen in within itself. It was difficult to tell with so much ivy covering it all, but I was sure all would be revealed in time.

When I got past all the debris of bricks and slate, the piles of spoil continued again, covered in the ivy that was so tough to pull out. As I reached the end of the row at Susan Matilda's grave, there was still a way to go before I reached the north boundary hedge that was so high and thick, made up of holly trees and other saplings that had grown out of control. When I was able to get close to the north boundary to look through a gap in the hedge, I could see the most wonderful view over the rolling hills that made up the local golf course. Its lush-green manicured lawns were vastly different from what lay on my side of the hedgerow, and as I finished cutting each row working south to north, I cut down the overgrown holly trees, using the long offcuts to lay in the hedge, an old country tradition often used to enhance the hedge row and make it stronger.

I worked my way across each row and through the debris that again finished halfway across, I finally reached a headstone situated on the right of the row to the north. It was a big, impressive work of art and even though it was covered in green mould and ivy it still had a majestic look about it. So, I cut away the ivy at the foot of the headstone so it would rot before it could be safely removed; to pull it off at that time may have damaged the stone since, as sometimes happens, stone becomes subject to frost damage and cause lime bloom so the ivy could possibly grow into the actual stone itself.

The second stone that I got to was a large cross and across the middle, I could just make out the words "Thy Will Be Done" that had been skilfully carved into the stone. As I stood and admired the craftmanship for a while and said to myself that, "Yes It certainly would", finding each stone as I had was quite emotional. To think they all represented a time forgotten and had to endure the neglect bestowed upon them on sacred ground and in view of the house of the Lord.

In time, when I was able to clean them and see who rested within, I became protective of them. It may sound stupid, but they were like friends, each one with its own identity and if you stood close to them it was like being next to an adult as a child, you felt safe. It was a strange spiritual feeling but the emotions the stones brought from me could not be completely explained, it was as if each one had a message for you. Sometimes if I looked back at the headstones from another part of the churchyard, and I could not see one of them I had to walk to a place where I could to make sure it was still there. Of course, it was my senses playing tricks on me.

So, when I had cut all the small trees, bracken, ivy and long grass from the wooded area, and left with a great pile of spoil, I had to move it but it was clear it would still need to be done by hand and, given how slow I now worked, it would be a long process. But I had the time and the will power and when I was in the churchyard I seemed to be energised.

I think it was because what I was doing was so interesting, I never had time to think about the aches and pains I had. But when I went home sometimes, I had a job to move around after six hours of steady work moving earth and rubbish from the natural woodland floor. But I loved working in the churchyard and could not wait to get there in the mornings. I was greeted each day by all manner of wild birds and I would bring food for them. They would sit on the headstones while I placed the food on one of the chest stone graves. While I stood very still, they would come and feed; it was a lovely moment each day to be around nature.

I had purchased a small van which was perfect for what I needed, and when I arrived some days one robin would come and sit on the wing mirror of the van to welcome me. When I started work, it would follow me around to see what I could uncover for it to eat. If I sat down, it would sit close to me and not move until I did. It is said that the churchyard robin represents the spirits that can be felt within the churchyard. The robin will welcome and watch to keep you safe, and if you do see it then it will come near you to indicate that all is well with your loved ones. A lot of wildlife was beginning to return to the churchyard again and becoming a place of welcoming peace once more.

I had been busy and enjoying the work and when I saw my mother at the weekend, I had plenty to tell her about what I had been doing. She liked to hear how everything was going and said that it was a good thing I was doing. Mum was still in good form and had her opinion on everything and everyone, but she more recently began to talk to me about what I had to do at her demise. She was quite serious about it and told me her 94th year was approaching and that she could not last forever, and that I may not like to talk about it. But I didn't have to because all I had to do was listen to her instructions; they would not be complicated and were easy for me to carry out. So of course, I said I would and asked her to tell me what she wanted me to do.

Mum took a list from her diary and began to instruct me as to what she wanted. First she said I would need to get my clever clogs head on, and would I be able to find out where my brother Melvin was buried. If possible, she wanted it in writing, meaning from the records office, then Mum said that I had to find out if her ashes could be put in the grave with her mother and father and if not, she wanted them placed, not scattered, under the trees at the crematorium where we placed flowers for my father. Dad's ashes had been placed at the old garden of remembrance by the undertakers but after five years the council decided to have a new garden at the cemetery that we went to now and that the top two feet of soil would be taken from the old place and put into the new garden. Mum said the undertakers sent a letter to everyone telling them what was going to happen. At the time she thought they must be bonkers if they thought people would fall for that. It was pretty clear that half the people's ashes would be on the tyres of the lorries moving the earth, and so that was why we found a spot where we always placed flowers for my dad. Mum then got onto the subject of her service saying she wanted 'Morning has Broken' played at the end of the service, that it was not to be drawn out, and it would be best if no one got up to talk because it was not fair to put pressure on people on a sad occasion. Given her age, not a lot of people were left who could talk about the past, and that if any of them were they may have lost their marbles by now.

She then told me all her paperwork was in order. It was an interesting conversation and I suppose one that many people have with an ageing parent, and I have to admit it was best to get it out of the way. Mum wanted it that way and I would make sure it was done. One of the first things I did was to get Melvin's death certificate. I contacted the curate at the church where Melvin had been buried and to asked him if he could tell me what area within the churchyard Melvin had been laid to rest. Then on my way to Durley church the following week I went to the cemetery, where my grandparents William and Lucy had been buried, to see if it was possible for Mum's ashes to go in with them. Unfortunately, their grave was a double depth and back then the undertakers placed a concrete slab over the grave before placing the kerbstone around it so it could not be dug. The only way I could have done it was to dig down at the side of the grave and place Mum's ashes into the side of the grave, but I was not going to do that; it was not respectful for my Mum or my grandparents. I was not going to tamper with their resting place, so I hoped by the time Mum next came to my house for Sunday lunch I would have some answers for her.

The next time Mother came for lunch I told her what I had found out about Melvin and gave her the paperwork. She took the envelope from me and held it close to her chest, closed her eyes and began to rock gently backwards and forwards cradling the information. This was the first time she had seen any paperwork regarding the child she lost some 67 years ago. I was able to tell her that Melvin was buried at what back then was our local churchyard, in an area set aside for child burials and that while Melvin had his own plot it was unmarked, but I had been told it was in a nice area of the churchyard. Mum asked me if I would go and see it; she did not want to go herself. My problem was that yes, I wanted to go and see it but what if the place was not kept up together. I would feel obliged to get involved and do it, but I had enough on my plate as it was. So I told Mum that yes, I would make the time to go and see the children's area of the churchyard. This seemed to please her.

I then told her that it would not be appropriate for her ashes to be placed in with her parents, and the reason why so Mum just said that I should put her ashes under the trees at the cemetery where we took flowers for Dad. Mum said she was glad things had been sorted out and that she could relax because it had been on her mind.

In July 2014 Mum had her 94th birthday. Her friends at the warden call flats had a small lunchtime tea and cake party for her, nothing big just the usual few people who all made up the small community of flats and bedsits. The residents came from all different walks of life and now found themselves together with people they may not have mixed with in bygone days, but who now made up this interesting band of associates.

The flat complex, like many others, are dens of knowledge if you can take the time to engage in conversation with the keen teachers that resided within them. While we enjoyed celebrating Mum's special day with tea and cakes for her and her friends, I could not ignore the fact that she looked very tired.

She was not sleeping that well and had told me before we went down to the common room, that she could hear in the night someone singing. It was wonderful, Mum said, but not in the middle of the night. She said it was sung in a foreign language and sounded like the same song repeated each night, starting low then becoming louder before fading away altogether. Mum's flat was on the first floor so had flats above and below, all of the same design. In the corner of the bedrooms was a wide ducting that housed the water and waste pipes from each flat. If someone played music in the flat above or below it was quite possible it could travel in the ducting; the construction was only a thin layer of plasterboard. When I told Mother this, it seemed to reassure her. I suggested she have her radio on low as that would maybe help her to get off to sleep and that she could ask if anyone else heard the same music. It was a big complex and noises in the night can be frustrating when you cannot get off to sleep. Mum didn't talk about having heard it again. Hence, I assumed everything was back to normal with her sleep pattern. The tea party did not go on for long, and when I took Mum back to her flat, she sat in her chair and before long settled into her afternoon nap.

Back at Durley churchyard another week began, and I was to meet for the first time the local gravediggers, Chris and his son Patrick. They had come to dig the grave of a local village person whose funeral was to take place the following day and would be buried at the northeast end of the churchyard. It was a new area only some 20 years old as a burial ground and that had not been looked after. The grass was very long, and Chris told me that a lot of churchyards that he dug graves at were very untidy, and the long grass in all of them was a problem on the day of a burial. I was to learn something interesting that day. I had never seen a grave dug before, and Chris used a small digger to dig the grave. He did so with great skill in such a tight area near to other graves.

When Chris had dug the grave, Patrick jumped down into it and shaped the sides of the grave with a shovel. The head of the grave would be wider than at the foot. The two men worked well together and what they did was indeed an art. While Patrick finished things at the grave, Chris walked with me down to the west end area of the churchyard that I had been clearing and was surprised to see what I had done. I asked him if he could tell me how so much spoil could have accumulated in the woods. He told me that when a grave is dug and they are all double depth, some 16 barrow loads of spoil is left over and that the church had the responsibility to deal with it. The spoil cannot be moved from a churchyard to another place or to landfill because it is regarded as possible contaminated soil.

The church council had always told the gravediggers to put the soil at the west end of the churchyard, in the woods and that each gravedigger had done so for many years. So, I asked Chris if he realised that the wooded area had graves within its boundary, to which he was not aware. He seemed to me like a decent man having only just met him, and my instincts were proved right in time because Chris and his son Patrick became my friends. Both I could trust, they each respected what I was trying to do with the churchyard and did a lot to help me. They were both very clever men and masters at the art of digging graves.

Back at the wooded area, I began the task of moving the earth I had a spade that was in the shed, a top-quality one. I may add, probably the only decent tool the church owned. I had an old rake from my daughter's farm, used to muck out the horses, and a long-handled shovel that I got on the internet for £13, along with a wheelbarrow the churchwarden brought in. I was set to go and tackle the moving of the spoil, as I had done when cutting out the bracken and small trees etc. working left to right across the west end of the churchyard. I would chop the spoil until I reached the natural churchyard floor, then I would loosen the earth, taking out any bricks or slate that I put further down on the south side of the wooded area. The ground needed building up and I used the soil to fill the sunken areas of the path that ran through the middle of the churchyard west to east. It was a laborious task but there was no rush. I took my time and if it had rained, the soil that I was moving was full of clay and got too sticky to move. I would work in the northwest area taking the turf off the kerbstone graves and levelled out the molehills.

After any rainfall, the wind would dry the clay content of the soil and it was easy to move it again, but if it was very windy the clay was like rock, so it was soon apparent that each day's work was dependent on the weather. If it rained too hard then I just worked till I was wet then went home. Durley churchyard was way up high on the hill and when it rained it rained, and the wind would blow so hard you could not stand up. If the sun was out, it was a wonderful place to be and on a clear day you could see the Isle of Wight. It was a fantastic view to all points of the compass.

Each week I learnt new things about the churchyard – how to read the soil, and by that I mean each old grave would be a mixture of soil that had been dug, disturbing its natural make up of turf, topsoil, sub soil, then layers of sand and clay. After a burial, the mixture of all the soil would be placed back in the ground and in time became firm. If it got wet, the water would sit on the top and not drain through the soil like the natural soil. Its water table intact so the ground reacted differently around the graves, the natural ground would swell and shrink while the soil in the grave would just sink and need to be toped up by man; it could not react as nature intended. It was something that, once disturbed, could never return to its natural form. It was still earth and things grew from it.

But it was not the Lord's earth, how it was intended to be but it was still sacred, whatever form it took. It housed his children and the Lord charged the living to protect them. One grave contained three children, none of whom survived past the age of two years, each one buried in front of the other, forming a long grave of about 12 feet that had been completely covered by the spoil that had just been dumped there without any care covering the kerbstone around it.

At the head of the grave was an impressive headstone and at the foot of the grave a smaller version known as a foot stone, with the children's initials carved and the date they passed away. On the main headstone, their full names had been skilfully carved with the inscription – "'Is the child well" asked the Lord to which the mother replied, "Lord the Child is well". Each headstone I found, I would know that something would be written but that I would have to wait to see it because I could not leave the primary task of clearing the spoil. However, as each area was cleared of the spoil, some headstones that had once marked a person's resting place had disappeared, only the plinth that it stood on remained. They must have been large headstones if the size of the plinths were anything to go by, but no sign of the headstone could be found. They would have been very heavy things to move and if they had fallen over, why move them from the area? It would have been a major task to lift and take away. If they had been taken to have another inscription cut into the stone, you would have thought it would be reinstated if they had gone to all the trouble of moving such big stones. The fact there was more than one headstone missing from its plinth in that area did give me cause for concern. I was sure that at some point I may find the answers as I went along.

The slow process of clearing the spoil continued and it would take me three and a half years to do so. Working now and then in that area and fitting it in with other work within the churchyard, I took on the task of cutting the grass. In the summer it was a full-time job. I split the areas into which needed more attention like the new east end area. All the graves in that area had regular visitors so it was important to make sure it was accessible. If there was a burial, it would probably be in that area, unless it was a second burial of a spouse in an already occupied grave at the northwest of the yard that dated back to the 50s. Any further back in time than that would not have been possible, only ashes could be considered and even then, it would depend on the state of the plot in question. Sometimes a grandchild wanted to have their ashes scattered on the grave of a grandparent but scattering of ashes is not always a good idea. If you tried to scatter them on a grave in Durley churchyard with the way the wind would blow, before the casket was empty your relation would be halfway to Upham, with a high chance of disturbing a golfer's aim on the way and make what was a melancholy occasion even more so.

All ashes should be in the earth, we are talking about human remains. Not everyone likes to be told what they can and cannot do within a churchyard, but it's the rules set by the top brass within the chancellor's office, that everyone has to abide by and if someone has a problem, they should always consult the chancellor's office.

At Durley, the church members make sure the place looks at its best when people attend a wedding, baptism or funeral. Word of mouth became the best way to get the message out that Durley churchyard was back in business after years of neglect. It was possible to allocate days that I would cut grass till lunchtime, and then for the rest of the day move more spoil from the west end area. If I moved half a dozen barrowloads each afternoon after cutting grass, I considered it a good day's work and the moving of the spoil would become the incentive, while the repetitive grass cutting was taking place to hurry and get back down to the west end area where something always seemed to turn up.

So, it was one day in the week leading up to the August bank holiday of 2014, I could not cut grass because there was to be an interment of ashes at the east end of the churchyard. Two young men had turned up with the undertaker to assist in digging a plot for their grandmother's ashes to be placed into. They did not take long and afterwards the vicar turned up with other relatives to hold a service. I had stayed down at the west end of the churchyard while the boys helped the undertaker, and just raked up residue of grass and weeds to put in a large bag to move out of the way, given that people would be in over the bank holiday. I wanted the place to look tidy. Then while the interment of ashes took place, I stopped what I was doing out of a mark of respect to the families and when the service had finished around midday, I decided to have my lunch before taking the large bag of rubbish to the compost heap at the other end of the churchyard. At around 1 pm all the people had gone, and I was left on my own to continue my work. I pulled the large bag to lift into the wheelbarrow and began to rake up the residue it had been placed on when I hit something solid with the rake. When I cleared the area, I could see it was a headstone but it was upside down. I could not see the inscription, the stone would have to be moved and it was pretty impressive. It had been broken off at its base – a clean break, it could have been done by a bow falling from the old oak tree it sat beneath or been caused by wilful damage. Other plinths further in the churchyard I had found looked like they had been struck at the base, the same as this one that had been saved because it had sunk into the ground and in time grass had grown over it.

I went to get timbers from the shed and some of the old bricks I had been digging out of the spoil and began to jack up the headstone on one side so I could turn it over. Its plinth, as like the others, was still intact, so once I moved the headstone away from the plinth, I was able to dig down next to the plinth with the intention of lifting the headstone back in place and securing it against the part that was left in the ground. It took me around an hour to get the headstone in position to turn over and when I did it was a moment I will never forget. The inscription was so wonderfully done in old English. It was the grave of a man who had died at the age of 30 years old in 1870. Cut into the stone were the words "In The Midst of Life There is Death" and the man had the same surname as me.

I was on my own and it was such a moment, I shouted out loud and my voice echoed around the silent churchyard. I quickly mixed concrete and stood the stone up and walked it into the hole I had dug next to the plinth, gently placing it back where it should be and secured it in place. I then washed the headstone, but where it had been under the ground it was so clean and was cut from of the finest sandstone. The inscription on the stone read "In loving memory of George Prowting the son of W. & M.A. Prowting he died on the 27th of December 1870 aged 30". I wanted to get home and find out all the information I could about him. It was as if I had meant to find George.

I had already found Susan Matilda's headstone but that was there to be seen and information regarding it could be accessed via the internet. I was protective of her grave each time I went to the churchyard. I did not start work without first touching her headstone and saying good morning. Likewise, on leaving at the end of work, I would look over and nod to her headstone. She had died very young, as George had done, and while I had not found any information regarding Susan Matilda, I had not delved too deeply into anything as of yet because I had been so busy. But now I had found George's headstone it gave me more information to work with. It had been a brilliant day for me and a day that would probably define my future at the churchyard. I was in for the long haul that was for sure.

So, I set aside the Saturday of the bank holiday weekend to concentrate on finding out all I could about George Prowting and on ancestry.co.uk I found information regarding his family. It was not long before I realised that his parents, William and Mary Ann Prowting (née Tomlin), were my three times great-grandparents on my maternal side. They had nine children, another one of them was William Henry Prowting and his wife Jane Prowting (née Hedges) who were my two times great-grandparents, also on my maternal side. Their son, George John Prowting 1861–1937, and his wife Emily Rose Prowting (née

Sparsholt) 1856–1924, were my Nan's parents, and it was George John Prowting who was responsible for all the stories that my father told me as a child.

When I worked my way through from George John Prowting, I could go way back. As I said, George John's parents were William Henry Prowting 1835–1913 and Jane née Hedges 1836–1887. William Henry's parents were William Prowting 1816–1899 and Mary Ann née Tomlin 1817–1895, then the father of William was David Prowting 1791–1866. The man that was said to be "the go-to man" of the Prowting family, he was referred to in many of the stories and his wife was Elizabeth née White 1793–1855 from Titchfield, Hampshire. Susan Matilda was the daughter of David and Elizabeth which made her the cousin of George, whose headstone I had found on the Friday.

I found I could go back further than David and Elizabeth who were my four times great-grandparents on my maternal side, to the five times maternal grandparents Robert Prowting 1755–1817 and his wife Mary née May 1759–1851. The sixth set of grandparents, Robert's father and mother another Robert Prowting 1733–1781 and his wife Mary née Woodman 1730–1767, then another Robert Prowting 1719–? and his wife Elizabeth Pratt 1716–?.

David Prowting 1677–1740 and his spouse was not known. Also with an unknown spouse was John Prowting 1634–1704 followed by another David Prowting 1601–1670. His spouse was a Joanna with no surname 1625–?. And finally, William Prowting 1580, with no death date or the name of his spouse. So, in all I could go back 11 generations, however I was confident with going back to seven generations and would seek help with going back further to the eleventh. But I was delighted with what I had found and all from finding the headstone of Great-uncle George Prowting hidden under the ground at the churchyard.

I was both happy and a little sad to think that I had so many ancestors who had been buried at Durley and may not have been able to afford a headstone to mark their final resting place. Then there was the thought of their children and children's children who may have moved on but would have been baptised in the church. The connection to Durley was amazing, and I could understand why my father was keen for me to know the Durley history and how important he used to say it was. It could be I was destined to do the work of saving the west end area of the churchyard, and now I had started and found so much in such a short space of time it would be very difficult to leave. Along with the fact that more interesting things may be found, not just for myself but whoever would need help in uncovering their ancestor's history within the churchyard. I would of course help if I was asked.

On the Sunday of the bank holiday weekend, I helped sort Mum's flat out as usual but she didn't want to come to my house for lunch saying she was tired and so we stayed at her flat and had sandwiches. I told her about the headstone I found and that it was a direct relation. Mum thought it was interesting but did not want to talk much about anything. After lunch, I noticed that on her leg she had a nasty sore and asked her how she got it. She said that her leg was itchy, and the sore was from her rubbing it and she also had some on the back of her leg. I decided that the doctor should look at them. Mum had an appointment anyway the following week for her MOT, as she called it. My brother was taking her so when I got home, I called him to tell him about the sore areas on Mum's legs that looked like blisters and asked him to go in with her and ask the doctor's opinion regarding what to do about them.

As it turned out, when they went to the surgery, the doctor arranged for the nurse to dress Mum's sores and she had bandages from her ankle to her thigh on one leg. The nurse even called at the flat to change the dressing every other day. Then I started to go in and get Mum's breakfast before going on to the churchyard each day. My brother got her meal each evening. Within a week, Mum's other leg had to be bandaged because of more sores, so both legs had bandages from her ankles to her thigh. My mother was not a good patient; when the nurses had left, she would take the bandages off and I would have to put more on, it was a horrid job. Mother's legs were in a hell of a state with the blisters and her legs had also swelled up and in places leaked fluid. The medics did not take kindly to having their attempts to make Mum well again interrupted by the removal of the bandages.

They also brought in a walking frame, toilet aids, special seats for her chair and all of a sudden, my mother had become totally dependent on people to help her. It all happened so quickly and on two occasions Mum fell over and would not pull the red cord – she had one on the wall and a panic button she had been given to have on around her neck, but instead she rang me and my brother and we had to try and lift her into her chair. The only way we could do it was to put a bath towel under her and both lift her back into her chair. For an old person to lay on the floor for any length of time, unable move or get up, puts a terrible strain on their organs. It was such a shame to see my mother suffering this way, she was so worn out by it all.

The nurses had a conversation with me and wanted to put Mum in respite, and I agreed and had to tell her she was going to go into a place where she would have 24-hour care. Also, to get her legs cleared up and she could recover properly. She didn't want to go and asked me why I could not look after her. It was difficult for her to understand but I had to say no and that she had to go away, and I felt so terrible saying it, but it was for her own good. The following day I had just given her breakfast and had a phone call to say that an ambulance was on its way to pick Mum up. I asked If they could give us half an hour to get Mum ready and quickly called my brother and asked him to go with Mum while I sorted things out with the warden. I told Mum it was time to get ready to go, and she stood up and, with no stick or walking frame, shuffled into her bedroom.

As I helped dress her, we looked at each other. We said nothing but I knew as well as her that she would not come back to her flat. To see your mum go downhill so quickly was hard to take, this once confident independent lady, a leader to family and friends was now, at the age of 94, in need of help herself and hated it. Being told what to do and when, was something she avoided in the past but now she was up against it and had to go with the flow and looked to me for direction. She trusted my brother and I to look after her best interests.

The ambulance came and Mum went off with my brother while I sorted things out with the warden. I had to tell her and Mum's friends at the flats what was happening. I also called Mum's brother to tell him what was happening. Everyone seemed surprised that Mum would need to go into respite. But she was worn out, poor love, and she was not made of rock; sooner or later people of her age need help and I was very glad she was getting it.

When I finished, I went to the churchyard and just walked round for a while trying to work out in my head what I would do if she could not go home to the flat. She would have to come with me or go in a home maybe. I could not think straight and went back home and got ready and went to the clinic where Mum had been taken. It was a very nice place and even after just the few hours Mum had been there, she looked much calmer and more relaxed. My brother, his wife and daughter sorted out what Mum would need from home and took things in each day and took away washing. I would go in every night and Mum's brother went to see her, as did her friends from the warden call flats. For three weeks Mum did very well. She had to show them she could make tea and toast and go for walks around the hospital, all to decide if she could go back to her flat and live independently.

After the three weeks, Mum said to me, "Trev what's going to happen to me? Please tell me the truth." So, I told Mum that if she went home, she would have help come in on top of what the family did, and the limited amount the warden could do and of course her friends said they would help but the firm that ran the flats made sure everyone knew that the flats were not designed for the disabled. I told Mum if she could not go back to her flat, she would go into a home that catered for the elderly, or if she wanted to, she could come and live with me.

Mum looked at me and said, "Well I would leave it to you, but I do not want to live with you" and laughed. It would not have been easy to have her with me, but I would have given it a go. I did feel some relief when she said she didn't want to live with me if I am honest and it let me off the hook a bit. I was not trained as a carer, so I told her we would all do what was best for her and that I didn't think it would be long before she would leave the respite after being assessed. It was while I was with Mum one evening at the respite when she told me that they had all been so good to her and that at night they showed films with wonderful singing and dancing projected on to the wall from the ceiling.

As I looked around, I could see nothing that would project something from the ceiling. Mum told me to ask the nurse when I went and that I should thank them on her behalf. So, when I left, I waited at the desk for the nurse to come out. When she did, I thanked her for making Mum comfortable and for the films they showed the people to help relax them. The nurse said that Mum was lovely but had no idea what I was talking about regarding films, and they did not show any. I left confused and when I got home called my brother to tell him that when they went in the following day to see if Mum said anything unusual. The following day my brother called to say that Mum had not said anything to his wife and daughter about the films and it took some time for her to realise who they were and seemed a bit down when they left.

But when I went in the evening, Mum had perked up a bit but did look at me for a while before saying anything. I asked if she had had a good day and she just looked at me. She was on a lot of medication, so allowances had to be made for that. She had become confused, so I just talked about things in general, but Mum did not engage in conversation. While I was talking, I said it would be my father's birthdate next week on the 19th of September, and Mum came straight back and said no it's the 18th and asked me what day that was. I told her it was the following Thursday, a week away, and she asked would I remember to take flowers and I said I would. Mum said in an excited voice that she had seen Aunt Doris and Uncle Laurence and had been round to their old home in Northbrook Road.

Northbrook Road was just around the corner from the respite where Mum lived as a child. Aunt Doris was one of the children that Mum's grandmother Draper had fostered and was brought up like one of Mum's sisters. Uncle Laurence was Grandmother Draper's son and the two of them had been dead for some 35 years, but Mum insisted they came in the night to see her. Mum was happy all the time she talked about them and was like a child when doing so and what with the story of the film with wonderful singing and dancing, it was clear my mother's head was full of jolly robins, but I would rather see her like, that connecting with the nice things of the past, than think of her sitting worrying about what the future held for her.

There is an old saying once an adult twice the child, and it was true in my dear Mother's case. But I held on to the fact that if she was not in any pain, then returning to the past was fine. She seemed to be locked into a time forgotten and I was happy for her. Within a few days, Mum was transferred to the hospital because the respite could do no more for her. On the 18th of September, on my father's birthday, my mother passed away on the very day she had asked about the week before at ten to midnight.

The hospital called my brother to tell him, and he called me. I called the hospital and said I thought they may have called if Mum was close to death. But the person said that Mum was not expected to go, there were no signs, in fact she was sedate, and her body was in effect being run for her. My brother later told me that he had been to see Mum in the afternoon, she didn't know him and was writhing on the bed as if to be trying to get out. I knew when

Mum asked what day my father's birthday was on the previous week that she would go on that day. Mum had not told my brother or his wife and daughter about going to Northbrook Road or seeing Doris and Laurence. She wanted me to tell them. She may not have known anyone at the end, but she knew what was going to happen, I was sure of that. After I called Mum's brother and my sister in Australia to say Mum had passed away, I felt sad and rather lost. I had my mother in my life for all my 64 years. We had our ups and downs and gave each other as good as we got but our mutual respect for each other always came through.

I can't remember my mum ever saying that she loved me and I never told her that I loved her, but our actions spoke volumes and we came from a generation that was not touchy feely. My mum was strict and sometimes hard on me but was always there when I needed her, as she was for everyone, and as I sat on my bed that night, just a few hours after Mum had gone, something happened to help me come to terms with things. The room was dark, and I was not sure if I was asleep, but the darkness exploded into bright light. As I was looking down, I could see an arm, its hand with its fourth finger pointing at clouds below and up from the clouds headstones appeared and one by one as they did, candles lit on each one and they formed a circle and inside the circle people gathered. They all seemed like the negatives of photos moving about and they formed a circle. Then two people, one from each side of the circle, walked towards each other. As they merged with one another, the rest of the people closed in on them until I could no longer see the two people. Then the headstones began to go back down, and as they did one by one, the candles went out until all that was left was the hand with its finger still pointing and then it all went dark again.

I sat up as if I had been pushed. I felt so calm and relaxed and when I feel asleep, I slept so well and in the morning all I could think of was what I had seen. Had it been a dream or was it something spiritual? Had I witnessed my parents back together again after so many years? If it was just a dream then so be it, but I prefer to think what I witnessed was real. I was so high above the clouds and the spirits had showed me something wonderful that I will never forget.

My youngest son, Wayne, said it was the churchyard's spirits thanking me for finding the graves, and that my parents were with them now. I believe if you are open to the spirits, they let you know that all is well. My brother and I let everyone know at the warden call flats and they had an impromptu get-together over tea and conversation. My brother left to sort out the banking paperwork and register the death, and I went to organise Mum's funeral. I used a firm that handled burials at Durley, Freemantle's of Titchfield and Botley, a well-established company with a good reputation. I told them what Mum wanted and they set about organising things. I met with the man that was to handle the service and gave him information regarding Mother's life and what music and song she wanted.

The service was set for eight days time so I let everyone know, but the following day Freemantle's called me to ask if anyone wanted to see my mum at the chapel, I said that I would not and that I was sure no one else would, except Mum's brother Ramon. They told me they would not advise it because edema had set in and my mother could not be dressed in her nice gown or placed in a coffin. So, I told the undertakers on that basis I wanted the cremation to take place as soon as possible. I was not prepared for my mother to have to wait eight days. She was a very dignified lady and would want me to get things over with. Within an hour, I had a call back to say the funeral would take place the following morning at 11 am. I went to see Mum's brother Ramon and told him and he said he wanted to see Mum, so I told him what the undertaker had told me and what I was doing was in the best interest of Mum. After we talked for a while, he agreed. I had to remember he was the last one left of the siblings, and he was very close to my mother, so it was obvious he would want to go. I never talked to him about it again or asked if he went.

On the day, only seven of us attended. I did not expect many before I changed the date, but it went well. Mother had nice music as we went in then the short service took place and 'Morning has Broken' played as we filed past Mum's coffin. I had done everything she wanted, it was heart-breaking to see her go, but she was at peace with my father, and a week later I picked up Mother's ashes. I burnt all Mum and Dad's love letters from their courting days. We had found in her affects and placed them in with her ashes and we all went and laid them at the place she had chosen. I have lots of good memories of times with my parents and I hope we each made them proud in our own way.

It took another month to clear Mum's flat and hand back the keys. Most of Mum's things went to charity; we left a lot of the furniture for the next resident. My brother and I still had some boxes to sort out, and we decided to do that another time. They were old photos and family things, but it was time to get back to normal. Mum's demise had been quick – from her birthday to my father's birthday was just 57 days. We all did our very best for Mother who had always done her very best for us, and all through the 57 days I had still managed to carry on with work at the churchyard for a few hours each day, cutting grass and still clearing the spoil. It was not long before I was fully back into the swing of things, I had not told anyone that my mother was ill or that she had passed away but had spent time in the church in reflection. It seemed to help and now my focus was back on looking after the churchyard and getting down to finding more about George whose headstone I had found before. I had to concentrate all my time and energy on dealing with matters relating to my mother, but now I was keen to pick up where I left off on all fronts.

Chapter 16
Back in the Swing of Things

It was in November 2014 that I got back into the swing of things fully at the churchyard, however some people had missed me being there and thought I had moved on. One lady in particular, who lived next to the churchyard, came by whilst I was working. She gave me a note with an address to go and pick up a book about the history of Durley that her gardener wanted me to have. I had not spoken to the lady before; I had only seen her and her husband in the garden of their home that backed onto the churchyard.

I took the note and thanked her, before heading over to the address on the note at lunchtime. The gardener and book owner was a man named Derick Strugnell, who was born in the village and had lived there all his life. He told me that when he had been told what my surname was, he asked the lady he gardened for to give me the note. He went on to say that the people from the village were grateful for what I was doing, and it meant a lot to them. I told him it was my pleasure and I enjoyed what I was doing and hearing the encouragement from the people in the village who came to tend to their relatives' graves kept me going when things became difficult at times

The book was called Durley in Old Pictures by John Bosworth. The gentleman wanted me to have it and said I should read it cover to cover. My family name was mentioned along with other historic local names of people who had married into my family, and of women members of my family who had married and taken other old local family names within the local farming community. I thanked him for the book and returned to the churchyard to work.

That night after my meal, I looked through the book and after reading John Bosworth's introduction where he thanked the villagers for the many photos and local stories that made up the book, on the first page was a picture of the road that ran past the Robin Hood public house and down into Ashton, and there was a picture of the small holding we would visit on a Sunday. To my great delight, I discovered that way back in time the small holding was called The Clump. One of the early families that had occupied it were members of my family, it was amazing to see our family name in print and that the small holding we visited as children was once occupied by a member of our family. Also, considering the many times I had passed it over the years, to find out now that ancestors of ours had lived there was interesting. I had no idea, and I didn't think my Uncle George would have known either as the John Bosworth book I was reading was not published until 1989, and the date our family members would have occupied the small holding was pre-1905. So, the very first story I read in the book made reference to my family name, but they may not have been direct ancestors. I would have to find out but they would have been related in some way.

Before I had my accident, I had done a little research into Durley with the limited amount of information I had remembered from what my father talked about. I did buy several record books in the post office regarding the burials, weddings and baptisms at the Church of the Holy Cross Durley. I had kept them in my office thinking one day I may need them and now, along with the John Bosworth book, I had plenty to refer to.

The record books covered the 16th, 17th and 18th centuries and had been transcribed by two ladies called Sheila Marshal and Shannon Abbott and published by Durley History Society. I had been told I should meet Adrian and Shannon Abbott, who had been connected to the local history group. The 19t-century records had been subject to data protection, however it was the earlier centuries that interested me. William Henry Prowting, my two times great-grandfather, and his son George John Prowting, my great-grandfather, had taken their families to live in the Shirley area of Southampton in the late 1800s. They still worked at Durley but lived in the town and that's where my Nan was born. The John Bosworth book, along with the Durley History Society's record books, would be of great interest to me, in finding all I could about the history of my family. In fact, I had more to work with than I did when I researched my Italian links. If information I hoped to find out about regarding my Durley relations went together and complemented each item found, as it did with the Italian research, then I would be very happy with that.

As I approached the end of 2014, the structure of my days took on a regularity. People got to know when I would be at the churchyard. I started each day at 10 am and worked through till around 4 pm. The busy times were between 11 and midday in the morning and between 2 pm and 3 pm when all the local people turned up and I was available to talk with them if they wanted to. I would leave it to them to talk to me, I found it was more respectful not to approach them each time they came to tend a relative's grave. They could be in a melancholy mood and the last thing they would want would be to enter into conversation. If people came who wanted to research their history, they tended to be very early and would often be in the churchyard before me. Often people would come up as I was going home but I helped as much as I could, however lots of people turn up at a churchyard not fully prepared. It is one thing to discover online that you have relatives in a particular churchyard, but it's another thing to hope to find them on your first visit.

You also need to dress for the occasion; a hat and coat along with a good pair of boots is a must at any time of the year. Durley churchyard, if it's not windy, often has a breeze being so high up and if you are standing around you would be surprised how chilly it gets. Pen and paper and all the information you can give to someone that's going to assist you should be high on your list of things to bring. Finally, a bottle of soapy water and an abrasive cloth to use on a headstone, if you find the one you are looking for – chances are it will need to be cleaned to read the inscription.

My time was soon taken up with my work within the churchyard by day, and in the evening I would research either for myself or someone who had come in and asked for help. It is always nice when you find what people are looking for, and I think that voluntary work is the most rewarding. One of the things I had to pick up on after the trials and tribulations of my summer, was to put down all I could find about Great-uncle George, whose headstone I had found in the week leading up to the August bank holiday.

George was in fact a shepherd and one of six servants at Great Stakes Farm at Upham from the age of 11 and worked there with his brother William Henry who became my two times great-grandfather. Great Stakes Farm was run by the Carver family. I went to look at the farm one Sunday morning. It is next to the Upham Brewery, a thriving local business. The main farmhouse looks very impressive and had not changed that much over the years. One thing I wanted to know was if the Carver family had family archives. While they no longer held the farm, they had been a respected family in the area before moving their farming operations to, I think, the Isle of Wight in the 1900s.

It was one iron I had in the fire, whilst gathering information on George who in November 1859, aged 20, married Mary Ann née Boyt at Durley church. Mary Ann was from the lovely village of Lytchett Maltravers in Dorset and worked as a domestic servant at Fair Oak near Durley. Sadly, George and Mary Ann were only married for 11 years before George's untimely death. Records show he had been sick with influenza for about four weeks and died as a result of it. It was also recorded that George had heart problems throughout his life. It was sad to read accounts of his illness, his death at the age of 30 must have been hard on his family but know I had found his headstone and placed it back at the head of his grave. George's resting place became a reference point for me within the churchyard, as was Susan Matilda Houghton's, together they would be the subject of many a conversation I was to have when telling the story to interested visitors keen to know some history regarding Durley.

Also, every day I would not start work until first walking to George and Matilda's graves and touching their headstones. It became a ritual; the two of them very much alive within my heart and mind and I hoped to find out more about each of them. The invention of photography came after their death dates so to find images of them would not be possible. I found records that Mary Ann moved back to Dorset after George died and that she lived to the age of 86 and is buried at Wimborne Minster Dorset.

As December 2014 approached, we had some hard frost and at the west end of the churchyard the spoil I was moving became crust-like. It was very easy to cut through and could be picked up in decent-sized lumps until thawed. I noticed that each time spoil was lifted partly frozen from the natural woodland floor, tiny plant shoots emerged. They were white and looked as if the moisture within them had been drained by the weight of the clay upon them. However, within a few hours as the day warmed, up the small shoots began to revive and slowly reached for the light that had been denied them from being dormant beneath the soil.

All the way along the rows that I worked on, new life was returning. It was amazing to see. In the afternoon, when the air became cold again, the plants' regeneration slowed down and froze like everything else as the hard frost returned in the night. The wildflowers were very hardy, and I wondered as each day passed if more plant life returned from their imposed slumber and what each one would become in the spring.

Also, on the days there was no frost, I planted daffodil bulbs. The wild deer would not eat them. I also found out which other plants the deer would not eat and could plant and bloom in the spring. Anemone St Bridget was one. It is said the beautiful anemone flower in Greek mythology grew from the tears of Aphrodite that fell to the woodland floor when her lover Adonis, a handsome young shepherd, was killed while hunting wild boar. Aphrodite was the daughter of Zeus, and it was Zeus who allowed the young shepherd to be restored to life for part of the year and before returning to the underworld for the remainder.

The underworld is where Dumuzid, the Sumerian god of shepherds and vegetation, lived for half the year, resulting in the yearly cycle of the seasons. There are many magical myths and legends surrounding sacred ground and the wildflowers that grow from its soils. The centre of the anemone flower is black, and its petals look like the eye lashes of Aphrodite, and it is said if the flower struggles to stay open in the windy conditions, then Adonis must return to the underworld and leave Aphrodite. But it is possible, that if you see an anemone struggle, place your hands around the plant and breathe warm air on to it, and the flower will then open in your hands and prolong the happiness of Aphrodite.

Most other flowers that people bring to put on graves get eaten by the deer at night; they are very destructive but if you are in the churchyard and one wanders in, they are the most beautiful-looking creatures. If you stand completely still, chances are they will come near until they pick up your scent and then they display their agility and are gone in a flash. The deer had been introduced by Lord Dene Wulf. King Edward the Elder AD 899–924 gave the manor of Waltham with all its lands to Dene Wulf Bishop of Winchester in AD 904. And it was Dene Wulf who created a deer park, so we have his bishop to blame for the wandering deer. People with a manicured gardens are not fans of the deer but within the boundary of the churchyard they are welcome visitors. Like all other wildlife that slowly returned to the churchyard, each with their own beauty, it's a pleasure seeing them in what is, after all their habitat. It is man who are the intruders, and we should remember that when blessed with witnessing them nature's way.

Christmas 2014 came, our first without Mum, and my daughters cooked Christmas lunch at my eldest daughter's home that was once a dairy farm. The lounge was the old milk parlour, and my daughters set the room out like a restaurant. My sons had come over from Spain, so I had all my children and grandchildren together. That, I am sure for many families, is an all-too-rare occasion, so when it happens it is always nice to remember.

2015, I started back at the churchyard with a renewed vigour and carried on where I left off at the west end of the churchyard. Still moving the spoil but at the southwest side, I came to the end of the brick and slate debris, from what I thought looked like the residue of some sort of dwelling. When I started working my way across from south to north again, beyond the bricks and slate residue, I found a floor of what could have been a shed or something.

The bricks had been laid flat in situ and covered an area of about six metres square. I had seen small buildings in several churchyards before placed in the corner, sometimes there were two, one in the east and another in the west. For instance, at Warblington on the Sussex/Hampshire border, the church of Sir Thomas Becket has two, one in each corner built in the image of the church. With red brick and knapped flint with each mortar joint filled with residue of the knapped flint that had been discarded by the master craftsmen then placed by hand into each joint, it must have taken an age to carry out such a precise task. The arched heavy door and tiny window painted royal blue indicated that money was no object; they had been built for night watchmen to guard the churchyard from grave robbers. The churchyard's remote position was accessible through the winding lanes or by boat as the coastline with its narrow inlets allowed craft to beach on the southside of the churchyard's boundary, because grave robbing was a lucrative trade at one time. Paupers' graves, who had no relations that could afford coffins or a proper service, would be buried in the churchyard of a village they came from, taken in a coffin probably on a cart! Their grave would have been just 36 inches deep and they would be taken out of the coffin, already wrapped in a shroud that was tied at the top and laid to rest. The coffin would be taken and used again for the next poor wretch with no money or relations. In some cities, the picking up of paupers was subcontracted out to anyone with a big enough cart who would run with the coffin on board, and they would sing 'Rattle their bones over stones it's only a pauper that nobody owns'. Then if the grave robbers turned up, they would dig at the top of the grave and cut the shroud and pull the body out, making off with their ill-gotten gains, probably to a medical doctor who could only have so many free per year. But like everything else in life, there are always some greedy people who want more. If the grave robber was caught, chances were he was let go because they would leave the shroud and you would not be prosecuted for stealing the body, but if you were caught stealing the shroud, then you found yourself up before the judge in the morning.

I thought it would be nice if Durley did have its own watchman's hut to guard the churchyard from intruders, who many have designs on recent paupers' graves or to inflict harm to the beautiful church that is situated in the darkest of rural places upon the hill. If the brick floor was that of a night watchman's hut it would be such a find, and if there was a record of such a thing being built then it would account for all the debris. I kept clearing the spoil that was, in places, becoming a little easier the deeper into the woods I went.

I wondered what else I would find in the John Bosworth book; the moving of earth sure gives you a reason to think of something else to do. That book became the carrot dangled before me, as I carried out more work natural to a machine than a human being, but using a machine was out of the question because graves may be found. Until I was sure there weren't any, I would keep going as I was digging by day and researching in the evenings.

I did find more interesting things in the John Bosworth's book on page six. It showed the farmhouse I worked on years ago for the local master builder Mr George Fry; the picture of the farmhouse was ancient. The road in the photo was just a narrow track that ran past it. I often drove by these days, and while over the years more work had been carried out, the place had not changed a lot. My external render work had seemed to have stood the test of time, given it was some 38 years ago that I had done it.

On the opposite page in the book was another interesting photo of a very smart grey-haired gentleman with a full beard. He was dressed in a dark suit with a watch and chain attached to his waistcoat, looking the smart gentleman he was. His name was Robert (Shoemaker Bob) Houghton, and he was the husband of my great-aunt Susan Matilda. He was the local cobbler. He and Susan Matilda lived just down the street from Oakland farmhouse that I had worked on all those years ago, Shoemaker Bob had a small area of land at the side of their cottage where he grew produce and the story in the book said he would take his produce, along with boots and shoes he had mended for people, to market.

I wish there was a photo of Susan Matilda but there was not, but I now knew where they lived. Their cottage had caught fire and Shoemaker Bob's hands were badly burned while extinguishing the fire. Susan Matilda and their lodger Caleb Houghton escaped the blaze, but they lost a lot of furniture. The villagers clubbed together and raised enough money to help replace the lost furniture. When Susan Matilda died at a very young age, I found the entry in the burial book that Shannon Abbott had compiled. Shoemaker Bob married again to a lady from Southampton who had a dress shop, Elinor Stebbins was her name and she outlived Shoemaker Bob by some years. While his death was entered in the burial book, it did not say if he had been buried next to Susan Matilda, as was usual back then.

Susan Matilda's headstone had her inscription at the top and room was left underneath for a second person's inscription – that was how the stonemasons set out the headstones. So, with only one name on Susan Matilda's, it was not clear where Shoemaker Bob was buried. I was given an account of his funeral by another local Durley man, Mr Stewart Collins. His father wrote an interesting book about the village. Stewart himself had many a story to tell whenever he came to the churchyard; he was another wonderful source of information that helped me help other people with information I always made sure to credit Stewart Collins for information. Another proper Durley man told me that Shoemaker Bob was a Methodist and his service took place at the Methodist church not far from their home on Durley Street. His coffin was then pushed on a cart from the Methodist church as far as Durley school, and then on over the field on the corps path, as it was then called, and is still in use today as a footpath. A record of Shoemaker Bob Houghton being buried in Durley churchyard was recorded however, just where he was laid to rest I could not find. I hoped it would have been near to Susan Matilda and when I touched her headstone in the mornings to say hello I would also say "and Shoemaker if you're there".

Susan Matilda and Shoemaker Bob had no children and that was unusual back then. Most of the Houghtons had a big family so I wondered if Susan Matilda's early death was anything to with childbirth. The problem is when you find connections to family members, even the fact that you didn't know them does not stop you becoming attached and protective of them. From the day I had found her grave hidden on the edge of the woods and cut my hands pulling off prickle branches from her headstone, I remember being watched by a small robin that sat on a branch above my head. Susan Matilda became real to me and I thought many times what she may have looked like. Now I was working in the churchyard, her grave, and the grave of George, meant a lot to me. The fact they have been almost lost for all time made them important, so much so I wondered if when it was my turn, who my ashes could rest with. They had been taken so young and neglected for so long, but then I think all spirits meet up anyway so it would not matter which one was chosen and their headstones were in sight of each other anyway, now that the woods had been cleared.

The John Bosworth book was to become a vital source of information for my research and to help others. The book had been discontinued and greatly sought after. At the beginning of February that year, I turned up at the churchyard and was approached by a lady who had come over from Australia to look for the graves of her ancestors who had lived in the village in the 16th century. Their name was Savage and were all together at the southeast of the churchyard. I had seen the headstones when cutting grass and was able to show the lady right to them, and she was very emotional saying that she had read about the family connection with Durley in family papers and on the internet. She had been chosen by family members back in Australia to travel over to England to find the graves, if possible, because the older members wanted to connect again with Durley, if only by the photos the lady had taken.

She knelt in front of the headstones and did not move for a while and said having travelled 11,000 miles and been directed right to the graves she could not believe it would have been possible.

I always felt it easier to let people gather themselves before saying anything and would walk away, because sometimes they would just sit and look at what are works of art with inscriptions. That would make anyone become emotional and more so if you had links to them. I understood fully how that felt after finding Susan Matilda's and Great-uncle George's headstones. This would happen often in the churchyard, if I showed people the grave they hoped to find, it became common practice to have people cry with happiness at finding something they had only read about and could now actually touch the headstone of an ancestor. Someone who lived way back in time and had been the person whose life history was the beginning of a family's particular tree that would span decades and travel to far off lands, and to think that every day the headstones sat proud waiting for such a moment.

That is why the churchyard had to be saved. What I had started would be ongoing and there probably would be barren years when nothing would be done, as my energy would decrease and render me useless for such strenuous works, till someone else came along and picked up the baton and continue the work. One thing was for sure, you could not trust the church or its councils to look after it, and all the English village churchyard's neglect was born from ignorance and sheer laziness by some, coupled with the changing of rectors who had no idea of the history of the village or church they would be responsible for. Nor did they show any interest in doing so and possessed an overriding demand that things would be done their way because they believed they had been sent by the Lord. But they missed completely the willingness of each village congregation whose love for the church, if tapped into, could move mountains but any hope of that was crushed by new blinkered rectors and council members. While being respectable members of the community missed the point completely, God was the only thing that drove them, and his word was manipulated by some to fit each of their individual thinking and sadly respecting the dead was not considered important and the proof of that could be seen in neglected churchyards all over the country.

The churchyard is a place where communities are brought together, people who travelled from all over the world on pilgrimages on behalf of others were proof enough. So, after a few months at the churchyard I discovered how important they are. Also, one day when I arrived in the morning, I was greeted by another visitor in the shape of a rather bedraggled ring-necked cock pheasant, who was sat on the bank as I walked through the gate. He was clearly too tired to move or fly away; he had obviously been in a battle of some sort and was lost and looked very sorry for himself. I placed some food on the ground next to him and he stretched out his neck and picked at it, but he was in need of rest. I got on with my work and kept an eye on him. He made his way over the north hedge and nestled right in under the prickle bushes and just slept all day and was still there when I left to go home. It was clear to me, because of the state he was in, that he could well be taken by the fox or would just die in the night.

However, in the morning when I arrived, he was sat under the old oak tree near to the headstone of my Uncle George. I placed food on the chest tomb grave for the birds as usual, the pheasant came over and joined them to eat breakfast and each day he looked better. He then lost all his long tail feathers and most from his wings and looked like a chicken, but the churchyard became his home and as the months passed, he became a topic of conversation among the people who came to the churchyard. The pheasant did not mind being photographed with the other birds while they fed, and in time he grew into the most handsome pheasant and followed me everywhere.

If I went to the van, I would have to tell him to sit like you would a dog, or he would have been in danger walking into the road. Several times he had seen me go into the shed but did not see me come out and shut the door. From a distance I would watch him as he would tap the shed door with his beak, thinking I was still in there and would give an almighty screech if I did not come out. But when I called out to him, and he could see me he would run over to me and settle down near to what I was working on. He was becoming even more handsome and after a year with the other birds in the churchyard, I thought he may have gone but while he was very happy in the churchyard, he needed a mate. Pheasants sometimes have two or three hen pheasants follow them around. I was also worried that he did not fly, he walked everywhere and that was not natural and could be dangerous for him if he did decide to go. Some people had a name for him, but I just said "Come on Mr Pheasant" if I wanted to know where he was, and after 18 months the pheasant left the churchyard.

When I got to the churchyard one day he was gone. I looked all over for him and it was a strange feeling to think that the pheasant would not come back. I think the other birds missed him, as did the local people who had got so used to having him around. He had been photographed many times and was a topic of conversation. I have to say that I missed him too; when I had been digging the spoil he would sit nearby and if I was cutting grass he would walk behind me. He was a good friend for the time he was with us, and the churchyard had been his salvation like so many others, but he gave a lot of people pleasure when they needed cheering up.

By Easter 2015, the churchyard was beginning to take shape, the main grassed areas all looked tidy. The main walkway leading to the church up the long-grassed path that I was able to improve was cut very short and had lines in the grass that gave pleasure to many people. Long gone was the tufty grass and molehills that formed the uneven path, especially for the men carrying coffins which had been difficult to negotiated. I made sure that when people made what was the last visit to the church, for their own funeral, that the walk was smooth and uninterrupted for the following family and friends. Once they got to the lych gate to be greeted by the rector and invited onto scared ground, the procession walked slowly to the church and passed under the great yew tree; white dust fell from its soft flora onto the coffin as it past underneath. The dust can only be seen if the light shines in a certain direction, and the cock robin flies from the great yew trees small branches when the coffin passes him by, to take up his position at the west of the church and perch on railings while the service takes place. The robin then leads the coffin around the churchyard, flying from headstone to headstone, to the person's final resting place. The cock robin is always the last to leave the churchyard when all is done and the person's rest begins at the churchyard upon the hill.

Easter, when the school had their service at the church, was well attended by parents and grandparents eager to see their children and grandchildren in full voice. After following a procession led by two donkeys around the church, the bells rang out their rich sound which was wonderful, and I for one did not want them to stop ringing so great was the sound. The church seemed to come alive as each toll demanded your attention but was not really appreciated by the rushing families eager to go home and back to their busy lives. This was just another date in the school calendar, something to attend and soon be forgotten. I was sure that back in time the service would have held more importance and been attended by more village people, but in the modern day was not so important. Indeed the school staff I noticed seemed keen to get away as well and always left lights on, the outside toilet left unlocked, and no one shut the gates each time they used the church. 'Use' would be the optimum word when the school came a calling and a lack of respect for the beautiful old building was an obvious conclusion one could draw.

However, the following day was Good Friday, breakfast was served at the early morning service at the church, and some members from Durley joined the members from Botley and Curdridge in the Easter walk. Starting at Botley after a service and on to Curdridge, before walking to the village hall at Durley for hot cross buns and beverages. They then walked to the church at Durley, taking the old route from the school where the stocks were once placed, and across the field on the corps path. It was a humbling thing to see all the people walking together and enjoying themselves before dispersing back to their families.

I got to know each church occasion in the calendar and would do my best to make sure the churchyard would always look nice, so there was always a target date to work to. I always hoped the weather was kind so the churchyard would be seen at its best. Also, that particular weekend on the Saturday, I had gone to finish some work in the morning and quite a few people came in with flowers for relatives and I noticed two people who came. It was clear they were old hands at negotiating their way around a churchyard, including how to look at a headstone from differing angles using the natural light to read the hidden inscription. As they made their way towards me, I took a guess that they might be Adrian and Shannon Abbott, the history people I had been told about. I guessed right and before they said anything I asked them if they were Adrian and Shannon Abbott. Of course they laughed and confirmed I was right, and they were impressed with my assumption. We began to talk about what I had taken on and Adrian and Shannon became from that day a very important part of what would go on.

The salvation of the churchyard so long neglected at Durley and their knowledge of how to find history was amazing. Shannon would dig on the internet and I would dig at the churchyard. Anything I found or some history that people would bring in and needed clarifying and added to then Adrian was the man; he could find chapter and verse on anything, in fact they both could. The two of them where so important to what I had started, and I trusted them both completely. I say that because sometimes with history some people find things and keep them hidden thereby changing or holding it up. As I knew from my mother's attempts at hiding history, hers was not in a malicious way but a generation thing, one of fear really of what people may think of a particular family or person, but there are also people who keep to themselves history that could benefit others, thereby changing the course of all things historic or leading people in the wrong direction.

I talked to Adrian and Shannon about the headstones I had found in the woods, about the spaces between each headstone that I thought were burials, so Shannon suggested that Adrian should come back another day with dowsing rods to go over the ground. I had not heard of this method before to find graves. I had heard of dowsing for water but never graves. I always had an open mind about everything, so a week later Adrian turned up with not only dowsing rods but a metal detector too and it did make perfect sense because if we went searching for graves, they all had cast iron numbers on the graves.

There were many around the yard on the kerbstone graves on the north side of the churchyard, but the area we would be looking had been lost in time. I told Adrian that I thought that the distance between the rows of headstones I had found was too wide, some 15 feet. In fact, in the other areas the headstones were much closer between one row and the next, around seven or eight feet, so we began to the right of the area. I had found old bricks and slate debris that was halfway across the last line. I had removed the spoil from this earth that had not been disturbed for many years.

When I had first started the project, I would get strange looks from the people playing golf and I got to know a few who in time did not think I was as mad as they did when they first spotted me moving piles of earth by hand. However, now they could see two of us and looked at us again in a strange way, as Adrian began to walk across the line of possible graves holding his dowsing rods. I was gobsmacked because as he walked from the edge of brick and slate debris to the north hedge where the golfers stood open mouthed, the dowsing rods began to move, indicating something was beneath the soil and they moved ten times as Adrian walked across the line. He said when the rods crossed it would mean something was under the soil, picked up by the energy between the rods and whatever was in the ground; if the earth was natural and untouched or disturbed in any way then the rods would not move. But because they had crossed so often in this row then one could be sure something was there; he could not say what but given it was in the churchyard then one would think it would be obvious – it was a grave.

So, the next thing we did was to measure six feet from what we thought would be the head of the grave and Adrian walked the same line across but this time with the metal detector. In each place that the dowsing rods had moved, the metal detector picked up something and began to bleep. I dug down and at the exact spot of the bleep, I dug up a cast iron number of the grave. It was an amazing feeling but also sad to think that people would have covered up graves with so much spoil.

We found ten numbers in that row – they were rusty and thick with clay, but we could just make out the numbers that followed on numerically. Some numbers had been damaged and part of the cast iron had broken down. But we could still make out the numbers or the residue of each one. We found numbers 3, 4, 5, 6, 7, 8, 9, 10, 11 and 12. Adrian and I had been both happy that we found them but also sad they had been lost.

Adrian, who was a very reserved person, was visibly shaken as we uncovered each number; he could not understand how something like this could happen. After finding the numbers all was quiet, we did not talk for a while. Then we both decided that it was enough for that day, and I remembered when I was digging the spoil in all weathers for so long when I would think to myself that people could be buried there, I was being optimistic they had been just run-of-the-mill thoughts. Now we had found the numbers it was a whole different feeling, one of shock and disappointment, also one of disgust in my fellow man. It did not matter if it was over 100 years ago, they had no right to do such a thing. I was almost too scared to think about trying to find any more and for the first time after being surrounded by death for so many months it started to affect me. Adrian left and took the numbers with him, and we agreed he would email me when he had cleaned the numbers he had in his workshop using a method of placing them in a chemical with an electric current running through it. That brought the numbers up like new so we could then, from the burial records that Shannon had copied from record books held by the verger Mrs Taylor, find the names of the people who occupied each grave we had just found. I packed all the tools away and, for a while, went and sat in the church. It was very peaceful. I reflected on what I had just done, and for a time, I did not like myself very much at all.

The people whose graves we had just found once sat in this very church, and had been baptised, probably married in it as well. When I had found the graves of Susan Matilda and Great-uncle George, I did not feel like this, probably because they had been relations of mine. I would have to wait and see if any of the names of the people we had just found would be related in anyway. Maybe that would make it feel better, I was not sure. Part of me said not to beat myself up over it and that's why I was there to discover what had been lost and neglected for so long. But I think the shock of finding them and the fact that I cared so much about the churchyard and all who rest within it was the reason for my melancholy mood. I now had to face the fact that we would find more and would have to look upon it as the rightful thing to do.

To have a record of a burial was all well and good but to know where the grave was would mean a lot to people related to them and so I felt I had squared things with the Lord. It was not often I asked for guidance, but when I left the church and looked out over the wide horizon, I felt better about myself and grateful for having learnt something about an emotion within me that I did not know I had. It was not to be frightened of what I was doing, after all I was digging for numbers to identify the occupant of particular graves in a respectful way. They had been lost in time, neglected by complacent people for reasons best known to them and I was sure when the names of the occupants of each grave became known it may shed some light on why no one cared about them.

The rest of the Easter weekend was spent with family. I never talked about my work at the churchyard at all with anyone. It was not really a subject for downtime with people who probably would not understand anyway. Unless you were interested in the subject, it could be very boring to put two and two together history-wise. Once you had done it, it was an interesting story with a beginning and an end, so it was best to stay focused on putting things together bit by bit until that time.

That Easter weekend was to become one of the most important times in my historical life. My brother had decided it was time to finish unpacking our mother's affects; we each had two boxes of her things. I had not had time to look through what I knew to be just cut-glass items, all really nice things that had been in the family for years. However, my brother called me to say that in one of the boxes he had was one of Mum's old handbags and inside it was a lot of paperwork she had kept over the years relating to my dad's work and Army days and that he thought he had found, inside a sealed envelope, another envelope containing the letter that my father received back in 1971 from the man wanting to know if they had been related. That letter had been talked about so much from the time my father died, all through the subsequent years. Mother could not have known she had it, I was sure of that. She may have wanted to keep things from me, however when she did eventually tell me the story of my Italian links, if she had known the letter was in my dad's affects she had kept, I think she would have told me. My brother, was now interested in the letter, but he had not been when Dad first received it, and in conversations down the years he showed little interest in its importance until now. So much so, he told me he had copied it and was on his way over with the original for me.

It was a great moment for me I had never forgotten the letter or how everyone reacted when it came. And now, if it was indeed the letter, then it would be such a find. My brother arrived a little less excited than when he had been on the phone, and he wanted me to confirm to him that what he had found was the real thing. But I had to tell him that I would need time because I had been hoping for so long that one day the letter would turn up, but I needed to be alone to open it. I wanted to look at every part of the envelope before opening it and knew it would take many reads to digest its contents. When I told my brother this, he did not really understand but agreed with my wishes to look at it alone. I told him as soon as I had we could meet up and talk about the letter. If I was to read it right then and it referred to anything I had worked on regarding the Durley links or indeed the Italian ancestry I had researched, he would not understand what I would be trying to impart to him.

One fact from the letter leaned to something not in the letter but in other information found in other family history I had found. I would know immediately if something did link the letter to other information. For my brother, it would be like him walking in halfway through a film and wanting me to bring him up to date while still watching it myself and being locked into the plot. The last thing anyone wants when engrossed in something interesting was someone who would need to be updated while you did so. You would actually miss something important. I found television adverts enough of a distraction when I was watching something on the television. So, if I had to stop to bring my brother up to date on what I had been putting together for ten years, that would be impossible. I would need to put things together in the order that I had found, for it to follow on so it would be easy to understand, in effect, ten years of research that could be read and understood if anyone was interested. I was not sure that my brother would actually want to wade through reams of research. He would prefer to cherry-pick the good bits whereas for me it was all good.

It was not till the following day that I looked at what my brother had given me. I had pen and paper to hand, ready to take notes, and then took out the envelope from the one it had been kept safe in and began to look at the envelope – our old address was typed neatly. The postmark was Salisbury! On the back of the envelope some numbers had been added up. I was not sure what that was, it had been done by my father along with several words, one being the place name of Oakhampton. I had worked for a time at Oakhampton in the West Country, so I was interested in what that could have been about and indeed if it was the Oakhampton I had been to.

Then I opened the letter and began to look at every single word one by one as they had been presented on the page, working my way slowly along the sentence of words as they began to deliver to me the lost information that had laid dormant for so many years. Each word, as on the envelope, had been neatly typed on the man's private headed quality paper that felt thicker than normal writing paper. At the very top of the page was the house name and address. The house the man occupied was called Beaulieu in Old Road Alderbury in Salisbury, Wiltshire. Under the address was his phone number, Alderbury 377, the date 14th January 1971. The first few lines of the letter blew me away. They began: "Dear Mr Prowting. I am interested in the Prowting family tree. I was born at Upham in Hampshire, the younger son of Alfred, who was one of ten sons of William and Mary Anne Prowting née Tomlin of Winters Hill cottages Upham. The names of the sons which I have taken from an old family Bible are as follows, William Henry, George, Robert, Walter, Alfred, Frederick, John Henry, Albert, Andrew and Edwin. In my boyhood days I heard of several of my father's brothers. George died in 1870 and Albert who I knew well in 1928." This letter was amazing. This man was indeed related to my father, a cousin in fact; and the William and Mary Anne named as the parents of his father Alfred were my Nan's great-grandparents. Alfred's brother, William Henry, was my Nan's grandfather, and to cap it all, this man's Uncle George, who he said he had heard of, was the same George whose headstone I had found buried under the soil at the churchyard, another son of William and Mary Ann Prowting née Tomlin.

I could not believe what I was reading and had to take time out to digest the first ten lines of the letter that had been lost for over 40 years. Now it was confirming to me that the stories told to me at my father's knee had all been true. I could understand why my father was so keen for me to not only know the family history of Durley, but to seek out more of it. Then it dawned on me that in 1971 the man that had sent the letter and indeed my father would not have had the internet to work with as I have now, so if what my father had read in this letter and already knew the family history. As he did, because his grandfather had told him, then that is why he did not contact the man that sent the letter because they both knew the same from the limited resources they both had to work with.

It was indeed food for thought. I also worked out what the numbers could be that my father had written on the envelope. He had written 14, that I thought could be the number of years left in the 18th century. Then 71, meaning the 71 years so far in the 19th century, that gave Dad the man's age. He was 85 years old when he sent the letter to my dad and his name was Arthur Prowting.

The letter went on with more interesting facts. You could tell that what he had written in the first few lines was nailed on definite facts handed down from father to son. Close family history from immediate members of his family in what you could call their own catchment area to which the boundaries did not extend far beyond the eldest person' recollection of events, sometimes could, for all one knows, be dressed up for effect, so to speak, and that was fine. Sometimes by reading between the lines, one gets the real story anyway.

The letter continued with the man telling my father how he had found his name in the Southampton telephone directory and was wondering if they could be related. I got the impression that this man was clutching at straws and also wondered just how many other Prowting families in the Southampton area he had contacted. To spread the net in such a way was not, I thought, the best way to go about finding direct ancestors. The rest of the letter contained information on the original Prowting clan coming from Normandy, some 700 years ago and after first settling at Shanklin on the Isle of Wight moved to the mainland. Some moved to Chawton in Hampshire – this was true, the Prowtings did live at the village of Chawton, and as the letter went on to say, many of them are buried in the churchyard however it was a big leap to try and connect our ancestors to the families at Chawton.

I had researched this line myself and while there are some interesting stories regarding our namesakes being friends with Jane Austen and living in a house called the Prowtings, of which a picture hangs in the house Jane Austen once lived in that is open to the public, it was a very romantic notion for all Prowting families to be linked with Chawton and of course some are but sadly not in our line.

It was obvious that this man had researched all avenues in his attempt to find family links and also in the letter he referred to his great-great-grandfather William Prowting, born at Chawton in 1708 and being an apothecary who went on to become a freeman of London. But again, sadly this William was not related to him, his two times great-grandfather was David Prowting, Susan Matilda's father, so in a way I was both glad that the letter had been lost and sad that I had not had a chance to meet this man. It could be said that my father not responding to his letter was cruel, but no one could have foreseen the death of my father at such an early age and it makes one think that we should not put things off till another day because sometimes there is no other day.

The letter was wonderful. The man had set out to discover if he and my dad had been related and I could prove they had been. The saddest thing was that they did not get to meet so I decided to try and find the family of the man who sent the letter all those years ago. It would take time because I was very busy at the churchyard and with research for myself and others but I was sure, as usual, something would turn up regarding all I had learnt from the letter. If I was to try and find relatives of the man, there would be no need to rush on my part, thinking back as far as I knew my dad never had a follow-up letter from the man. So, if it was, as I had suspected having read the letter many times, that the gentleman had been spreading the net wide to then trawl in his catch of possible ancestors, that would have been I am sure from differing walks of life, and only he would have known as to what to keep and to throw back into the sea of life's differing personalities, some of whom may have been quick to take the bait, eager to find out if the bait would be beneficial to them. By casting such a net, the man risked missing special species such as my father who would not be fooled by the beginning of the letter's factual information followed by facts that had been wishful thinking on the part of the gentleman who would by casting his net in that way become just a fisher of men. I put all I had researched and what I thought of the information in the letter in a file for my brother to have when he was ready to read it.

With Easter out of the way and the long, drawn-out dissecting of the letter putting it into perspective information-wise and what I thought relevant to me, I got back to my work at Durley. Any time I had been away from the churchyard, if only a day, it seemed an age somehow. I was drawn to the place by a strange desire to just be there and had the feeling that much more history was in store for me to connect with. While I carried on with the daily task of cutting grass in the morning and devoting the afternoon to the history side of things, I did not forget I had important things on the back burner, for instance census records of the refuge regarding my Nan's position there. Also the Italian link to Miceli and the R.N. Libia . All the things that would bring about the ending of each thing I had researched, it was rather like spinning plates.

I would remember just in time to reconnect with each of the things that needed to be finalised. I was indeed wealthy with information if not so rich finance-wise. While I was working at the churchyard, I was funding my living costs and did afford myself a small amount of funds when needed, but I saw my work as a means to an end and could not stop to consider that I could in the end have nothing but a pile of information only relevant to myself.

However, I would have helped save the churchyard, not that I would shout from the rooftops that I had done so, it was enough for me to know I had. I had lived on the edge most of my life, I had many a fall but always bounced back and managed to remain keen and wide-eyed. I was told by an old gypsy woman many years ago things about my life that had all happened so far as she had predicted. She told me I would inherit and that it would not be money but that I would be alright for money and should follow my instincts. So maybe what I was to inherit was the knowledge of all I was learning now. The gypsy woman also said that something beautiful would happen and that I would know when it did and not look for it because it would find me. I would be blessed with this beautiful thing; I often thought about the gypsy woman and what it all meant but could never work it out.

Each time I did ponder the subject, I seemed to get very busy, and thoughts of it just slipped away. It was at the beginning of March that Adrian Abbott contacted me with news that he had cleaned the numbers we had found along the first row of lost graves and when he returned to the churchyard with them, they looked as if they had just been cast in the foundry. To handle something so old that had been lost for so long felt like handling treasure. They were heavy for their size and cold to touch but somehow they looked majestic. They were only made of cast iron but as far as I was concerned they could have been gold. I worried about placing them back in the ground upon the graves we had discovered.

My intention was to, once we had identified the occupant of each lost grave, lay a memorial stone on each one with their name and date of death with the number next to the memorial stone. I would have to fund it myself and thought about making the stones myself and cut the inscription. I had the skills to do it and I wanted to do them justice. That was my only concern. I felt once I had the names of the people and we found information about them then the work could not be done cheaply. The church council had made it clear to me that they would not fund anything but would insist on deciding the size and type of stone used and what inscription would be on each one. For a body of people who inherited the complacency and neglectful attitude down the years and who did not care that the graves had been forgotten, it made me feel sick!

I could see that I would have a problem with a few people within the church council; as it stood; most of whom I did not know. They would meet in secret and the meetings closed to the public, and some of them who had watched me move the earth by myself for four years and did not lift a finger to help would have the final say. But in life you have them that do and them that don't and them that don't try and make life a misery for them that do. But it is a sad fact of life that within all churches and organisations there are ongoing conflicts between them that do and them that do not, whose only wish is to try and crush people's enthusiasm with harsh words. But it was the villagers who helped when I needed it and encouraged me in my dark moments when I could have given up the mammoth task I had undertaken at an age when I should be retired. I tried to put to the back of my mind that I would have opposition and that I had right on my side. Still, life is never easy, and that problem was never far from my mind. It was like a stone in my boot. It was irritating and made me angry still. I used that anger as motivation sometimes. If you have something to be angry about, you work harder and become stronger in mind and body.

The first ten numbers to be researched starting with number three, found to the right of the brick.and tile debris along the last row I had cleared of spoil came up with no name, nor did graves four, five and six they showed in the church burials. But with no name or date just a blank space next to each number, it was confusing but the next grave, number seven, had a headstone. I had cleaned this headstone: it was the grave of a Florence Mary Churcher née May and her husband George, he was a private in the Royal Marine's Light Infantry. He died at Haslar hospital at Gosport of his injuries on 13th January 1913 at age 29. He was also buried at Haslar and his inscription was on his wife's headstone. At Durley, Florence Mary Churcher née May, died on 22nd June 1913, of a heart condition just five months after her husband.

Adrian found information regarding the couple who had only been married for four years. There was also a newspaper article about a married woman called Henrietta Moore of 39 Union Street, Southampton.

It said she was charged with stealing clothes valued at £2.15 shillings, the property of Florence Mary Churcher. The latter was the widow of private George Churcher R.M.L.I., an invalid attended by nurse L. Arnold attached to the R.M.L.I. infirmary. The nurse identified the property as belonging to Mrs Churcher. She and a private, W.G. Sultburn R.M.L.I., also identified a suit and other articles as having belonged to private Churcher who had died in Haslar Hospital on 13th January. Nurse Arnold said Mrs Churcher was taken to Durley about three weeks ago suffering from a heart problem. The prisoner had assisted in attending Mrs Churcher for some time between the end of November 1912 and the beginning of January 1913, Police Sergeant Tarrant arrested the prisoner at Union Street Northam Southampton. In answer to the charge, Henrietta Moore said she lived apart from her husband for 15 years and got her living from going out nursing. The Police Sergeant said it was the first time that Moore had been in the hands of the police and that she knew it was wrong to steal. But she did so because she had no money and had been tempted by drink and drugs. The bench sentenced Henrietta Moore to two months in prison in the second division, and the chairman remarked that she would have an opportunity to give up drink and drugs.

It was a sad affair all-around. George Churcher had died an invalid at Haslar, his wife Florence also passed away just a few months after him. While Henrietta Moore still lived, she had what seemed to be a rotten life with not much to look forward to and had been reduced to stealing from a widow. Poor Florence was buried at Durley on her own, and then the grave had been forgotten. A man who died from his injuries for his country was not remembered. But now the grave and its headstone had been found against all odds, the two would be remembered. And I wondered what happened to Henrietta Moore. I hope she escaped her poverty and had some sort of life. Yes, she had stolen, but sometimes people are at the mercy of circumstance.

The next grave number eight also had a headstone, but it was too dirty to see anything of the inscription and I had not had time to clean it. I had cut the ivy growth at its root and once it had died off it could be cleaned, however this headstone was very close to the Churcher headstone. Too close as if it had been placed there, moved from another place. It was much smaller as if it had been broken. So, for now we decided that it would be our number eight but with reservations once cleaned. We would have more idea as to the owner of the stone. Moving on to number nine, a grave with no headstone just the number and we had more luck. This was the resting place of a man called Alfred Primmer born in 1864 who lived in a cottage with his wife and children in Church Lane. The lane leading to the churchyard from records found online Alfred was a thatcher and hurdle maker, an important trade of its time. Alfred died in 1921 aged 75 years. Next to Alfred in number ten was a lady called Hanna May. She was born in Henley Dorset in 1823, and she married James May. His trade was a carter and worked out of Little Snake Moore Farm in Durley.

Hanna May died in 1889 aged 66. Along from Hanna May's grave was number 11, another Hanna, this time Hanna Primmer née Banham. She was born in 1808 and was the mother of Alfred Primmer, in grave number nine. She was married to William Primmer and as well as having Alfred she also had seven other children. Hanna died in 1882 aged 74 and buried next to her in grave number 12 was her husband William Primmer. He was another member of the family of thatchers and hurdle makers.

So, the end of row (A) had given us some names and an insight into who they were and what they did to make a living. It was also clear that there was some sort of agreement between the villagers as to who occupied an area within the churchyard to be buried. The first row was mainly for the Primmer and May families and records show that at one time more Mays lived in the village than any other family. Later it was the Houghtons who took over that mantle, and today over 250 Houghtons are buried in Durley churchyard. Lots of the big families intermarried – you would not have to look far in your family tree to find you had a Houghton as a relation if you came from Durley.

The rectors at the time would have had no say in the matter who was buried, and where all they needed to do was to record the event; the members of the leading families called the shots. The rectors in the 1800s did not even live in the village, most of them had caused too much discontent within the community. There were regular conflicts, and it was once reported that the Bishop of Winchester was threatened. Hence, the rectors were wise to stick to all things religious and leave the village's more prominent figures to know what was best for Durley.

The first row where we found graves gave us food for thought and a completely different feeling now we knew who was buried there. In row (B) I had a little work still to do before we could go through with the rods and metal detector, so on the Saturday I decided to stay till I had got that row done. This row ran the width of the churchyard from south to north and was in front of the brick and tile debris; this was the last of the soil I had to move. I had a feeling of achievement as I moved the last barrowload, the only way I can describe the feeling was the same as when I was in football management. It was the 89th minute of the last game of the season with the referee about to blow his whistle and our team would be champions. It was very emotional. Then, as it was now and for the first time in a while I could relax, it had been a mammoth task to undertake. I felt the need to kneel down and thank the Lord for the energy I had been blessed with and Mother Nature for the season's changing weather conditions that had been the indicator as to when I used that energy, given my age and restrictions in all my endeavours.

Chapter 17
Continued Investigation

After identifying all we could in row (A) and clearing the rest of the spoil, we were ready to investigate the area we referred to as row (B). This row also ran the width of the west end of churchyard south to north and in front of the area where I found all the brick and tile debris stood three headstones. I had first noticed them hidden by small trees and bracken, but now they stood completely visible to all and in remarkably good condition given their imposed exile. I had taken most of the variegated ivy from their base, leaving what was left to decompose and become compost to help regenerate the soil in that area. The ivy had been a contributory factor in the survival of these headstones. Cutting the ivy away could be considered detrimental, given it had been influential in the protection of such fine works of art. It's a well-known fact that ivy covers and protects things that have suffered neglect and been forgotten.

So, cutting it should be an indication of intent to make sure this neglect never happens again, an assurance to Mother Nature and a willingness to work with her in the regeneration of this fine meadowland, and you're rewarded with a colourful spring display of all that's wild. The headstones became the reference point, if we started under the south hedgerow and walked northward, crossing in front of them, we would not go far wrong.

I had found one rusty number caked in clay when I was digging early on in my work, and I had made a trench through the spoil some 16 feet away from Florence Mary Churcher née May's headstone. I had put the number in the shed after taking a photo of where I found it, thinking it to be just another discarded rusty number. Still, now we had confirmed row (A)'s existence, it could be that the number, when cleaned up, could be from another line of graves that would become our second find referred to as row (B).

Adrian began to walk along row (B) from left to right from the south hedgerow and started to pick up energy with the rods as he had in row (A) and found that the rods moved on 18 occasions across to the north hedgerow. The metal detector picked up 17 signals and when I dug at each signal, I found another 17 numbers. The interesting thing was the number I had in the shed that I found in front of Florence Mary Churcher née May's headstone, the rods crossed when Adrian walked over that area, but the metal detector did not pick anything up. So, the number in the shed could belong in row (B) depending on how all the numbers followed on numerically, but we would not know that until they had been through the cleaning process.

In all we found another 17 rusty numbers caked in dirt and clay and with the number I had in the shed it would mean that 18 graves were in row (B). All we needed was for them to run numerically on from the last numbers in row (A). It was another amazing occasion, all the work I had done moving the spoil was now beginning to pay dividends and pleased we had found two rows of graves, we decided to see if I was right in thinking the vast void between row (B) and the headstones situated on what was the edge of woods before any spoil was moved could contain more graves.

Such, a big void in what was not a very big churchyard where all the space would be needed was a good enough reason to look, so we decided to have lunch and continue in the afternoon. After our welcome break, we set out with a tape measure and placed a marker eight feet away from one of the three headstones in the new row (B). We chose eight-foot because if the grave was six feet long, a two-foot walkway between it and the next grave would have been required. We could measure six feet from the walkway, if there were graves, they would be in what we would call row (C).

After setting up and armed with a bucket of wooden marker stakes, Adrian began as he had in row (A) and (B) walking from south to north across the cleared earth; and to our amazement discovered another 19 numbers, one of which was right next to a buried stone plinth. This, as we worked out, was connected to the broken headstone that we found next to Florence Mary Churcher née May's headstone; there could be no other explanation for it being there. The headstone must have been moved because it had been broken by the roots of the big cedar trees. The only difference between the numbers we had found in row (C) from the ones in rows (A) and (B) was they had been broken; they were caked in mud so the process of cleaning them would take longer. We didn't consider this a problem, but the fact we had them was so important and confirmation of where the broken headstone could go back on or next to its original plinth as I had done when putting George's and one other headstone back in place.

It was like putting together a big puzzle and would take time, but I had plenty of that. Having no more spoil to remove from the west end area, I began to take the soil from on and around the kerbstone graves in the northwest area. Over the years the areas had been covered by huge molehills that had become home to all manner of weeds and long grasses, making it impossible to read the inscription on the side or head of each kerbstone grave.

This area was part of the second extension to the churchyard and began in the 1940s. Like the rest of the churchyard, it was overgrown with many graves unkept, because people who had tended them had themselves either passed away or had become too old to look after their relation's graves. Also, if they could get to the churchyard, it would have been impossible to find the grave given the neglect inflicted by the church council who used the feeble excuse that they had left the area to nature. What rot that was, and I heard about many churches adopting that line of excuse to make up for what was in fact pure laziness by people who just could not be bothered if truth be told. Many churchyards do have working parties who work hard to make a difference; however, it is a sad fact that church councils up and down the country don't care about the churchyards or indeed the people who come to try and find a particular grave.

With all the soil and turf that was being removed from the northwest area, many old kerbstone graves were revealed. The soil and turf from on and around them, I started to place around a large mound down in the wooded area at the west end of the churchyard. The mound had a tree growing through it, and over the years as more spoil had been placed against it, its roots had travelled into the spoil making it impossible to remove this tree.

I had cut down about 18 small self-seeding trees that had also grown from disturbed soil that I had identified as possible graves. I had been told that the archdeacon had given permission to take out all the self-seeding trees and that Durley churchyard was in fact his favourite of all the churches he had to visit. I did find this comment rather confusing. Given the state of the churchyard, it was so obvious nothing had been done for many years. I made no comment on what had been imparted to me, but I did think the archdeacon must have walked round with his eyes shut if he did indeed walk round his favourite place of rest. Just why his name would be used in vain I was not sure, but I said nothing.

The two bigger cedar trees had grown from graves and their roots had travelled into and over some dozen graves. These trees were over 80 feet high and far too big a job for me to handle, So I reported that the trees would need to be moved because they were either dead or dying. They also leaned terribly and were a real danger to the public. If they fell over, many graves would have been affected. I pointed out the church councils had a responsibility to protect all human remains in the graves had they been disturbed by falling trees and the Home Office would have to be called in, bones would have to be identified and the churchyard would probably close because of the risk of contamination.

All the things I was pointing out were in the book called churchyard rules, set out by the main chancellor's office. However, my concerns fell upon deaf ears and just confirmed the obvious reluctance of the church council to do anything to make the job easier at the west end of the churchyard. It was also then I realised that they would use the archdeacon's name as a tool to halt any unwanted questions. A stock response, if you like, to anyone connected to the church who if told that their question or action would 'Offend the archdeacon greatly' would recoil and shrink back into line, if they believed in God that was. If they thought they would have displeased their cherished saviour it would cause them much sadness. It was in fact a horrible way to treat a believer. However, to a spiritual person not used to such controlling comments it still left a bad taste in the mouth.

So, while I worried about all I was doing could be a waste of time, I managed to put things to the back of my mind. I needed to finish what I had started before walking away. The mound with the permanent tree growing from it was about four feet high. I had fashioned it, so it ran from its high point of four foot down to meet a circle of red bricks around the base of the mound that abutted the turf I had brought from other areas.

I also placed ancient bits of headstone, flagstone and cornerstones that had once been part of the first structure built by fine craftsmen. Many churches have Saxon foundations supporting a newer structure built with Oligocene Quorn stone from the Isle of Wight, stone used by the Saxons from the 8th century. The stone, when shipped over from the Island, would be taken on smaller boats on rivers that ran right up into the Meon Valley as far as Droxford in Hampshire's Meon Valley. This quality stone was very much like Dorset's Portland stone and caused some confusion among craftsmen, but in more recent times with the help of technology the stones can be identified when cut through, revealing its micro-organisms.

While it's hard to distinguish between two sets of stone when the stonemasons carry out their craft, both sets are beautiful to the naked eye. Much of the stone I had found buried in the churchyard must have been from the original structure. I found an old arched stone window frame, very small in size. Back when the first structure was built, they wanted to see out more than wanting other people looking in. All of the things I had found and was still finding were all interesting, as was working out where they were used before the church had been altered over the years.

One thing that did survive was the plans and letters relating to the works. They were all at Winchester in the records office, which was lucky for anyone interested in the architecture of this beautiful building. At least something survived for prosperity and not ignored by previous incompetent rectors whose attitude was if they did not understand it then it could be thrown away. There must have been, down the years, someone who would use a common-sense approach and who realised the importance of keeping such records. But unfortunately, too many oddball rectors seemed to have held that position at Durley through to the 19th century, after which more intelligent intellectuals who would think things over and consult more informed people than themselves before deciding what to do regarding matters of importance. It could be that by burying the stone, entombing it away from uninformed eyes, was in fact, their idea of the best way to preserve things for the people that followed who possessed a better knowledge of the stone's history. Stone that seemed to be everywhere, each bit discovered in the order it was buried in the earth.

Two large bits of a headstone that had been placed against the east wall of the church were very old and covered in green mould took pride of place on the mound. They must have been part of an impressive headstone at one time, that was clear. It must have been about three months after I placed these bits of headstone on the mound, that while working at the east boundary moving old piles of molehills away from the front of some headstones, I came across more broken bits of headstone. Buried in front of them and thinking they would look good down on the mound, I dug them out and took them to the mound and as I looked for a good place for them, I noticed that two of the bits were the other half of the headstone I found placed against the east side of the church.

Once I put them together, they formed a fine-looking piece of art and after being cleaned up I could read the inscription. The headstone belonged to a man called Richard Hickley, who died in 1741 aged 75. The carving on the stone was wonderful with a cherub in one corner and a skull in the other. Lots of headstones back then depicted things like that referring to birth and death. Across the middle of the stone, written in fine old English, were the words "Upon They Hill". I had seen those words on several other headstones at the front of the church, and It could be Richard Hickley was a member of that family. But why was one half of the headstone against the church and the other half buried in another part of the churchyard?

Also, right in the middle of the stone was a hole the size of a teacup. It could have had a tree bow fall on it, or another headstone had fallen against it. It would be another thing I had to investigate. I had several things on the back burner that needed clearing up. For instance, what to do regarding the letter my father had. I was unsure what the next move was regarding that, and until I was clear about what to do, I would do nothing. But first I wanted to find out why Richard Hickley's headstone was in two different areas of the churchyard. Things became more confusing when I searched the burial records and found no sign of Richard Hickley's burial. I did find a record of his marriage to Elizabeth Houghton, she was born in 1682 and passed away in 1762, outliving Richard by some 21 years. Richard and Elizabeth had three sons, John Hickley 1712–1733, Robert Hickley 1707–1781. The third son, William Hickley, I could only find his death date of 1717. Adrian thought they could have farmed at Hill Farm in Durley.

I looked online at the Winchester records office; it was a good way to find things. Any records held would be shown with a reference number if you put the person's name into the search engine and if you wished to order copies you could. Several reference numbers came up for the Hickley family, one (65m89/z72/9) referred to Richard Hickley being mentioned in the vestry records of the Church of The Holy Cross Durley. The vestry records from 1560–1900, had been recorded in a book written by Mr George Molesworth. It was an analysis of the vestry records issued by the Parochial Church Council of Durley in 1961. The good thing was I would not need to order a copy because it was in the pile of books that one of the frequent visitors to the churchyard – a Mrs Batchelor – had given me. I had two copies; they had been freely available at the time to villagers when they had historic meetings. Mrs Batchelor attended with her friend Ms Gwen Houghton who worked at Winchester either in the records office or in the same building and she would copy anything relating to Durley. Over the years she built up an impressive collection. Ms Gwen Houghton was now housebound and had given all her historical collection to the History Society, which Adrian and Shannon Abbott were involved in. Adrian had told me the collection was amazing and would take some time to put it all together in order for it to go on show to the public. So, we had to be grateful to Gwen Houghton for compiling such a collection.

I found out sometime later that Gwen Houghton had wanted a photo of me because her great-grandmother was called Elizabeth Houghton née Prowting. I cannot be sure if she was related to any of my ancestors but given that Durley was a small village there was a good chance someone may have been.

I found the George Molesworth book with the others that Mrs Batchelor had given me. On page five, it was indeed all about the vestry and how things had been run before the introduction of Parish Councils in 1890. Before that, all parish administration, as well as church matters, had been controlled by members of the vestry, i.e. the rectors, churchwardens, and poor law overseers as well as some other vestry officials. To finance their activities, they were empowered to levy rates upon the community at large, since Holy Cross of Durley was the Chapelry of the Blessed Mary of Upham. The rectors of Upham cum Durley had a major responsibility through two sets of churchwardens, one for each parish. In practice, the rectors seem to have taken little interest in Durley and left church matters there to the curates, because the rectors found parishioners and yeoman farmers far too difficult to deal with.

The parishioners refused to allow the rectors a free hand on anything relating to Durley, because they did not trust the administrators at Upham and didn't want money collected from Durley used for the need of the Blessed Mary at Upham. In one reported case, they refused point-blank to allow the rector of Upham cum Durley to nominate one of the churchwardens. The parishioners and yeoman farmers at Durley wanted a chief say in anything that was done either in church or lay matters concerning the village; they made sure that Durley's interests were looked after. Now the rector of Upham cum Durley, the Reverend Mr John White, was rector from 1720 till 1738. Sadly, for the Reverend John White, he proved to be very unpopular and misjudged the Durley community. In 1723 he fell out with the parishioners when he endeavoured to nominate a personal rector's warden named Mr John Hickley, the brother of Richard Hickley. So, the leading parishioners of Durley, led by Mr Richard Hickley, caballed against the Reverend John White and brought a successful lawsuit in the Ecclesiastical Court at Winchester to restrain him. The money to pay for the legal costs was paid out of the public funds. The people of Durley did not mind public funds used against the rector of Upham cum Durley. If he wanted his own warden, then he could pay for him. So, the people of Durley backed their leading parishioners if it meant the rector at Upham would be kept in check by the likes of Richard Hickley and other parishioners.

Richard Hickley and the parishioners' drastic action was repeated two years later when the Reverend Mr John White was again back before the Ecclesiastical Court, this time for refusing to do statute duty on the highways in Durley, i.e. filling in the divots on the king's highway. Again, he lost but this was seen more as a malicious act, a reminder if you like that no one disrespected the village of Durley, and people like Richard Hickley. The leading parishioners, who would have things done the right way, seemed to have a following of like-minded people and is just what every village needs. So, it wasn't hard to see why the headstone of Richard Hickley had been discarded, probably smashed from the state I found it in and placed in different areas of the churchyard. His enemies in the church waited 18 years to get their own back and it shows what a vindictive lot they must have been back then.

I admired Richard Hickley and his parishioners and was pleased I found his headstone purely by chance, as I had George's buried under the soil, yet another event that was meant to be. Richard had been given a new lease of life so to speak, and to be able to tell his story after so many years after his demise was a pleasure. We have the advantage of time and coincidences that have led to this story being told, little did George Molesworth know that his interesting book about the events of 1723 at Upham cum Durley would reach its final conclusion via first Gwen Houghton and her devotion to the village by gathering all she could about the place she loved. Then Mrs Batchelor and her gift to me of the books. We have all been led it seems, maybe by the spirit of Richard Hickley. A spirit that was so strong in life and continued after his demise, I am sure he would appreciate having the final say. For me, to rob someone of their history is the cruellest of acts, to remove all traces of the man ever having lived is deplorable. So, I say 'rest in peace Richard Hickley, you have waited long enough, my friend'.

One other coincidence regarding Richard Hickley, in the winter of 2019, as I was clearing things away after a funeral, four people came into the churchyard, a couple and their son and grandson. The man, a recently retired American who now lived in Spain, was showing his family where his ancestors once lived. He told me he had been to the church before and seen Gwen Houghton, who showed him the Hickley graves at the front of the church. I asked him if Richard Hickley was one of his ancestors which he was, so I told them the story from the George Molesworth book. The grandson recorded what I was saying. Of course, they loved to hear about him and then when I asked if they would like to see Richard's headstone, they were blown away. Of course, I could not show them a grave, but the impressive headstone upon the mound was enough and a great end to a great story. I was pleased I could help yet another person with his historical past, and the man's son said to me as they left in his strong American accent, "My friend, you have made my father's day, today, tomorrow and forever more."

The George Molesworth and John Bosworth books would become a great help to everyone; I lent them out to people to read or copy, no one let me down. They came back on the date the people said they would, people I had never seen before, all keen on the history of Durley. Eventually, when Adrian Abbott sorted out over 200 photos that Gwen Houghton and other villagers had given to John Bosworth for his book, those that did not make the cut for the book Adrian gave me copies. They too were also given to people to copy or look through and see if they could name anyone that was not named in the original batch of photos. It brought people together. Most of the people in the book now rested in the churchyard, even more reason to get the place back as it was because living relations of the Durley people buried at the west end of the churchyard had no idea they were there.

Once they did, I would often see small posies placed on graves at that end of the churchyard that had headstones. As soon as we could identify more people in graves without a headstone, I was sure more people would come. One other interesting thing I came across in the George Molesworth book was regarding the Reverend Mr John Rodgers, who was curate at the Church of the Holy Cross Durley for 65 years and did by all accounts try to be the peacemaker in the rift between the people of Durley and the rector of Upham cum Durley. It seems this man was well respected and tried to help each side without taking either one and tried to encourage a common-sense approach by both sides. He must have been well thought of by the people at Durley, because on his death in 1741 he was buried inside Durley church, a privilege only bestowed upon very special people. It was good to know someone like the Reverend Mr John Rodgers seemed to be able to keep order while remaining impartial. George Molesworth wrote of Durley, "There is little doubt about this topographical isolation led also to, isolation of thought and ideas and a somewhat limited outlook perhaps it was for that we find the inhabitants a close-knit but somewhat isolated community hardly at all affected by what was taking place in the country outside the parish and immersed in their own local problems while being protective of the village from outside interference."

Well, you could probably have that opinion regarding most villages, not just Durley. The smaller the village, the bigger the family-like protection for its well-being. To be a villager in a small community brings out the supportive nature in people, they may not all get on but try and come between them, you will soon find out which way the wind blows. Also, many villages like Durley, when asked to help the wider community, do so without question and the George Molesworth book of vestry records have noted a few interesting collections made in the church.

Recorded as follows: "August Ye 4th 1666 collected for loss sustained by fire in ye great cities of London ye sum of three shillings and four pence."

The Great Fire of London was in 1666 so this entry must have been regarding Durley's help to restore damage. Then in 1662: "Toward ye briefs for employing poor people in fishing and making of nett's six shillings and six pence." To make sure people overseas had the good book the entry reads: "Forward presenting of Ye Bible in Lithuania beyond ye sea", and finally 1670–1700 several collections one of nearly three pounds for the redemption of poor prisoners taken by the Turks. These were prisoners taken and held to ransom by the Barbary Corsairs or Sallie Rovers gangs of pirates who operated from Sale, Sta, on the Moroccan coast and were harboured by the Sultan Moulay Ismail. Their raids extended as far north as the English Channel and were greatly feared, in Giles Milton's book Forgotten White Slaves he tells of the Salle Rovers pirates of the narrow seas who kidnapped thousands of English people mainly from the West Country.

They raised the Islamic flag on Lundy and in one raid dragged 60 men, women and children from St Michaels Mount to become Christian slaves kept in dungeons, whipped, burned and compelled to work 15-hour days until they expired. Some were ransomed hence the collection in English churches, the attractive European women were sent to the Sultan Moulay Ismail's harem, and it is said that Moulay Ismail fathered 1,000 children. He sent the strongest slave men to breeding farms to mate with black Senegalese slave women; the Sultan Moulay Ismail believed they produced the most trustworthy workers.

One Frenchman was enslaved and kept naked in a cage with four slave woman and plied with drink. Each time he attempted to impregnate the Sultan's slave women, a slave drummer would beat the drum to indicate to the Sultan that possible reproduction was taking place. The Sultan Moulay Ismail led with his iron will and put his strength of power at the service of this unyielding will. "If God gave me the Kingship Man cannot take it from me," he was reported to have said. This will was always apparent in his actions and decisions. The colour of his clothes was linked to his mood, green is the sweetest colour, white was a good sign of those appealing to him. But when dressed in yellow, all the world trembles and flees his presence because it's the colour he chooses on the days of his bloodiest executions. One of his normal entertainments was to draw his sword as he mounted his horse and decapitate the slave who held the stirrup.

When Christian churches collected funds for the release of captured Christian slaves, the congregations like the one at Durley would have little idea what went on over the seas but still gave freely. I am sure some slaves were released when a ransom was paid, however thousands of white slaves had been captured and no amount of money collected in Christian churches would be enough to make a difference. Slavery was big business in the world, black and white, and always has been. Many wealthy families in England owned slaves, there is a list of who they are, however, it's a well-guarded secret if you ask to see government records of slave owners – you will be turned away. You can ask if a certain person or family owned slaves and get an answer but no one can see the list. We would be shocked I am sure to see who is on that list. When the bill was passed for the ending of slavery, forty per cent of government funds was paid out to slave owners in compensation, so the owners of slaves had been well paid for giving up the slaves. If they had not been paid, the bill would have never got through Parliament, a sad state of affairs indeed. No one man should own another or indeed profit from the misery of it, so what a wonderful book George Molesworth had put together. Every single page gave the reader something to think about and find more information on those days. All from vestry records written when the outside world seemed large beyond the seas to the hard-working agricultural workers who cultivated lands on tithes, they would receive little profit from themselves.

To give a tenth of a successful year's turnaround of all that's grown and nurtured from Mother earth brings a satisfaction that they can start the seasons again with a clean slate. However, in bad times when the harvest fails on sodden soils and a tenth of nothing was still expected was a disaster for the agricultural workers. The rich landowners, they could be the lord of the manor, men of state, universities, or the church itself who held grain in tithing sheds from successful seasons, gave nothing back in times of crises. These same people who made a profit from slaves inflicted the same misery on people in their community. It is difficult to understand when you walk around beautiful English villages, what price the ordinary village families paid trying to survive the hard injustice of times gone by. But the stories are there if you wish to scratch the surface and set memories recollecting and arouse forgotten hatreds.

The George Molesworth book had recorded many things relating to the clergy throughout the 1800s. Mr Molesworth would not have known about the lack of keeping proper records, regarding where each of the graves numbered in the burial records were or who rested within each one. However, he did report in some depth about Durley's long-established almshouse, used to house the aged when their energy had finally deserted them after a lifetime of working on the land. Prior to the introduction of the Droxford Union Workhouse, when without warning the elderly found themselves in an institution hardly beneficial to their needs, it was the end of the line! Life was over, and death was waiting in the wings.

The village almshouse, a picture of one which could be seen in John Bosworth's book, gave the older adults the dignity they had earnt over the years. George Molesworth reported that in 1821 William Becket (illiterate) and a Mrs Gaynor (relationship not stated) kept the poor house at £8 per annum paying for "their own tea and sugar and kept the profits of the garden". The vestry supplied the food and necessaries for the almshouse at the cost of around £500 per annum. The accommodation in the house was for six people, sex unstated, there was a sitting room, kitchen pantry, wash house, a little bedroom for two, and a double for four beds, chests for clothes and bedclothes (16 blankets and one quilt) provided. From 1813, there are entries for "earnings of the poor", mainly stone picking on the farms amounting to one year, some £32, credited to the account of the house.

Items purchased for the house included malt and hops so the paupers could brew their beer, considered safer than water back then and beneficial healthwise; other items such as meat, bacon, flour, split-peas, bread, etc. were purchased and from time to time a pig was brought and fattened on "fine pollard and barley". With most of the items purchased locally, from farmers, the last entry for the "expenses of the house" was in 1834. Any of the elderly who had passed before that date would have been considered local, with a good chance after their demise of having some record of where they rested within the churchyard.

Then in 1835 the Droxford poor law union was formed and overseen by an Elected Board of Guardians and representing its 11 constituent parishes in Hampshire. These included: Bishops Waltham, Corhampton, Droxford, Durley, Exton, Hambledon, Meonstoke, Soberton, Upham, Warnford and West Meon. Later in 1894 three other villages of Curdridge, Shedfield and Swanmore joined making 15 parishes in all who became dependent on the new Droxford union poor house. This spelt disaster for the people who had reached the age where energy had been their primary bargaining tool; without it they would have been no use to man nor beast. Feeding people who could not work and sustain a living put pressure on everyone.

The new Droxford Workhouse was one of 350 constructed, many of them in the South's more rural areas considered to be more pauperised. The workhouse at the northwest of Droxford was built at the cost of £5,738, its architect Sampson Kempthorn who designed many early workhouses. The one at Droxford was an unforgiving place and whilst from the front it was an impressive building, behind its facade created by skilled tradesmen it was a place of poverty and despair.

The accommodation wings and segregated exercise yard of different classes of inmates old and young, male and female, this told the real story of life in the workhouse families, separated on admission and set to work and earn their keep. The only people the workhouse benefited were the people who earnt the money to build such places, institutes that took away the dignity of people who at an age when life should have been easier found themselves locked into a system designed to benefit only the rich. The site at Droxford, even though the workhouse has long gone, has a strange and unhappy dismal feel about it. The houses built there seem sad and to live on a site that had seen such suffering would for me be impossible and to think that place housed many of the elderly from Durley made me cringe.

The burial records transcribed by Shannon Abbott show who and how many ended up there. The last death in the poor house at Durley was in 1827

– Ann Mead aged 90. It's hard to imagine someone of her age would have to go to the workhouse but still they did, maybe not all as old, but old enough to be frightened by the prospect of having to go there and some took the drastic action of killing themselves rather than be taken to a place where they would die anyway.

In 1844, George Goodwin of Durley aged 73 "cut his throat", later in 1898 John Goodwin of Ashton aged 48 a relative of the above "hung himself" rather than being sent to the workhouse. There were plenty of others, James Walker of Durley found hanged in Mosses row near the Vaseny ground, he hanged for days before he was found. They all took the only way out they could, and they all rest in the churchyard at Durley but it's not known where. The people who did die in the Droxford Union Workhouse, they rest there too but again no record of where. Only their names are recorded: 1841 Molly Bigwood aged 78, in 1842 William Colyer aged 75, 1843 John Scorey aged 80, 1844 Abraham Warner aged 69, 1862 Richard Carter aged 83, 1865 Maria Bridges aged 79, 1866 Ann Browning again aged 79, and also in 1866 I was devastated to see recorded David Prowting. Susan Matilda's father, one of my great-grandfathers, he of "yum Retor pray for rain", he died in the workhouse aged 76. How on earth that happened, I do not know. All information I had found up until this record had been positive, but it would be something I would certainly try and find out.

In 1869, Charles May aged 79 also died in the workhouse, as did James Short in 1869. He was only 26 years old, God knows how he ended up in that godforsaken place. In 1879, Ann May aged 77, 1880 Mary Evens aged 51, and 1881 aged 61 George Shaw also passed away in that horrid place, and finally in 1887 Jamima Chalk aged 84. All of them perished in the workhouse, all of them buried at Durley and to add insult to injury, none of their graves were recorded as to where their final resting place is. Grandfather David could be next to his late wife Elizabeth. She had been dead for some time, but there was no record of where she rested either, and given it was so long ago the only thing I could do was to try and find out who the rector was back in 1866 and that was the Reverend Thomas Scard.

His coachman and servant was Frederick Prowting, another brother of Great-uncle George's. Now the Reverend Scard MA had popped up in some records I had seen before, mainly about how long he served as the rector of Durley. Also, I found that his wife Elizabeth Eliza Scard née Veck had died on 9th March 1866, aged 76, and she was buried just outside the west door of Durley church.

That year, ten burials took place between March and December when both David Prowting and Ann Browning had been returned to Durley, having both died in the workhouse within two weeks of each other. So, my question, if it were possible, to the Reverend Thomas Scard, would be why did all the burials after his wife Elizabeth's not carry on in the same row as hers and why didn't he record where they were. The thing was back then if you were in the employment of someone like the Reverend Thomas Scard, as Uncle Frederick was, he would not have questioned Thomas Scard's decision, he would have kept his head down, his livelihood depended on his job. Frederick's father, William, Grandfather David's son, would have kept his nose clean because the family lived in a house rented from the church as well as working a tithe also rented from the church that the Reverend Thomas Scard was responsible for.

Grandfather David himself rented a tithe called the Gully with a house and garden attached to the land he worked. So, the church had a major hold over many people, and it paid not to get on the wrong side of the rector. It's true Susan Matilda may have had something to say where her father should have been buried and probably knew, but she would not rock the boat either because she and shoemaker's cottage and land could have also been rented from the church and the responsibility of the Reverend Thomas Scard.

So, I decided to find out more about the Reverend Thomas Scard. Adrian Abbott had told me there was some sort of problem surrounding Thomas Scard's tenure at the private school he was master of at Bishops Waltham. It would be more to research, but I was used to spinning plates, one more would be no problem to me. The Reverend Thomas Scard was born at Eling in Hampshire in 1789, the son of Thomas Scard snr, and his wife Mary Scard née Yeats. She was the daughter of a wealthy Eling Mailteser. In 1809 it became apparent that young Thomas's father was having financial problems, with prison a reality, Thomas Scard Senior's three siblings were called on to help their brother, and while his sister Susannah and one of his brothers, John, agreed to help his third sibling, Benness flatly refused. This did not go down well with their father Thomas Scard the Elder, and Benness was disinherited from his father's will.

However, Benness was later reinstated and still there was great pressure on the family to preserve the family name. This put a great strain on young Thomas Scard's father, not only from his debts but the effect it would have on his family.

Then In 1816 on the 23rd of December it was reported in the Hampshire Telegraph newspaper that Thomas's father had died at the age of 41. Thomas Scard's father's premature death was partly put down to financial pressure and that his family faced ruin. However, Thomas Scard's wealthy Uncle William Yeats Esquire made sure his sister Mary's family would not be ruined, and this was the beginning of young Thomas Scard's lucky life, never having to worry about money because William Yeats Esquire would eventually make Thomas Scard a beneficiary. This allowed the young Thomas Scard to concentrate on his education, backed by William Yeats Esquire and his paternal grandfather, Thomas Scard the Elder. Thomas had an uninterrupted education, he was academically gifted and chose the clergy as a way of life. Back then, many wealthy families had sons who would be encouraged to become men of the cloth, mainly because they were not much good at anything else. Thomas Scard matriculated at Oxford and in time he became chaplain to the Duke of Cambridge, then at 25 and Master of Bishops Waltham Grammar School, he married Elizabeth Eliza Veck, daughter of Richard Aubury Veck and his wife Elizabeth née Bulpitt. Her father, famed for his cricket career and business interests at Bishops Waltham, would mean that Thomas Scard's association with the rich would continue. In 1824, Thomas's paternal grandfather, Thomas Scard the Elder, died, Thomas, his mother and siblings all benefited from his grandfather's demise. Then two years later Thomas inherited again when his maternal Uncle William Yeats Esquire also passed away. His will had been made some six years before and just six months before William Yeats Esquire's death it was ruled at an inquest that he was insane and certified as such.

In 1846, after many years as master of the Grammar School, Thomas Scard was praised at a dinner given in his honour for the work he had done and over 50 former pupils attended along with nine fellow rectors and many leading businessmen of the day, including Mr William Gunner Esquire, Mr Thomas Clark Merchant of Bishops Waltham, and Mr Hash Stare's Land Surveyor of Droxford Hampshire. All three men were keen to keep on the right side of the Reverend Thomas Scard, as the rector of the Church of the Holy Cross Durley.

The problem for Thomas Scard was, while the great and the good would heap praise and gifts upon him for outstanding work in the education of young gentlemen, the rector was falling into a trap – wealthy businessmen were keen to exploit the man they saw as a bit of a wuss. Who on receiving one fine silver plate costing 17 shillings, stood up after being presented with the special gift and put on an act of being so emotional he was unable to deliver his speech and had to "Take a Moment" as one report commented, until having collected himself he delivered a speech worthy of any trained actor.

Thomas Scard had a wonderful run, however, now as rector of Durley, dealing with local farmers who would know the time of day and see right through the manipulative individual he was. It would not be long before the people who had applauded him would turn on him once they worked out he was not the full shilling and a schemer for his own ends. History recorded Messer, Gunner, Clarke and Hash-Stares, along with others, came down on the Reverend Thomas Scard like a tonne of bricks. Thomas Scard may have been skilled at turning silly young boys into even more silly young men, but he was silly himself if he thought he could bullshit his way into kidding hardened businessmen, with all their faults and one of them was not being silly where money was concerned.

Thomas Scard had bitten off more than he could chew; he owed money to everyone and you did not mess with Messers Gunner, Clarke and Hash-Stares. They would have his shirt off his back and they did. They took Thomas Scard to the cleaners after giving him enough rope, silver plates, wonderful dinners, and cream teas. Thomas wandered into no-man's land, a land he had never been before. After a lifetime of luck, it finally ran out. Messers Gunner, Clark and Hash-Stares, along with others, made Thomas enter into agreements to put up lands and property as security against what he owed to them signed on the 1st of July 1857. Over the years with all he had inherited he should never have found himself in such a position. As rector of Durley, that alone brought in £500 per annum, and a fine home in Durley.

So where did it all go wrong? Who knows. And so Thomas Scard entered into an agreement with the gang of three and others promising to pay what he owed or forfeit his assets. Job done, everyone happy!

But just when the rector thought he was clearing things up, other creditors entered into the fray in the shape of farmer Abraham Edwards. He also trusted and was ripped off by the rector Thomas Scard. Close behind Abraham Edwards was Mr John Sanger, Mr Edmund-Etherington and Miss Sarah Long. They all on hearing about the deal Thomas Scard had struck, scuppered the whole agreement by taking out writs at the high court in London that would supersede any agreement Messers Gunner, Clark and Hash-Stares had made with Thomas Scard who by then was in a real mess.

The writs were taken out separately over four months beginning with Miss Sarah Long whose levy was taken out on the 21st of August 1857 for the sum of £53 and 19 shillings, a lot of money back then, and in today's comparison some £6,000 was owed. Then on the 27th of October 1857, Mr John Sanger took out his writ levied for the sum of £183, which in today's money amounts to £20,829 – a vast amount. On the 19th of November 1857, Mr Edmund Etherington took out his writ levied for the sum of £252, in today's terms £28,683. Each writ amounting to more and when Mr Abraham Edwards took out his writ for the sum of £296, in today's terms a whopping £33,692, Thomas Scard owed the four creditors £784. Its value today would have been £79,204. Thomas Sard was not just stupid, he was a crook.

The Bishop of Winchester took over the fiscal running of the church. There was a problem when the sheriff of Hampshire returned to the courts, and what follows is taken from the original document. "The sheriff of Hampshire returned to Westminster and reported that the said Thomas Scard had not any goods or chattels in his Bailwick, of which he could cause to be made the sum and interest by that writs directed to be levied or any part thereof. He did thereby further certify that the said Thomas Scard was a benefice clerk 'having no lay fee in his Bailiwick', that is to say the Rector and the parish Church of Durley in the county of Southampton and which the said Rector and the parish Church were within your Diocese: Therefore we command that you enter into the said Rectory and parish Church of Durley and take and Seqester the same into your possession and that you hold the same in your possession, until you shall have levied the sum and interest aforesaid of rents, tithes, obligations, conventions, fruits, issues and profits thereof, and ecclesiastical goods in your diocese of the said Thomas Scard to be rendered to Sarah Long, Abraham Edwards, John Sanger, and Edmund Etherington." Well, what a mess. The church could have lost possessions if Thomas Scard did not pay the money back.

I did find records in the Scard family's archives, letters to the affect that Thomas did indeed dispose of some of his assets and after two years had settled with the preferential creditors Sarah Long, Edmund Etherington, John Sanger and the family of Abraham Edwards. Because on the 29th of November 1859 Abraham Edwards passed away at the age of 52, and maybe not knowing his writ had been settled in full, it may well have been the stress and strain of the whole situation that contributed to his death. Thomas Scard would have known first -hand how that felt, having lost his father in similar circumstances.

Abraham Edwards had worked his way up from nothing and made something of himself. In the census forms it showed how he became better off each time the reports came out every ten years. I could follow his rise from a one-man band to employing men and boys to help run his vast acreage. He had house servants, a groom and all the trappings of a successful man. Abraham rests in grave number 252, his wife Jane is next to him in grave number 253 and their daughter Fanny in grave number 254, just outside the west door of the church, just five graves away from Thomas Scard and his wife Elizabeth in grave number 247.

Thomas Scard tried to leave his job as rector of Durley when the writs had been issued but the Bishop of Winchester refused his request and made him stew in his own juice and did not give him an easy way out. And if anyone tells you he spent 50 years at Durley and how wonderful he was, remember half of his term was enforced. In all, Thomas Scard was no good for the village. Abraham Edwards proved he was a proper Durley man.

Chapter 18
The Letter

After finishing with George Molesworth's interesting book and more or less up together with the creation of the mound at the west end of the churchyard, I decided to take another look at the file I had started regarding the letter my father had received. I usually had files on the desk in my study and, although looking like a rubbish tip, I knew where everything was. However, I had kept that particular file on the dining room table and after each meal would just look at it, recalling how far I had got with it – in reality, not far at that stage. I would take the letter and its original envelope out of a second envelope it was in for safekeeping, then place it back when I had finished looking at it. I could in fact recite the letter without even looking at it, but I was still stuck in respect of what to do about it going forward.

One evening when I put the letter back into its original envelope, I noticed something written next to the place name of Oakhampton. I had seen that name so often each time I took the letter out and knew my dad had written it on the back of the envelope, but I had never bothered looking at it because I was more interested in what was inside of the envelope. However, this particular evening I noticed some individual letters written in pencil that had faded and the imprint of the pencil could clearly be seen with the aid of the natural light coming in via the window next to the dining room table. I had not noticed it before because I had sat with my back to the window through the winter therefore there was no natural light to cast such a shadow as it did when the clocks changed; and I also changed chairs so I could have a good view over the valley that my house backed onto.

The pressure placed on the pencil when written all those years ago, even though the lead had faded, revealed these initials 'A.E.A.' before the name Oakhampton. They most certainly had been put there by my father and once again, as I touched each imprint, I imagined what my dad had been thinking as I was now regarding this mysterious communication. I put the letters, followed by the place name of Oakhampton, into the search engine of my laptop and waited for modern technology to weave its magic wand and what it brought forth was bloody amazing or words to that affect, if you get my drift.

I had – or so I thought – gone as far as I could with finding things about young Arthur, the person who, when reaching the age of 85, had written the letter to my dad. Now that I had more information, in fact so much information, I didn't know where to start. The fact was that Arthur's made-up stories of his lineage most certainly worked for him in the opening of doors;

he had started a business, A.E.A. Prowting, in 1928 that went on to become one of the biggest construction firms in England, acquiring other construction companies along the way. From his humble Upham beginnings he became mega rich. This letter, as we know, was just made-up bullshit to impress the great and the good at the time and seemed to have most certainly worked.

So I set out to find his family. It was the easiest research I had ever done and it didn't take long to track them down. However having found the family of the gentleman who sent the letter to my father, I could not just ring and ask if they were interested in a letter their ancestor wrote to my dad 43 years ago. They would, I was sure, tell me what to do with the letter. They were, after all, very wealthy and may think I was out to fleece them in some way and probably had regular requests from people wanting funding for various projects. They may think them all a scam, the same as my mother had thought when the gentleman's letter first arrived at our home.

Anyway, I had to call them now I had got this far, so I decided to do so one Sunday evening. I found when I was in business that early Sunday evening was always a good time to talk to people, it was the end of the weekend and there was never much on television. At that time, only Mr Attenborough spoiling everyone's tea with his wildlife programmes, showing animals killing each other and close-ups of big cats with blood-soaked faces. It was either his programme or Songs of Praise held at churches with standing room only, its congregation swelled for the week all trying to sing and smile while following the camera, pretending they knew the words.

So, I called the family's home, and the telephone was answered by a very polite lady who asked me how she could help. I told her who I was, and the story verbatim then asked if they would be interested in the letter written by her ancestor to my father 43 years ago. After a slight pause she handed me over to her husband, the son of the gentleman who wrote the letter and, far from being disinterested, said he would love to see the letter.

Over a period of around 18 months, we kept in contact by phone and email, he would dictate to his secretary what he wanted to say because he could not use a computer. He was also by this time himself getting on a bit and was interested in what was going on at the churchyard and even asked how he could help financially. Well, what could I say, at the time I was not in need of money because most of the work was just manual. So, I told him that at that moment I didn't require any funding, kicking myself as I said it but it was the best thing to say right then and we agreed to discuss it when it was time.

I sent him the monthly parish magazine. He enjoyed reading about what went on in the village. In one addition he asked me to give his address to a lady who had written an article about the place she once lived, that he himself had lived in the same area. So, I contacted the lady, Josie was her name, one of the many interesting people in the village. She was pleased to correspond, and I was glad I managed to put them in touch with each other, something I would do for many other people who wished to talk with others regarding things from the past. I also sent him a full lineage of our ancestors that Shannon Abbott did for him. He was a thoroughly decent man, and we discussed his father and who, after the First World War, in 1922 worked as a jobbing builder in the Harefield area and then Ruislip. He was elected as councillor to Ruislip and Northwood District Council and was instrumental in persuading the council to rename West End Road from Ruislip Station to Midcroft as an extension of the High Street. His father had purchased for a song the whole frontage on the east side of the road, from Brick Wall Lane to Midcroft which he then sold off following the renaming at a substantial profit.

I had no idea where all the places were that he referred to, but it was interesting that his father was a councillor. Having first got his foot in the door, he then went on to, if you like, feather his own nest. Later he also went on to build the Westminster Bank on the high street followed by the Catholic church. There was a lot of controversy when his father was awarded the contract to build the Catholic church because he was not Catholic. However, the funds for the building were being provided by Miss Warrender, a member of a very wealthy family, and owners of the Highgrove Estate at Eastcote and Miss Warrender insisted that the contract be awarded to his father.

So, I was beginning to see how the made-up stories in the letter had indeed helped his father climb the ladder of success. As well as the bank and the Catholic church, he also built a house for himself that he called Beaulieu, the same as the house he wrote the letter from in Salisbury, Wiltshire. Interestingly he named two houses the same. By 1930 the young gardener's son from Upham, Hampshire, set up a company that would become the forerunner of all his subsequent Prowting activities. In the following 11 years he went on to build Ruislip Post Office, Hillingdon Hospital, Potters Bar Telephone Exchange, 24 flats at West End Road Ruislip, The George public house in Ruislip, and the Grey Stoke public house in Ealing, as well as other ministry of works private projects.

It was a remarkable story. I was later sent the autobiography notes of my cousin; he was keen to know what I thought. Most of what he told me that I had written was contained in the autobiography, so of course I said he should write more. I did send him the original letter after copying it for myself. We talked about what was in the first ten lines as being spot on. I did say I didn't think that the rest of it was correct, I wanted to say I disapproved about lying about your family links. But I didn't because it was just a personal opinion, also it could be that the first time he had seen what his father had made up was when I sent him the letter. All he said about the freeman of London stuff, and links with the family of Jane Austen etc., was in a soft voice "No it was not correct" and we never talked about it again.

In January 2018 I had an email to say he hoped to come to the churchyard in the spring. His grandson Kevin was to bring him, so I arranged with the family that owned Winters Hill Hall to show him where his Grandfather Alfred was a gardener all those years ago, before taking his family to live at East Wood Hay. I would also show him where the family lived as well as the church and its churchyard along with George and Susan Matilda's graves in the churchyard. Then about a month before he was due to come down, I had an email from his secretary to tell me that he had sadly passed away.

So, we never got together, nor did we finish what our fathers began. It was such a shame, I didn't meet him or had any idea what he looked like. I was just glad we talked and communicated through his secretary. He was a very wealthy man but he was also a very nice person and that was more important to me. He liked what I was doing and would have helped but we never got that far, I have never asked any of his family if he told them it was his intention to do so or if he had put anything in place for the project. I would not anyway, if something was supposed to happen in that respect then it surely would in time, and if he had thought about helping it may not be the wish of the family who may have known nothing of what we discussed together. I suppose the concept of doing something like saving something while important to us is not really everyone's cup of tea. Unless of course you see what's been done.

When people arrive at the churchyard, they cannot immediately see what's been done, however when they do see activity has taken place but still not completely sure it makes them curious enough to find out. If I am there and conversation begins then they are hooked, so without seeing what's gone on I could never expect anyone to be interested in funding something that would seem impossible because I didn't understand it myself. I have done it single handed with a spade and a long-handled shovel I got for £13 pounds from Amazon, a rake from my daughter's farm, and a barrow supplied by the church, and it took me four years to move the largest pile of earth you have ever seen.

Come on, who is going to believe that, unless you see it or photos of each stage? But I thought funding would one day turn up but in what form or from what direction I had no idea. All I could do was what I was already doing and wait for what the old gypsy lady told me many years ago, that something beautiful would take place. She said it would find me and I must admit that sometimes I wished it would hurry up.

Chapter 19
Back to the Project

So, after the disappointment of losing a cousin I continued with the project. Adrian Abbott had by this time brought back more of the cleaned numbers and as before they looked impressive. Even the ones that we had to piece together to photograph, they too looked fine. The broken ones had all come from row (C), so what we did was to place the numbers from that row back into the ground, and again mark the spot with a wooden grave marker as we had done with all the graves we had found up until then. The numbers that were still intact I kept in the boxes because whenever it would be possible to mark the graves with proper stone markers, I intended to place the numbers next to them, but that seemed a long way off at the time. So having got as far as the grave of Mr William Primmer in grave number 12 in row (A), it was time to work out who rested in row (B). I could be very flexible with this research, most of which I could do at home in the evening. This flexibility gave me the freedom to take each day as it came, if I had to get things ready for a funeral or had to work with someone who wanted to find a family grave then I had the time. There was grass cutting, as well, that needed to be kept in good order so nothing I had to do required me to work that hard as I had done when clearing the spoil. As long as I had all the records to refer to then I could work at home or in the churchyard, so all of a sudden the work became a pleasure and not a chore.

I still had the PCC to worry about, that was always at the back of my mind. I made sure that nothing I did could be considered as assuming too much. Something that had been levelled at me early on, I had no idea who by and I was not really that interested but I kept my nose clean so to speak. Because sooner or later I would have to ask them again about removing the two intrusive cedar trees that grew from graves, given it was already collectively considered it was just me being dogmatic and wanting the trees moved just for the sake of it and not because they were growing from people's graves.

So, keeping my head down and making the churchyard presentable would, I hope, sway some of the unknown members of the PCC to vote in favour of having the trees moved and not dig their collective heels in and make things difficult for everyone. After all, they ran the show and having cleared everything away from on and around the headstones at the west end of the churchyard, many people's questions when they came in was when will 'They', meaning the PCC, move the trees. It was going to be a bone of contention that was for sure, and I could wait because the ball, as they say, was firmly in their court.

Starting with number 13 in row (B) this was another family affair, rather like the Primmer graves in row (A), further proof that families picked the area they wanted to be buried in the churchyard. It was the resting place of brothers Harry and Robert Charles Cowdrey who had been buried one in front of the other. Harry died in 1933 aged 33 years and Robert Charles in 1945 aged 55. The interesting thing about the Cowdrey family graves was they were on the main grass path under the south hedge row and had not been covered in spoil. They were also from a much later date than graves in the area just to the right of them going north where I had moved all the spoil. Behind Harry and Robert Charles was the grave of their brother Wilfred and his wife Violet Ann. They didn't pass away till the 1980s, in Wilfred's case 1980 aged 86 years then Violet followed six years later aged 88 years.

In the church burial records, they are recorded as being in a double grave number seven-two-seven. Double graves began in the 50s so it could get confusing when looking for graves. If number seven-two-seven is actually behind number 13 at the west end of the churchyard, when it should be if following numbers numerically and the burial dates in the records, that grave should have been at the northeast of the churchyard but trying to work out the numbers in relation to where a grave should be was one of the biggest challenges we faced.

Families selecting areas to be buried in is fine, but the church would not or could not be bothered to map out the churchyard to show this. There was no map of any kind and I had asked frequently, insisting there would be one. All churches had them but again my request fell upon deaf ears, the determination by unknown members of this PCC to obstruct me at every turn was nothing short of vicious. A spiteful act designed to halt progress, but in fact they only succeeded in shooting themselves in the foot because sooner or later if there was a map it would have to be displayed where it could be seen by the public who had every right to see it.

The church and its churchyard belong to the many and not the few, so the closed-shop attitude in time would be banished and just like the money lenders in the market place an interesting biblical story. Their days were certainly numbered and would have to embrace the wider public if they wanted to be taken seriously, shape up or ship out I think the term is. In time I hoped everything would turn out for the good of the churchyard; each grave we could identify and who rested within it gave us more information. If living relations could be found, we had more chance of help if we needed it. Not manual labour but from relatives' own professions we would in time need legal advice, new tools, people to go and research in the archives of Winchester. If we had found and identified where people's relatives had been laid to rest, the amount of people only too willing to assist us was heart-warming and to have that sort of backup energised me and the project I had started. I never thought of how the project would develop and snowball, no one had a title that was irrelevant, the same vigour was instilled in everyone, and everyone always said yes to anything that was in the best interest of the village church and its revitalised churchyard.

Continuing along row (B) in grave number 14 rested a member of the White Family. Mrs White, with no headstone or first name recorded to help identify who she was or what family she was connected to. However, from the date and year of the burial no other Whites had passed away that year, and it did take time trying to work out who Mrs White was. At times we had to keep some on hold and continue with the next grave's occupants and that was fine, there was no rush. For all I knew, I could have had a line of spirits lining up, all itching to be found after their imposed exile but as with any cue they would have to be patient a little longer. After all, I only had one pair of hands and I was as keen to know who they were as much as they wanted to be found.

I also found myself talking to them when they had been found. Not about anything in particular and quietly so not to be seen as having lost the plot by passers-by. They could have heard talking from behind the south hedge row that was just high enough so people could not look over unless on horseback but then I would hear them coming and was able to wish them good day.

Keeping my reputation intact and not be considered barmy if overheard talking with headstones, one's whole reputation could be ruined in one fell swoop if Bush Radio reported that the sexton was bonkers!

Moving on to number 15, Mr Hugh Charles Croswell – he was a journey man bricklayer and a member of one of the many Crosswells at Durley. The family had built lots of the big homes at Durley including the Methodist Church and they were very important members of the community. Many of them were Methodists and as well as their day job, some were Methodist preachers. Given that this whole area had been neglected by members of the Church of England, I had the terrible feeling that this could be why.

Conflict was rife in the past and old habits die hard, so I was interested to try and find out how many dwellers at the west end of the churchyard were indeed Methodists. So, when finding out who was in each grave if it was possible, I would try and find out if they were Methodist or Church of England. I looked online and apparently many attempts had been made to try and reunite the Methodist Church with the Church of England, however it's been the latter who have rejected such attempts for whatever reason. To be honest I didn't really care, all that concerned me was when people are dead, they should be respected and judged on what they did when they lived. Settling old scores when a person has passed over is hardly a respectful way to behave.

But remember the problems Richard Hickley had with the Church and what they did to him. If they treated old Rich with contempt then neglecting a few Methodists would not bother them and probably vice versa. I could be opening a big can of worms but being the seeker of truth and justice for anyone treated unfairly no matter what denomination, they supported things needed to be put right and, as Lonnie Donegan sings, 'It's a Hard Road Dead or Alive'.

Grave number 16 was occupied by Mr George Cowdrey and his wife Mrs Kate Cowdrey née Houghton. They had a small dairy farm at Job's Corner and as well as running his farm, Mr Cowdrey also worked as a woodsman at the Greenwood Estate. The Greenwood Estate's land once abutted the churchyard and was owned by Colonel Sir William Jenner 1st Baronet G.C.B.Q.H.P. F.R.C.P. an English physician primarily known for having discovered the distinction between typhus and typhoid. He was also Queen Victoria's physician and his whole family rest within the churchyard at Durley. When he died on the 16th of December 1898 aged 88, attendees at his funeral were representatives of H.R.H Queen Victoria, H.R.H the Prince of Wales, the Duchess of Albany, widow of Prince Leopold Duke of Albany and youngest son of Queen Victoria. The Colonel was a very important man in the village, his own capacity for hard work made him a difficult employer, expecting the same commitment from people in his employment. It was said he took umbrage easily and showed no tolerance for other people's opinions; he was by all accounts a miserable so and so. However, I am sure he would have been more courteous when attending to Queen Victoria.

His grave plot has never been looked after as it should be. Mrs Batchelor told me the story about when her father, along with other men, had been sent to the church to carry out a few urgent jobs. Whilst they were at the churchyard, they began to tend the Colonel's family grave plots but when the Colonel turned up to see why the men had been so long away from Greenwood he gave them all a dressing down for wasting time. The grave was never touched again by any of the farm workers.

George Cowdrey also had a tentative link to Queen Victoria. As a young 22-year-old he served in the Royal Marines including time on the Royal Yacht Osborne. Another sad coincidence was that Mrs Kate Cowdrey and Queen Victoria were both carriers of the disease haemophilia. Queen Victoria had passed on the disease to three of her children, Leopold the late Duke of Albany, and daughters Alice and Beatrice were carriers. Beatrice's daughter married into the Spanish royal family and passed on the gene to the male heir to the Spanish throne.

Alice also had a carrier, daughter Alex. She became Empress Alexandra when she married Russia's Tzar Nicholas in 1894. Their son was born in 1904 and named Alexis. He inherited the disease from his mother, and the young Alexis was treated for bleeds by the mysterious Rasputin, known as a holy man with powers to heal. The story of the royal family's battle with haemophilia is told in an interesting book titled Nicholas and Alexandra by Robert Massie, who himself was the father of a son with the disease. It seems that back in the 1800s little was known about haemophilia and while the stories can be followed regarding the more powerful families who were touched by the disease, it must have been terrible for country people like Kate Cowdrey who had the disease but almost certainly didn't know. Kate and George Cowdrey had eight daughters and four sons so you can never be sure if the disease remerged further on in her lineage.

In grave number 17 was Mrs Florence Windsor née Symonds and the wife of Mr Tom Windsor. Florence's headstone was the first one I reached when cutting down the small bushes and bracken that clung to this lovely cross. Its inscription I will always remember as pausing to read it said "They Will Be Done" and back then I thought to myself that yes, it certainly would be. If I am honest, at the time I had no idea what I was letting myself in for if it had said "They Has Been Done" I could have left and saved myself a lot of time and expense, but I was caught in the grip of these spiritual moments when things happened with no rhyme or reason.

Once the spirits that had waited a lifetime to be discovered and got their hooks in me, I wasn't going anywhere soon. The coincidental happenings they placed in front of me were like hurdles in a race against time, the spirits knew I was old and would eventually be too tired out to do much at all in the way of digging. They were eager to keep dangling this historical carrot before me, somehow knowing I would follow. And it would take four years before I was able to say those four simple words, 'They Has Been Done' as regards moving the spoil from the west end area. With many of the inscriptions I still had to uncover from beneath the dirt and grime that covered the headstone, I was sure there would be more profound messages to set me thinking. Challenging me to work out what the person sending it wanted me to understand, it had been important enough for the incumbent to instruct such an inscription so I felt obliged that in time I would read each one.

Florence Windsor died at the young age of 31 years, Tom Windsor survived Florence by some 39 years and he died on 10th December 1953 aged 70. Again, I could find no record of where he was buried or his grave number, I would like to think that he would have been next to Florence – there was enough room, and the dowsing rods did move when Adrian walked across the space between her grave. Also, in the next grave number 18 were Tom's grandparents Henry Smith and Harriet née May. So, even more reason to think that Tom's grave would be between his wife's and grandparents. Tom's parents, Emily and George Windsor, made my assumption even more likely when I discovered that they rested in grave number 19. Emily Windsor, Tom's mother, was also Mrs Batchelor's great-grandmother and Henry and Harriet's Smith's daughter. After being widowed losing Tom's father George aged 40, the whole family occupied a house called Rodlands that Henry Smith had built opposite Parsonage Lane on Mays Corner.

The house was on a sharp left-hand bend, and I remembered as a child that the bend seemed to take ages to negotiate when travelling in Uncle George Wilber's old Austin 7. We would all lean over to left when going to Uncle's mother's small holding, and then on the way home we had to lean over to the right when momentarily Uncle George's head seemed to go out of the open car window as we did so, before the car righted itself and Uncle George returned to his more natural driving position. The sharp bend at Mays Corner remains, so too does Rodlands, but it is now much bigger. Over the years I have seen it grow from the double-fronted cottage it once was. It also has a small annex, the home of Gwen Houghton. She and Tom Windsor were related in some way and Gwen Houghton being Methodist, I did wonder if Tom had also been connected to that church. It could be why no record of his burial had been recorded by the rectors at Durley church, the same as Shoemaker Bob.

If I found proof of one more unrecorded Methodist burial it could be there was indeed some sort of conflict between the Methodists and the Church of England, because by using three to determine anything takes away the notion of a coincidence and gives rise to something more sinister going on by the powers that be, who back then did seem to be the role model that down the years collective narrow-minded councils had followed.

As I have said, in grave number 19 rested Tom's parents, George and Emily Windsor. Both Emily and Tom's wife Florence worked in the service of the Reverend Mr John Jenkin's at the rectory in Greenwood Lane. Florence was the parlour maid at the rectory and Emily the cook. A fine photograph was in the things given to me by Mrs Batchelor, it was taken in the garden of the rectory depicting three servants with the rector. Also, along with the photo was a postcard sent from Bishops Waltham to Emily on her birthday from her mother in 1905.

So, the closeness of many families at Durley all together in life continued after their demise and with each person I found and identified I began to develop a story that had waited for so long to be told. I took much pride in the fact that it was I who had been chosen in a spiritual way. It was hard to understand and best not to try but just go with the flow.

Further along row (B) at rest in grave number 20 was a man called Peter Houghton, born in 1824 and died in 1896 aged 72. His wife Caroline Houghton née Churcher, was in fact related to George Churcher, the man that had died at Haslar Hospital and whose wife Florence occupied grave number seven, more family connections it seemed. Peter and Caroline had 11 children – four daughters and seven sons. Three of their daughters, Esther, Caroline and Elizabeth, all married and moved away from Durley, however the fourth daughter, Kate, became Mrs Kate Cowdrey who was in grave number eight. The seven sons, Peter, Richard Charles, Harry, Edwin, Frank, Jess and Wilfred, I was shocked to find, had all died young. Peter at 30, Frank at 23 (which for the time was not that unusual) but then I found that Richard Charles died when he was nine years old, Harry at 15, Edwin four, Jess at five and Wilfred at 19 years old. It must have been difficult for Peter and Caroline Houghton to deal with the loss of all of their sons and I became convinced the boys may have been victims of the disease haemophilia, I knew their sister Kate was a carrier so it must have been one of their parents who handed the disease on to the boys and back in the 1800s I was not sure what, if anything, would be known about the disease by the average farm workers.

I wanted to find out so I would try and get the death certificate of one of the seven sons. I had always been reluctant to buy such things from Ancestry because it was a sure-fire way to lose money. However, on this occasion I considered it important. I didn't do it straight away, but it was one of the things on my list of things to do. I also found in the photographs Gwen Houghton gave to Adrian a nice photograph of Peter and Caroline smartly dressed in the clothes of the time. Peter had an impressive full beard, if I had not known they had lost all of their sons I would have commented on the fact their persona looked somewhat melancholy. However, having got the information I considered them brave to even try to conjure up any expression at all.

In the grave number 21 was a child, Fanny Elizabeth Houghton who died on 30th July 1877 aged just four months old. Baby Fanny Elizabeth Houghton was the daughter of Frank and his wife Fanny Houghton née Roberts. She moved to Durley from St Germain in Cornwall. She and Frank also had a son named Frank after his father. Frank Senior was the son of Peter and Caroline Houghton who died at the age of 23. Frank Junior was a year old when his father died on the 10th of February 1883, and more tragedy befell young Frank Junior when his mother passed away just three months after her husband on the 9th of May 1883. Young Frank went to live with his grandparents Peter and Caroline Houghton and his parents were buried next to each other. His mother in grave number 22 next to her baby daughter and Frank Senior in number 23. Then in grave number 24 was Frank Senior's brother Wilfred, another early death at the age of 19. Wilfred's cast iron number was the one I found when digging towards Florence Churcher née May's headstone early on in the project, so I decided to get Wilfred's death certificate.

I needed to know what it was that was killing these young men Wilfred died on the 20th of December 1886. Even looking through records finding information of what had happened to this family was, I wouldn't say upsetting, but made me a little angry, I can't explain why. Each one I found was one grave nearer to the end of row (B) and with four to go it didn't get any easier because in grave number 25 I discovered that young Frank Junior had himself passed away also at the tender age of 19. If I had not already ordered the death certificate of Wilfred Houghton then I would have got young Frank's, because, don't ask me why, I have no idea. I just wanted to do something for him, I suppose that's how I felt. Now I knew where they all were, walking in that area was completely different; there was no headstones, just a wooden stake for the time being with the grave number and most of the numbers had faded somewhat, but I knew them all off by heart as to where they rested.

As I moved on ever nearer to the end of row (B) I found in grave number

26, Peter Houghton's widow Caroline. She passed away on the 8th of February 1898, two years after Peter. She was 73. They had both had a horrid time of it and lived to witness each heart-breaking moment as they buried all their sons, grandson and granddaughter. I did wonder if the first graves in row (A) with no name, only numbers, could have been Peter and Caroline's youngest children, but I think it was wishful thinking on my part. I was hoping they may all be near to each other but in reality, I had no idea where they were. However, they were there somewhere in the lost woodland at the west end of the churchyard, and their spirits live in this story. Some of their graves can be seen by living relatives who would, I was sure, eventually come.

The last three graves in row (B) began with number 27. This was the resting place of Mr Arthur James Eades. He died on the 28th of June 1913 aged 58 and after the information I had uncovered regarding the Houghton family, Arthur James Eades brought back some normality to proceedings. I had felt as if I was never going to read anything normal again, so I was pleased when Arthur came into the story. I was sad he was dead of course but he did lift me from the melancholy mood I was in as I researched row (B). It had been like a long dark tunnel but now, almost at the end, Arthur seemed to brighten things up. He had a simple life, it seems, born in Compton, Hampshire. Arthur worked in the timber yard in the village. Durley had one of the main sawmills around at the time and employed many people from Durley and surrounding villages and was probably work that brought him to Durley. He lived for a time with his grandmother, Ann Littlefield, on her farm at Twyford.. Eventually he married his wife Julia. She was born at Hove in Sussex and worked as a domestic servant. Arthur and Julia had been married for 30 years when he passed away in 1913. I could find no record of Julia in Durley after that. The couple had no children as far as I could tell and Julia may have moved back to her home town, I hoped to find in time some form of record of her having done so just to square things up record-wise.

The two last graves in row (B) numbers 28 and 29 had no record of who rested within and in a way, it was good to have a couple of spares, to coin a phrase. What I mean by that is, if I had not done my homework properly and got something wrong or another record emerged from another source it could be everyone from the last headstone of Emily and George Windsor would need to shift up one place or maybe two. If more than two turned up, I would be in trouble, because back then no double graves existed so there would be no room on top, if you get my drift. Sometimes a couple were buried one in front of the other and we had several of those, but they would be almost joined seamless, in fact as if they wanted to be as close to each other in death as they had been when they walked God's earth. But in the area of row (B) there was no such graves, mainly at least from the Windsor's grave onward towards the north hedgerow. Most of the people were too young to have built up such a desire to need to be with someone. Death robbed them of the chance to love and embrace life; we can only hope they found it in the spirit world, that's why I speak of the spirits, not because I am bonkers, but it's the only way I can cope with farming the dead. So, I create a world of spirits where no one is spoken of in a past tense; they are within many hearts and minds and at no time are they ever without.

Moving on, the row (C) was the row where we found all the broken numbers and the plinth that matched the headstone placed next to the Churcher headstone in row (A) and while there were 23 graves in row (C), only one had the broken headstone halfway across the row, and only two other names were recorded buried one in front of the other on the path under the south hedge row. Number 31 was Daisy Caroline Freemantle née Cowdrey, daughter of George and Kate Cowdrey née Houghton. Daisy died at Winchester in 1964 aged 70 and was returned to Durley where her plot had been booked years in advance of her death. According to the burial records she should be in plot seven-four-seven at the east end of the churchyard. But the Cowdrey's occupied the southwest corner of the churchyard, and it was named Job's Corner by locals, the area in the village where most of the people buried in that corner lived. Then resting in grave number 32 we have Peter Frank Freemantle and I am not sure if he was Daisy's son but he was another victim of haemophilia.

He ran the local barber's shop in nearby Bishops Waltham, an unusual job for a haemophiliac and dangerous if he cut himself. One of his relations told me he would take Peter to the hospital for regular blood transfusions. These transfusions worked for Peter; he had more energy going home than he did travelling to Winchester to receive new blood. Peter Frank Freemantle died in 1987 aged 58. The only other record of people buried in row (C) was number 47, Abraham May and his wife Sarah Ann née Steen. Sarah died aged 41 in 1864. Abraham outlived his wife by 40 years and died aged 78 in 1904; their headstone was cleaned and placed back at the head of their grave. I can't think of a reason why there were no other names to go with the broken numbers on graves in row (C), just three names in that row is a tragedy.

Chapter 20
The Plot Thickens

After the death of Thomas Scard MA, the London Pall Mall Gazette informed its readers that the vacant situation worth £500 a year which is a gift of the Bishop of Winchester passed to the Reverend Mr Richard Ferguson MA by induction mandate on 10th May 1878. The presentation of the deed of Durley vicarage on 8th April 1878, was issued by the Reverend Mr Augustus Selwyn Lord Bishop of Litchfield and former Lord Bishop of New Zealand. The Reverend Augustus was well documented in the Hampshire Telegraph as being a famous champion of the poor and working-class.

Well, I wonder where he had been hiding. Forgive me for being a tiny bit cynical, these clergymen love to heap praise on each other do they not, remember how they praised their reverend friend Mr Thomas Scard, and a right wolf in sheep's clothing he turned out to be. If this alleged famous champion of the poor and working-class was the role model Thomas Scard followed, then it was not difficult to see why the poor and working-class people had such a hard time of it. However, we must trust till betrayed, I suppose, and cannot tar them all with same brush. History would reveal in time if the Reverend Mr Richard Ferguson would be any different, so I will give the new rector the benefit of the doubt.

Adrian Abbott was looking into records at Winchester regarding the alterations carried out to the church sometime after the Reverend Richard Ferguson had taken over. So, he decided to look into the history of the rector both before and while he was incumbent at Durley's Church of the Holy Cross. To be honest, I was all 'rectored' out after researching the Reverend Thomas Scard, reading about him completely drained me at times.

The summer was progressing well at the churchyard. Plenty of grass-cutting needed to be done because we had few weddings that year. We also had several funerals including one for Ms Gwen Houghton. I had never seen the lady, but as I said before I had heard a lot about her from various people who told me that she was pleased someone had started to clean up the churchyard. She would have known if we were related because her great-grandmother was Elizabeth Prowting, and she did send someone to the churchyard to take my photograph, not because I was a handsome beast but to see what I looked like!

Gwen Houghton was supposed to be buried next to her parents, Jacob and Alice Houghton, in the northwest corner of the churchyard. It was taken as read as in other areas of the churchyard that Gwen Houghton's wish would be carried out. However, her plot was used in 1965, and out of respect to the people in the village who were around at the time I am not going to write about who rests within that grave. Only to say that the special one's grave like all others is checked out every day on my way around the churchyard to make sure all is well. So, Gwen Houghton is buried next door but one to her parents. The verger, Mrs Taylor, asked if we could check out the area behind Gwen's parents grave and have her grave there. We called Adrian Abbott to come and use the dowsing rods to see if it was possible.

We had to do this because that area was at one time all grave mounds and, believe me, I am not complaining about the PCC again, but the decisions of the past still affect the current layout today, as the PCC decided to take out all the grave mounds some years ago because they thought it would be easier to cut the grass. This didn't go down very well in the village, and I have to say I don't blame the villagers who still talk about it today. The people that took out the mounds also lost most of the cast iron numbers so no one had any idea where anyone was buried. The other thing was after taking out the mounds they let the grass grow again right up to your nether regions. So, it was a waste of time and energy and caused unnecessary stress for the local people worried about their relatives' graves.

A few days before we dug the grave, Adrian Abbott came and walked over to the area at the back of Gwen's parents and there was a grave already there. We worked out it was the grave of a lady called Alice Winifred Oakley who died in 1964. So, Gwen Houghton was to be buried next door but one to her parents. It was on the Bank Holiday Monday when Chris the gravedigger turned up. It was a fine day so we didn't have to rush. It was a single depth grave and would not take long with the machine, then at midday two people turned up out of the blue asking if I could help find their relative's grave. The person they were looking for was, believe it or not, Alice Winifred Oakey, whose grave we would have opened if Adrian had not walked the area.

The people were impressed that we could show them the grave straight away but if it had not been for Adrian, they could have been introduced to Alice Winifred Oakley in person. It was a close shave and could have been embarrassing for the church and the people who took the mounds out, and by doing so lost a third of the village's history in one fell swoop. Some of them come in from time to time but keep quiet about their involvement; it was many years ago that it happened but as in all villages no one ever forgets or forgives such an inhuman act.

Gwen Houghton's funeral went well. It was a fine sunny day and the mourners were in no hurry to go. So, we reinstated the earth manually; it was a nice thing to do for Gwen, I know what a difference she made history-wise, and we would be poorer without her contribution. She is part of the history herself now and is at peace in the last grave in the northwest corner of the churchyard number (840).

After completing the research into rows (A), (B) and (C), I began looking into row (D). This row was on the edge of the wooded area and had never been covered in spoil but left to the elements. All the headstones had become filthy and covered in ivy that I had cut at the base of each one when I first discovered them, and over time the ivy had died. So, I began to remove it to clean the headstones, each one a pleasure to work on. In row (D), only six of the 21 graves had a headstone, the rest just had the residue of visible mounds. Each afternoon after a morning cutting grass, I spent time cleaning the headstones and revealing the very moving inscriptions. Messages from the past that gave an insight as to what the incumbent believed in respect of their religious beliefs. A line from a prayer hymn, or a reading from the good book, each headstone had something like that and after being cleaned up brought many an admiring comment as to how good they looked.

The start of row (D) began once more under the south hedgerow. The graves again from a later date and in the burial records were recorded as grave number 415. But they will be in fact numbers 54 and 55 when a new map of the churchyard is created. The double kerbstone grave is occupied by Mr Walter Hounsham and his wife Annie née Churcher. She died in 1936 aged 65, followed eight years later by Walter in 1944 aged 86.

In a small grave next to them is their three-year old granddaughter Barbara Kathleen Hounsham who died in 1938. Some people remember what happened when they were children and now in their senior years often walk over and pay their respects to Barbara Kathleen Hounsham. Two fine oak trees separate the Hounsham graves from the rest of row (D), and to the right of the trees looking west is grave number 56. In the records, only the number identified this grave, however, a lady who had come to the churchyard on a pilgrimage pointed out this was the grave of her mum's brother William Heath who died aged 13 months. The lady said she would never forget the place of his grave, having visited it many times over the years with her mother. The child had died in 1916. So based on what the lady told me, I recorded the name of William Heath to grave number 56.

Moving on to grave numbers 57 and 58, this was a double plot and must have had a headstone at one time but only its plinth remains. It is twice the size of a normal one but there were no names recorded, and I wondered what happened to the actual headstone. Grave number 59 and 60 is the family Carpenter's plot, Henrietta Kate née Hankin died aged 39 in 1891. The headstone is probably one of the best in the churchyard, made of fine white marble and at the top of this beautiful marble headstone are fine carvings of trailing wildflowers, obviously carved by one of the finest stonemasons at the time. Henrietta's husband, James Carpenter, was a thatcher by profession and was the grandson of master thatcher William Primmer who rests in grave number 12 in row (A). James Carpenter outlived his wife by 31 years and passed away aged 81 in 1922. Two fine photos of James can be seen in John Bosworth's book, one of James working in the fields at his farm and the other a head and shoulder portrait of this rugged country gentleman. The couple's headstone was once surrounded by railings, the four corners of this large plot in front and to the sides of the impressive headstone has the residue of corner stonework that has been broken away to take out the railings, probably in the Second World War as many of them were.

However, outside of the west door of the church are graves with railings that were never touched. Charles Whale, a wealthy farmer, and his family are buried there. He also has a plaque inside the church, a tribute to the man who did a lot for the village. Also, another wealthy gentleman farmer, Mr Richard Gibbs, a bachelor who rented and farmed 323 acres at Netherhill Farm at Durley, employing eight men and six boys. Mr Gibbs came from the Isle of Wight where his family farmed some 600 acres run by his five siblings – three sisters, Ann, Frances and Margaret, along with brothers Robert and George. The interesting thing about the Gibbs family was none of them seemed to have married. They had been devoted farmers all born in Bowcome cottage at Carisbrooke on the Isle of Wight. Richard Gibbs left a fine sum of money to the church when he died for the upkeep of this impressive plot. The only problem with that request was the money left for the upkeep of his plot was the responsibility of the rector at the time and guess who that was? Why, the Reverend Thomas Scard MA.

So, Richard Gibbs had no chance of his plot being looked after, he would have been better off flushing the money down the toilet than trust the Revd Thomas Scard who we know had already fleeced Abraham Edwards, another hard-working farmer. I am sure Thomas Scard praised the Lord when Richard Gibbs' money dropped into his lap, manna from heaven indeed. Of course, the Revd Thomas Scard and his good wife have railings around their plot. So, when the church had to decide what railings to give for the Second World War effort they took apart James and Henrietta Carpenter's fine marble plot. Another example of out of sight out of mind, given by this time, the Carpenter's plot was lost in the woods. More proof, if you needed it, of the 'them and us' situation.

Moving on to grave number 61, occupied by another member of the Carpenter family, Frederick Henry Carpenter, the son of James and Henrietta. Frederick passed away in 1926 aged 40 and beside him in grave number 62 rests Susan Game née Chandler. She passed away in 1890. No other family members seem to have been buried at Durley. Adrian Abbott came up with some facts, regarding the Game family that are important from an historical point of view, but why was Susan buried alone?

Adrian said she was born in Bishopstoke, Hampshire, in 1828. She married James Game at South Stoneham, Hampshire. James was born in Haydon Dorset near Shaftsbury, and in 1881 they lived at Water Lane Farm in Ashton that was just down the road from the Robin Hood public house in Durley. In 1881 they lived at Warblington in Sussex where James was a farm bailiff, then in 1891 the couple moved back to Bishopstoke with their two sons. James was described as a dealer, but there was no reason for why Susan was buried alone at Durley. She would have been entitled to be laid to rest there because she did live in Durley and I believe that Bishopstoke came under the same ecclesiastical umbrella, Bishopstoke not having a church at the time could be the reason. This information may not seem important to us; however, it may be to someone looking for Susan Game née Chandler's final resting place.

Graves number 63 and 64 we have William and Mary Denham née Lamond. William died in 1888 aged 75 and Mary followed in 1908 aged 73. They are buried side by side with one headstone. The inscriptions are a work of art carried out by two different stonemasons but equally skilled in their art. Then in grave numbers 65 and 66 is the resting place of Mr James Houghton and his wife Harriett née Denham. She was the sister of William Denham from grave number 63. James Houghton, also known locally as 'Skinny Jim', was a woodsman and farmed 25 acres of plantation. He planted hundreds of trees and was the man who would start the Durley sawmills, a business that grew and gave employment to many local villagers in the future.

James Houghton and the sawmills are well documented in John Bosworth's book, Skinny Jim was also a Methodist preacher. Before Durley had its own Methodist church, he would preach in people's houses and in one of the pictures he can be seen smartly dressed holding the good book. He looks impressive, clearly a man of importance. James Houghton died aged 85 in 1890, whilst wife Harriett passed away ten years later in 1900 aged 85. Their graves are side by side and had been lost in the woods. A man who had the vision and drive to help put Durley on the map, should not have been left neglected in that way.

The next six graves in row (D) from number 67 to 72 were all without headstones, just numbers in the records with no names. It was also the area where the great cedar trees were, with their intrusive roots still covering many of the graves like giant hands whose fingers seemed to have grabbed the soil around them and would not let go. It would be possible to cut the roots down just below ground level and make them invisible once the trees were taken down, then let nature take its course and regenerate the area. However, the removal of the trees seemed way off at that time. The PCC voted against taking them out at every meeting, but not all the members were given the reasons for my wanting them taken from on the graves. As I said, they thought I was being dogmatic and just wanted them out of the way to win some battle of sorts. After one meeting, I was told by one of the wardens that she thought the people at the west end of the churchyard died a long time ago, so it didn't matter about them and that most of the PCC liked the trees. It was after that comment I never asked again but took a leaf from Richard Hickley's book and looked into taking the PCC to the Ecclesiastical court. It was a battle I would win whenever I wanted to and, in the end, it was just sport to me.

The PCC did make an effort and had a tree firm come and cut them down, however the firm's instructions were to only cut them in half. The trees were dead, they would never regenerate from that form of pollarding to be carried out. Anyway, I still went ahead with taking the PCC to the Ecclesiastical court using the rule book to back me up. It would then be a question of waiting. So, I carried on with the research as to who rested at the west end of the churchyard.

The task of finding who was in the graves around the trees would be difficult; you could use Harriett and Skinny Jim Houghton's headstone as a reference to work from by their burial date, but you would need to have another headstone further along the same row. As well as finding out from the burial records dates of people who died after Skinny Jim. We already had his death date of 1890 on the headstone, and given people wanted to be buried with or near their family, chances are that these graves would be occupied by either a male Houghton and his family or a female Houghton that married out and returned when she died.

So, it would be very difficult to find out who rests in these graves but not impossible. There was a picture on one of the ancestry sites of a headstone that was no longer there in row (D) behind Susan Matilda's headstone in row (E). It is just visible in the photo and from the burial record it was the grave of Mr John Dangerfield, in grave number 73. He passed away in 1925 aged 71. So, you would need to find out how many people linked to the Houghton's died between 1890 and 1925, and if you waited long enough maybe something would turn up.

Talking about something turning up, Wilfred Houghton's death certificate finally arrived and haemophilia was not the cause of death, but pleuritis and exhaustion after 14 months of suffering. Wilfred died on the 13th of December 1886 and his grave number 24 was the first one I found under the spoil in line with the Churcher grave.

It could be that spiritually I was supposed to find his number first, a reminder to me how lucky I had been to get through the experience of these dreadful chest conditions we shared. Wilfred had been buried twice; once with love and affection by his relations then a second time when covered in spoil by the complacent individuals with a complete lack of respect for the likes of this young man whose death had been witnessed by his father. One of seven sons' deaths the Houghton family had to endure, and then with the mark of an X, Mr Peter Houghton signed to confirm he witnessed the death and understood the description of the condition that killed his son. The man could not write, and chances are he could not read either, so would only know the sound of the disease when pronounced. It would have been difficult for him to pronounce exactly the cause of Wilfred's demise.

So, from finding Wilfred's number to receiving his death certificate, any affinity I had with the boy back when I found the number multiplied ten times now that I knew who he was and how he died. As I have said, there was a photo of Wilfred's parents in Gwen Houghton's historical papers that were given to Adrian and Shannon Abbott. Many of the photos were returned by John Bosworth to Gwen that did not make it into his book and the sorrow that was evident in Houghton's eyes would make it impossible to leave the west end area of the churchyard in the hands of the church again.

The clergy had demonstrated their contempt for their fellow man, at least for the poor among them anyway. So however boring as it may seem to some people, the act of identifying graves and who rests within each one – at least the rows I moved the earth from – that became the project. Despite what anyone else thought, I regarded it as a duty to put right the wrong carried out upon this worthy collection of villagers. That's what this was all about, the sooner I could get to the end of the row (F), the better I would feel. I only hoped there would not be more heart break to uncover and again have the spirits urging me to put things right as they had done from day one.

Every grave has a story, so I had to stick with it then all this can be recorded before a return to normality is afforded. My time was not all taken up with research, the number of local people coming in meant I would learn more from each one. It was like witnessing a historical masterclass, many of the older people could not use a computer. Their historical knowledge was in their heads and having all been born and raised in the village could collectively recall and deliver events from the past, and it was easy to see why John Bosworth had tapped into this local knowledge to produce his wonderful book of the history of Durley.

Many of the people I spoke to said it was their parents that had told them the stories and showed them the photographs and were now passing them on to me. They were exceptional people who found that being together brought back long-forgotten memories. They all gave so much information to me, and the mutual respect we held for each other was something I would not like to lose. They understood completely the feelings I had for everyone buried in the west end of the churchyard because these people were living relations of them. People who had lived in the village all their life and had only heard of ancestors that were buried at the churchyard, not knowing that the wooded area was once part of its fabric or that there were graves beyond what they believed to be the boundary at the beginning of the woods. The more I learnt from them, the more I understood what had spiritually drawn me to undertake the project that had cost me a lot in terms of money. But had given me so much back that money could never buy, so that's why the research into who the people were that rested there was important and, in time when I finished the research, would become part of the history of the village.

While I was keen to finish researching the rows (E) and (F), as summer drifted into autumn, I had to break off from it because Adrian Abbotts' research had brought forth new information both good and bad. His trips to Winchester had been well worth the effort. He had found many maps of the church and the churchyard that showed how things looked way back in time and an exact size of the original churchyard and showed where the newer extensions to it began. Adrian had made several copies and coloured in each of the yards before being extended; his meticulous work was both easy to follow and backed up with a written explanation of how he thought the churchyard once looked and just how small the original yard was. Adrian had also found many photographs of the church dating way back before any work was carried out to the fabric of the church. What he found was amazing and showed how important it is to have a team who contribute together in search of a common goal. Adrian Abbott is a genius. However, he also had some bad news to impart. It centred around the Reverend Richard Ferguson who, as it turned out, was no better than his predecessor, the Reverend Thomas Scard. I was pleased Adrian had found the information. If I had produced it, people may think I just had a dislike of all things ecclesiastical and its clergy. That was not the case, I may have found nothing good about any of them thus far however one can always live in hope. Maybe one day a leopard really would change its spots, but it wouldn't pay to hold your breath because the Reverend Richard Ferguson was as bad as you could get.

In the case of Thomas Scard and his inability to handle money had been discovered far too late, the property and lands he owned or managed caused him to become complacent as well as ruining other people's livelihoods. The fact was he was just like his father; when he was in too deep he just gave up. You could argue he had not seen the trouble coming and it was not premeditated. However, in the case of the Revd Richard Ferguson, most of his actions were intentional without any thought at all for people's feelings or indeed any respect for the church he had taken over. And, with others set about changing the very fabric of the place that while old had stood the test of time and should never be touched, you would need permission in triplicate to change even a pane of glass these days. Given that it's a grade two listed building of special interest, these rules did not come into being until the County Planning Acts between 1944 and 1947, and any change to the fabric of a church or building of great interest is illegal. You can repair and maintain things, but they must be like for like and cannot be carried out without written consent from the relevant authorities, and once listed then a building is safe from the kind of abuse carried out at Durley's Church of The Holy Cross.

The lack of good judgement in the past left the church unprotected. And, as reported in the Hampshire Advertiser county newspaper on 28th May 1879: "Durley Church – this very curious old Church, dedicated to 'A Holy Cross' and situated in a pretty but rather out-of-the-way Country Village, is about to undergo a necessary restoration and repair and to have required additions made to it from the designs and plans of Messer's J Colson and Son, the well-known architects whose taste and care of and for antique details are not only guarantees of good work but a safeguard against that which is not restoration but destruction."

Well, what a build-up. One of the top architects famous for the great work they did at Winchester Cathedral was taking on the responsibility of the restoration and new addition to this wonderful old house of the Lord. The work was to be carried out by local builder Edward Heath, a well-respected member of the community. He was to work under the direction of the Revd Richard Ferguson MA, what could go wrong!

Well, let me tell you, reported in another edition, an article reported that, "The parish Church at Durley some parts of it are of Norman origin and some Saxon." The paper then banged on again about how great J. Colson and Son the architects of Winchester were. Then in the very next sentence delivers to its loyal readers news that says, "It is matter of great regret, however, that the removal of the pews and the uncovering of the inner walls of its plaster as well as the removal of the plastered ceilings all took place without the supervision of the architects. The work of demolition was so vigorously executed that there is nothing left of the groundwork for a guess as to the General design." It was clear the Reverend Richard Ferguson had no idea what he was doing, and Durley had another useless rector who in his wisdom was determined to completely ruin the internal fabric of the church. The newspaper continued: "By instructing the scrapping of the walls of their accumulation of plaster that brought to light but alas not to permanent recovery, a series of frescoes and polychrome decorations, of great interest, marking as they did three different periods – the transition, later gothic, Reformation mural ornamentation, the work extended round nearly the whole of the walls. But it was consigned to oblivion by hacking off the walls and re-plastering the internal walls, followed by six or seven thick applications of whitewash doubtless executed at the time when a similar agent performed similar duty in many an ancient fabric." So, the ceilings were removed and not replaced. True, the beams look very impressive, and if it were not for the nail holes that once fixed the laths you would think that's how the ceilings were originally. But by taking the ceilings down, you lose the beauty of its curves and arches and took away the acoustic echoes of singing voices, long after they had ceased. It would have been warmer too by the retention of the congregated heat, but the church was left unfinished, as it still is to this day. The abuse of the place was not over yet, the Reverend Richard Ferguson, possibly with others, also decided to remove from under the sacred floor of the church several skeletons. One of them recorded in the archives of the diocese a will of one William Oysell, who directed his internment at Durley church and left some small sums of money to provide lights for the altar to secure 300 masses for his soul.

Also buried in the church, as previously reported, was the Reverend John Rodgers, curate at Durley for 65 years. He had worked hard to keep the peace between the Reverend John White of Upham and Durley's Richard Hickley and co. in 1728. There were more burials, two in the chancel, the first close under the wall and communion table, were those of the Hersent family who occupied Durley Manor down to the close of the Merry Monarch's reign. As well as the Hersent Family were the Pope family, one of whose graves Thomas Pope, was accidentally opened. Found with the dried skeleton was the remains of the coffin "an Oaken one" with remnants of cloth fastened with brass nails and the deceased's initials. Curiously enough, the coffin lid had once been secured with a lock and key, and the upper part of the lid provided with a winged flap to view the features of the deceased and proof he was kept from the earth for some time to probably sooth the feelings of a bereaved wife or loving mother.

Also taken from the church were two old stone coffins, one believed to be from Norman times and the other Saxon. These are outside the church, one to the right of the south door and the other to the left, but no record of which is which. One was said to have on it a floriated cross, but this would have been ruined when it was moved. The other thing was Adrian Abbott couldn't find records of where the human remains taken from within the church had been reburied. You would have thought that would be the first thing to do when removing such important things. I would ask the question, why move them at all, they should be left to rest in peace. I think you may find, between them – Ferguson, Heath and Colson and Son – they had no idea the remains were there in the first place, and just went at it like a bull at a gate shouting 'Whoop! Look what we have found, what's that doing there?'

'Well gentleman,' the spirits would cry, 'we have been here since the year dot didn't you realise?' But as we know, keeping records was something not considered important by the clergy. Ferguson, like most of them who became the incumbent before and after him at Durley, had no idea of the local history or any intention of finding out. He was from Carlisle, for Christ's sake, so far away from the rural village of Durley, the only thing in common the two places had was a church and the worshiping of the Lord. I wonder what would have happened if it was the other way round, and the church authorities sent a useless rector to Carlisle who didn't care for their local history. J. Colson and Son covered themselves by including in the architect's instructions that said any human remains found should be dealt with in a respectful way, but he didn't say in what way or if they meant human remains found inside or outside of the building.

Some of the work was close to the outside of the church and soil that was taken out for revamping the boiler room had to be taken no further than a specified distance away from the church because they may well have come across old bones from older graves. Mr J. Colson was clever, he well and truly covered his bottom, nothing, would come back to haunt him. Edward Heath, well he just wanted to earn a living having supplied all the materials and priced every job covering every usual eventuality that may turn up. But it was not in his remit to have to look for things like bones, he wanted the money back he had laid out, so that was it and all about it.

The person I felt sorry for was Adrian Abbott. He had worked for months after finding the first records at Winchester and it was something I know made him unhappy that he could not complete the story of the lost remains of these important people. He was used to having some sort of conclusion at the end of each research he carried out, and I have to say I did feel a little guilty having got him to research the two things that turned out to be lost causes. These remains had been lost for all time, by the actions of a few people who did not research their project. Personally, I would not blame Mr Heath, the job was too big for him. It was clear there was a lack of direction from J. Colson and Son who should have been on site anyway, if they knew the history or not, chances are they wouldn't care.

When taking old work apart it should be done forensically, Mr Colson would have known that. If you came across something like they had then the job stops, and plans are changed to make allowances and incorporate the findings into the historic life of the church. Any extra work needed to be done by Mr Heath should have been agreed before any more work continued. And then we have Ferguson. Well, what can you say about him. Adrian had found out that Ferguson, or rather his wife, was very well off and thought the Fergusons may have put money into the project given the amount of authority he had. His signature was on many of the documents relating to all sorts of things, and if he was calling the shots and paying for works to be done then Mr Heath would have been keen to please whoever was picking up the bill. For me, you would have to blame the church authorities, they placed Ferguson to run loose like a headless chicken surrounded by an historic place that he probably thought was just old.

After destroying many frescoes, plundering Dick Ferguson decided he would replace the drawings with a few of his own. As reported in the county newspaper, "The Revd Mr Richard Ferguson's contribution to the refurbishment at Durley Church was that of drawing nude figures, and others clothed, apparently in the act of kissing each other, and with the saintly nimbus, a scene of the last judgement and the happiness of the blessed in paradise." Well, what can you say, after reaching a deadend in respect of what Adrian had found at Winchester, he didn't give up hope of the possibility that the human remains taken from within the church could turn up one day in some other record.

In the meantime, he and Shannon began to sort out all of Gwen Houghton's historical documents, one of which was yet another newspaper article that would prove that a building once stood where I had discovered all the brick and tile debris. Clarification of this fact was enhanced when I found a photograph in John Bosworth's book stating just that fact. I had used the book more as a reference than reading matter and referred to its index only to establish the answer to a particular question I received from people who visited the churchyard.

Anyway, let's begin with the photograph because it also referred to another dastardly deed carried out by the Revd Richard Ferguson, who by this time was public enemy number one even in Adrian Abbotts' 'benefit of the doubt book'. The photograph, taken in the late 1800s after the refurbishment, showed Samuel and Fanny Crosswell with their two daughters probably after church. Mrs Crosswell was sat on the side of a grave mound facing the camera to the northwest and Mr Crosswell and his daughters were looking on. Now please make a mental note of this photo because all will become clear how important it is further on. Anyway, in the write-up under the photograph it refers to, as I said, the Reverend Ferguson who it says "Almost caused a civil war in the Village" when he decided that some of the older headstones should be moved from the head of their graves to make pathways. One idea was to cross the graves with the headstones that had been removed from the head of each grave. I mean, you could not make this up, could you? This man was an utter moron!

This path will also come into the story again later. To continue, regarding the building the write-up said that next to the churchyard to the right once stood an old cottage where old Roman bricks and tiles had been found. Brilliant proof indeed of what I first thought was a structure was correct, but as for the bricks and tiles being Roman, that was not right. In Gwen Houghton's newspaper article that Adrian had discovered said as follows: "A Terrier of House and Glebe land belonging to the Reverend Rector of Upham and lying in the hamlet of Durley, in the parish of Upham taken on 21st June 1635. One house now adjoining to the west end of the chapel at Durley containing two rooms below and two lofts above with an outhouse hereunto. Adjoining with gardens and plot laying on the northsides of the said house, contained by estimate three perches square, i.e., fifty square feet. Bounded on the northside with lands of the Philpot family, and at the east end abutted on the Churchyard." You could trust the documents Gwen Houghton had given to the history society, they confirmed to me that what I had found was the cottage because each row of spoil that I dug out was full of bricks, tile and slate. I was not far out in thinking it was a watchman's hut to stop grave robbers. It was a building after all, and the rubble was tangled in old ivy from near the south hedgerow moving north until you reached the middle of each row where the cottage ceased to exist, where digging became a luxury to look forward to when digging forensically virtually inch by inch.

In the church's information sheet, it referred to the Roman tiles and a settlement was somewhere nearby, but the bricks and tiles I had found were from the cottage so the information sheet could be misleading. Roman tiles had been found in Durley, and in the British Museum they have the tiles that were found in the waste field to the east of the churchyard. The waste field is now part of the churchyard and everything of age that was and still is being uncovered all came from another place. The waste field was once part of a farmyard that in winter months was churned up by animals and carts. To counteract this, the farmer would bring in good rubble to cover the mud, and over the years all this would sink, and we often find things from the past when graves are being dug.

Adrian once took tiles and the remains of clay pots to Winchester for ageing. They had all been unearthed by the gravedigger in an area we think was used to cook things. Animal bones and the residue of burnt material were evident when the top layer of subsoil was disturbed and many oyster shells were found that were part of the staple diet for farm workers back then. In the dry weather you can see the outline of the structure that may have been stables and a barn. A massive hinge was dug up, that was thought to be used on a barn door, it was all fascinating. We were advised the pot was medieval and the tiles were of interest to the archivist. However, if we wanted the things aged, we would have to tell them where we found them, and the fact it was a churchyard on sacred ground was something we agreed on without question. The decision made was not to reveal where the artefacts were found, it all just added to the history for the villagers and would have been of no interest to anyone else but them.

From that one photograph in John Bosworth's book, we had clarification: first there was a building to the west, second that the Roman tiles referred to in the church information sheet was not correct. Thirdly, more damming information about the rector of Durley at the time who I can't be bothered to name, and finally we also found it was the Reverend Rector of Upham who owned the land at the west end of the churchyard that bounded land to the north once linked to the Philpot family who were wealthy landowners from Compton in Hampshire.

Their family had very strong links with the clergy. I could not be certain if one of them was Rector at Upham at the time. The Philpots also moved within high society; they held and managed lands at Pitt in Hampshire as well as Durley, Bishopstoke and Lymington. They had manors in Middlesex and Herts, as well as many houses and properties in the city of London. One member of that wealthy dynasty was Sir John Philpot the Lord Mayor of London in 1378, whilst another member of the Philpots was the Reverend Mr John Philpot. He was burnt at the stake when he broke away from the traditional Catholic faith of his family. He was described as a man of uncompromising views and always keen to defend them; his courage in facing death at the stake is honoured by a golden circle of flame around his name in his family tree of 1620. All he had to do was return to the faith he once held and was begged many times to return to the fold, but he would not give up his newfound faith. After walking through the mud to the stake refusing to be carried by the jailers, when he reached the stake, he kissed the wood that was to burn him. A brave man indeed or stupid depending on your point of view.

This story, while not directly connected to Durley, is of interest because the area of the woods that I cleared keeps giving me at least one more reason to talk about it. Its historical interest all brought about by Gwen Houghton's newspaper report and John Bosworth's photograph of the person sat on the grave mound. The fifth thing I found out was the possible names of people who could have occupied some of the graves between James and Harriett Houghton and Mr John Dangerfield. Clarification was needed but as 2017 ended, I did some more research as to who they may have been. It took me a while to get back into the swing of things again regarding them. I knew that the completion of rows (E) and (F) needed to be finished as well and would signal the end of what I had set out to do.

That was finding graves and who rested within them. While I had not neglected the spirits of the people in the remaining rows, I must admit trying to sort out the work carried out to the church by Ferguson and co. had been a lot easier as well as everything else that I seemed to have used as an excuse before getting back to the primary task that was the project.

I think part of me knew some of the people rested within those graves had more sad stories to tell and part of me didn't want to find anymore because I felt I knew these people now. And if they had all died in their sleep at a ripe old age, I would be happy to report that fact and rejoice in their passing. But I knew that wouldn't be the case, so had to build up to it and I did get a break from it on occasions when I was asked to show people around.

One Thursday afternoon when I was about to go home, I noticed a minibus in the lay-by outside the church. Not overthinking things, I continued to put the tools away, but out of nowhere came a small Japanese man. At first, I just looked and turned away then when I looked again, he was gone. As I walked from the shed down past the church, he appeared again, this time with about 18 other Japanese people who were all smiling and nodding as if to say hello. They began to spread out over the churchyard, amazed at what they could see. Most of the old headstones seemed to be bigger than them, and as they clipped away with their impressive cameras, two more people came in and joined me. There was one English man, the minibus driver, and the other man was the interpreter for the people who by this time were all over the place, enjoying something they had never seen before – a real old English churchyard.

The minibus driver asked if they could look inside the church and of course, how could I say anything but yes. Then the interpreter called them over saying in their language that I would let them inside and as one they all hurried over surrounding me like small school children eager to be the first one inside. When I took the large key out to open the church the people began snapping again with cameras, this time in amazement at the size of the key that I had to hold up while they photographed it. After opening the ancient old door, I stepped out of the way as one by one they walked slowly into the impressive church itself and, like many people, the sight of it took their collective breaths away.

They remained remarkably quiet, and it was some time before they began to lift up their cameras again, looking at me first as if to ask if it was allowed. When I nodded yes, they enjoyed photographing just about everything they could see inside the church. I was then asked if I would talk to them through their interpreter and as we gathered outside, I did my best to give them chapter and verse about the history of the church, pausing after each sentence while what I said was translated to them. I showed them the stonemasons' initials that were carved into the stonework, and the hidden cross on the stonework that surrounded the original chapel door, possibly made by a knight before going off to fight in one of the seven crusades.

If the knight had come home then another cross would have been struck into the stone underneath it, but this was a single cross that indicated our knight never came home. After that fact had been translated to the group, there were nods of understanding and a sadness that our knight did not return home and, for a moment, we were all one people brought together by the story of our knight's unsuccessful crusade. To think we all stood on the same spot as he did makes everyone think, no matter where you are from, their mood was lifted when I told them the history of the large yew tree that is over 1,200 years old to which Oliver Cromwell tethered his horse.

From their response, I gathered they had heard of Oliver Cromwell, and they all hurried down to the tree to take photos of it and each other around it and on low branches that they climbed onto. I told the minibus driver that it was time for me to go and the interpreter told the party and, as one, they all stood in line and applauded me as I left the churchyard. It had been a pleasure to be with them all; they had filmed and recorded it all and was to go on a blog that at the time I had no idea what that was but over time I have been on a few, all promoting the Church of the Holy Cross at Durley. It was events like the one with the Japanese tourists that summer that made working and meeting people in the churchyard so enjoyable.

But I did have to try and complete the identification of who rested in the graves in rows (D), (E) and (F) and in total had another 36 graves to investigate, most of which I would research in the evenings. With the onset of winter, I didn't need to be at the churchyard for so long each day, and if the weather was harsh there was no need to go at all. I had a list of things I wanted to work on, and several people asked me to clean their relatives' headstones. As I would be cleaning some of the older ones at the west end of the churchyard, it wasn't a problem fitting them in, and besides, the money came in handy. I didn't have a set rate, I just asked people to give what they could afford. It was not really about money, everyone likes their relations' graves and headstones to look tidy and I can honestly say that those with living relations looked after them well.

There were many very old headstones that had either sunk or were leaning to one side or the other. So, managing them from time to time was essential if the history of the village was to be preserved because someone would turn up one day to look for a relation as sure as night turns into day. However, my focus was to clean the old headstones at the west end area to coincide with trying to find out who was in each of the 36 graves in rows (D), (E) and (F), of which only nine had headstones, and in the whole of the six rows I had cleared the spoil from only 20 of 112 graves that had headstones.

As well as pictures of some on the Ancestry sites that were no longer there, it really was a dismal place when I found it but now its bright and we have some idea of who rests within. They number some 129 people in just six rows that had been cleared of spoil, quite a small community when you think about it. I am sure there could be more burials in that area, however Adrian Abbott and I did all we could in our endeavours to put things right on their behalf. I created the mound in memory of all who passed this way before so no one is forgotten, and I am satisfied that in the first six rows of graves at the west end of the churchyard all who rest there can now do so in peace.

Regarding the remaining graves in row (D) where the cedar trees are, I only found two possible ladies whose graves could have been between James and Harriett Houghton and John Dangerfield. One was Emily Lampard née Houghton. Emily was related to James Houghton, as well as having strong links with the Methodist, she and husband Joseph Lampard's farm was close to the Methodist church they attended to the west of Durley. The other lady whose grave may have been in row (D) was Avis Crosswell née Lampard, the sister of Joseph. Avis married Hugh Charles Crosswell who rests in grave number 15 in row (B) who passed away in 1918. The reason he is in row (B) is that he and Avis had three sons, two of them Harold Joseph Crosswell and Percy Crosswell both died on the day they were born in 1889, and the third child Perry Crosswell lived for just 11 months (June 1890 till July 1891). All three children rest just behind their father, who would have made it known to everyone in 1891 when his 11-month-old son died that he would go in front of the children. Back then, all children were laid to rest on the boundaries of the churchyard, which was in front of where the cottage once stood. I had not looked for graves there but after finding records of Hugh and Avis Croswell's children, Adrian walked over the area with the dowsing rods that indicated that the graves were small.

Information was added to the mix by Mr Ron Gibson (Littleen as he was affectionately known). Ron was a great help to me; he knew where many people were buried because he was related to many of the families. His older brothers were at one time the gravediggers at the churchyard and frequent visits to the churchyard to talk with me was a real masterclass for me. When Ron was a boy he would help his brothers with the graves, and also ride his bike rounding up the cows on the land that's now the golf course. He would fetch water from the river for the chickens with a yoke and was also in the church choir and pumped the organ on Sundays. Once after a Sunday out on his bike with best friend Alan Munday, he fell asleep and missed the signal to start pumping.

Ron Gibson teaches me so much whenever he comes in, and now in his 90s is still a fountain of knowledge. Ron talked about a large whale that came up the river from one of the inlets to the Hamble River. The whale, Ron said, got as far as the Horse and Jockey pub a few miles from Durley and many of the villagers made their way on whatever transport they could muster. At first, the story sounded like one of my Uncle George Wilber's yarns, however Ron then brought in a photo of the whale with many villagers standing with him and his father. Ron Gibson and his late wife moved away from the village a few years ago so he has planted many wildflowers at the west end of the churchyard so we can remember him. Ron's late wife was a Tomlin and may have had links with Mary Ann Prowting née Tomlin, Great-uncle George's mother and one of my maternal grandmothers – so it's a small world.

So, once the grass was cut very short in the area where the Crosswell children were buried, I could recognise the soil conditions that show signs of disturbance. When old graves have been left and unattended, not much grows from them and what does is mostly weeds. Stinging nettles and giant hogweed, sometimes called 'Break your Mother's Heart', but it's just rubbish that grows and by the time autumn comes it looks a mess. Dumuzid, the ancient Mesopotamian god of all shepherds and vegetation, works hard in the underworld to prepare what grows in spring but leaves it to the living to arrange what stays and what does not. Wildflowers or weeds to him, they are all the same.

Today's weeds were yesterday's flowers according to one of the village gentlemen who comes to the churchyard, Mr Jim Hack another fountain of knowledge regarding anything to do with the countryside. He can name any wildflower or weed, what its benefits are, if any, and he qualifies his knowledge by eating many of them as he makes his way around the churchyard while tending his loved ones' final resting place. A proper country gentleman is Mr Hack, another man I respect greatly who's liked by all who enter his space. With Adrian's dowsing rods, Mr Ron Gibson's knowledge of the area and Mr Jim Hack's teachings of wildflowers help to work out things for me. Teamwork, it never fails.

It would be another 27 years before Hugh Charles Crosswell died and took up the unwritten rule that grave number 15 in row (B) was for him. When his wife Avis Crosswell née Lampard passed away two years after him, there was no record of where she is buried. She would not be next to him, the plot is not wide enough. I did think she could have been in front of her husband, as many couples are. When I talked to Ron Gibson about it, he told me that a lady called Dorrie Gibson née Cowdrey wanted to be buried near to her parents, George and Kate Cowdrey née Houghton, in grave number 16 in row (B) at the west end of the churchyard. But when his brothers dug the grave there was already someone there, so Dorrie Gibson is buried at the east end of the churchyard. If it was Avis Crosswell née Lampard in front of Hugh Charles

Crosswell, the church had no record of where Avis rests. She could of course be in row (D) with Emily Lampard née Houghton, because Emily was Avis's mother, and the lady sat on the grave in row (D) in the photograph in John Bosworth's book was Fanny Crosswell, her mother-in-law.

So, we have two places where Avis could be, in front of her husband in row (B) or with her mother in row (D). It's a complicated process working out who rests where, and time consuming. You can only look into things if someone provides new information and that can take ages. But from that one photo in John Bosworth's book, we learnt a lot from different people and one of the ladies who is a regular visitor to the churchyard and looks after several graves is Mrs Monica Whale. She is also a mind of information and could name everyone in that photo because one of Fanny Croswell's daughters in the photo was Mrs Whale's grandmother. Word of mouth really does help and while the remaining graves in row (D) will stay on the back burner, something will turn up eventually as sure as dogs chase cats.

The first grave in row (E), number 74, was Mr William Lever, who died in 1925 aged 34, and next to him are his parents David and Elizabeth Lever née Collis. David died aged 69 in 1936 and Elizabeth passed away in 1949 aged 82. The two of them are in the burial records as being in grave number 418; that would have placed them at the east of the churchyard, but the parents of William wished to be near their son. Hence their collective grave number is 74. I found out later that David Lever's grandmother was a Cowdrey, which answered that question as to why they were in that corner of the churchyard.

In grave number 75 is David Houghton. He died in 1928 aged 82. David was the brother of Emily Lampard née Houghton and worked as a wood-hoop maker. A skilled trade working with timber, making hurdles and splitting timber to lay in a hedge that strengthens its regeneration after having the deadwood cut from within. David was also a carter and sold produce grown on his land that he and his wife, Pricilla Houghton née Denham, would deliver to outlying districts each week with their horse and cart. Pricilla rests next to David in grave number 76. She died three years before him aged 80 in 1925.

I wondered why if Pricilla died before David she would not be in grave number 75 and David in 76. It was one of many puzzles relating to the churchyard. Maybe picking your final resting place was taken seriously back then more than we thought, and in John Bosworth's book is a fine picture of the couple with the horse and cart. The book says, "Empty after another profitable trip" and points out to us an umbrella that's fixed to the side of the cart for use in all weathers if it's warm or it's wet. This hard-working couple have no headstone, but I found the numbers and the place where they rest and with the help of John Bosworth's book, I could see who they were.

David and Pricilla had one son, Edmund William Henry Houghton, and he married Elizabeth Jane Cowdrey, the daughter of George and Kate Cowdrey née Houghton, who rest side by side in grave number 16 in row (B). Edmund and Elizabeth had eight children, and one of their sons, Robert William, died aged 15. I could not help but think that the blood disease that would have been passed down through the generations had struck again. It's hard not to think that if you see one so young has died knowing as I did of the disease that followed that family around.

Robert had a brother, Corporal David Josiah Wilfred, who is a war hero killed in action at Salerno Campania, Italy in 1943 aged 25. He has a war grave over in Italy so far away from his family, however those cemeteries are well maintained, and the war grave commissioners look after the interest of all military. If a person dies in battle, then the War Grave Commission look after the headstone, however if a person dies not in action, then the graves are looked after by the MOD. It is a big concern and many former military personnel are involved in it , and at Durley, there are three graves looked after by the War Graves Commission, and one other is the responsibility of the MOD. We also have many like young Corporal David Josiah Wilfred Houghton, who never came home. I found if I wandered off base whilst researching the six rows, it was easy to end up looking into other areas of history. Some were even more lost than what I was supposed to be uncovering, and if I allowed it would take me away from my primary task. Keeping me locked into a never-ending story of historical dross that made me think nothing happened back then that was nice.

So, it was best I didn't stray if possible and stay on track to finish the six rows that were difficult enough. I suppose I went off base looking for better things that in reality were not there, and each time I did look for things I could almost feel the soft breeze of the spirits shepherding me back to the real point of it all, and that was to save them and return them into history where they belonged.

I would try and keep to the primary task; I had come a long way from the beginning when there was just a pile of earth and then finding numbers followed by the shock that there were actually people buried there. I can't explain how or why the spiritual feeling is so strong in that area and I challenge anyone to do and see what I have and not be moved. You see it's important I finish the six rows from (A) to (F) because I released the spirits from the lamp, so to speak, and it would be a devil's own job to get them back without first telling their stories so they can all rest in peace.

Grave number 77 in the burial records only showed the number but, one thing we could be sure of in my opinion, was whoever rested there would probably be a Methodist. I thought there must be a way of finding Methodist burial records. Adrian was not convinced that the area was mainly for Methodist. But I thought there was enough evidence given how many people buried at the west end of the churchyard had links with the Methodist church and these thoughts were enhanced when local farmer and Methodist, Mr John Spreadbury, gave me chapter and verse regarding Methodist burials records at

Durley. John is another proper Durley man and Chris the gravedigger's uncle. He also liked to see the path's neatly edged, he would say as he stood next to the church, "I do like to see a proper bit of edging", so if it needs doing I get the guilty feeling if it's left too long.

Moving on to grave number 78, this grave had no headstone, but the names of Robert Houghton and his wife Matilda Jane née Moody were in the records. They ran a market garden in Heathen Street at Durley. The couple had one daughter, Eva Elizabeth, who became Mrs Frank Taplin, a member of another old Durley family. Robert Houghton died in 1927 aged 78, Matilda Jane outlived her husband by eight years and passed away at the good age of 90. Graves numbers 79 and 80 didn't have any names, however I had better luck with grave number 81. Edmund Houghton and his wife, Emily née Denham, rested there. They were the parents of Robert Houghton in grave number 78, Edmund was a woodsman and also farmed. He began with 11 acres of land in Durley, and when he passed away in 1887 aged 67, had worked his way up to farming some 40 acres and employing two labourers. Emily survived her husband by 13 years, and she died in 1900 aged 81.

Grave number 82 was occupied by Thomas Houghton, one of the eight sons born to Robert Houghton and Sarah née Wadmore. Robert's great-grandmother was Elizabeth Houghton née Prowting. He was a direct relation and uncle to Gwen Houghton, his brother James being Gwen's great-grandfather. Grave number 82 was to give me more information than I could imagine relating to Thomas Houghton.

Born in 1881, Thomas never married and worked as an agricultural labourer on his parent's farm at Winters Hill. In 1830 his younger brother Stephen Houghton died aged 26, leaving a wife, Matilda Houghton née Watkins, and four young children who lived at the Houghton's farm after Stephen's death. Thomas took on the role of stepfather, and two years after his brother's demise, had a daughter with Matilda. They stayed together at the farm for 50 years. Matilda would be described as the housekeeper on census forms. Back then, if a woman became pregnant when single or widowed, most would be entitled to help from the church. However, there was something called a bastardy examination, carried out by the churchwardens and Poor Law overseers where the woman was subjected to the most rigorous questioning as to the identity of the father of the child. If the woman refused, the child would become aware from the time it was old enough that it was a bastard child looked after by the church and others till it became of apprentice age.

This following indenture is one sent to me by someone in my family tree, not a direct relation but linked somehow down the years, Philip Prowting, son of John Prowting from Emsworth in the county of Hampshire. Philip was indentured to an Uncle William Prowting, a cooper (barrel maker) of London. The indenture reads: "That Philip Prowting doth put himself Apprentice to William Prowting citizen and Cooper of London. To learn his art, and with him after the manner of an apprentice, to serve, from the day of the date hereof until the full end of the term of seven years, thence next following, to be fully complete and ended. During which term, the said apprentice his said Master faithfully shall serve, his secrets keep, his lawful command's everywhere gladly do. He shall do no damage to his Master, nor see it done of others, but that he, to the utmost of his power, shall let, or immediately give warning to his said Master of the same. He shall not waste the goods of his Master nor lend them unlawfully to any: he shall not fornicate, nor contract matrimony within the said term: he shall not play at cards, dice tables, nor any other unlawful games, without licence of the said Master's service day or night unlawfully; but in all things. As a faithful apprentice, he shall behave himself towards his said Master, in consideration of his said Apprentice, in the same art and mystery which he useth, or cause to be taught and instructed, finding, into the said apprentice, meat, drink, apparel, and lodgings. And all other necessaries, according to the custom of the City of London, during the said term, and for the true performance of all and every these present. In witness, of which of the parties above-named to these Indentures interchangeably have put these hands and seals, the seventh day of February in the thirty -second year of the reign of our Sovereign Lord George III of Great-Britain, France, and Ireland King, Defender of the faith, and in the year of our Lord 1792."

Well, what a hard life awaited an apprentice back then. I wondered if a child who became apprenticed – and they were children, let's not forget that – carried the burden of being bastards, a fact thrust onto them as soon as he or she could understand they were considered second-class citizens by the church and others.

Thomas was a strict Methodist, like many others buried at the west end of the churchyard, and would have, I hoped, not let anything like that happen to Matilda or the child. Thomas and Matilda's daughter was named Caroline and when she was 25 married George Crosswell. Together they had eight children. Caroline lived a full life, and when she died in 1935, she was 101 years old and left more than 100 living relations. Caroline rests in grave number 408 with her daughter Alice who died one year before her mother in 1934 aged 76. Sadly there is no headstone, but I do know where the two rest close to Caroline's son, Frank, who does have an impressive headstone. Some of Frank's family live in Australia and have come to the churchyard. I can't show them a photo of Frank as a child but have a picture of the pram he was in with his cousin who just happened to be Mrs Monica Whale's mother.

Thomas and Matilda would have been proud of their daughter Caroline and any harsh words spoken at the time regarding them not being married, well they were just words, sticks and stones and all that jazz, best forgotten, I think. If it were possible to pop my head around the door into their world, I think I would have liked Thomas. Records show him to have been a hard-working man and his loyalty to Matilda was mutual. Thomas died aged 87 in 1887 and buried next to him in grave number 83 rests Matilda who died just 10 months after Thomas, aged 86. One headstone marks the two graves and once cleaned revealed this inscription: "We Speak of the Realms of the Blest, That Country so Bright and so Fair, and of its Glories Confessed, but what must we do to be There." I am sure it meant something to Thomas and Matilda. It was one of many inscriptions I would uncover, and if Thomas and Matilda's inscription was supposed to get you thinking it most certainly did that.

The cleaning of each headstone was quite a job, needing plenty of time and effort to then see the words come to light. I have to say it confused me somewhat in the beginning because I was not ready for anything too profound that would stop me thinking of anything else. I figured if I had found their graves and revealed the inscriptions – their message to the world if you like – then that was enough.

I am sure the spirits would understand, however, I did look into the verse and it was from a hymn and had about four other verses to go with the one on the headstone and I have to say the words were beautifully written by a lady called Elizabeth Mills née King. This wonderful poetry can sometimes be intoxicating, and I began to look for something more beautiful and more meaningful to feel as I did when first reading the words on Thomas and Matilda's headstone of "We Speak to The Realms". But the reality is it can be like the second cup of tea is never as good as the first, so why bother pouring one. But you do and it would not be long before I did find a more meaningful inscription – to me anyway – because resting in grave number 84 is Mary Ann Houghton née Dodd, the mother of Emily Lampard née Houghton, who I think may be in row (D). Mary Ann's headstone was one I came across when I first arrived at the churchyard to begin the project. Her grave is seven plots from my great-aunt Susan Matilda's, and the census records informed me that in life they lived next door to each other on Durley Street. So they would have known each other well. Therefore, Mary Ann Houghton née Dodd's grave would get a little more attention from me because her headstone was face up, lying on the floor having been separated from its plinth by the intrusive roots of one of the big cedar trees having grown against it causing it to break.

A photograph of the headstone was on one of the Ancestry sites just lying on the floor covered in ivy. I thought it was rude of whoever photographed it to just leave it there with no attempt to clean all of it. Only the name of the person buried there was visible, so I spent time digging next to the plinth and manoeuvring the headstone into position, making sure that when it was lifted into place it faced to the east. I used old round fence posts found in the shed and once the headstone was levered onto them, I could use more stronger timbers wedged under one end to slowly ease towards the plinth. Once in place, I put bricks at one end then with timber placed on the brick and wedged under the end of the headstone. I stood on the timber to lift it enough to get bricks each side of the headstone that would then rest on the bricks, the round fence post could then be taken out from underneath the headstone and used again, this time they were placed in the hole I had dug next to the plinth. The feet of the posts would sit against the residue of the plinth left in the hole and the middle of the posts would be leaning at a 45-degree angle. My theory was if I could jack the headstone up on bricks one at a time. The headstone should in theory slide off the bricks onto the posts that would then, with the force of the headstone, strike the bottom of the round fence posts in the hole to cause the posts to stand upright stopping the headstone falling to the other side of the hole.

It should, if I had my sums right, be wedged between the residue of the plinth in the hole and the upright round fence post. I hadn't figured out how to get the fence posts out of the hole afterwards, if I could get that far. I would cross that bridge when I came to it. But first I had to get the headstone up on more bricks before that problem arose, and the job became difficult when it began to rain and I got wet through, jacking the headstone up into position. It was at such an angle that the back of the headstone pinched against the post in the hole and the bottom of the posts were wedged against the residue of plinth left in the hole. All it needed was one good push on the headstone that was resting on the bricks, and it was job done. However, I was soaked to the skin by this time and decided to finish the operation the next day. If when I got back to the churchyard the headstone was still as it was when I left, then all I would have to do would be to push the headstone off the bricks with another timber, a T-shaped piece. We used to make them when lifting plasterboard into place and wedge the T piece between the floor and the plasterboard leaving both hands free to nail the board to the ceiling timbers.

If I pushed the T piece against the face of the headstone it should slide off the bricks, hit the timbers in the hole and stand upright next to the plinth. I had done the job several times in my head between leaving the churchyard and arriving back the following day. I approached the headstone like an athlete about to throw the hammer, walking around it because these headstones were heavy, if it did not go in first time then starting again would be difficult. So, after walking around it for the umpteenth time I picked up the T piece and walked up to it. I was on my own and while still going over things in my mind I sang to the spirits. "It's quarter to three there's no one in the place except you and me, so set them up Joe, I've got a little story I think you should know, I think my friend I want to bring to an end this episode." So, make it one push for Mary Ann Houghton née Dodd and one more for row (E), eat your heart out Frank Sinatra!

Then to the imaginary applause of the spirits I pushed the T piece as hard as I could against the headstone that slid off the bricks, and Mary Ann Houghton née Dodd's headstone shot right down into the hole. The two posts in the hole stood upright and slapped against the headstone, sending echoes around the woods, and the spray from the water in the hole went everywhere and soaked me. Once again, it was a great moment. So, she and I have a kind of bond, but should I take all the credit? Maybe the spirits had a hand in helping Mary Ann back to a more dignified position, who knows.

All the time I was working to get the headstone back in position no one came in. It was a solitary task, just myself and the spirits as my witness. They had been around for many of the tasks I had undertaken that just seemed to work first time, lifting things that never felt heavy, cutting down small trees with an ordinary standard wood saw that took no effort to cut through and just fell into the area I wanted it to. Mary Ann Houghton née Dodd's headstone was the first one I had cleaned properly because I had found her in such a mess. And like a child coming in from the garden covered in dirt, your natural instinct is to clean the child, it was that sort of duty feeling.

Mary Ann's headstone had an inscription on it as well, with words I will never forget; they were not like any others but as if she was telling me what it would be like when I meet her for real. The inscription was a verse from a hymn called 'There is a Land' and the full text reads: "There is a land of pure delight, where saints immortal reign infinite day excludes the night, and pleasures banish pain. There everlasting spring abides, and never-withering flowers. Death like a narrow sea, divides this heavenly land of ours, sweet fields beyond the swelling flood stand dressed in living green. So, to the Jews of Canaan stood, while Jorden rolled between, but timorous mortals start and shrink to cross the narrow sea, O could we make our doubts remove, those gloomy thoughts that rise and see the Canaan that we love with un-beclouded eyes. Could we but claim where Moses stood and viewed the landscape O'er not Jorden's stream, nor death's cold flood, should fright us from the shore." Well Mary Ann Houghton née Dodd's inscription just blew me away from the first sentence to the last and afterwards, I had no fear of what the future may be like beyond this precious life.

One month after my encounter with Mary Ann Houghton née Dodd, I found Great-uncle George's headstone buried under the ground, and 52 days after finding him, my mother died. I put the first verse of 'There is a Land' in her obituary. I had told her about it when I found it, but Mum was away with the fairies at the time. Her head was full of jolly robins, not much went in. Still, I knew she would have liked it. I remember that time well.

I have not had much to say at all to Mary Ann Houghton née Dodd for a while because I had been busy. I knew she would be fine with that. Still, now I have reached her headstone that rests neatly in place at grave number 84. It's quite nice to be reacquainted, if only for a while. Mary Ann Houghton née Dodd was born in Bishopstoke Hampshire, the daughter of a Ms Charlotte and her father is unknown. I wondered if her mother Charlotte had to go through one of the bastardy examinations carried out by the churchwarden and Poor Law overseers. Nothing like being kicked when your down, is there folks?

I asked Adrian Abbott for help finding information regarding Ms Charlotte, and after looking at several records, he found information about her. Her parents were Richard and Ann Dodd née Cox. Charlotte had kept her maiden name when she gave birth to Mary-Ann, an indication the father was no longer around. When Mary-Ann was four years old, her mother, Charlotte, married William Alfred Denham and had more children, so Mary-Ann had half-siblings, two of which were William Denham who, with his wife Mary née Lamond, are resting in grave number 63 and 64. The other half-sibling was Harriett Houghton née Denham who, with husband James (Skinny Jim) Houghton, rest in graves number 65 and 66. Then Adrian found a record that Charlotte Denham née Dodd had died in the Winchester district in July 1843, she was 46 after which William Alfred Denham re-married to a woman called Ann Orman on the 7th of October 1847.

Mary Ann Houghton née Dodd's husband was Robert Houghton who she married in 1834, and he was the brother of Thomas Houghton in grave number 82 in row (E). They were another two of seven brothers born to Robert Houghton and wife Sarah née Wadmore. Robert and Mary Ann Houghton née Dodd had six children. One of their son's David married Pricilla Denham who rest in graves numbers 75 and six in row (E). Their daughter, Emily, became the wife of Joseph Lampard who I thought might be buried somewhere in row (D). Mary Ann's other children were Solomon, Charlotte, Caleb, and Joshua. Mary Ann was related to many people at the west end of the churchyard. I had enjoyed researching her life, getting her headstone back in place at the head of her grave number 84. She died aged 79 in 1883, having been married to Robert for 51 years.

Next to her grave number 85 just had a plinth with no headstone, possibly another one broken by the closeness of the big cedar tree. The occupant of this grave could have been one of her children, what made me think that was because the next grave along number 86 was her husband's Robert Houghton. He had followed the rural family tradition making his living as a wood hoop maker. Robert died aged 74 in 1885.

Grave number 87 was the resting place of Caleb Houghton, his wife Eliza née Misselbrook, and their son Harry. Eliza died aged 46 in 1885, son Harry also died that same year aged only 20. Caleb died in 1898, he was 57 and the son of Robert and Mary Ann Houghton née Dodd, so that would rule him out of being in between his parents' in grave number 85, and leave four options: Emily, Solomon, Charlotte and Joshua. Caleb must have booked his family's resting place well in advance of any deaths, so picking your place was important. In fact, most of row (E) seemed to be close family members of Robert and Mary Ann Houghton née Dodd.

Grave number 89 is the resting place of three children who had all died before the age of two. Their kerbstone grave stretched some 15 feet, each one laid to rest in front of each other after each unexpected death. At the foot of the grave is a footstone with the three children's initials and at the head of the grave is a replica more impressive headstone with the three children's names. On 1st August 1881, George Houghton died aged 11 days, then on 8th August that same year Robert James Houghton aged one year passed away, and on 24th June 1895 their brother Dennis Houghton passed away aged two. The three boys were the grandchildren of Edmund and Emily Houghton in grave number 81. The children's father, also called Edmund, was the trustee of one of the local Methodist churches, as well as having local businesses with his wife, another Mary Ann Houghton but this one was née Cooper.

You see the reason for all the nées, one can get confused if you don't add them! The two parents are buried further in the churchyard while not in the wooded area, their grave could not be seen for long grasses and smaller trees. The reason I mention the parents is next to their grave, when everything had been cleared revealing their headstone next to it, I found the kerbstone grave of Mary Ann Houghton née Cooper's brother when I was planting daffodils.

The planter had struck the side of the kerbstone that had been buried under the ground for God knows how long and gave me a further insight as to how the church treated the villagers. The gentleman buried there was Walter George Cooper who died in 1926 aged 75, nothing strange about that you may think. But the inscription on the side of his kerbstone said: "Walter George Cooper 25 years Sexton of this Church." He also served on the parish council, and it seems the church forgot all about Walter George Cooper, a man devoted to the church and his village. When I started clearing the earth from the children's long kerbstone grave, the headstone was hidden beneath thick ivy, and once removed revealed the words taken from the Bible: "The Lord asked 'Is the Child Well', and the Mother replied, 'Lord the Child is Well'." The long kerbstone grave gets a lot of attention these days when visitors come, and people don't walk by this impressive grave without first touching the headstone. People who know what it's like to lose a child maybe, and those of us who cannot imagine what it must be like losing a child, touch it and think there for the grace of God go I.

Grave number 90 is Susan Matilda Houghton née Prowting, my great-aunt. I had little information about her, and she died aged 45 of tuberculosis in 1881. With the absence of any photographs from her era, I would try to imagine what she looked like dressed in the clothes of the day. Was she tall and had long hair? What colour were her eyes? I could find no record of her, and Shoemaker Bob having had children, which was unusual back then. It was frustrating being unable to find more than just the basic information, however I should be grateful I found her headstone at all, discarded in the woods it could be that one day something more may turn up.

The last grave in row (E) number 91 was Albert Stubbington who passed away in 1897 aged 25. The grave number had a question mark against the entry. There were other members of the Stubbington family in the record books but with no specific graves recorded, Shoemaker Bob's mother was a

Stubbington so maybe that's why they are all together. Albert Stubbington's grave was the last in row (E) and it was time to research the last row (F). There were many graves before you reached the wooded area, they too were left unkept, but people knew they were in the first area I had cleared. Before I realised there were more in the woods, so while they would need researching and recorded it was not so important at that stage of proceedings because I had not cleared any spoil from the area. There was plenty of long grasses, small bushes and giant hogweed that had hidden the west end area completely. But this was not part of the project I set out to do, so I felt comfortable with what I had decided.

I did have to draw the line somewhere because I wanted to move on from long evenings of researching families from the past who I had the utmost respect for having got to know them as I had. I had been looking at census forms that revealed who they were and what they did in and for the village. This modern way of researching brings to light many things some people would rather forget. However, history will never die nor will the spirits whose insistence lead you to a bygone age and sometimes you have to pinch yourself to return to the here and now. You get so wrapped in the past, it as if you were there. The strange thing is, after researching from home when returning to the churchyard, what was just a grave marker of a person the day before, changes and turns into someone real who you have got to know. You feel a sense of obligation when walking by the grave in the mornings and saying hello because if you don't you get the feeling somehow, they will know.

I began row (F) with what you could call an end-of-term attitude after the rigorous research. Grave number 94, I was not surprised to find, had no record of who rested there. In grave 95 was Mr John Penney. He had died in 1937 aged 76, and his wife Mrs Jeanette Penney née Chalk was next to him in grave number 96. She passed away in 1932 aged 69 years. The strange thing about this couple was that they chose to return to Durley after 34 and 38 years respectively to be buried next to their son Frederick Penney, who occupies grave number 97. He died in 1894 aged one year and ten months. This added even more credence that people picked their grave plots. John and Jeanette Penney once lived with their family of seven children in a fine home called church cottage at Durley that backs onto the churchyard. There was one other Penney buried in the churchyard, Earnest Penney, son of John and Jeanette. He died in 1947 aged 56 and rests in grave number 522, at the northwest of the churchyard. Earnest Penney married Annie Sophia Woodhatch; she was from another well-respected Durley family.

Now for the link as to why John and Jeanette Penney came back to Durley for burial, I found in Earnest and Annie Sophia's marriage certificate, that I discovered online, the two witnesses to their union were Edmund W. H. Houghton and Elizabeth Jane Cowdrey. Edmund's parents were David and Pricilla Houghton and their grave numbers are 75 and 76 in row (E), just behind the Penney graves in row (F). Elizabeth Janes Cowdrey's parents were George and Kate Cowdrey née Houghton who rest in grave number 16 in row (B), which also suggests that the Penneys were Methodists and that the west end area was for the Methodists of Durley.

To give a bit more information as to why I think the Penney's were Methodists, Earnest and Annie Sophia named their son Hiram, taken from the Hebrew name meaning 'my brother exalted'. The Hiram first Methodist church is very big in America with a great number of licenced ministers, such as Hiram Franks, Hiram Edson, Hiram R. Revels, and Hiram Wesley Evens. The list is a long one and includes Hiram Ulysses S. Grant who was President of the United States of America for eight years. So if the name was good enough for that lot, then it was for little old Hiram Penney from Durley in Hampshire, England.

Grave number 99 has an impressive headstone that needed rescuing from beneath the flora that had encased it. After cleaning, it revealed the simple inscription that this was the grave of John and Anne Staphnill of Rectory Lodge Durley. Mrs Anne Staphnill was an invalid and died aged 47 at Durley, after which Mr John Staphnill moved to Great Malvern. The 1891 census detailed that he married again to a lady called Clara, whose maiden name is unknown. However, even though John Staphnill's name was on the headstone at Durley, he is not buried there, as John died in 1924 aged 78. It's not clear why his name would be on the headstone, or they could well have had a son named John after his father, but I could not find a record of a son. So, it must have been when his wife died, and he expected to remain at Durley. Who knows, grief affects people in different ways, but it is a very impressive headstone whatever the reason.

The next six graves in the row (F) numbers 100 through to 105 had no names at all to go with the numbers. So, moving on to number 106, this grave had been affected badly by one of the big intrusive cedar trees. Its roots had grown into and over it and affected both the end of the Houghton children's long impressive grave as well as Susan Matilda Houghton's both situated in the row (E). Number 106 was the resting place of Elizabeth Noyes, born in Middlesex England in 1832, then when she moved to Durley she worked in service and in later life worked for the Compton family for over 20 years. The Comptons were another Durley farming family. I think Elizabeth remained a spinster all her life she died in 1892 aged 70 years. Her affairs were dealt with by Mrs Mary Ann Robinson née Compton, the daughter of John and Mary Jane Compton who employed Elizabeth Noyes for all of those years.

The intrusive roots within her grave would eventually rot away once the rest of the cedar trees were removed. I had not mentioned their removal again to the PCC. I had no intention of doing so because of information I had from a very helpful lady, let's call her C.E. who worked at the Diocesan office. I had asked her for help regarding the rules to see if I was right after I was put off by one of the churchwardens when they said the archdeacon would be the one to say what happens with the trees.

C.E. told me that he was just one of a team of people who would look at the matter and if the rules set out in the churchyard regulations regarding trees in all churchyards that the archdeacon and his merry band of ecclesiastical investigators would have to go by, then the answer would be the trees would have to go. The archdeacon and his team would probably get it all done over lunch between the sweet and a drop of fine sherry before nodding off, no doubt.

Elizabeth Noyes would have to wait a little longer for the roots on the surface to be gone, except there was just a small lilac heather that grew near to Elizabeth's headstone. A gift from Dumuzid, for what Elizabeth had to put up with in death. Elizabeth Noyes brought to an end my quest to discover all that had been lost at the west end of the churchyard. In the beginning, I had no idea where to start or indeed how things would turn out in the end. What I had created I would most definitely look after for as long as I was able to.

The northeast area would need volunteers to look after it, and once a map of the churchyard was created anyone wanting to find a grave would be able to, but all these things take time and Rome wasn't built in a day. As for the northeast end, this was a new area and the most important to tend, first impressions mean a lot when people visit and should always come first. As for the southeast area, well apart from finding Richard Hickley's headstone and his story, this area remained virtually untapped history-wise. I did cut the grass and strim tight to the foot of the impressive headstones in that area but as for research, nothing had been done by myself. It was the original churchyard from around the 13th century so many a fine story to uncover there for people if they knew what they were looking for to take on a project.

Chapter 21
Seeking Justice

At Durley I could now pick and choose what I did at the churchyard and was comfortable with the way things fell into place. Whatever turned up seemed to come in stages and intermingled; the conclusion of each research never got in the way of each other. You would be busy with one thing but have time to investigate another.

At this time, it was all change, especially for the personnel regarding the parochial church council. The main two churchwardens had stood down from their voluntary positions; they had contributed much to the church during their tenure. The new churchwardens began their duties, and the changeover was seamless. I had plenty of irritating conflicts with the previous incumbents. So, whether that would change remained to be seen, however the early signs were good – the first thing the new churchwardens did was to order the rest of the great cedar trees to be cut down. So, this was good news, not just for me but many of the villagers who came and took the timber for winter and there was plenty of it. One gentleman made me a pen out of some of the timber he had, something I will keep for always. I had to cut the tree stumps out; each one took me a month to move. Working in the afternoons, I chopped away until each of the tree's roots were no longer visible. And to look at the area, no one would think there were once two massive cedar trees in that area; they had never grown properly because they grew from graves and were unable to establish a proper root system so they suffered too in a way from a lack of respect for one of Mother Nature's wonderful gifts. So, things began to change for the good of the churchyard at last, and after many months of searching, Adrian Abbott found a record of where the Reverend Richard Ferguson and co. had put the bones from inside the church. Listed in the grave numbers, one small line entry read: "Number 398 bones removed from inside the church 1879."

For Adrian, this was a major find, and as we know people chose where they wanted to be buried. So, if we found graves 397 and 399 it may not follow that the grave where the bones were was in between the two of them. Adrian found that grave number 397 was occupied by Robert Pink. He had died in 1820 aged eight. There were many of the Pink family buried at the east end of the churchyard, just a few yards away from church cottage. In fact, if you were to stand in its garden and look westward to the churchyard, on your left would be the original pre-13th century churchyard, and on your right would be the first churchyard extension when the first north boundary hedge was taken out in 1878. So, the numbering of graves Adrian believed would have been done in 1935 and ran numerically from the west end area up to the boundary at the east end.

However, in the 13th century area there were only a few headstones that could be seen and nearly all of those were impossible to decipher given their age and condition they were in. But there were 12 rows of graves from the south door of the church from (A) to (L), and Robert Pink's grave number 397 in row (L) was right on the boundary looking west. Take a step to the left and you would be in the southeast area of the old pre-13th century churchyard where 398 and the bones were supposed to be. But next to Robert Pink's grave to the south there was no headstone, just the residue of three grave mounds with no record of their numbers or who rested within each one.

The next three headstones on from Robert Pink's were some 15 feet away and were in a mess and impossible to read. The records showed the first headstone was the grave of Stephen Holmes, son of John and Elizabeth, who had lost his life by accident on 8th September 1827 aged 28 years. Next to Stephen was Margaret Holmes, the daughter of John and Elizabeth Holmes who died 20th February 1827 aged 39, and the third headstone after these two was William and Rachel Windust. William died on 22nd August 1833, he was 76. The records showed that Rachel had died in 1800 in November with no date just a question mark; there was also a question mark against her age – she was 5-? something. The last four headstones in the row were about 30 feet away, the first being in loving memory of Sarah, wife of Jonathan Misselbrook. She died 6th September 1843 aged 39. The inscription on the headstone read: "This stone placed to the memory by her Master and Mistress as a token of respect for many years devoted and faithful service."

Next to Sarah was the grave of her husband Jonathan who died on 21st October 1839 aged 37. Also on the headstone was a tribute to Henry Misselbrook, son of Jonathan and Sarah Misselbrook who died on board HMS Simoomine, China on 26th February 1861 aged 19 years. The last two headstones were next to the lych gate, Edward Barfoot who died 11th January 1855 aged 89. Then to complete row (L) the last headstone said: "Sacred to the memory" of Edward Martin who died 25th June 1849 aged 66 also Eliza Martin, wife of Edward, who died 26th November 1863 aged 76.

So, it was quite sobering looking at these records and if I did not have to find the bones, I would have found out more about each family and I could not see these graves being of interest in the search. To be honest, they were from dates well before any work had been carried out by the Reverend Ferguson, and not even he would use old graves to dispose of old bones from inside the church. We were stuck and no matter how many times you read the small entry in the records "398, Bones taken from within the Church", given Robert Pink's grave was 397 in row (L) you would automatically think the bones were in the same row, but which of the graves was 398?

Adrian walked the length of row (L) but the metal detector gave no indication of any cast iron numbers in the vicinity at all. So near yet so far, and complicated to boot! Just to complicate things a little further, in 2016, in the old 13th-century part of the churchyard, I had found a number purely by chance. The only one, I might add, that at the time I thought must have come from somewhere else, so I dug a hole at the back of the headstone where I had found it. The headstone leaned to the left and was impossible to read and while Adrian was scratching his head and complaining to the spirt of Robert Pink Esquire, I went and dug the number out and believe it or not it was 399. In the records, this grave was in row (J) and 66 graves away from Robert Pink's and the resting place of a Mr and Mrs Charles and Martha May.

Martha had died aged 38 in 1864. Charles May died 40 years after Martha in 1904 aged 81. He was also village clerk during the time when the work was carried out by the Reverend Ferguson. Charles and Martha May were also the parents of Abraham May whose headstone had been broken at grave 47 and moved next to the Churcher grave in row (A) at the west end of the churchyard. It was ironic that the May family seemed to be leading us toward where the bones might be buried. The fact that the number 399 was the only one in the southeast of the pre-13th century churchyard could be considered a clue or a sign. Because as village clerk, Charles May was around at the time of the renovations to the church, and something so amazing as finding people buried inside the church would have swept around the village in no time at all.

Even if Charles May was no longer the clerk, he would have been kept in the loop so to speak. The work and what was found was well documented in the press at the time, copies that are still around today, some 140 years on, kept in the records office at Winchester. In Durley, at the time there were more members of the Mays than any other family in the village, so direct relations of Charles May would have known all about this part of his history. His son Abraham and his wife Sarah had eight children who would have known what was found in the church. Information that would have been handed down through the generations. The children would not have known what happened to the bones, but I would think that Abraham May would have because grave number 399 was the grave of his mother and he would have made sure that his father Charles May had been laid to rest next to her and shared the same number. So, it would have been a number of some importance around the time the work had been carried out in the late 1800s. It could be that some members of the May family always knew where the bones had been buried, which if it was next to Charles and Martha's grave, then this grave only had a small headstone, more like a footstone, in fact a marker maybe.

Adrian and I were back on the trail of the bones and the big question for me was why Robert Pink's grave would be included in the renumbering in 1935 and given the number 397. When it was so obvious, he died 115 years before the renumbering and over 50 years before the first extension to the churchyard where this renumbering took place. Records showed that Robert Pink's parents were Thomas and Sarah Pink, Thomas Pink's grave was number 393. Sarah's 394, then two of their daughters, Caroline occupied grave number 395, and Sarah's grave number 396.

This line of graves must have been set aside well in advance for the Pink family and further research brought to light that Thomas Pink once farmed at the Greenwood Estate, next to the church. A pattern began to emerge. We had the rector, Richard Ferguson, the parish clerk Charles May – whose father by the way was once the sexton and parish clerk – then the Pink Family, whose business interests with the church must have helped them secure the plots for their respective burials. Not all of them came from Durley but were favoured with plots in a prominent area of the churchyard, and Robert Pink's grave was used as a reference i.e. 397, and people who were around at the time of the restoration work to the church could have known where the bones went that were taken from within the church.

It must have been descendants of some of them who were involved with making sure the grave numbers continued to be on future lists. A list that must still be around somewhere with more information regarding the bones and where they are. But without it we were stuck, the only real clue we had was the bones were between Robert Pink's grave and Charles May's. So, we had 65 options between numbers, 397 and 399 to work out where 398 was.

The metal detector had not picked up anything next to Robert Pink's grave. The headstone next to the May's grave was more like a footstone, a marker but I could not see this being the resting place for the remains of people taken from the church during the restorations. It was not wide enough for a start, although it was long enough and I didn't know what the remains of the people taken from within the church would have looked like.

The Reverend John Rodgers, who had been the peacemaker in the conflict between the Reverend John White and Richard Hickley and co., had himself been buried for 140 years before being moved in 1878. There would have been more of him left than the rest of them one would assume, but none of them should have been disturbed in my opinion. It made me go cold thinking about it, because I would imagine once you started you would have to see it through, and you would not know what you had to deal with until you took the lid off the coffin to see what's what.

One of the Pope family's coffins, Thomas Pope's, did have two viewing points, one each side, as the newspaper had reported because his wife or mother, it said, would want him kept from the earth until their grief had eased. Well, they would turn in their own graves if they had known what plundering Dick Ferguson and co. had done to their loved one. So, was this grave next to 399 narrow as it was the resting place of the people taken from the church? It would hardly be dignified, to gather them all up and pop them in with each other.

Anyway, Adrian walked over the plot with the rods and the grave was longer than usual. It could have been for more than one person, just like the Houghton children's at the west end of the churchyard. I did dig and remove the molehills from around the footstone and cleaned it, but it just had the initials in bold lettering of someone who had died in 1810. So that was it. We had to face reality and admit the lead had gone cold once more.

Adrian's hard work looking for records had drawn a blank again, much to his annoyance, but he was very dignified in the way he took his disappointment. When we left the churchyard, he said it was not about us and what we wanted. I had to smile because as we walked, his camera case strap was down by his ankles. If I had not stopped him, he would have fallen arse over 'breakfast time', because his next step caught his foot inside the strap. Whilst taking retrograde steps, he became more entangled to the point I made him put everything down so he could climb out of the camera strap as if taking off a pair of trousers.

It had been a disappointing morning, and we were no further forward in the search for the blessed bones from inside the church. And to be perfectly honest, I hoped we never would find them given how long it had been. After lunch, I tidied up and placed the soil back around the footstone we hoped would have been 398. This grave was five rows away from the church. As I worked my way back to the church, I tended around the headstones immediately in front of what we had thought was our grave number 398, tapping the soil like a cricketer gardening his wicket with my spade.

Before I knew it, I was standing in front of the only chest stone grave at the southeast area of the original churchyard. The chest stone measured some eight feet long by three foot wide, built of brick, and it stood around three feet high. I had spent time cleaning the top of the stone before when, if you remember, I was looking for Richard Hickley's son, John Hickley's tombstone that I had found records of at Winchester. But this chest stone, while also named in the same record that a photo existed at Winchester of the two, I didn't get it because by the time the art of photography had been invented the chest and tombstone were covered in mould and grime.

I never found John Hickley's tombstone because it was not there like his father's, it had gone for whatever reason. This chest stone was the resting place of the Mears family, at least that's what it said on its stone lid – the name Mears was all I could make out when cleaning it the first time. I had made several attempts at deciphering what else was on it, but the years had not done the stone top of this chest stone any favours, also the age of it looked to pre-date the bricks used to build the chest stone. Adrian, with others, thought the stone top could have come from another area of the churchyard close to the original structure. My thoughts were, it could have been inserted into the floor of the original structure in memory of a Mears.

Now after gardening around the headstone of Charles and Martha May's grave and others, I began to chop the longish grass down with my spade that had grown up the sides of the chest stone. I would normally strim this grass tight to the ground, and as I worked my way around the chest stone the spade hit a row of bricks at the base of it and when the residue of grass was removed it revealed another row of bricks underneath and descended into the earth pyramid style. Each row about the width of a brick, there were five rows in all that made me think the chest stone was built on top of something else as the brickwork that formed the chest stone didn't match the bricks underneath – and to my amazement, I was right.

At the east end beneath the chest stone was the top of an archway, in front of the arch was an independent wall about seven feet wide that blocked off the entrance under the arch that seemed to me could be a tunnel. At the west end of the chest stone, while there was also an arch, there was a very wide footing on each side of what looked like a bricked-up entrance that was about two feet wide and situated within the arch. The wide footing each side of what I thought was an entrance indicated that this structure continued further to the north and south and may well have been part of an original building.

Also, there were headstones each side that dated back to the 17th century so the structure, whatever it was, predated them. The fact the arch at the east end was underground, meant the only way to access the structure was from the west end through the bricked-up opening. If it was a tunnel, then the independent wall at the east end sealed it off completely from what it had been used for. If the structure was a crypt or family vault then the back wall at the east end would have been tied into the two side walls, and the only way in would be via the opening on the west side that had been bricked up.

Many old churches had secret passages that would lead in and out of the church without anyone being seen, or to escape the clutches of troops in the time of the Civil War or the Reformation, if you did not conform to Parliament's decision in 1543, through the Act of Supremacy that declared King Henry VIII to be supreme head of the Church of England that would be called Anglican a Ecclesia. The well-documented rift between King Henry VIII and Pope Clement the second forced the clergy office holders and others to choose allegiances. For many it was a case of falling into line or getting away from King Henry's powerful followers. It was not just when the Reformation started that people in the clergy fell out and needed to escape, it was an occupational hazard not only in England but France too. People needing a place to hide away from the eye of the storm, recouping their losses and building up a network of people to trust. All these escape routes were very important but were lessened with the dissolution of the monasteries.

Many rural village churches continued to be used, to get people to and from the coast and Titchfield in Hampshire, not far from the Meon Valley and its many medieval churches and chapels, was one of the main ports in those days. The abbey at Titchfield would have been used in escapes, and legendary stories of escapes through certain rural villages in Hampshire were often talked about. It was interesting to say the least having found this structure when I was not looking for anything like it, but then history finds you if it is meant to be.

I rang Adrian and suggested he came back, because I had found what I believed to be a tunnel. He did so quickly and was amazed to see what was discovered; we had to tell the new churchwarden who would then inform the rector. As sexton, my first port of call was always to the churchwarden with all information, and with change in personnel within the church council it was not a good idea to assume too much. The dealings I had with the new churchwarden had all been positive, but he would have to be the one who told the rector. There was still a protocol to follow if you find something that looked to be part of another structure; that history said was once at this churchyard when in medieval times monks travelled to outlying districts from Titchfield on pastoral missions and served as parish priest ministering to the spiritual needs of all.

Titchfield churches construction was influenced by St Wilfrid who had also built the chapel at Church Norton Castle in Sussex. He was also responsible for the creation of other churches in Hampshire such as St Nicolas Church at Wickham, Corhampton Church, The Church of our Lady at Warnford, all in the Meon Valley of Hampshire. St Wilfrid, in the 7th century, had set out from Northumberland and travelled south converting people to the Christian faith in areas more in touch with pagan ways. The Jutes and Meonwara people of the Meon Valley were the last people it's said to learn about Jesus from St Wilfrid who settled among them. His influence is evident in many of the churches that are said to have a secret entrance attached to their historical stories, some had been found and others just remained legends.

Secret tunnels that when talked about went further than was possible, stories embellished over time. There was a legend of a secret tunnel being at Durley. The story had been told down the years and if it was true and what had been found was part of the first structure to be built on the site, then this was a major find. The first structure built was said to be in the mid to late 12th century and before that the area was said to be just a religious venue dedicated to "A Holy Cross". People gathered long before the 12th-century chapel at the Blessed Mary at Upham cum Durley was created. Then in the 14th century, when the north and south transepts were built along with the bell tower, it remained a chapel until it became a church in its own right around 1853. That's how it stayed up until 1878/9 when plundering Richard Ferguson and co. got their hands on the place.

So, first question, how did this structure remain a secret or did it? And if it didn't, then who knew about it would be the second question. So, it was all hands-on deck for the research team that had increased in my time at Durley. I decided to take out more soil from around the structure. What we couldn't work out was why the chest stone was built on top of it. After digging about 18 inches down around the perimeter of the structure, it increased in size; as the width of the arch seemed to become wider the further down, I dug. One spit of the spade each time forensically, and when I reached halfway at the east side I had to stop when Adrian noticed a small child's skull. It was face down in the soil so not in a grave. It was also laid south to north, a normal grave at Durley would be west to east and the skull's features would have been facing up.

We wanted to call the police and coroner because this skull was not buried in a conventional way, the grave was shallow and there was no coffin. Nothing about it indicated it was a genuine burial so who was it and why was it buried against the independent wall that blocked the arch and why was it only 18 inches down in the soil.

All these questions would need to be answered, and what were the circumstances surrounding it being there. So, the work stopped, and the churchwarden was informed. He would then tell the rector who would in turn inform the archdeacon. The problem with that was the higher up you go, what was more likely to happen was we would be told to stop the excavation and backfill what was taken out. The archdeacon would tell the rector to say a few words over the child's skull and that would be that job done as far as the clergy were concerned. And that's exactly what happened, the archdeacon had ruled the area next to the east side of the structure was now to be considered a grave.

However, the rules of the Chancellor's office state that the PCC of all churches are responsible for the protection of all humans remains. I was not prepared to leave it at that, or was I worried that we had a major find? Yes, I wanted to find out what it was, but first we had to sort out the skull and if it was still attached to the rest of the remains. Articulate is the term used, then you can't touch it, if it's a de-articulated skeleton, i.e. in bits, then you still can't touch it because it's archaeology and in each case it's a job for the coroner as I understood it.

As sexton of the church, people trusted me with looking after their loved one's graves, so I was not going to be involved with covering anything up. I talked to the new churchwarden who was a military man, a Major General, in fact, from one of the most important families in the village, and the nearest person to a Lord of the Manor you could get, living as he did on his large estate at Wintershill, where many of my ancestors had worked as gardeners. It was the Major General I asked if I could take Peter Brian Prowting to his estate and show him where his grandfather once worked, but sadly Peter died before we could keep that appointment and with him any hope of a financial boost to keep the churchyard going as we once talked about.

So now as the General's sexton we had to sort out what to do about the structure and the skull which we called A.N.Other; we couldn't keep calling it the skull, we needed to do the right thing in both respects. The conversations we had with the General up until then were all lively, he was as keen as we were to make the churchyard a going concern. He got involved with everything and showed good leadership as you would expect from a man with his background who would lead by example and was a pleasure to have him on board. My work as sexton became a lot easier as the General understood what I was endeavouring to achieve. The only problem I could see regarding the structure and A.N.Other, was how long things would take once the PCC got involved. Their decision would then go to the Diocese for approval, if indeed they all agreed that we should do the right thing regarding A.N.Other and the structure.

However, the General decided the excavating around the tunnel could continue, but the northeast corner had to be left while he looked into what to do about the remains of A.N.Other. So, it took me a day to dig out enough soil and expose what a fascinating structure this was. We asked for permission to drop a camera down into the tunnel to see what was inside and on the General's say so permission was granted, so all the early positive signs of the new regime was encouraging. Unlike the problems I encountered with the other lot. In fact, the transition from working at the west end area to breaking new ground, so to speak, at the southwest of the churchyard was actually seamless and all of a sudden, I found myself back in business, only this time there were no great piles of spoil to move before I could do anything.

It was rather like finding yourself in next door's garden. Everything that was familiar looked a little different from where I was now standing. Also, the headstone and accompanying spirits were much older at the southeast area. Rather like having been with your grandparents and then finding yourself in the company of your great-grandparents who you would have to earn the respect of and who may not appreciate you taking things for granted as you had done, having once got to know what we're after all the children of these spirits who were at rest down at the west end of the churchyard.

Adrian and I agreed he would return to the churchyard and take photographs of structure both inside and out in a week's time, allowing me to prepare the area and work out the best place to remove bricks from the structure. The two side walls were each over 18 inches thick and spread out like a bell the further down you went. So, cutting out bricks at the sides was not an option, the best place to access the tunnel was on the west side of the structure facing the church. Although the west end wall was also 18 inches thick, where the entrance was bricked up it was only the width of one brick and the best place to drop the camera in.

The brickwork there had been affected by frost damage. For many years the wind and rain had battered the chest grave that was built on top of the old structure. Underneath it, the bricks down there were much older and longer in size, and as well as being a lot softer they retained the water that ran down from the chest grave. In winter they would become frozen, causing the old lime mortar joints to blister, swell up and return to a dusty state, and once dry it was easy to rake out the joints without having to use a hammer and chisel that would have damaged these fragile bricks.

The few days I spent preparing the structure for its photoshoot gave me time to appreciate what an amazing find this was, and understand just how clever the tradesmen were. The biggest question though, what was this structure? If it were a family crypt or vault, then the bricked-up opening on the west side would make perfect sense, since when a family member died and the coffin placed into the crypt/ vault, it was sealed up again and so on till the last person of that particular family joined other relatives to rest in peace. But, this structure was open at the east end and sealed by an independent wall from more recent times, so my theory was what we had was a tunnel that allowed people to go from the church into the churchyard without being seen. An escape route for want of a better word. I also thought it to be part of a bigger structure that was once linked to the church and the tunnel could have run into and under the floor of the church.

That is how I saw things at that moment in time. It was only an opinion based on what I had seen before in other buildings I had worked on in the past. I had seen many a priest hole used to escape the aggressive unwelcome intruders. There would be other opinions of course but that was fine, we would find out in time what it was.

Just in front of the structure on the westside was a row of headstones about ten feet from the church, and in front of them was a stone path that ran across the graves south to north. This was the path that caused so much anger when the Reverend Richard Ferguson took out headstones and used them to make a path. In John Bosworth's book it said that civil war almost broke out in the village when the rector took out these headstones to make the path, showing a complete lack of respect toward people's graves. I could see what made the villagers angry, the headstones still had some inscriptions that were still visible to the naked eye having been worn down by many years of excessive use as an unwelcome path. But as we know, the rector at the time, Richard Ferguson, had little respect for anything regarding the church or indeed the villagers' concerns, he was a law unto himself like many other of the rectors before him.

With the General's permission, I took up the old headstones and gardened the area in front of the graves then laid a shingle path closer to the church. It ran the same length south to north but did not go over the graves and didn't take long to do. I did have help from local villager Chrissy Rumbold, a retired front-line ambulance worker who had no trouble moving the old broken headstones, having lifted heavier things in her previous occupation. We soon removed the stones that had caused so much anger back in the late 1800s. If we were going to open this area for the public to view, then we needed things looking tidy in that area and if people kept to the new path, they would be able to see everything.

So, by the time Adrian came back for the photoshoot, I had the area up together. I had raked out the joints of the brickwork so we could lift two of them out and put them back with new mortar when we had finished. We were ready to see what was in the tunnel! How big it was and what direction it took, other than what we could already see. Adrian positioned himself in the surrounding trench, tied the strap to his wrist and dropped the camera into the tunnel which immediately lit up and the camera began to take pictures. Adrian skilfully moved the camera around; he didn't have much room and stopped once or twice to reposition himself, then after 15 minutes the work on the westside was finished.

Of course, we wouldn't know what we had till he went home to process his work. We talked about what we may see while I made good the brickwork. It reminded me of when we discovered the first cast iron number at the west end of the churchyard, it was a sort of feeling of melancholy, excitement and fear, if you like, the mixture of the two made your chin shiver as you began to speak.

The cold chill I felt back then was present again. I knew I had done nothing wrong the same as back then, but it was a strange feeling all the same. When the dry mortar I used began to cure, I rubbed dry earth on the two bricks I had removed to make them look old and untouched. Once the air had dried the area, Adrian asked if we were going to take photos from the east side. However, the situation regarding that was, as I had agreed with the General, that I would not move the earth from the area where I had found A.N.Other.

The only way we could drop a camera down into the tunnel was by removing a broken brick from the centre of the arch, situated behind the independent wall that had sealed off the tunnel. The brick was loose anyway and its soft mortar easy to cut through, so there was no need to use a hammer because if I cut through the mortar each side of the brick with a saw, its weight would allow it to drop into the tunnel. It would mean Adrian had to crouch right down to operate the camera, and because he was confident he could do it, we made an executive decision to remove the brick. Adrian had to kneel and lean against the chest stone and could not see where the opening was that the camera had to be dropped into.

It was a job for a long-armed gynaecologist really, rather than a very tall cameraman but he managed well enough. Mind you, there were some extraordinary looks on his face as he propped himself up against the chest grave above to support himself and, if I had another camera, I could have got some wonderful pictures of his face as he grimaced and tried to keep himself upright. Needless to say, he did a great job and while I set about repairing the arch, Adrian went home to process the many photos he had taken, copies of which would go on a memory stick for me.

After our successful morning work, I cleaned the tools and had just put everything away when my mobile phone rang. It was Adrian saying he was coming back up and for me to wait there. I didn't have a chance to say anything because he rang off and I thought the worst that the photos had not come out and he would want to try again. Anyway, within half an hour he was back, not with his camera as I expected, but with a large A4 envelope and he looked pretty concerned. We sat down on the old chest stone and Adrian took out three photos and the memory stick and handed them to me.

The three photos of the inside of the tunnel were amazing, the camera had captured perfectly the arched brickwork ceiling of the tunnel, so I was pleased with what we had found. However, Adrian wasn't and handed me more pictures of the tunnel floor and they were gruesome. The tunnel was full of human remains and broken coffins. Adrian was shaken having seen them first, and what had been found was, we thought, the human remains from inside the church. Well, what would we do now, how could we prove that these bones were from inside the church? We discussed the situation and what our next move should be. No one had any idea we had taken the photos that day and it was a good job they didn't because we were in no mood to talk about this find. We, or rather I, had only seen a few of the pictures, whereas Adrian had seen them all and was beside himself having searched for so long for records of where the bones were. He would not have expected to find them in an old tunnel obviously abandoned there, after already having received a proper burial which was many years ago.

So, what happened next was each of us went home. We decided to talk later on to swap opinions regarding the photographs. Later on, turned out to be six days because that's how long it took to look through and make notes of what we could see so when we did get together, we could discuss each photograph frame by frame. Each one a still of a moment in time when the actions of a few people who represented a body such as the church disregarded the human remains, of some of the Lord's children and confined them to this hidden cave of a tunnel for them never to be heard of again.

Not until then, that is, so I looked at each photograph and made notes. I had to get over the shock of what I could see that looked even more gruesome when blown up on a full screen that enlarged everything, picking out all the things of importance, the many bones and skulls, none which were attached as you might imagine. When I got used to that after many looks, then I could view each frame with the respectful intention of sorting this gruesome problem out in their memory. These people should have been resting in peace and not in pieces as they were at that moment in time.

I copied each of the photos onto A4 extra white paper and placed each one in clear multi-punched A4 poly packet and put them in a file. The first half of the file was of wonderful photos of the outside of the structure and the impressive arched brick ceiling inside. Then if I were going to show anyone, I would tell them that if they looked further on in the file, they might find the photographs rather disturbing.

However, because I had taken the trouble to tell them the whole story regarding the removal of human remains from the church in 1879, and the story right up to and including this point, people wanted to see for themselves what this was all about and I wanted them to. I was sure the clergy would try and qualify doing nothing was the only option, just say a prayer or two and forget we ever found the human remains. I am not talking about the PCC, this was far too big a responsibility for them to make a decision on nor was it fair on them. We may have had our ups and downs in the past but in reality, they were good people. They just fell short when it came to admitting they were not qualified to make certain decisions and they were also reluctant to put themselves out to try and understand and learn from people who knew what they were talking about. But this problem was not going away and there would be a standoff with the clergy before anything happened.

It was very important to try and gain some breathing space and not push for an early conclusion to this problem; we needed to let things calm down while we worked to find out as much as possible to make a case to hand to the General. You have to remember it was members of the clergy and the powers that be who had tried to hide all this in 1879. But by bragging about what work would be done to the newspapers and who was going to carry out the work, it was not surprising when things went wrong that the newspapers of the day would pick up on it. Dishing the dirt in newspapers is nothing new, articles that back then would only be around till the next edition came out, unlike today when the world and his wife can see what's going on as it happens, and with the internet we can bring the past right up to date. True, there would be no one around to blame but that wasn't my motivation, if it was then I would have gone public but that would not make what needed to be done any easier. Each person I showed the file to said we should try and do the right thing, so when I could work out what we had then it would be a question of who to ask for help in a covert way. I had to do this because if the clergy had got wind of what I intended to do, they would find a way to block me. As sexton, after building up people's trust over what was years of hard work, I could not be seen to be doing anything other than what was right in this situation. I also knew I would have to go it alone; I could not drag anyone else into it, especially not Adrian, he would stay in the background. I hoped he would back me up if I needed help with things of historical nature, so for the time being I said nothing to the General. He had already said we should do the right thing but "not yet".

If the General said "not yet" he meant it with knobs on, as he had several things he wanted to look into, and when he was satisfied then we could talk again. Until then I was told to follow the archdeacon's instructions, that the tunnel would be classified as a grave. So, the longer I left things the clergy would think I had bitten off more than I could chew and back away from what was, in their eyes, none of my business. If that's what they thought, then it was good news for those of us who were active in gaining all the information possible to present the case, first to the General and hope to convince him that what was found in the tunnel was linked to what had come out of the church in 1879.

You may say it was years ago and why bother now, well everyone has an opinion and if that's yours, it's respected. So, what did we have? Well let's forget the tunnel for a moment and the photos and remind ourselves of the newspaper article that gave the names of people buried in the church. The first record of a Durley dedication was in the will of William Oysel dated the 1st of August 1410. He was said to be "sick in body but sound in mind" and left a sum of money for the masses for his soul and sanctuary and desired to be buried in the "Capella de Santa Cruce", under the low arch of the south transept window housed his tomb where he rested for over 400 years.

Then we have the Reverend Mr John Rodgers Curate at the "Capella de Santa Cruce" for over 65 years, a man dedicated to the people of Durley. The peacemaker in the disputes between the Reverend John White of Upham cum Durley and Durley's favourite, Mr Richard Hickley. John Rodgers' interment in the church showed the respect the villagers held for him, and he lay peacefully undisturbed for over 137 years. The newspaper article continued, amongst more recent burials there were two series in the chancel. The first, close under the wall and the communion table, are those of the Hersent family, who occupied Durley Manor down to the close of the Merry Monarch's reign, after which the family became extinct in Durley.

Also buried in the chancel were members of the Pope family, one of whose graves – Thomas Pope – was opened accidentally. The dried skeleton and the remains of the oak coffin with the remnants of cloth fastened with brass nails and the deceased's initials. But curiously enough the coffin lid had once been secured by lock and key, and the upper part of the lid provided with a winged flap to view the features of the deceased. Proof that he was kept from the earth for some time to sooth, perchance, the feelings of a bereaved wife or loving mother.

So who were the other members of the Hersent and Pope families buried within the church? Well Elizabeth Hersent died in June 1639, then just over 12 months later in August 1640, Henry Hersent passed away. The two of them had been buried for just under 235 years before being disturbed. Then 45 years later, Mr Peter Hersent died in June 1685. He rested peacefully for 194 years inside the church. The last member of the Hersent family recorded in the burial records I could find was Mr John Hersent the elder, who died in 1705 and he only had to wait 174 years before he was removed. The Hersent family must have had some influence at Durley given the length of time between the first and last burial, just like outside in the churchyard maybe people picked their spot inside the church as well. The only difference being the people outside could rest easy for all time.

Now regarding the Pope family, other than Thomas Pope, whose place in the church was well documented, but no record of when he died, there were two more Popes, Susan Pope who died in September 1688 and following Susan was William Pope who died in May 1707. So, their time in the church was 172 and 197 years respectively. Then Adrian found a record of the will of William Munday drawn up in 1572, and he directed that his body should go alongside his father in the north chancel. No dates of each burial were recorded so assuming William Munday's wish was granted, that indicated 11 people were buried inside the church.

We also had the occupants' names which should have made the research easier, but the problem was there didn't seem to be enough bones in the tunnel, not for 11 people anyway because, we could only see five skulls. The Hersent and Pope families, so the newspaper article said, were in the chancel close under the wall and communion table. Above the newly created furnace vault, the removal of William Oysel's remains was also well documented. Nothing though about the Reverend Mr John Rodgers' remains.

As for William Munday and his father, if they were under the floor of the north transept, they could still be there as not much work was carried out in that isolated area. So, we have the remains of eight people to account for, and that was just the ones we knew about back then. Many people wished to rest within the church, that's if people could pay that is, a fact commented on by Robert Philips, a gravedigger in Kingsbridge, England. His epitaph read: "Here I lie by the Chancel door, Here I lie because I'm poor, The further in the more they pay, Here I lie as warm as they." It seems our eight deserving souls went to some lengths to rest in peace within Durley church but are remembered more for being cast out and into the chilly confinements of a medieval tunnel by the actions of a few people who then tried to cover their tracks and blame everyone else when things went wrong.

In another newspaper article it said of the three series of frescoes that were destroyed, that the architects J. Colson and Son, who are zealous antiquaries and ecclesiologists, were not appraised of the fact the frescoes were even there. That the clergymen of the parish seemed to have been untold of them by the workmen. Well what rot that is! I doubt that the workmen, agricultural labourers most of them, would start work without first being told what was needed of them. Nor would they know what a fresco was in the first place. In fact, if they did see things written on the walls, chances are they could not read it anyway so would ask someone who could, and that would be the people running the show – J. Colson and Son or the Reverend Richard Ferguson.

As for the human remains being removed from the church, I am sure the workmen would have questioned that. The churchyard was sacred to them – they may have had relations resting there – so would resist because, if word got round the village that they were involved in removing human remains, they would have been questioned forcefully no doubt. The removal of the human remains would have been carried out by the clergy, and in secret. The church was closed to all during the refurbishment and that made it easy for them, and when the church reopened, a task carried out by the Bishop of the Diocese, no less, who I am sure would be completely unaware of what had gone on during the refurbishment of the Church of the Holy Cross at Durley.

So, I looked at the photographs forensically, starting with number one, a view from the west looking east, inside the tunnel. The first few photographs were mainly of the top half of the tunnel, and if this discovery had not involved such a sorry tale, it would have been easier to admire the craftsman's art. However, my primary task was to look for clues as best I could and one thing I did notice was the side of one of the coffin's separated from the rest that laid at a 45-degree angle southwest to northeast. The camera seemed to have been right on top of it, and you could even see the grain of the decaying oakwood – the picture was so clear. Also, more importantly, its faded brass handle that had turned to the colour blue was still intact, and right down the side of this section of the coffin were signs of fabric that had rotted over time and left the imprint of the fabric that was once fixed with brass tacks or something like it that had also turned parts of the oak coffin to the colour of blue. Blue stain in the wood could be a result of the tannic-acid-rich log moisture mixing with the iron of the saw blade that had cut the wood or a metal that had been fixed to the coffin. I immediately thought of the description in the newspaper article regarding Thomas Pope's impressive coffin and was convinced what I was looking at now was indeed part of the side of his coffin; it was so obvious.

As far I was concerned, what I thought to be a well-constructed tunnel had become a crypt by default. So, this was my first clue in the attempt to get enough evidence to present to the General. If I could convince him then I stood a good chance of getting what I would like to happen, and that was a proper resting place for A.N.Other, and then remove the independent wall from in front of the arch at the east end of the structure. Then put all the human remains into new coffins and leave them where they were. If I had been allowed to bring in a bones expert it may have been possible to match certain bones with the help of DNA. Anything of historical interest could be recorded and left inside, we could then brick up the east end once more making the old structure secure again. People would know what was inside and probably interested in both stories – what the structure was and who the people were inside.

It was no good pretending there was no cover up in 1879 because there was, and by putting things right now would show respect for the families who when they had been alive had a significant standing in the village. But this one bit of evidence would not be enough to convince anyone. I would have to find more than that solitary item, because the 'big cheeses' in the church's hierarchy would want the whole thing to go away. And if I presented them with just that photo, they would laugh me out of court. I would need more evidence to give to the General before I could expect him to go and fight what was in effect my battle.

Another photograph showed a faded name on a steel or brass lid that would have covered a coffin when under the floor; sometimes people take rubbings of such things. Trying to make out the name on the lid was impossible, even trying from different angles; there was too much dust on the lid. Further back in the tunnel on another steel lid I could make out two symbols of the fleur-de-lis one in each corner, finding this stylised emblem in a small out-of-the-way medieval churchyard was interesting. The fleur-de-lis, French for the lily flower, symbolised the crown of France for one thousand years and could mean an important person's connection with the village and links to France. In the 12th century, a French monarch used the emblem on his shield, English kings later used the fleur-de-lis on coats of arms to emphasise claims to the throne of France. The symbol could mean anything when you research its origin. In Mauritius, slaves were punished for stealing food or trying to escape and branded with the fleur-de-lis symbol. And Lord Robert Baden Powell, the founder of the Scout movement, adopted the fleur-de-lis symbol. So there were many reasons for the symbol's use but whatever it was in the context of this coffin lid would remain a mystery, at least for now anyway.

Adrian thought the name on the steel plate said 'Mears', and in the burial records there were plenty of them dating back to 1611, the first being John-De-Lyon-Mere. The word variation would eventually become Mears, as many names changed as the years progressed. For instance, if you have an 'I' in your name, it would have been a 'Y' back then. In 1465, Richard Prowtyng worked the lands around Durley, and with the advancement of years the surname became Prowting. The Mears family were well-to-do farmers in Durley and nearby Bishops Waltham, and one of the families had a large headstone built into the original external wall of the south chancel of the church, to commemorate the life of an infant child. So, if the Mears family had that much clout within the village, one of them may have been laid to rest within the church. If the name on the metal coffin lid in the photo was Mears or Meere, then the plot would thicken even more, an indication that a Mears or Meere would have to be added to the list of people buried within the church proper. The name Meere or Mears derives from the old English word 'mere' meaning pond, so nothing to do with France.

When word got around that what had been found was to be put on hold, people came in and asked why. So I told them more evidence was needed and if anyone could remember anything about the legend of the tunnel or things connected to it, maybe stories handed down through the generations like this one from 1879 that could have spanned the years, then to let me know. At least that's what I hoped; it was a long shot, I know, but you have to be optimistic or you get nothing.

I still had plenty to do in the churchyard and had no intention of looking at the east end of the churchyard as another project, not with the tunnel on hold, it was not worth it, as nothing would be more important than what we had found already. We had found the Motherload, so to speak, and it was just a question of sieving through the information we hoped would come in. So as autumn 2019 approached, I made sure the west end area of the churchyard was ready for winter, falling leaves from the great oak trees would in time cover a vast area and would protect the deep-rooted bulbs from the frosty nights. The whole of the west end area had completely changed, and with Dumuzid's efforts in the underworld, each spring brought with it a vast amount of colourful wildflowers so kind on the eye. I had completed the removal of the cedar tree's roots by just chipping away at what was left and my expectations were high as to what wildflowers Mother Nature would bless that area with come the spring.

New life from sacred old lives in the rejuvenated area that was the west end of the churchyard. It had been a busy year, what with one thing and another, mostly peaceful and quiet. It was good to see everyone and enjoy our conversations that while serious were also informative. There were lighter moments as well. One summer's day, I was with a regular visitor, an elderly lady who I would walk with to her husband's ashes plot, then when she had finished, I would walk her back to her car. On the way round the yard, I would look into the outside little boy's room to make sure no one had received a visitation from God while in there. It was always a relief to see that no one had, or that the Grim Reaper was not sat there, maybe waiting for me. When we reached the gate at the south hedgerow, on opening it, I noticed another lady in her 50s coming across the road. So, waiting for her to come into the churchyard, the elderly lady and I moved back so she could come in, as the gate opens inwards. If you needed to go down the west end of the churchyard, as this visitor did, then we would all move back up the path so the gate can be closed to let the visitor walk by. As she did, she looked at us and said what a nice day it was, and that she had scattered her husband's ashes under the big oak trees to the west. To which we replied that was nice, but then she said it was done without permission and all of a sudden, she began to fall backwards down the slight incline as if she had been pushed by an angry spirit. I put my arm out to try and stop her, but her rotation backwards just pushed my arm away. The lady dressed for summer fell through the hedge backwards and wedged herself between the steps and the hedge. Well, what could I do? My elderly lady, by this time was shaking on the top step and gripping my arm wondering what on earth was going on. I released myself from her grip and told her to hold on to the gate while I worked out how to get the other lady out, but when I got down onto the road things looked different than from above. Her legs were up in the air and her summer dress up around her chest. Whatever underwear she selected for the warm summer's day had disappeared into the two available orifices and looked like a wrong-sized band aid covering a rather nasty scar. I had seen a woman's nether regions before of course but never of someone I had not been properly introduced to.

So, once I had worked out how to go about getting the woman out, I leaned over her and placed my hands under her buttocks and lifted her up and, with her legs still spread, I had one on each of my shoulders and my face smack in the middle of her you know what. Her head was between my ankles and her hands gripping my legs; she was stopping me from bending my knees. So, I had to stride backwards from side to side till we reached the grass verge on the other side of the road, where we flopped down on the ground in a position that looked even worse, and both struggled to separate ourselves from each other's grip. If we had been seen, we would have surely been arrested. My regular elderly lady, who was still shaking on the top step and gripping the post, just stood open mouthed, so what would we say.

Well, we said absolutely nothing right then, but after taking the shocked elderly lady back to her car, I walked back to the churchyard and said the first thing that came into my head. That was to ask the lady if she would like a cup of tea – well what would you say? – and while she brushed herself down and declined my offer of tea, she said that she really should get back and off she went, looking like something that had been dragged through the hedge backwards, which of course she had been.

So, the life of a sexton is a varied one. The lady comes in from time to time and we talk about things like the weather but never mention the day we would both rather forget. You see, when people say I must have seen it all as sexton, I smile and say I most certainly have.

It wasn't long before people began to come and talk to me about the legend of the tunnel and the many different places it supposedly ran to. All the stories were interesting, and I took them all seriously. They were mostly the same version of a subject handed down through the years that, if you had not seen it, as these people hadn't, they told the story with an air of disbelief – almost embarrassment, you could say. However, when I showed them a photograph of the tunnel, a legend they had only heard of, they were all amazed at what they could see – it was such a wonderful structure, but it was very sad that it now represented something so unbelievable, even more than the legend itself. Each person's comment to me after they had seen the photo of the arched tunnel roof was "I told you so" but when they had seen the photos of the rest of the structure that comment was followed by "Oh my God, look at that" and from a moment of elation was born deflation in what they could see. Everyone agreed that we should do the right thing in this matter. It was also strange because having been told about the skull, A.N.Other was referred to as a real person and came up in conversations as to who it might be and was accepted as part of the fabric of the churchyard. No one had seen the skull apart from myself and Adrian.

But A.N.Other became real, just like Richard Hickley. His headstone was enough to convince people he was real, as did this small skull with two teeth that was A.N.Other. One gentleman told me that in the mid-70s he had worked as a security guard for the probation services and that very early one Sunday morning, he came with a work party to Durley churchyard and took away bones. He was quite adamant that it was bones when I asked him if he was sure, and told me the bones were in large bags that went to Gosport in Hampshire. He had no idea where they ended up, but I thanked the gentleman for the information and decided to contact the probation services to find out if they had archives of previous work parties' contracts. I eventually found the right offices, and after giving a lady all the information the gentleman had given me, it was a question of waiting to see what materialised. So, it was another iron in the fire, and slowly a story began to take shape, and within the month there was more relevant information.

Adrian had been active in the process of finding things out and one of his neighbours, a retired builder, told him that in the 1970s he was contacted by the church to repair damage done inside the church after a break-in. Also there had been extensive damage out in the churchyard. Now, not far from the church in Durley there was an approved school. I had been told of damage in the churchyard before by local people who said it was caused by youths from the school. The school had shut down in 1990. I had been to the place after it had closed because of a fire. A teacher had been overlooked for promotion and ran amok and burnt the place down. The youths from the school could cross the fields to the church without being seen and if they had found their way into the tunnel and trashed the place and scattered bones, then it could tie in with the story the security guard told me about the bones. Also, if the churchwardens had known it was the youths from the school, they would expect the school's management to sort things out. If the school used the probation services, then they could have set up the early Sunday morning removal of bones. If that was the case, I could forget about hearing back from the probation office if the removal of the bones wasn't official. This theory had legs but not easy to follow up because there wouldn't be a record kept by the church.

It would be easy to find out who the churchwardens were at the time but hardly worth it because if they dealt with the matter in-house, it would seem the right thing to do. If we were faced with the same scenario now, we would probably do the same thing. We would keep a record of events but that would be the only difference because we knew about what happened in 1879 and it is unlikely the churchwardens in the mid-70s would. They would have been shocked to have to deal with the situation surrounding the bones and the less said the better would have been the order of the day.

I talked about my theory with the General, who kept an open mind because he knew I was searching for proof to put before him so then he could take the issue up with the church authorities. The man was as straight as a gun barrel so would give me all the time I needed. I suggested it may be an idea if he called in all paperwork that may be held by recent church officials. So, he set up a meeting with all former officials that he would chair at his estate on the outskirts of Durley. The General was a dynamic character and set up everything with military precision. His expectations of other people were high. He knew everyone's strength and that's what he focused on; he knew how to get the best out of people and for a small church council to have someone like him at the helm there was only one way to go and that was avanti.

The meeting was arranged with former church officials, and it was no surprise that several documents turned up out of the blue. One being a full-scale map of the churchyard that I had asked for so many times but told there was no such thing. The person that came forward with it was the same person responsible with others who took out all the grave mounds in the northwest area of the churchyard. If I had the information when I asked, it would have saved about two years of trying to work things out. The map was very professionally done and covered every area in grids and even had the names of people who had headstones as well as the grave mound numbers. While I was annoyed, I also thought if I had seen it two years ago it could have made me complacent, and I would have missed some of the graves to the north in rows (A), (B) and (C). They had not been included because the numbers were buried under the spoil, and as for the rest of the map, well that matched perfectly with what Adrian and I had worked out. If it had been an exam, we would have passed with flying colours, so the General's request for information was a success. He also gave me some information of his own, telling me that one of the churchwardens in the 70s was his late father, the Commander. He held the position of churchwarden for 25 years. The Commander was a very popular figure in the village; he was spoken of with a warmth and respect by people who had known him. They could have been describing the General himself, who said he would look at the Commander's own personal records of his time as churchwarden and we left it at that.

So, after finding the tunnel, there was plenty to get on with; if anything else turned up to prove this theory wrong then it would be back to the drawing board, but the story was plausible. I had not tried to make things fit or to deceive anyone into believing what I said. They were the facts as I saw things and only my opinion, of course. With things left in the General's capable hands, I took a look inside the church for signs of the original structure.

I had sat in the church a few times when I was working at the west end of the churchyard. I never felt that welcome then,Only when the musical director Mrs Catherine Mc Clurg was in the church practicing for the Sunday servise ,she was allways interested in the project ,Catherine and I enjoyed many a conversation while sitting in the churchyard that she loved, sadly Catherine passed away but our conversations continue all be it one sided these days while tending her grave, but her spirit lives on she was a good friend of mine I am proud to say. So, looking for signs of the old structure took up a lot of my time; each day for about a week I would have my lunch in the church looking around as I did so because looking at areas as if in a grid was a method I used to try and understand buildings and work out why a craftsman did a thing a certain way.

The information is there if you look, you don't have to knock the place about to receive messages from the past. On the second day at lunchtime, I sat in the north transept, the seating there faced the centre of the church and while enjoying a rather nice doorstep cheese sandwich I noticed something within the roof. The original roof beams of the first structure that predated the work done in the 1400s when the north transept, south chantry, and possibly the bell tower were . It was quite a eureka moment – seeing proof of the original roof made it easy to imagine each stage of its construction and how small the building was to begin with. Then when somebody built the 14th-century additions, they went around and over the top of the original structure. You would have to know what you were looking at to understand its glory. People just in the church to pray would not notice these treasures on the earth or of man's ability to create and craft such a wonderful building that over the years had become annexed by predatory individuals who couldn't see further than the end of their nose. So, these eureka moments bring a warmth to the soul, whether you're in the church or churchyard. I often spend time in the church after that find, not necessarily looking for other things but just to feel part of it all. That find was as important as finding the tunnel, not in their present state but back in time when they served the purpose they were built for.

Having found some of the old structure hidden within the fabric of the church as it is now, it didn't take long to find information online. It was interesting to read what the Hampshire Field Club and Archaeological Society said about the Saxon charter and landscape evolution in the south centre basin. The actual boundary of Durley and East Horton leads to Durley's medieval church that stands alone "Upon They Hill", and it's believed the earliest part of the church could be pre13th-century and an earlier Saxon building preceded it. It was interesting reading a more in-depth opinion by well-informed people whose job it was to gather information and make it much easier for the likes of yours truly to learn more about the area. So, when asked why the church is so far away from the village, I can answer that it is not, nor is it, as many people think, the last remaining building in a village wiped out by the Black Death or built away from the village because of some other harmful disease that caused devastation in the community.

Durley, like any other village, had its fair share of diseases – consumption and scarlet fever, all responsible for many children's early deaths. In some years, Durley folk buried up to 22 loved ones, poverty laid many people low, inviting diseases in to cut short a life prematurely. Once a child contracted scarlet fever, they were taken quickly as there was no cure, in 1839, three Prowting siblings, Ann nine, Emma eight, and David ten, all died of scarlet fever, taken between the 6th and 9th of June. Their two Houghton cousins, Charlotte two, and Ann four, perished with the fever in the month of May that same year.

Open graves were created in churchyards when the fever struck, each child buried with siblings and cousins as they died. These graves, known as public graves, have no markers of who is in them, only the death dates of the children and young adults were kept in the burial records. To be poverty stricken was a way of life in rural England and groups like Hampshire Field Club and Archaeological Society are a great source of information and clever people who share with others their research into history as it should be done. I have enjoyed interesting conversations with people who share with me an opinion they hold that may be different than mine, but on the same subject and to share is to learn and understand who went before us and what they had to endure.

The best information I have seen regarding the church's location, development and archaeological features is in work called The Ancient Parishes and Chapelries of Hampshire. It is over 300 pages of fascinating information, and Durley is just one of the many church sites covered in this survey. The report introduction said: "It's frequently thought that the Manorial Lord sited many small rural churches on land often close to the Manor House. A manorial lordship was not a noble title, but a semi-extinct form of landed property, historically a lord of the manor could be tenant-in-chief if he held a capital manor directly from the crown. Many of these sites have a considerable bias of slope-located churches towards the east. It would be odd if church sites had been chosen after the siting of the settlements on these slopes, as east-facing slopes are not an ideal location for an arable-based community-as the land is slower to warm, on both a daily and seasonal basis."

Therefore, the possibility that the site was chosen first because of its suitability as an early graveyard to be followed by the rest of the settlement is examined. The introduction of this report makes sense to me, if you're starting a settlement, you need somewhere for the dead to be buried. Also, many Saxon churches are built on hills with the altar always facing east and at Durley the church could not be in a higher position – it's possible to follow the horizon from the northeast at Greenwood Lane all the way round to the northwest corner of the churchyard and the old Greenwood Farm Estate. This site, when it was chosen, really was in a prime location. The report continued, discussing how the Bracklesham beds of the Durley parish are indicative of a former heathland economy and this in turn, will have influenced the settlement pattern, which is essentially one of dispersed isolated farms.

There is no evidence suggesting that the Church of the Holy Cross at Durley has ever been the centre of a nucleated settlement. It is not associated with a plantation or a manorial building. In short, there is no obvious reason why Durley's medieval church is on this site. The dedication might be an indication that it was the site of a preaching cross; the report suggests that this hypothesis is conjecture only and as a precautionary measure, any opportunity for archaeological investigation within a 200-metre radius of the church could be of significant value in understanding this site.

So, Durley was never a village to begin with but a cluster of small settlements that in time would spread closer to each other and once there was more than

2,500 residents the settlements became a village. The Ancient Parish and Chapelries of Hampshire's interesting papers answered many questions and helped me understand how the Church of the Holy Cross came into fruition. With their knowledgeable report, coupled with my knowledge of what to look for in this ancient old building and a possible structure that may have preceded it, I was confident I could converse with an archaeologist much more experienced than myself who would, I hoped, teach me even more skills of what to look for. I felt we needed an archaeologist involved now so we could move forward, but that was out of my hands; I couldn't do anything about that, it was for other people to decide, and for me finding out who was in the tunnel was the primary task, but I would have to be tolerant in that respect.

As December 2019 arrived, I spent time making sure the churchyard would be ready for the many visitors who came to pay their respects to relations and leave many colourful Christmas wreaths, some of them homemade. They made the churchyard look wonderful; we would have over 140 wreaths as well as cards and small gifts from children to their grandparents. I never placed anything at the graves of Great-uncle George or Susan Matilda, I would see them every day, touch their headstones and say good morning. I felt if I placed a wreath on their graves then I would have to do the same to the rest of the graves at the west end of the churchyard. I would get a sort of guilty feeling if you like, because the spirits would know and probably frown that I favoured them over the others. Not only that, there were so many it would cost a small fortune.

So, I would wish them all a merry Christmas and leave it at that. I did, however, place a wreath at the head of Gwen Houghton's grave, for what she did for the history of the village and having few relations left who could visit and it was a pleasure to do it. I also continued looking at the inside of the church for possible clues to be added to the list of alterations I had not seen yet; there would be more I was sure of that. The only thing that looked out of place were four plaques on the walls, one on the south wall that praised architects J. Colson and Son, which was a bit rich in my opinion. On the north wall to the west was another strange memorial plaque reminding everyone that the Reverend Thomas Scard MA was once in residence and how wonderful he was. Also tucked away on the south wall was a small copper plaque in memory of Thomas Pink, which was strange given he was not born in Durley but proved he was well in with the church for whatever reason that may be. But the most amazing and pathetic plaque on the north wall was said to be from the villagers a dedication to the Reverend Richard Ferguson, thanking him for the years of service as rector of the Church of the Holy Cross.

It is a pathetic tribute and made me laugh loudly, thinking it was probably drafted by himself before his demise and I was surprised he hadn't sainted himself in the process. This dedication completed the cover ups that this individual instigated to hide the wrongdoings he presided over, not knowing of course that one day the truth would out. It was all flannel of course, made out to look impressive for future generations of honest souls tricked into believing the writing on the wall was gospel. It was also an insult to other genuine dedications that followed. The Jenner and Palmer families, Clarke, Whale and the Reverend Jackson all more deserving. And of course the many brave men and boys who gave their life for their country, in wars fought far away and who never came home but who are remembered for the ultimate sacrifice; they became heroes one and all.

Chapter 22
Anne with an 'e'

Early in December that year, a lady came to pay her respects to her ancestors. I noticed her standing at the west end of the churchyard just looking at the old headstones. Smartly dressed in a long high-collared coat that reached down to a bright pair of fawn ankle boots, hardly suitable for walking around churchyards. She wore a fur hat that sat low on her forehead and covered her ears. It was clear this attractive lady was probably in her 70s. As I turned away to go about my business thinking she had a touch of class about her, when I looked again, she was approaching me, and I tried quickly to tidy myself – because as usual, I looked like an unmade bed when working at the churchyard.

Anyway, I touched my hat and said hello, to which she smiled and said the churchyard looked a lot different from the last time she came. Then, taking my arm as if to steady herself, we began to walk with an eagerness back down to the west end area of the churchyard where she had just come from. When we reached the bench that overlooked the golf course, we sat down and, still holding my arm, she asked me what all the white markers represented.

I explained what we had done and how we found many graves, mostly without headstones, and that I had just finished identifying the people that could afford headstones. I also mentioned the tunnel at the east end of the churchyard that had just been discovered, However the lady didn't seem that interested in the east end of the churchyard, telling me her name was Anne with an 'e' and that she had come over from Australia on a cruise.

Her family had migrated there in the late 1800s when her mother was a child and had joined other members of their family already in Australia. She said her mother's maiden name was Houghton who had married a Denham. I explained that many of the graves at the west end of the churchyard were occupied by members linked to the Denham and Houghton families and in fact we had over 250 Houghtons buried in the churchyard.

It was around 2 pm and as the afternoon chill began to set in, we stood up and walked back towards the church. She still held my arm, and the warmth of her coat made my shirt sleeve feel damp. We stopped several times on our way to the church as she began to tell me a story of the agricultural riots of 1830. I had not heard of the riots before, so I was quite interested. She told me many of the Hampshire rioters were transported to a place called Van Diemen's Land in Australia and she had been to the cemetery there when on an organised pilgrimage to Tasmania.

We made our way into the church, and I offered her a candle to light which she did and walked with it to the front of the church. I stayed at the back and watched as she slowly knelt before the altar, and on removing her hat I could see the lady was completely bald. It was then I realised this lady had little time left on God's earth. I had seen people before who came to the church when they were dying, but with them I had seen a gradual change over time. We had a chance to talk about many things that were important to them that they found difficult to share with family and friends. They saw me as a friend to confide in, knowing what they told me would go no further, and I knew when they came to talk I could go on a sort of automatic pilot to listen intently to what they said, and be able to store what they said when they left and not think about it too much, otherwise you could end up in a dark place yourself.

But I had just had the pleasure of meeting this woman and the feelings I had were very different. I didn't see this coming and felt quite useless, if truth be told. Then the lady walked back to me and held my arm again but this time more firmly; she had recognised I was uneasy, shocked if you like; and I didn't make a very good job of hiding the fact that I was shocked. We left the church and didn't say anything as we walked quietly down to the lych gate, then turning around and looking back at the church the lady smiled and said, "Well this little church would be worth committing bigamy for" and laughed. I told her she looked fine for the occasion, smartly dressed as she was, but I would have to play the part of the chimney sweep and found myself at ease again.

We continued the walk back to her car, stopping several times on the way to finish parts of the conversation. To reach the car too quickly would mean the end of our meeting, one I felt I wanted to go on and got the impression that she did too. But it was past half-light in the afternoon and the lady had to go. She asked me if I would look into the history of the riots, if only out of curiosity, then opened the car door and said she was glad I was in the churchyard when she came but was afraid she could never come back to see me again but would always remember our conversation. I told her I had enjoyed talking with her and would not forget the time we spent together and said I would look into what she had told me about the riots in 1830. It was very difficult to say goodbye to each other, so we didn't but embraced each other warmly and she got into her car and drove away, sounding the car horn loudly as if in defiance of the disease that was killing her. That was so obviously 'the big C'. I watched till she was out of sight, thinking in another time we would be friends. She was a very attractive and brave lady called Anne with an 'e'," who I will remember always.

The rest of December that year my time was taken up doing normal everyday things that go on in a churchyard, too mundane to talk about actually. I did send for information from the archives at Winchester regarding the agricultural riots of 1830. I also used the quiet time to file things away and in particular everything regarding the tunnel and A.N.Other; we could not forget whoever that turned out to be, could we. I anticipated it could be some time before anything positive would happen regarding those issues, and I wanted to have everything ready to hit the ground running once the General decided if we could go ahead in whatever form that would be. The longer he took to decide the better as far as I was concerned because I had a sneaky feeling he was beginning to enjoy working in the churchyard. In fact, he began cleaning and weeding the old graves like a veteran sexton, and when his doctors told him his blood pressure was perfect he put that down to working in the churchyard. It was wet there sometimes and cold but also relaxing and good for the peace of mind.

I couldn't get him interested into believing the spiritual side of things, but in time certain things happened coincidently that did make him think I was not completely bonkers when I referred to them. I also filed away everything I discovered inside the church regarding the original structure and the timeline of events that led up to the creation of settlements in medieval times, as well as the interesting information about the siting of the Church of the Holy Cross.

2020 I hoped would bring about the conclusion of everything I had started back in 2014, however life as we knew it was about to change. COVID-19, a disease no one had heard of, hit the world hard, taking many people's lives and changing many others for good. Orders to be locked down affected many people. Working from home became the new way of business. Social distancing and the separation of families became the normal way of life. At the churchyard, things changed; more people were coming in, observing the safe distancing rules. The place became important to them. The church became the halfway distance for people's walks; when they reached it, they would walk back from whence they came as per the government's instruction. If you were not locked down because of some underlying illness, people were encouraged to walk, run or ride bikes; in fact, keeping fit was best for both mind and body alike.

The churchyard became busy because this virus had frightened everyone and, just as when we were children, it was Mum and Dad we went to. I noticed this trend grew by the week and people openly talked over their parents' graves. It was good to see but while the circumstances in which it happened was not, people came together and helped each other more than usual. Artists came to paint, readers to read, and students to study, cyclists left their bikes and went walking, joggers and dog walkers were many and such a lot of people to say good day to.

Of course, all things were on hold regarding everything linked with the tunnel; when things became clearer there would be plenty of time for that. The General devised a way to open the church. He was determined to keep the place open, if only for a short time each week. So, people would come in one door and out through another, sanitising hands was the order of the day, masks worn and homemade ones too showing the person's artistic vent. If this was the new way of life there was a need to embrace it.

My life didn't change much apart from not seeing my grandchildren, but I coped. I could talk on the phone as usual and if everyone was fine then I was. I used my time in the lockdown still looking after the churchyard and looking into the agricultural riots of 1830. I needed to do it, it kept me interested because I had always had some form of research on the go for the 20 years leading up to 2020. Of course, Anne with an 'e' had suggested I should, I thought about her a lot and had no idea if she was alive or dead. But she was alive in my head and all the time she was, then to me she wasn't dead, spiritually she never would be.

When I started researching the agricultural riots, I did so with less vigour than usual; this was often the way things started with me until I found something to cling to that would lead to something else. Protecting the initial information was like keeping the flame alive from the last match in the box; you should never forget your first lead, it's what takes you to where you need to be. What follows that lead determines how far you run with what you first discovered, and with everything I had ever researched it would not do to try and make things fit just for the sake of it; if your research had legs, you would need to be fit mentally to keep up with it if the research dried up for a while. Then you have to be patient because sooner or later something would turn up.

So, with Anne with an 'e' in mind, I began my research. Google and Wikipedia were good places to start for a general overview of things. From 1800 to the 1853 abolition of the penal transportation, Van Diemen's Land was the primary colony in Australia following the suspension of transportation to New South Wales. All transported convicts sent to Van Diemen's Land totalled some 73,000 convicts, about 40% of all convicts sent to Australia.

Convicts served their sentence as assigned labour to free settlers or in gangs assigned to public works. Convicts completing their sentence or earning their ticket to leave often settled in the new free colony of Victoria in an attempt to earn enough money for their passage home. But many stayed and formed a new life, never to return to the land of their birth. So, my first look at the information regarding Van Diemen's Land was straightforward enough, but what did the convicts do to be there? To find out more about this, I asked Adrian Abbott what the local History Society had on the subject.

He gave me a look rather like my mother would when I was embarking on something she considered a lost cause. However, he produced two books for me to read, one called The Hampshire Machine Breakers written and published by a lady called Jill Chambers, and the other book was a guide to Enclosure in Hampshire 1700 to 1900 by John Chapman and Sylvia Seeliger. I would use these books for reference as I had with both John Bosworth and George Molesworth's important books. But my primary task was not to repeat verbatim what Jill Chambers had said in her book because that would defeat the object of the exercise.

What I wanted was to find out what Anne with an 'e' was referring to and her eagerness for me to look into it. So, I did what I always did and looked what was online in the archives at Winchester and by just putting in the search engine 'agricultural riots Hampshire' plenty of information came up on my screen.

The agricultural riots in rural England, also referred to as the 'Swing Riots' began on 28th August 1830, and spread quickly through the rural communities of Norfolk, Cambridgeshire, Suffolk, Berkshire, Kent, West and East Sussex, Wiltshire and Hampshire. The introduction of the threshing machine was put at the heart of the problem. Landowners, lords of manors and wealthy farmers looked to the threshing machine to maximise their profits. The farm workers saw these machines as a threat to their jobs, and by October 1830 over 100 machines had been destroyed by gangs of farm labourers. It was, however, a battle they would have no hope of winning. The threshing machine was here to stay and there would still be the need for men to work in gangs to operate the machines but the old way of dealing with the harvest was about to become a thing of the past.

The agricultural riots of 1830 were a result of a number of things that would have a devastating effect on rural England. The ending of the Napoleonic Wars, where men had been taken from the land to fight for their country. Landowners thrived while the war continued, grain to feed the troops was needed and prices were good. There was also something called the Enclosure Act, when six million acres of common land was enclosed between 1770 and 1830. Common land had been used for centuries by the poor of the countryside to graze animals and grow produce for themselves.

Once the land was enclosed it was divided up among rich local landowners such as universities, the church and wealthy individuals. While it's true the common lands at Durley were not fully enclosed till 1858, you could be sure that all the good land was taken first and what was left would be of no use at all. The 17th-century folk poem by James Boyle called 'Stealing the common from the goose' sums up perfectly in a few lines the process of fencing off common land and turning it into private property. It's said, "The law locks up the man or woman who steals the goose from the common but leaves the greater villain loose who steals the common from the goose."

The controversial nature of property rights left the landless farmer dependent on the local tenant farmers to give them work for cash wages and this was fine while the wars raged In France. Corn prices were high, and the shortness of labour would mean longer periods of work for the people that were left. But then when the war ended, and men returned home to their villages coupled with the terrible harvest of 1828 and 1829, farm labourers faced the winter of 1830 with despair, as did the tenant farmers they worked for because the landlords of these rented farms still wanted their rent and refused to lower the tithes. So the tenant farmer and the farm labourers were in the same boat.

Basically, they were up the creek without a paddle; if the landowners would not reduce the rents of the tithes for the tenant farmer, then he could not up the wages of the agricultural workers, if indeed he had enough work to go round. Originally tithes were payments in kind such as crops, wool and milk, a proportion of the profits from the farming year made by the parishioners for the support of the parish church and its clergy. Tithes were divided into great and small tithes i.e. corn, grain, hay and wood were considered great tithes. All their predial tithes, together with mixed and personal tithes, were classed as small. It was common in some parishes for the great tithes to be paid to the rector, and the small tithes to the vicar of the parish. The custom of tithing is biblical, and the word means 'tenth' in Hebrew; many Christians and Jews practise this as part of their faith. The Bible encourages people to give generously far and beyond the ten per cent, the giving of time cannot replace the tithe.

So, after looking into how the tithe system worked, I didn't think it was a fair system, not when things were bad anyway. What was clear to me was the fact the church had a tremendous hold on the village population; the church-owned properties were many as well as actual land. I have records of my ancestors renting their home from the church as well as the tithes. For me, I think when times were good the system worked well; people could pay their way and live maybe from hand to mouth, but that's keeping your head above water, and back in those days if you could do that then you had a chance of a decent life.

However, when the times were bad, and through no fault of their own if the crops failed, then that's when the system broke down and people ended up with debts and owing money for what was after all an act of God. If the crops failed from circumstances beyond anyone's control, then I think the church should have made allowances for that. After all, the good book says you should "love they neighbours" and "do unto others as you would have them do unto you". So, the church couldn't preach one thing and do another themselves, I understand why the farm workers got involved in the riots if the landlords were too stupid that they could not use common sense to sort the problem out.

Moving on, the riots covered many counties, but it is the Hampshire/Sussex riots I want to concentrate on to begin with. The first report I looked at was regarding letters sent to the local landowners well in advance of any rioting that took place. The letters said: "Sirs we will give you till a fortnight to Destroy your Threshing Machine, if it is not Destroyed by that time you must face the consequences" signed "Captain Swing". Clearly these letters were ignored, and no action was taken by the owners to protect their threshing machines. I find this amazing; if you are given notice that this would happen surely you would want to protect your property?

This was the first information I had seen and I thought then that something was not quite right. It was as if the landowners' neglect of their machinery could have been somehow orchestrated to give the machine breakers a free run so they would fall into some sort of trap or other. At the time of reading it, it didn't make sense to me. Anyway, the men in Sussex were stirring up trouble in the small villages, informing the residents that teams of machine breakers were on their way from other county parishes and that the agricultural labourers should join the movement in an attempt to have the tithes reduced. It was also reported that these gangs were offering to break up the local landowners' farming machines for the sum of two pounds, while the local people could join in the dispute and demand money and food. So it was that the travelling gangs stirred up the local community who may not have rioted themselves had it not been for the instigators who first came to the villages. Further reports of incidents indicated that the people who whipped up the farm workers into a frenzy did not take any part in the riots themselves and were nowhere to be seen, leaving the farm workers smashing up their own village. Hardly the way to get a reduction in the tithes.

Don't forget, we can look at this with all the information from reports in newspapers, and from people who wrote about what happened at the time and became folklore in the Sussex villages. For the people around at the time, it must have been a job understanding what was going on.

Looking at what happened at Durley, Bishops Waltham and the village of Owslebury, firstly on 20th November 1830, letters were sent to landowners at Durley: "Sirs We give you till a fortnight to destroy your Threshing Machine. If it is not destroyed, you must take the consequences". The letter again signed by the fictitious Captain Swing and sent by penny post with a Southampton postmark. As in Sussex, several men came to Durley to stir up the local villagers into rioting with the same offer to break up the threshing machine for two pounds. The problem with this was the riots kicked off two days after the landowners received their letters; and if you had a letter like that then why wasn't the threshing machine well-guarded against any attempt to destroy it?

Again, something didn't seem right to me. The other thing is no right-thinking Durley man would pay someone two pounds to break up a machine when they were skint, even if the travelling machine breakers did do a good job of it. At the same time, giving the local farm workers an alibi who could prove they were elsewhere when the alleged incident had taken place. So, the whole episode of rioting was very well organised; it was not a spur of the moment thing, far from it, someone was pulling the strings and using the agricultural workers' desperate situation for their own ends. What that was I have no idea, not yet anyway.

In the Hampshire Chronicle on the 29th of November 1830, they reported: "That on the 22nd November 1830 riots occurred in Durley when an assembly of the peasantry at Durley near Bishops Waltham demolished the threshing machine of Farmer Mr Thomas Pink of the Greenwood Estate." Well, this was the same Thomas Pink who was so well in with the church and who had his impressive headstone at the southeast area of the church. The headstone was also damaged at some time so it would be interesting to find out why. Then the rioters proceeded to Upham where they conducted themselves in a riotous manner at the parsonage. The Upham peasantry had previously been there, and with threats and menacing conduct demanding a reduction of the tithes, this would enable their employers to pay better wages. The same day during the absence of Walter Long Esq., a numerous gang appeared at Preshaw and by threats and imprecation obtained a supply of provisions and destroyed a machine. A large party then went to Bishops Waltham and demanded money from the Reverend Thomas Scard MA.

Well, our old friend Thomas Scard has popped up again. It's not difficult to see why he had a dislike of the farming community. Clearly he held a grudge against the likes of Abraham Edwards, for instance, who dared to rise above his station and make something of himself, but in Thomas Scard's eyes, Abraham Edwards would never have been his equal. So, this newspaper report, interesting as it was, made me wonder if the reporter went with the gangs. If so, he would have had prior news of when they would take place, and maybe who had instigated things from the start because Durley to Upham walking is 3.7 miles and takes 1 hour and 15 minutes, then Upham to Preshaw 3.6 miles takes 1 hour and 12 minutes. From Preshaw to Bishops Waltham is 4.7 miles as the crow flies and takes 1 hour and 29 minutes. Then back to Durley from Bishops Waltham the 2.9 miles under normal circumstances should take 57 minutes. But you can add a bit of time to that because these men had been out all day walking and destroying every machine they could lay their hand on. For me having got this far in my research, these agricultural workers were being given enough rope to hang themselves eventually, with no opposition at all from the landowners who owned these machines if we believe what the newspapers reported.

The reporters knew the rioters' every move so were the machine breakers set up? I am not sure yet, let us dig a little deeper. So far we have machines broken up with no opposition, preceded by letters from fictitious individuals, a newspaper reporting events as they happened and if they knew where the riots would take place, chances are they would know who was involved (bad news if you're a machine breaker).

Now we were in the fourth month of these riots and the government were getting pretty fed up with what was going on in the countryside and there were calls for reform. Enter into our story Mr William Cobbett, the well-known journalist, farmer and radical politician who made speeches in defence of the swing rioters and blamed those in society who lived off unearned income at the expense of the hard-working agricultural labourers and called for parliamentary reform.

William Cobbett was one of a large number of politicians who were not happy with the government's handling of the riots and wanted the prime minster out of office. As a farmer himself at Botley, not far from Durley, William Cobbett was committed to supporting the rights of the small farmer and peasants against the wealthier in society. He backed low taxes, the reversal of the Enclosure Act and the return of common land for communal use. So, you could say he was sympathetic to the rioters' cause, and while he may have been in the majority of politicians who wanted the prime minister out of office, he wouldn't have sided with fellow politicians who wanted drastic action taken against the agricultural workers. Much of his writing was in support of the people who worked the land and as an orator he could make his feelings known and this would have got him into trouble, no matter who the prime minister was.

William Cobbett also coined the phrase a 'red herring' and the more I was finding out about the riots there seemed to be plenty of those banded about. Eventually William Cobbett was put on trial charged with seditious libel for an article he wrote in the political register called the rural war. Defending himself, he subpoenaed six members of parliament including the prime minister of the day, Cobbett went on the attack and tried to ask government ministers awkward questions supporting his case, at great embarrassment to the government, and he was acquitted.

Now at the time of the riots, the prime minister was Field Marshal his Grace Arthur Wellesley 1st Duke of Wellington KG, GC,GCH,PC, FRS. He thought the measures in place to deal with the riots were good enough, and he should know, he ended the Napoleonic War when he outwitted Napoleon at the Battle of Waterloo. So as a strategist he should have been able to have the trust of the ministers around him, one would think. His Grace was against any reform, his government though were struggling because as prime minister he was unpopular.

I am sure, like all great men, he was not there to be liked but to do his best for the country as he had done in the battles he fought and won. But back in civvy street he was up against an enemy he couldn't see in front of him because like all cowards they attack from behind and were probably people he thought he could trust. After the statement he made regarding the measures in place to deal with the rioters, his home was attacked by rioters and, to add insult to injury, on 15th November 1830, his government lost a vote of confidence. Field Marshal his Grace 1st Duke of Wellington KG, GCB,GCH,PC,FRS, was replaced by Charles Grey 2nd Earl Grey KG,PC, who was asked to form a new government by the new King William, son of George III. Who, as it happened, had only been king for five months and still finding his way around and was not as interested in politics as his brother and father who had both preceded him in office. He relied heavily on the advice of people around him while he settled in. Lord Grey's new government would be more in tune with what parliament wanted.

Now the thing I found strange about the attack on the Duke of Wellington's home was this. He had said that the measures in place to deal with the rioters were good enough. So, if you're a rioter you would know that the measures were not because each time a riot occurred nothing happened in the way of anyone being arrested. The Duke of Wellington's statement was as good as a compliment, so why would the rioters make such an attack? I don't believe they did and think it could have been the same dark force that had been working in the shadows. With the promise of an important position in Lord Grey's new government, and the person who was alleged to be behind the manipulation of events both in regard of the riots and the downfall of the Duke of Wellington's government, was Lord Melbourne who on the 22nd of November 1830 – the exact same day the riots occurred at Durley and eight days after the downfall of Wellington's government – he became the new home secretary.

His full title was William Lamb 2nd Viscount Melbourne of Kilmore, later he would become Lord Melbourne, Baron of Kilmore, Baron Melbourne of Melbourne Australia, so named on the 10th of April 1837 by Governor Richard Bourke, Melbourne Australia was formally a settlement known as 'Batmania', named after John Batman who claimed to have found it in 1835. The colony was Victoria, named after the reigning English monarch Queen Victoria, and the main town Batmania was renamed Melbourne in honour of Lord Melbourne. William Lamb was well educated and attended Eton and Trinity College, Cambridge, where he became part of a group of radicals that included Percy Bysshe Shelly Poet and Lord George Gordon Byron, poet, British peer and politician.

But William Lamb was more intent on following a career in politics, and romantic revolutionaries didn't fit the bill. His mother, Elizabeth Viscountess Melbourne, had promoted her son William whenever possible and wanted to move her family's interests up in polite society. Her wish to promote William before his elder brother, the Honourable Peniston Lamb, member of parliament for Newport Isle of Wight, did not go down well with her husband Sir Peniston Lamb 1st Viscount Melbourne. It was alleged that, like many others in polite society, he believed that Peniston was his only true son and that William and two of his other three siblings were the children of Lord Egremont, George O'Brian Wyndham 3rd Earl of Egremont FRS. It was also alleged that Lord Egremont had bought Lady Melbourne from her previous lover Lord Coleraine for £13,000. Well, what a palaver, it seems to be the only true-blue bloods in polite society were the people's racehorses.

Anyway, Lady Melbourne had many men friends that became lovers and lovers who remained friends. She also wanted to instigate a match between her son William and Lady Caroline Ponsonby and why not when climbing the social ladder? The Ponsonby family were very famous and steeped in history, but the eldest son Peniston would become Lord Melbourne when his father died and leave William without a title to offer Lady Caroline Ponsonby.

But when Peniston died of tuberculosis in January 1805, unmarried and without children, Lady Melbourne again became matchmaker, orchestrating a match between her son William and Lady Caroline Ponsonby. A match more beneficial to the Melbourne's than the Ponsonbys, one would think. Lady Caroline was the only daughter of Frederick Ponsonby 3rd Earl of Bessborough and Henrietta Countess of Bessborough. Lady Caroline was exceptionally well educated at home and at Hans Place School, named after Sir Hans Slone 1st Baronet, a physician and collector, notable for his legacy which became the foundation for the British Museum. Lady Caroline wrote prose and poetry, took to sketch portraiture, all courtly skills that stood her in good stead. She was fluent in French and Italian, skilled at Greek and Latin, music and drama, and at the age of 19 married the honourable William Lamb, the up-and-coming politician. His mother had achieved what she had hoped – she would by seeing a union between the two families and the advantages it would bring to her rise in polite society.

At first, William and Lady Caroline enjoyed a happy marriage and had a son, George Augustus Frederick Lamb, born the 11th of August 1807, but the child had severe mental problems. Lady Caroline became a devoted carer to young George when other aristocratic families sent mentally challenged relations to institutions. Lady Caroline was both mother and carer. Then in 1809, Lady Caroline was again with child. She had been considered ill-suited to childbirth after suffering long periods of recovery after the birth of her son. The stress of her son's illness and her husband's consuming career made things difficult for her. All this drove a wedge between them and on top of all that, Lady Caroline's second child, a premature daughter, passed away after only 24 hours. So with her marriage on the rocks, she became involved with Lord George Gordon Byron and had a well-publicised affair, intending to cause embarrassment to her politician husband.

Lady Melbourne, however, while she approved of her son's marriage on social grounds, she disliked Lady Caroline intensely and the feeling was mutual. Their relationship was always bad and while Lord Byron's affair was going on, Lady Melbourne became his confidante. Lady Caroline wrote a book about the affair and made unflattering comments about many in polite society and saying Lord Byron was "Mad Bad and Dangerous to know". While the names were changed, people knew who she was writing about. She was, in my opinion, cleverer than her three enemies put together – Lady Melbourne, her son William Lamb and Lord George Gordon Byron – and it's said after Lady Caroline's affair with Byron had cooled, she had called on him and finding him not at home, she left a note that said: "Remember me."

An angry Lord Byron wrote back to Lady Caroline: "Remember thee remember thee till lathe quench life's burning streams, remorse and shame shall cling to thee. His aye, doubt it not thy husband too shall think of thee, by neither shalt thou be forgot thou false to him, thou fiend, to me."

Well, Lady Caroline certainly rattled Byron's cage, and good for her as he was in league with her mother-in-law and between them ruthlessly destroyed her. And as for Lady Caroline's husband, well, as we are about to find out, the son of a bitch inherited all of his cunning mother's political tricks. Lady Caroline's torrid life ended when she became reliant on excessive alcohol and the use of drugs to forget her torments and died on 28th January 1828 aged 43.

Her invalid son Augustus, aged 29 with a mental age of seven, outlived his loyal mother by eight years and died on 27th November 1836. Elizabeth Lamb Viscountess Melbourne died on 6th April 1818 aged 67, and her husband, Sir Penistone 1st Viscount Melbourne, died on 22nd July 1828 aged 83. Neither lived to witness their son's rise into government circles, so researching that sorry tale it seemed to me polite society was not all it was cracked up to be and as troublesome as any other class in society. I think it was important to research Lord Melbourne and his family's past in order to try and understand the man and what happened next.

To continue with the story, we have to go back to 22nd November 1830, the day of the Durley riots and Lord Melbourne's appointment as the home secretary, where he would pick up, no doubt, where he had left off before the collapse of the Duke of Wellington's government. It's alleged that Lord Melbourne played a big part in that and had things already in place for when Charles Grey 2nd Earl Grey KG, PC became prime minister. The reason I agree with that is because on 23rd November 1830, the day after the Durley riots, at Lord Melbourne's insistence the new King William produced a proclamation on rioters. It could not fail because the proclamation would test the loyalty of the agricultural community to each other like never before, and the new king, by putting his name to the proclamation, would risk becoming a figure of hate if things began to get nasty.

Lord Melbourne looked to be setting King William up as he had been doing all summer to the agricultural workers. The new king was dubbed the 'Sailor King' because of his connection with the navy, or 'Silly Billy' because he was not at all political. However, he was responsible for many reforms such as updating the Poor Law, Child Labour Restrictions and Abolished Slavery in nearly all of the British Empire. So, in all he seems to have been a good person who it could be said became king too late in his life at the age of 64 when he inherited the title. His successor to the throne was his niece Victoria, the only daughter of his brother Edward Duke of Kent, who, like the Sailor King, had no legitimate sons, and it was alleged that Edward Duke of Kent was the father of one of Lord Melbourne's siblings, the Honourable George Lamb MP.

When King William died on 20th June 1837 aged 71, he had held on long enough to hand over the reins to Victoria who had turned 18 the month before on 24th May 1837. Whilst the Sailor King had no surviving legitimate children, he did however have ten illegitimate children with actress Dorothea

Jorden, his long-time companion of 20 years.

The Sailor King's proclamation began under the heading "Claims for rewards for the capture of Rioters" and continued, "whereas great multitudes of lawless disorderly people have for some time passed, assembled themselves together in a riotous and tumultuous manner in the counties of Wiltshire, Kent, Sussex, Surry, Hampshire, and Buckinghamshire. For the purposes of compelling their employers to comply with certain regulations prescribed by themselves, with the respect to the wages to be paid for their labour. And have actually committed various acts of outrage in different parts of the counties above mentioned. Whereby the property of many of our good subjects has in several instances been completely destroyed and their lives and properties are still greatly endangered. We therefore, being duly sensible of the mischievous consequences which must have inevitably ensure as well to the peace of the Kingdom as to the lives and properties of our subjects for such wicked and illegal practices. If they go unpunished; and being firmly resolved to cause the laws to be put in execution for the punishment of such offenders. Have thought fit by the advice of our privy council to issue this Proclamation hear by strictly commanding all Justices of the Peace, Sheriff's, Under Sheriff's and other Civil Officers whatsoever within the counties of Wiltshire, Kent, Sussex, Surrey, Hampshire, and Buckinghamshire. That they do use their utmost endeavours to discover apprehend and bring to justice the persons concerned in the riotous proceedings above mentioned. As further inducement to discover the said offenders we do now promise and declare that any person or persons who shall discover and apprehend or cause to be discovered and apprehended. The authors, abettors or perpetrators of any of the outrages above mentioned so that they or any of them may be duly convicted thereof shall be entitled to the sum of fifty pounds for every person who shall be so convicted and shall also receive our most gracious pardon for the said offence if the person making such discovery aforesaid shall be liable to be prosecuted for the same. And were certain wicked incendiaries have destroyed the corn, hay, buildings, and other properties of our subjects we do now promise and declare that any person or persons who shall discover and apprehend or cause to be discovered and apprehended the authors of the said fires so that they or any of them may be duly convicted they shall be entitled to the sum of five hundred pounds for each person who shall be convicted and shall also receive our most gracious pardon and to be except if was an actual perpetrator of any of the fires in case the person making such discovery shall be liable to be prosecuted for the same. The Lords commissioners of our treasury are hear by required to make payment according to the said records, circa to our court at St James this Twenty Third day of November One Thousand Eight Hundred and Thirty. In the year of our reign, God save the King."

So, the proclamation was in place; the first thing to do was to understand it. Up until then, not many people had been before the local magistrate's courts, whose powers were limited anyway and could not prosecute anyone on alleged hearsay evidence. However, the proclamation was about to change all that, because if someone said they had seen a certain person do something against the law, that was all the law needed to place the individual under arrest. While the home secretary had given the local magistrates full powers, few felt qualified enough to impose them. But Lord Melbourne made allowance for that too; all the local magistrates needed to do would be to remand the prisoners in custody and send them to the county gaol at Winchester to await trial. Lord Melbourne had put in place a special commission where every rioter would go before Lord Justice Parke in a mass trial set to start in December 1830 and would last several weeks. If prisoners were found guilty, they would be either sentenced to death, transported or put in prison. Because if someone said you took part in the riots, then in the eyes of the law set out in the proclamation then you were in trouble. It was a show trial, it was as simple as that, if you were named there was no way out and the trial at Winchester was a sham, men and women sentenced on hearsay evidence.

So let us go back again to 22nd November and the release of the proclamation. It would have taken some time to filter down to the villages, and even then, the average agricultural worker wouldn't truly understand it, if they saw it that is. Lord Melbourne made sure that the proclamation went to the respective high constables and magistrates first. In the case of Upham cum Durley, Owslebury and Bishops Waltham, that would have been Mr Edward Wyatt High Constable of Bishops Waltham and Mr Walter Long Esq. Magistrate from Pershaw House in the Parish of Corhampton.

The other people that would know about the content of the proclamation first would be the sirs, lords (if there were any) and, get this, the churchwardens, rectors and poor law overseers. Yes, if anyone wanted to claim a reward for giving information and someone's name to say that person took part in the riots, the information went to the churchwarden first. Can you see where this is going?

What happened then was the people in the know became bounty hunters, 'posse comitatus' – it's a group of people mobilised to suppress lawlessness and the rewards were great. Lord Melbourne relied on people's greed to get what he wanted. All the posse comitatus had to do was sit tight and wait, as the rioters who were unaware of the proclamation continued to riot, falling as they would right into the trap set way back in the summer by Lord Melbourne. He couldn't introduce his plan then because the Duke of Wellington was still the prime minister, he would never agree to the plan because the measures he had to deal with the rioters were sufficient enough. It's worth thinking what would have happened if the Duke of Wellington had not lost the day in regards to the confidence vote. No proclamation, show trial or Lord Melbourne to contend with, all three a disaster for rural Britain, and on the day of the proclamation, 23rd November 1830, 171 rioters gathered on Owslebury Hill in Hampshire, and after a few encouraging words – probably from the same group of people travelling from village to village to stir things up as they had done in Sussex and at Durley – the rioters split up into smaller groups and proceeded to go in search of provisions, drink and machinery to destroy.

It must have been a frightening thing to see for the people who didn't want any part of it. Owslebury was just five miles from Durley and not a place you would expect to find rioting. Some residents troubled by this went for the help of local yeoman farmer, Mr John Boyes.

John Boyes lived in the village with his wife in the small hamlet of Hensting in the parish of Owslebury. He farmed sheep at Hensting Farm which he inherited as a copyholder that was part of the Manor of Marwell. Copyhold was a form of land tenure now obsolete which was similar to a lease but subject to rules and customs of the manor.

So if John Boyes was to be seen with a riotous mob and thought to be part of it, he could well lose his right to farm land on the Marwell Estate. But John Boyes, along with another farmer, Mr Dreacal, went to confront the rioters who, when they saw John Boyes, stopped to talk with him and Mr Dreacal. The men said they would draft a letter on behalf of the mob to be taken to other leased farms to be signed. The letter said they the farmers would do their best to give work to the men if the landlords would reduce the rents of the tenant farms. This seemed to satisfy most of the men in that group taking part in the riot and they began to disperse.

However, John Boyes did not want to take the letter. He would agree to its contents and would sign it himself but as for having it in his possession he refused, only to be reminded of the consequences by the mob if he continued to do so. Now the story of John Boyes is a very famous one and has been written about many times. Works by Mr Mike Pearson, who is one of John Boyes' ancestors, also Helen Boyes, she gives talks on the riots and is also a relation of John Boyes. So, I will not repeat what people may have read before because it's the Upham- cum Durley stories I am interested in finding out more about and what Anne with an 'e' had referred to.

Anyway, the riots continued after the proclamation came into being and it was not long before the people in the know became bounty hunters, who encouraged men that had been involved in the riots to come forward with the promise of the money on offer. The main man was the High Constable of Bishops Waltham, who would receive the information from the churchwarden or poor law overseer given to them by the informant who would remain anonymous. The High Constable would then ask for warrants from the magistrates for the arrest of the individuals named by the informant who, while they would have anonymity at the time of their accusations, would however be named when the show trial started.

The informants would receive a pardon if they had taken part in the actual riots themselves but, what they would not have known when they gave up the names of their fellow agricultural workers, was that the £50 reward for each rioter would be shared out among the rest of the bounty hunters.

But £50 in 1830 is the equivalent of over £5,000 in today's money, so a lot of money when the wage of a married agricultural worker was around nine shillings per week. Whilst I would like to think I wouldn't give anyone up, we just don't know until you're faced with the poverty our ancestors had to put up with back then. That's what the Home Secretary Lord Melbourne played on. It was not greed but need that led to the person giving up the names of people they knew. In the paperwork obtained from the records office regarding the show trial, each informant is named. I am afraid I will never name the informant because they may have living relatives. You can access the names yourself, but first ask yourself, what would you do if your family were starving? Of course, I will name the bounty hunters, churchwardens, overseers and rectors if they have already been named in black and white for all to see; no need to use the word 'alleged' regarding those greedy sods who, before the Sailor King's proclamation, all turned a blind eye to what was going on but as soon as there was money to be had they were in like flynn. The church should have been offering sanctuary to the men wrongly named, not help Lord Melbourne send them to the gallows. But you can make your own mind up when I have given you the facts, and I will just make this point – in the months leading up to and including the riots in November 1830, one man was killed in Hampshire. He was shot by a soldier or farmer, the report was not sure which.

So, to see a full-scale riot must have been horrible; it was a class war between those who had and those who had not and those who had wanted more. The first bounty hunters to move into action at Upham were Mr Edward Wyatt, High Constable of Bishops Waltham, the Reverend Mr John Haygarth MA Rector of Upham cum Durley, Mr Walter Long Esq. Magistrate MP and former High Sheriff of Hampshire and the occupier of Pershaw House Corhampton where the riots took place. The problem I found researching who the high constable and magistrate were, when they talked about who they were and what they did, I suppose for affect they used their full titles. However, when it was time to divvy up the cash for rewards that are published for all to see, they became plain old Mr Edward Wyatt and Mr Walter Long Esq., as if trying to hide the fact of who they were. So, when I refer to who picked up the rewards and how much they got I can use the titles because from old records and the passage of time I am quite sure they are the same people.

Just another one of William Cobbett's red herrings to put us off the scent, me thinks. The other posse comitatus members were Mr Thomas Newlyn, Mr John Watts, Mr Edward Everalls, Mr Thomas Bennett, and the informant who will remain nameless. Now the men accused were Mr William Primmer aged 34, who it was alleged fired a pistol in the air to start the riots, Mr Benjamin Harding aged 38, Mr James Cropp aged 25, Mr Charles Brummell aged 23, and 30-year-old Mr James Glasspool. All charged with the offence of having, on 22nd November 1830 at the parish of Upham with menaces and force, feloniously demanded of and from Mr John Haygarth Rector of Upham cum Durley aforesaid a sum of money with intent to steal the same, the Reverend Mr John Haygarth informed Mr Newlyn that the rioters had robbed him and directed Mr Newlyn to apprehend them. The Reverend Mr John Haygarth afterwards laid information against the rioters before Mr Walter Long Esq. Magistrate who issued a warrant to Mr Edward Wyatt High Constable of Bishops Waltham for the rioters' apprehension with which he proceeded to search for them, but met Mr Newlyn with the rioters already in his custody and received them from him.

Mr Walter Long Esq. Magistrate talks very favourably of Mr Edward Wyatt's activity during these riots. He also thanked the informant for coming forward to give his evidence and that he would recommend the informant should have some small share of the rewards on offer. Mr Walter Long Esq. Magistrate then charges the rioters with crimes they committed at Upham on the testimony of the Reverend Mr John Haygarth. Then more charges were laid against William Primmer, Benjamin Harding, James Cropp, Charles Brummel and James Glasspool. This time by Mr John Watts who was one of the posse comitatus who said that he was robbed by three members of the riotous mob on the same day in the parish of Corhampton in Hampshire and that witnesses Mr Stares, Mr Edward Everly and Mr Thomas Bennett, all of Corhampton, Hampshire, will confirm the attacks took place. The anonymous witness had confirmed who all the men were. The incident was reported as follows: "Benjamin Harding 38, stands further charged with having on November 22nd 1830 at the parish of Corhampton feloniously made an assault on one John Watts and put him in fear and danger of his life. He took from the person of the said John Watts one piece of current gold coin of the realm called a Sovereign, and three other pieces of the like coin called half sovereigns the property of the said John Watts.

"It was also reported that James Cropp 25, stands further charged with having on November 22nd 1830 aforesaid at the parish of Corhampton in the company with persons feloniously robbed one John Watts of the sum of five pounds and ten Shillings. The same charge was laid against James Glasspool 30, that he as having on November 22nd at the parish of Corhampton with others feloniously and with threats demanded from John Watts the sum of ten pounds with the intent to steal the same, and with having on November 22nd at the parish aforesaid, feloniously robbed the said John Watts of the sum of five pounds ten shillings. It was also reported that William Primmer 34 and Charles Brummel 23, stand further charged with having on November 22nd 1830 at the parish of Corhampton did act in a riotous manor and put John Watts life in fear of danger."

Mr Walter Long Esq. Magistrate charged the rioters with crimes committed at Corhampton on the testimony of Mr John Watts, Mr Stares, Mr Edward

Eversley and Mr Thomas Bennett. The anonymous informant was again thanked, and Mr Walter Long Esq. Magistrate committed the rioters to the county gaol at Winchester where they would await their day in court. Well, where would you start if you had to try and defend what they were alleged to have done. You could ask if the Reverend John Haygarth did give them any money after it was demanded at Upham, he did tell Mr Newlyn he had been robbed so how much did they take from him, and did the Reverend tell Walter Long Esq. Magistrate how much the rioters took? I assume he would been under oath. Walter Long Esq. Magistrate would have to hear their statements under oath, even then it was hearsay evidence given by the rector against the rioters if there was no witness. It would be the rioters' word against the rector's and informants' allegations and to be honest what magistrate in his right mind should take the word of an informant who had been promised money and a pardon from prosecution if he was involved in the riots himself. The King's proclamation had made a mockery of the law and took away the element of innocent until proven guilty.

The report tells us everything that was said between all the posse comitatus, Mr Walter Long Esq., Magistrate MP and former High Sheriff of Hampshire, Mr Edward Wyatt, High Constable of Bishops Waltham, Mr John Newlyn, Mr John Haygarth, Rector of Upham cum Durley, Mr John Watts, Mr Edward Everalls, and Mr Thomas Bennett, and even mentioned the informant who named the men involved in the riot at Upham and Corhampton on 22nd November 1830. But his accusations were unsafe, if you want my five pence worth. There were no witnesses, at Upham all charges were laid by the rector Mr John Haygarth and he waited four days to do so when warrants were issued for the rioters' arrests after the proclamation was issued.

I think the rioters were on a hiding to nothing, but they would have to wait and see because the show trial was not due to start until the middle of December 1830. So if they showed good character while awaiting trial that may count for something. These young men were in their prime, probably with families or dependent parents. It was a horrid time for them all and even after all this time, the more I read about the riots, the more it makes my back go cold.

Now we find out what happened to the rioters from Durley, and we have to remember that they too travelled to Pershaw House at Corhampton on the same day and could have been part of the same mob. In the Durley men's case, there were more posse comitatus, 12 in all, and again to head up this posse was the High Constable of Bishops Waltham Mr Edward Wyatt. His posse included Mr Thomas Pink whose threshing machine was alleged to have been destroyed by the Durley men. This was the same Mr Thomas Pink of the Greenwood Farm Estate and who was so well in with the church and I am starting to see why. Then we have Mr James Chidwell, Mr Thomas Tier, Mr William Pink. I am not sure if he was a relation of Mr Thomas Pink of

Greenwood. Also in the posse comitatus were Mr John Apps, Mr Richard Austin, Mr John Hatch, Mr William Simpson and Mr Eli Windebank. So quite a large posse comitatus to have looking out for you, and the men that had been pointed out by the informant who will again remain nameless. Five in total and they were Mr John Chalk 32, Mr John Stonage 49, Mr Richard Etherington Junior 20, Mr James Houghton 39, tithingman, Mr Peter Houghton 34, also a tithingman.

It's interesting to find the two tithingmen involved in rioting because the description of a tithingman or tythingman (over the years it has been spelt both ways) is a sort of local peace officer, a kind of chief charged primarily with preserving order and enforcing the observance of the Sabbath. One of their key responsibilities was keeping order in the church. Sometimes the services were long and tedious. If you were a landowner who rented land to various tenant farmers employing agricultural workers, you would have a tithingman to make sure things were in order, so it was a responsible position to hold and a very dangerous one at that if you were seen flouting the law, which in this case it looks as if these tithingmen could have been. Or it could be they were trying to keep some sort of order or try and stop the riot happening as John Boyes wanted to do at Owslebury the day after the riot took place at Durley.

So, what were the charges against the Durley men? They should help us understand more of what happened. As we know from the newspaper report, a letter was sent but things kicked off prematurely, and from records I was able to obtain from Winchester I could see what happened and it was pretty straightforward really. The five Durley men were all charged with the same offence set out as follows: "Having on November the 22nd at the parish of Durley 'With Others', unlawfully and riotously broke and destroyed a threshing machine the property of Mr Thomas Pink of Greenwood Durley Aforesaid Yeoman." The warrants were dated 26th November 1830, four days after the event took place and three days after the Sailor King's proclamation.

The warrants instructed Mr Edward Wyatt High Constable of Bishops Waltham to act on information received from Mr Thomas Pink and Mr James Chidell who had both laid information against the Durley men that eventually lead to their apprehension. What I noticed about the alleged Durley machine breakers' charges was they were all the same, unlike the charges laid against the rioters who it was alleged robbed Mr John Watts at the parish of Corhampton in Hampshire. Those charges were more detailed and more or less what each individual had done; the Durley men's charges were exactly the same with no variation whatsoever as to who did what or if anyone tried to stop what was going on.

It seems Mr Thomas Pink and Mr James Chidell just stood by and let them get on with it, and there were more than the five Durley men involved as the newspaper reported there "Were Others", so who were they? If Mr Pink and Mr Chidell could pick the five Durley men out, why not the rest?

I think the answer to that is simple. Mr Pink and Mr Chidell were not even there but relied on the information given by the informant. By the time that information got to the magistrate for the warrants to be issued to the High Constable, the accusations were not only fourth hand, but hearsay evidence given by an informant who could pick out whoever he liked. And to bag two responsible tithingmen in the process would be quite something. Especially if the informant had some sort of grudge against the two men, who as tithingmen would decide who worked and who wouldn't when times were hard.

I had a bad feeling about these planned machine attacks after reading the reports about the ones in Sussex that they were all an orchestration for something else. The other thing I found very strange was why break a threshing machine at the end of November, surely the time to disable it if you were going to would be when it was most needed in the summer season at haymaking time. Why wait four months after the Swing Riots had started and then decide to break the machine up?

So, I looked into a few of the men's history when they lived at Durley and Upham, starting with William Primmer from Upham. He was a thatcher by profession and lived with his wife, Mary Anne and two daughters, six-year-old Mary Anne and one-year-old Fanny. It must have been a worrying time for the Primmer family.

One of the other men arrested was John Stonage from Wintershill at Durley. He and his wife had three children – John Junior 22, Elizabeth 14, and nine-year-old Emma. So the first two men had great responsibilities to keep up as family men. The third person was Benjamin Harding from Upham. He and his wife Charlotte also had two daughters, Maria five and three-year-old Ellen. Then John Chalk and his wife Mary, who were neighbours of Benjamin Harding, and had two sons, Charles three and two-year-old Henry. So far what I had found was that these were all family men in their prime who needed to work to look after their respective families. I could understand why they would march to try and get the tithes reduced in order to have better wages, but if there were characters among them who were just out to cause trouble then they would all be tarred with the same brush as far as the law was concerned.

On top of that, if someone said they had seen them do something against the law because they were being paid to, then there was not much room for manoeuvring their way out of that situation. I then looked at information regarding Richard Etherington Junior. He was the youngest of the Durley men, just 20 years old. He was single, and there was not much more I could find out about him.

I moved on to the tithingmen. James Houghton, 39 of Wintershill and his wife, Sarah née Pink who may have been a relation of Mr Thomas Pink of Greenwood which was interesting. James and Sarah had four children at the time of the riots, James Junior 18 who, believe it or not was Skinny Jim Houghton who went on to start the sawmills in Durley. He was also a Methodist preacher, and he rests in grave number 65 next to his wife Harriett Houghton née Denham in grave number 66 in row (C). He had three siblings, Sarah 15, Mary Ann 12, and nine-year-old William.

So, James Houghton senior was another hard-working family man who somehow had been drawn into the riots with his younger brother Peter. In fact, the two men had six brothers and I felt as if I knew some of them because Thomas Houghton, who was 30 at the time of the riots, lived at the family farm with his late brother Stephen's wife, Matilda Houghton née Watkins. They had, if you remember, a daughter, Caroline, who lived to the age of 101, and Thomas and Matilda rest next to each other in graves 82 and 83 in row (D).

Then brother Robert who was 20 when the riots took place at Durley. He married Mary Ann Houghton née Dodd and they lay near to each other in graves 84 and 86 in row (D). Edmund Houghton, who was ten years old when his brothers were arrested, married Mary Ann Houghton née Cooper who were the parents of the three children who lay together in the long grave number 89, also in row (D). Two more brothers, William married Mary Ann Stubbington and I think they were Shoemaker Bob's parents, and lastly Anthony who married Mary Powell from Winchester. Tithingman Peter Houghton and his wife, another Sarah Houghton née Godwin, had six children at the time of the riots – Edmund 11, Elizabeth nine, Peter Junior seven, who I can't forget because he and his wife Caroline Houghton née Churcher lost seven of their sons who all rest in the graves I found at the west end of the churchyard. Peter himself rests in grave number 20 in row (B). His other siblings at the time of the riots were William four, Mary two, and one-year old baby Robert, all of them far too young to understand what was going on at the time. Nor did anyone at the heart of the rural county of Hampshire.

Many lives were about to change. Just the Durley and Upham men's wives, children, parents and grandparents amounted to 140 people who would be affected by the trials before the Special Commissioners at Winchester. It had been interesting, and I have to say disturbing, to read about what happened at the villages of Upham cum Durley in 1830 and the way the bounty hunters rounded up the rioters just for the sake of the money. While of course I didn't know any of the rioters, having found many of their relations graves, I had a feeling I did.

Research on Ancestry sites and looking at census forms gave me information about each person after finding their lost cast iron grave numbers in the neglected wooded area of the churchyard at Durley. So, I was already close to the people's history. I also wondered which of the Houghton families had links with Anne with an 'e'". She had said her mother was a Houghton and there were plenty of them to choose from. She also mentioned her mother married into the Denham family. All I would need to do was to look at the families that migrated at the end of the 1800s, and work from there but searching the hereditary links to Anne with an 'e' would be for another day.

I had been eagerly awaiting information regarding the show trial from the Hampshire Records Office at Winchester. When it arrived it, all came in an impressively large carded A3 envelope containing everything needed to try and make sense of what went on in the courts. The contents were mostly newspaper articles covering the build-up and then what happened each day.

So, what I write now is as I read it, selecting the relevant information about the Upham come Durley men, with a few comments I think appropriate. But not to influence anyone one way or the other. The first article introduced the calendar of the prisoners in the county gaol at Winchester for the trial at the Special Commission of Assize, Holden at the Castle of Winchester on 18th December 1830. Before these gentlemen, the Hon Sir John Vaughan, Knight (One Baron of the Exchequer), the Hon James Parke (One Justice of the Court of Kings Bench), the Hon Edward Hall Alderson, Knight (One Justice of the Court of Common Pleas), his grace the Lord Lieutenant of the County the Duke of Wellington; his grace held that post for 32 years so he would have been very interested in what was happening in his county of Hampshire. His grace was a brilliant man, and his role in this show trial was to make sure that justice won the day and the disturbances that posed a direct challenge to the law of which the duke was the head. It needed someone like him to oversee things then maybe some prisoners on trial would have a fighting chance. I think his grace the Duke of Wellington would have tried to see to that. Other commissioners included the Right Hon William Sturges Bourne, Mr Richard Pollen Esq., George Purefoy Jervoise Esq. High Sheriff, the Grand Jury Foreman was the right, Hon Sir George Henry Rose, Bart MP, and along with 13 sirs and 12 plain old esquires that made up the rest of the jury.

So, 33 gentlemen would decide the destiny of many; if all the gentlemen were true and just remained to be seen. What I didn't like was a few members of that jury had property damaged and machines broken, so had a conflict of interest and would have a chance to make judgement on men who it's alleged caused havoc at their property. It could be said that a small number of jurymen would influence other jury members; it is human nature to want to get your own back and these gentlemen had the perfect chance to do that and it would be legally right even if it was morally wrong. Now where have I heard that before!

On 28th December 1830, ten days after the trials began, the Durley and Upham men were included among 345 names on the county gaol list of offenders. Charges ranging from rioting, robbery, destroying equipment in factories and iron works, and destroying threshing machines and other farm machinery. Many of the men charged were from Hampshire and most of the offences took place throughout 1830, and the last being on 26th November 1830. So it was obvious the money offered to induce the agricultural workers into betraying their fellow men is what Lord Melbourne had hoped for and any form of united front the men promised each other had been shattered.

On each day of the show trial, Winchester became busy very early in the morning with family and friends gathering outside the county gaol in the hope of seeing their loved ones as the prisoners left shackled to each other. Taken on fast-moving carts, flanked by equally fast smartly dressed trotting soldiers in red and black uniforms. Their loud stomping boots announced their arrival at Winchester Castle where the trials were to take place. Women and children called out to husbands, fathers, brothers and uncles, hoping above all they would see each other again soon. But the reality was that some of them may not; it must have been distressing for all of them, and if a father could hear his children's calls but could not see them among the bustling crowds, then that must have been an even worse heartbreak to endure.

I am sure that even Lord Melbourne would have hidden his head in shame if he witnessed that, but maybe not. He thought the working class and their plight was their vocation in life, an obvious condition if they were born into it. Talk about the great and the good, neither of those words should ever be used to describe that man. Historian Boyed Hilton concluded when writing about the home secretary, said that Melbourne's personal life was a mess and that Melbourne hated the working class. Boyed Hilton thought that Melbourne's alleged spanking sessions with large old consenting aristocratic trollops was harmless enough, not so the whipping administered to the orphan girls and boys taken into his household as objects of charity. It's alleged Lord Melbourne had plenty to be ashamed of and it could be said this show trial was one such thing.

At 10 am each day, the trial resumed. Many of the public managed to scramble into the courtroom taking up every available space. At the same time, the people left outside just waited, some whispering, others silent, but all were very worried about what would become of the prisoners. The judge, the honourable Sir James Parke Knight, after acknowledging the jury and legal representatives set out the business of the day. He started by telling everyone in the court that the prisoners brought before him today on the most "Satisfactory Evidence" would be dealt with as all other cases had been in the days leading up to this one. The tenth day of the Special Commission of Assize, the judge then tells the prisoners that he would be failing in his duty to the public if he didn't visit these offences as in most cases tried, with the highest penalty which the law awards against it – that of death by hanging, transportation for life, 14 or seven years, and in other cases long imprisonments to serve as an example to others in their station in life.

The judge then continues by saying that having made a selection of some cases, in which the parties if convicted could not have been affected by the use of these machines, such as carpenters, bricklayers, joiners, blacksmiths, mechanics, thatchers and shepherds, these were marked for the severest penalty which the law attaches to the offence. The judge continued by saying he had no doubt that there were, perhaps some persons engaged in those acts of violence who may have been ignorant of the law as it applied to these machines. But that it is hard to suppose that any of the parties so engaged could have been deficient in common sense as not to know that in the destruction of any property belonging to others, they were committing a violation of some law. In some cases, the machines destroyed were the property of neighbours of some of the prisoners and others of their masters. They must know therefore that they had no right destroy them. Well the judge certainly made his point and all the prisoners on trial had some idea of how things could work out for them. If any of the prisoners were tradesman, then it didn't look good for them, the judge had been clear about that.

In the previous ten days of the trials, many of the prisoners found guilty of machine breaking had been sentenced to death but then in most cases that sentence was commuted. Apart from just three men, the sentences were changed to that of transportation or imprisonment. The three men sentenced to death were found guilty of burning down buildings and barns as well as breaking into properties and attacking people. They were men who would have travelled anywhere to break any machine. One of the prisoners even boasted to the judge that he would go anywhere to smash machines. So, they were to hang on a date to be arranged.

In the meantime, there were plenty of people not happy with the way the trial was proceeding and petitions signed by hundreds of people were sent to parliament, in protest of the way cases were rushed through and the unreasonable sentencing of many of the prisoners. The Upham cum Durley men were among 345 prisoners who in groups of 20 were ushered in to receive sentence after being found guilty. Some pleaded so and hoped the magistrates would have mercy on them, others who would not plead guilty to anything because they had done nothing wrong but had been pointed out by informants who had taken the Sailor King's coin.

First to go before the judge were the Upham men William Primmer, James Cropp, Charles Brummell, Benjamin Harding and James Glasspool, and as expected they were all sentenced to death by hanging. That sentence was then commuted. In the case of James Cropp and Charles Brummell, they were both sentenced to 18 months imprisonment and kept to hard labour. Benjamin Harding and James Glasspool, however, were not so fortunate. They were both told they were to be transported for a period of seven years, for their part in the riots that took place at Upham and Corhampton on 22nd November 1830. Even though the men had all been charged with the same crime, although Benjamin Harding and James Glasspool did not demand any money that counted for nothing, the fact they were there and had a trade is what did for them.

Then things got even more confusing because William Primmer, while also being part of the mob and he didn't demand any money either, he did fire the pistol that set the riots off. William Primmer was sentenced to transportation for the rest of his natural life. As the judge said, "taken from these shores never to return." What was going on? To take a man away from his family was bad enough but never to return and see them again? Well, that sentence was a criminal act in itself. But William Primmer was a thatcher and the judge did say he would throw the book at all tradesmen. So why was that do you think? Well having the advantage of time I was able to look at other sentences and many of the tradesman that were transported I found that what could be considered a trade to some people would not be to another.

Most agricultural workers were multi-skilled – they had to be able to turn their hand to anything – so a pattern emerged. Certain trades were selected and the interpretation of who was a tradesman and who wasn't must have been decided by someone who needed men with particular skills. The judge had more or less indicated that in his opening address to the court, so why was that? Let me give you a clue – it could be in one of Lord Melbourne's titles!

So now it was the turn of the next batch of 20 men to be sentenced, including the Durley men. Remember they had all been charged with the same crime, no variation as in the cases of the men mixed up in the riots at Upham and Corhampton. From what I had seen, the reported charges did not differ at all, but before this unpredictable show trial continued, the Judge called a halt to proceedings while the names of 65 prisoners who had pleaded not guilty were read out to the court, including that of James Houghton Tithingman of Durley. The judge ruled they were all to be acquitted, nothing was reported as to why.

The only thing I could see on the original charge sheet of the five Durley prisoners was that next to James Houghton's name, and rather faded by the years, was that he had pleaded not guilty when asked by the Magistrate Walter Long Esq. This was after James Houghton had been apprehended and before being sent to the county gaol at Winchester, so was he told to say that? After all, he was married to Sarah Pink, she could have been a relation of Thomas Pink whose machine had been destroyed and what James Houghton had been charged with along with the other Durley prisoners. So, if James Houghton pleaded not guilty it would have been his word against the informant who had told Thomas Pink and John Chidell that he saw James Houghton breaking the machine. It was on the strength of Thomas Pink and John Chidell's accusations that the Durley prisoners were apprehended and charged in the first place.

Thomas Pink risked destroying himself, never mind his machine, so by taking James Houghton out of the equation there wouldn't be any awkward questions asked. James Houghton was not the informant; it would be easy to think that he was. I did myself when I read that he was acquitted but the informant's name appears in more than one document and it's quite clear who he was.

The show trial was a sham, it was as simple as that. The Durley five became four and on their charge sheets they all pleaded guilty, hoping for mercy from the courts no doubt and it makes you wonder who told them that it was a risky thing to do. They must have been frightened even if they were grown men, but they had to face the judge no matter what.

When John Stonage, Richard Etherington Junior and John Chalk faced the judge they were each sentenced to 12 months in the house of correction and kept to hard labour. So, the gamble paid off for them, but when you thought the show trial was starting to show some sort of justice, Peter Houghton, tithingman of Durley, a married man with a wife and five children and another on the way was sentenced to seven years transportation for his part in the riots. His charges were the same as the other men, so why was Peter Houghton more severely punished? Well again with the advantage of time I could see that it was recorded that his occupation was that of a mechanic, so obviously the judge threw the book at Peter Houghton as he had done with William Primmer, Benjamin Harding and James Glasspool. Even then, these four sentences were hard to fathom. It must have been difficult to understand for the men as well as their families, who would now face such an uncertain future.

To have your families torn apart in that way is something I for one could never comprehend. So what happened next? Well, after the four Upham cum Durley men's terrible miscarriage of justice they were further kicked in the teeth, if you like, because two days after they were ordered to be transported the Reverend Mr John Haygarth MA reduced the cost of the tithes by 15%, but it was too late for that. If he and the other landowners had agreed to do that in the first place, when it was obvious that after the difficult seasons that it was bound to affect the farming community, then none of this would have happened. It would be the agricultural workers and their families that would be the ones to suffer the most.

Life was hard enough as it was, but even more so for Benjamin Harding, William Primmer, James Glasspool and Peter Houghton's folks who would now have to rely on help from family and friends. Also, what would they have told their children who must have missed their fathers during the time they had been awaiting trial at the county gaol, but now they would not see their dad at all. These children were also victims of these miscarriages of justice, and their mothers would have to work hard just to get by. Given the severity of the sentences and the bad feeling that would have been born from the Swing Riots of 1830, it was clear to see why the west end of the churchyard at Durley was mostly taken up by the Houghtons. The fact they were nearly all Methodists as well just added to the mix. Why that end of the churchyard had been left neglected in a further attempt to cover up the behaviour of the clergy of the time who, after been given information from the informant as to who was alleged to have taken part in the riots, passed that information on to the likes of Thomas Pink and other bounty hunters who then organised a posse of men to round up the accused and by doing so changed so many lives.

So, shame on these people, and let's take a look at how much these bounty hunters made and try and work out what went on in their greedy little minds. And first up we have the Reverend Mr John Haygarth MA, the rector of Upham cum Durley, who became a target of the rioters. I do have some sympathy for this man and his situation, having found himself caught in the middle of a riot at Upham and felt his life was in danger. Yes, he told Mr Newlyn the mob had robbed him, and he gives information to Walter Long Esq. However, it was not him but the informant who came forward voluntarily to give the main evidence and named the men who carried out the attack that he had taken part in himself and knew the men.

Their apprehension that leads to them being charged and convicted was on his testimony alone. Also, the Reverend Mr John Haygarth and Mr Stares did not desire to partake of the rewards on offer as the other bounty hunters did. As a man of peace, the whole episode of what went on and its disastrous consequences distressing as they were for the families, I cannot help thinking he was as much a victim as them, believing as he did the home secretary's actions were honourable regarding the proclamation when in reality it was a trap.

So yes, reducing the tithes by 15% may seem like closing the stable door after the horse has bolted, but it was a start because over the next ten years the Reverend Mr John Haygarth worked on behalf of many families. In particular, William Primmer whose life term of transportation to New South Wales Australia was seen as a miscarriage of justice by just about everyone at the time, but it would be the Reverend Mr John Haygarth's efforts to put things right in that matter. Not because of a guilty conscience, but his realisation that the Home Secretary Lord Melbourne was himself alleged to be guilty of instructing the judges to give severe sentences to tradespeople. As in William Primmer's case, he had been with the rioters at Upham and Corhampton, he didn't ask or steal any money at either parish. As early as 3rd January 1831, the Reverend Mr John Hagarth wrote the first of many letters he would write to the Home Secretary Lord Melbourne with requests for mercy for William Primmer. These letters were to the Crown via the Home Secretary, they were precise and to the point and the contents were for the Crown to observe so Lord Melbourne or anyone else could not keep the contents of such a communication from the Royal Majesty.

They would begin by saying: "To your Gracious Majesty I the Reverend Mr John Haygarth a dutiful Loyal subject of your Majesty, most humbly as your Majesty's subject may approach your Majesty under the firm conviction that due observance of the law will ensure the most significant possible amount of rational and practical liberty. That my infraction must be injurious to the truth of these sentiments your loyal petitioner approach your Gracious Majesty, regarding the case of one William Primmer who in December 1830 was convicted of rioting and was transported to New South Wales in Australia for life and as your Loyal Majesty's Petitioner may approach your Gracious

Majesty to ask for mercy for William Primmer and returned him to the bosom of his Family."

The Reverend Mr John Haygarth regularly wrote to the Crown, at first to the Sailor King and then to Queen Victoria. The Reverend lobbied that William Primmer's wife and children could maybe join him in New South Wales and that the local community had raised funds for them to do so, and that William Primmer was working hard for a free settler who himself offered to build a small shack on a parcel of land so William Primmer could live with his family. But all requests of that sort were frowned upon, but then in 1837, six years into his life sentence, William Primmer received an unexpected conditional pardon and returned to England to live among his family and friends at Upham and again worked as a thatcher. He was ever grateful to the Reverend Mr John Haygarth, rector of Upham cum Durley who continued to lobby on behalf of men directly involved in the attack on him at his parish.

As for the rest of the Upham bounty hunters who did partake of the rewards on offer, the first being Mr Thomas Newlyn, he received £50, Mr John Watts £15, Mr Edward Wyatt High Constable of Bishops Waltham £10, Mr Edward Everalls £10, Mr Thomas Bennett £10, and the informant who will of course remain nameless he received just £5. So in all £100 was paid out to the bounty hunters who tracked down and apprehended the men who took part in the riots at Upham and Corhampton,

I think greed and not need filled these men's pockets, apart from the informant that is. £5, would not go far and he must have wondered if it was worth it. Now the bounty hunters of Durley seemed to have done somewhat better, their total amount to be shared out came to £415. The lion's share of that went to the High Constable of Bishops Waltham, Mr Edward Wyatt, his reward for services rendered was £210. People must have found it difficult to understand how Mr Edward Wyatt could justify receiving that amount of money if he was High Sheriff. Still, the Sailor King's proclamation and Lord Melbourne's reward scheme would override any rules. It would have been a retrograde step for the police force because the right honourable Sir Robert Peel BT FRS had already changed the way of policing in 1830 when he founded the modern Metropolitan police force leading to a new type of officer known in tribute to him as 'bobbies' or 'peelers'.

Sir Robert Peel was also Home Secretary at the time under his political mentor the Duke of Wellington when he was Prime Minister. But then the honourable Robert Peel was replaced by Lord Melbourne in November 1830, about the same time as the Duke of Wellington lost the vote of confidence. Lord Melbourne would have encouraged a rule allowing anyone to partake in such rewards on offer, to have a High Constable in your grip, so to speak, would be like having the keys to open any door. For Mr Edward Wyatt High Constable, farmer and altogether a greedy so and so, would be like winning the pools if they had things like that back then.

Next on the list of greedy bastards was Mr Thomas Pink, and having already been compensated for his threshing machine, also received £50 from the Crown for his bounty work. Mr James Chidell was a miller and became a little richer to the tune of £40, a good reward it seems for saying he was at the scene of a crime when more than likely he was not. He also received a bounty for apprehending rioters who broke one of his machines at his farm in Droxford, Hampshire. Mr Thomas Tier didn't shed many when rewarded with £40 for his efforts. The bit-part players in these outrageous miscarriages of justice got their hands on what was left over, Mr William Pink picked up £15, and the rest of the posse, Mr Richard Austin, Mr James Stonage (not related to the John Stonage, the alleged rioter), Mr John Pearman, Mr John Hatch, Mr William Simpson and good old Mr Eli Windebank, all received £10 reward for their treachery. Most of the bounty hunters were from the town of Bishops Waltham, and in the cold light of day probably advised each other to stay well away from the people of Durley, who would have taken stock and kept their own council as usual and helped each other come to terms with what had happened.

In the space of 27 days, so many Durley people's lives had changed, and after the shock of Peter Houghton's transportation, his wife Sarah would have to bring up her children on her own. She would get plenty of help from other Houghton families but as for funds, things were bad enough for everyone already. First her main desire would have been to see her husband Peter before he was transported; one can only imagine what a desperate meeting that must have been like. To be torn apart for the second time while still so very numbed by the first, Sarah Houghton would get no help from the clergy, even though she would have been entitled to some. But they had been instrumental in her husband's capture, believing as they did the word of a hungry man who gave the Durley men up. I wonder who told Peter Houghton and the others to plead guilty, and did they know that James Houghton had already pleaded not guilty, were they apprehended, charged and kept apart after Walter Long Esq. ordered them to be taken to the county gaol at Winchester?

All the warrants for their arrest were dated 26th November 1830, their offence numbers all ran numerically: Peter Houghton number 88, brother James 89, John Stonage 90, Richard Etherington Junior 91, and John Chalk number 92. So the paperwork indicates that it was all done at the same time, no dates though of when each arrest took place. The bounty hunters knew who they were looking for but finding them all together and charging them together? I don't think so, the paperwork was all done at the same time, individual numbers and all it could be when each man was picked up, they went straight to the county gaol at Winchester. That's when they were asked what each individual pleaded, and other questions like age, occupation, date of birth and so on, all that information could have been filled in if and when. Furthermore, who told the court Peter Houghton was a mechanic? Who ever said that was very much mistaken and last but not least who told James Houghton to plead not guilty?

So many questions would have been asked, and if it had been possible for the people to have seen what's available these days. If only they had someone who would have asked leading questions on their behalf at the time. But the sad fact is they did not and would have been victimised if they did speak up or caused problems. Their livelihoods depended on them working the land owned by landowners such as the church, and things were bad enough anyway, that's why the riots started in the first place. However, we can try to unravel things in memory of them, the most important thing for me was the feeling I had when I first looked at the newspaper article regarding the riot in West Sussex close to the border of Hampshire. They had been stirred up by unknown people, then again when everything kicked off early at Durley on the same day as the rioting took place at Upham and Corhampton in Hampshire. As well as the following day's riots at Owslebury, the fact is in my opinion they were all orchestrated, four riots in a short space of time locally as well as many more in other areas of Hampshire in the days leading up to the weekend when the Sailor King's proclamation came into being.

Lord Melbourne struck hard and fast from early November up until the end of that month, because if those riots took place any later then people would have known about the proclamation and if there were rewards on offer then there is no way they would riot. But they did and fell right into Lord Melbourne's trap. Remember one of his titles was Baron Melbourne of Melbourne Australia, that was a clue in itself and would become clearer as the show trial continued and more tradesmen were transported.

There was another movement in England that would keep the disruption going: they were called the Luddites, a secret oath-based organisation of English textile workers, worried that unskilled machine operators would take their work. The Luddites spent years learning the art of weaving and objected to the increased use of mechanised looms and knitting frames. The Luddites rebellion against the mill and factory owners started in 1811 and ran to 1816. Machine breaking was the only way to put pressure on employers to stop lower paid workers competing for their jobs. The Luddites organisation continued well into the 19th century, their oath was sacred and any industrial unrest involving machinery, the Luddites could be involved. Infiltrating other organisations, unrest was common and it could be what happened in the case of the agricultural unrest and the sabotage of many threshing machines. The Luddites, if they were involved, became part of the problem for the agricultural workers and their fight to have the tithes reduced.

The more disruptive things got, the more reason Lord Melbourne had to use greater powers to put an end to the riots that he was alleged to have helped orchestrate in the first place. There was also something else that would become, in time, an obvious reason for the very harsh sentences given to tradesman like Peter Houghton of Durley, and William Primmer of Upham. John Boyes had been accused of being part of the riots gang that gathered at Owslebury the day after the riots at Durley and Upham. He was accused of assaulting with others and obtaining, by threats and force, from Mr Long the sum of five pounds. He was also accused with others of having robbed Mr Moses Stanbrook at his property of a five-pound note of the Bank of Knapp & Co. In the parish of Owslebury on 23rd November 1830, John Boyes was also charged with conspiring to lower the price of the tithes. It was Moses Stanbrook who informed on John Boyes and others at Owslebury and insisted he should be rewarded, and he received the sum of £25 for his efforts. But when John Boyes was tried, he was found not guilty of all charges, but the judge, unhappy with the jury's not guilty verdict, ordered that John Boyes should go on trial again and at the next trial he was found guilty of the same charges and sentenced to be transported for seven years.

His occupation stated on his charge sheet was that of a yeoman farmer and shepherd, one of the trades that Lord Justice Parke said he singled out for a heavier sentence. So being tried twice was a clear indication that Lord Melbourne had something up his sleeve. John Boyes' sentence became a talking point in the Houses of Parliament as soon as it was made public. Lady Mildmay of the Marwell Estate had a close working relationship with John Boyes, having known him for many years. She, with other important people, petitioned Parliament in protest at the transportation of John Boyes. There was also an unexpected supporter for John Boyes, Lord Palmerston wrote a letter to the Home Secretary. That said: "Dear Lord Melbourne my indefatigable Philanthropist from Hampshire has brought these papers about Mr John Boyes which especially the Affidavit. He is very anxious that I should submit to your consideration, could you not take an indulgent view of Boyes case on condition for which I would be responsible that no other Hampshire men with any claim to mercy, would receive it. The poor devil has been pretty well punished for besides his transportation he has lost his little property he had which has been forfeited by his becoming a convicted felon."

So, we had Lord Palmerston writing to the Home Secretary, even if it was a bit patronising, it was in support just about, Lady Mildmay and others had petitioned Parliament, so things were moving in the right direction in the case of John Boyes. The Reverend Mr John Haygarth of Upham cum Durley moved heaven and earth in support of William Primmer. Who wrote in support of Peter Houghton? Well there was a letter written to the Home Secretary Lord Melbourne on 5th January 1831, that was also written by the Reverend Mr John Haygarth whose reputation by that time for promoting the welfare of others preceded him.

However, the good rector must have forgotten to put on his pleading hat that morning in his letter to Lord Melbourne, that was supposed to plead Peter Houghton's innocence, co-signed by William Gunner landowner and the Reverend Thomas Scard. The letter was nothing like the letters written in support of William Primmer and John Boyes. The letter was addressed to Lord Melbourne, not for the attention of the Crown. It simply said they, "Haygarth, Gunner, and Scard", would like to point out that three others found guilty of the same offence as Peter Houghton were sentenced to 12 months imprisonment, and they believed Peter Houghton was given a harsher sentence on account of having been described as a mechanic rather than an agricultural labourer. Although he was frequently employed in what's called coppice work, he is to all intents and purposes a farmer's labourer, and during the last and preceding winters he has been in receipt of parochial relief as a distressed pauper. They hoped his sentence may be reduced to imprisonment for 12 months.

Well, I wonder why they bothered writing at all! Nothing in that letter would cut any ice with Lord Melbourne, who hated the working class and would never help a pauper. The authors of the letter had no intention of helping Peter Houghton. The Reverend Thomas Scard's premises at Bishops Waltham had been attacked by the rioters the same day as Thomas Pink's threshing machine had been broken. So quite why he would put his name to anything to help an agricultural worker was strange to say the least because he hadn't any respect for that class of person. If he had and cared, he would have kept a record of where they were buried. His signature to that letter was probably for effect only. William Gunner was a businessman and would need to be seen to be making the right noises and indicate to the men that worked his tithes he cared but his signature was just sweet-talk. As for the Reverend John Haygarth, if he was not going to go the whole hog and address the letter for the Crown's attention, then why bother, which is basically what they did. They said nothing about Peter Houghton's family and that wife Sarah was pregnant with their sixth child. Peter Houghton received a rotten deal from the judge like many others at the show trial at Winchester, then from the people who were writing to beg mercy for the man. But as we know from the state of the west end of the churchyard at Durley, the Houghton's as well as being Methodists received no favours from the clergy regarding anything.

So, what happened next? Well I hate to think what state Sarah Houghton must have been in, knowing she was about to lose her man and I hope she had no idea of the contents of the letter written by the clergy. If she did, it would have fully broken her will, as her heart was already broken with the intense sorrow she had endured. Peter Houghton and John Boyes were among 224 convicts described as machine breakers that sailed from Portsmouth aboard the hulk ship Eliza, captained by Mr John Groves on 6th February 1831, their destination was Van Diemen's Land, Tasmania, part of the British Colony of New South Wales that became independent in 1824. The first Governor was Mr George Arthur. The problem with Van Diemen's Land for the free settlers and convicts was it was a dismal place and trying to get free settlers to go there was a big problem. It was an out-of-the-way place, with the added problem of the gold rush in Victoria, and the population of Van Diemen's Land dwindled. Working-class people didn't want to go there as free settlers, preferring instead to try their hand at gold prospecting, so a request for more British emigration to make up the numbers was needed for the place to survive.

The British were worried that the French would colonise part of the island so needed the infrastructure to continue to attract more free settlers; who would in time realise all that glitters is not gold and would return to a more sensible way of making a living. The more people that became free settlers would mean the place would grow. In 1788, the British claimed sovereignty over the area, claiming the land belonged to no one (Terra Nullivs). It's legal jargon that's hard to explain or understand, so I will not try either one, but basically it means the land is ours now.

The British ignored the Aboriginal people who already lived there and the conflict between the British colonists and Aboriginal Australians, known as the Black War, dragged on for years. It was not difficult to see why no one wanted to go there. Hence the transportation of British convict tradesmen was just what the doctor ordered. The tradesmen would work for the white settlers and help get the infrastructure up together. These British convicts were in fact white slaves, no other word for it, they had been stitched up. Shackled to each other, and shipped off to the back of beyond, and it's alleged that Lord Melbourne had a hand in that and why the main town in Victoria Australia, Batmania, became Melbourne and why Lord Melbourne became Baron Melbourne of Melbourne Australia as a tribute to him. You see the Slavery Abolition Act of 1807 would become law in 1833 after 26 years and British slave owners would not and could not move slaves around from one British colony to another because of it. Something Lord Melbourne was against becoming law, it meant the owners of black slaves would be well compensated. So their now valuable black slaves would stay where they were and were replaced by white British convict slaves used to complete the infrastructure of Van Diemen's Land. With the benefit of the history books, that opinion is not that far-fetched, so while the hulk ship Eliza sailed the 13,000 miles to Van Diemen's Land, a journey that would take roughly 110 days to arrive there, back in England moves continued to get John Boyes transportation overturned, with many letters sent in support of his release. This would continue for some time.

The Reverend Mr John Haygarth had been successful with helping William Primmer return to England from New South Wales, using the method of keep writing to the Crown. In the months since the transportation of Peter Houghton, just one solitary letter was sent to the Home Secretary and nothing else, nor was there anyone likely to help. If you were a Houghton, you would be hard-pressed to trust anyone outside of the circle of family and local village friends. But the main thing for Peter Houghton's wife, Sarah Houghton née Godwin, was to try and make a new way of life until her husband returned.

With children to look after and no wage coming in, she would have to have asked for parochial help from the church for which she was entitled. She was also heavily pregnant with their sixth child, so whatever farm work she was doing at the time, she would need time away from the farm. On 26th June 1831, Sarah Houghton gave birth to a baby daughter. She was named Sarah after her mother and also took Peter Houghton's mother's maiden name of Wadmore. I am not sure why that was; it could be the grandparents would take the child on, given their daughter-in-law had rather a lot to worry about at the time, trying to adjust to the situation she was in. By the time Sarah Wadmore Houghton was born, her father Peter Houghton had arrived In Van Diemen's Land and was obviously unaware that his daughter had arrived. It should have been a joyful time with the arrival of a new daughter.

Peter Houghton would never see her because 20 days after Sarah Wadmore Houghton was born, Peter Houghton died of consumption in the Hobart Town Hospital, Tasmania, aged just 35 years. He was interred at St David's Burial Ground Hobart, with no family members in attendance.

This was the graveyard that Anne with an 'e' told me she had been to, so quite what Sarah Houghton must have felt at the time is hard to imagine. She wouldn't have the facts that are available to everyone in our timeline. Having researched things as I have, I can't quite believe it happened and my Lord I felt for Sarah. She didn't just lose her husband but as I found out later on in her life, she also lost five of her grandchildren and they rest at the west end of the churchyard.

Remember the first cast iron number (24) I came across when clearing the soil in what would turn out to be row (B)? The number was Wilfred Houghton's, her 19-year-old grandson, son of Peter Houghton Junior who rests in grave number 20 also in row (B). Peter Houghton Junior lived well into his 70s and looked after his mother. The census records show where Sarah lived, first with son Peter Junior and then with one of her daughters. The census records describe Sarah as a 'widowed pauper', and when she was 58, after such a hard and sad life, on 11th July 1859 she married again in the Church of the Holy Cross, Upon They Hill. Records show her son Peter was her witness and the gentleman she married, his witness was a relation. Each person signed with an X.

The man Sarah married was 62 and together they lived and worked together at Hill Farm in Durley. I am sure the gentleman she married would have looked after Sarah, well in fact I know he would have because she married my four times great-grandfather David, he of "Yum Rector Pray for Rain" and father of Susan Matilda Houghton, wife of Shoemaker Bob. I didn't find this out until after I had seen Anne with an 'e' and kept the information till now because I like a happy ending and after so much sadness, I have had to report I think we deserve one, don't you?!

I also think I have done what Anne with an 'e' expected of me. I hope I have and at last, I understand why I went to the churchyard in the first place. It has taken a while but has been worth it, and the way everything has fallen into place has been quite amazing. Sarah and David were not married long, Sarah died aged 60 in 1861, and as we know, David died in the Droxford Union Workhouse in 1866 aged 75. They are both buried in the churchyard at Durley, but I have no idea where, and I do blame the Reverend Thomas Scard for not keeping records at the time.

John Boyes, after four years at Van Diemen's Land, received a pardon and between 1836 and 1838, most of the agricultural tradesman were granted their pardon. John Boyes wrote about Peter Houghton and said he was sick on the hulk ship Eliza most of the way to Van Diemen's Land and was a broken man when he died so far away from his home and family. John Boyes said they were all slaves and treated like them too. So what next? Well I think the only thing to do is write a letter to the Home Secretary for the attention of the Crown to try and get Peter Houghton his pardon, because over 240 other agricultural tradesmen got theirs and justice must be seen to be done.

Chapter 23
The Tunnel Structure

After the shocking revelations regarding the agricultural riots of 1830, it was time to resume investigating the structure I found southeast of the churchyard. I was told by the General they were to be minor investigations and care had to be taken around the headstones and footstones situated on all four sides of the structure that pre-dated any of these works of art. The first area I looked at was to the north, just below the chest grave, that was built on top of the tunnel structure at a much later date.

The first headstone situated on the northside of the tunnel structure was that of two brothers and the inscription said: "George and Thomas Mears sons of Richard and Elizabeth Mears". George was born on 26th April 1826, and died on 22nd December 1846, aged just 20. His brother Thomas Mears was born on 18th May in 1811 and died on the 6th of December 1852, aged 41. There were many graves with headstones containing members of the Mears family buried in the southwest of the churchyard. In one of the photos from inside the tunnel there was a large coffin plate with what looked like the name Mears on it, but it was difficult to read with so much dust on the item

Thomas and George Mears' headstone next to the tunnel had earth piled against it and on top of the grave itself. Once the earth was moved, this impressive headstone was over five feet high and measured 30 inches wide. It was also clear the earth on top of the brother's grave was imported and could have been removed from within the church as well as earth dug out to make the new boiler room situated under the present-day vestry. The earth and the headstones in the vestry area would have been removed along with any human remains. In J. Colson and Sons' instructions it said: "Any earth that was dug out to create the boiler room could not be taken further than thirty yards away from where it was removed." Through our investigation we now understood why all the headstones looked shorter than they actually were.

I had found out when levelling the earth around the grave of Thomas and George Mears that many bones had been placed on top of their grave, then covered with earth. With the evidence from the gruesome photographs of inside the tunnel I could now see what I was up against, and that the whole area where the headstones looked shorter was in fact a burial ground for old bones, mainly broken bits and pieces.

All the large bones were inside the tunnel and what was left had been smashed up, laid out and covered with soil and the discovery at the time made my blood run cold, as it did when I had first seen the gruesome photographs of inside the tunnel and looked at them forensically in order to work out what certain things were. Back then I could set aside the feeling aspect of the situation, as if I had become numbed by the sight of what I was looking at because each photo was so shocking I became immune to the shock of it all.

That was some months ago and I hadn't looked at the photos again nor did I want to. I felt nervous about what would need to be done with what I may find now, but if I was to get this situation over and done with, I had to push on with all the things I could make a difference with. But I couldn't in this area of the churchyard without the help of the archaeologists. Without them it may never be done, because for a start we had no money to pay for such things as ground radar.

I could still look in what direction the thick 18-inch walls ran, some of that was at ground level. And with a long metal rod, I could feel in what direction the wall went, but as for digging into the spoil I had to think about that. Unlike the west end of the churchyard where everything was lost in the woods, those graves were not covered with bones from another timeline. If they had been, I would have left it. The reasons for their neglect were much different from the situation we had now. The southeast of the churchyard, as far as I was concerned, was a crime scene from yesteryear and any investigations into those responsible were of no interest to me. What was of interest is who the victims were, as their treatment was a crime against humanity itself. I could work and remove the imported soil from on top of the graves and sieve through forensically removing any bones, but it would take some time, However, I had plenty of that. By collecting the broken bones and putting them into a proper grave, then the area around the headstones could be properly gardened and the headstones could be seen at their full height.

It could take years to do it all and the work would be done by many people who would follow on with what I would start, separating the human remains from the soil that also contained coffin handles, broken tiles, bricks and so much slate all of it in bits. So, I talked with the General and Adrian and told them if we were to do the right thing in respect of all who passed this way before, then it was important to get the job started. I planned to work in grids, one grave at a time. I knew if I found the plinth at the foot of each headstone then the resting place would be well below that. What was on top of the graves is what needed moving and sieved through forensically, if we did that then we may find more of the original structure as we went along.

So what we had were three investigations. One was to find out about the original structure with a tunnel. Two was to remove the soil from on top of the graves forensically. These first two investigations could be done if and when. But the third investigation would be ongoing to find out all we could about who had been removed from inside the church. We knew the names of the families that had people buried within the church from the old newspaper reports we had seen. So, there must have been records, but what happened to them, God only knows! There were three individuals named the Reverend Mr John Rogers, whose history was in George Molesworth's book. Thomas Pope, we had plenty of information about his coffin, but who was Thomas Pope? Not even Adrian could find that out and he could find a needle in a haystack.

Thomas Pope's name was not in any of the burial records we had seen. I had looked long and hard after first reading about him and looking at photographs of inside the tunnel, at what I thought could be the remains of not only Thomas Pope but what was left of the coffin. You could see where the fine fabric had been secured with brass nails that over the years made the timber on his coffin turn a shade of blue. Finally, there was William Oysell, and the only record of him was that his will dated from 1410, a copy of which had been found in the Muniment room inside a book at Winchester College.

These Muniment rooms were used to keep valuable information regarding each college or university. They had to be kept in the safe room, where the walls and floor were constructed with fine stone and above flood level to ensure the history of each place of learning was preserved. So, if William Oysell's will was considered important then he must have been too.

The will indicated he was to be buried in the chapel at Durley and he left enough money for masses to be said with candles lit in his honour. He had gone to a lot of trouble making sure those wishes were carried out. He had been laid to rest in a stone coffin and on the lid was a French floriated cross. Even with all this information to hand, the only reference in the burial records was where he was put after being removed from within the church on one brief line. So, if William Oysell's remains were in the tunnel along with Thomas Pope's, that would account for two of the skulls that were each close to separate piles of de-articulated bones. But there were more skulls that lay isolated away from any bones they may have been articulated to. But it was more than likely these skulls related to the bones broken and scattered at the southeast of the churchyard. Given that the skulls were thrown into the tunnel, this indicated to me that whoever smashed the rest of the bones up didn't have the guts to destroy the skulls. Which didn't exonerate them from any criminal act; far from it, they were just guiltless.

I decided that William Oysell and Thomas Pope would be the main people I would concentrate my latest research around. I contacted the archivist at both Winchester College and Winchester Cathedral to ask if any historical documents were held regarding William Oysell. I knew this would take time so meanwhile, I tidied up the area to the north of the structure where the soil had been laid on top of Thomas and George Mears' grave next to the structure. What bones I had found before I realised what had been done were respectfully buried in the area next to A.N.Other and blessed by the rector.

It was a shock to find those bones, and why I needed help from the archaeologists. But it could be they would not be interested anyway, looking at bones found in a sacred burial ground was hardly a major find for them. If the remains were still inside the church, then that could have been of interest to them, and they would probably find out who was who in that respect. I was sure if they could get inside the tunnel they would love to have worked on those bones, but there was no chance of that because whoever was in the tunnel had been disrespected enough having been moved once from their resting place within the church. They would not be taken away in boxes to be prodded about with, then stuck in the bowels of a university. I didn't like the fact they were in the tunnel, but the tunnel was in Durley, the village where they wanted to be laid to rest.

If it was at all possible that they could be removed again, it would be to respectfully place them in a proper coffin and into a proper grave within the churchyard. Sometimes I wondered how the hell I had got into this situation, worrying about the remains of people who died many years ago. Yes, I had been looking for where they were buried but uncovered so much more that needed sorting out, so like everything else in the churchyard I could not leave things as they were or walk away and forget about it. As I saw things, Thomas Pope and William Oysell were the people I wanted to concentrate on – who they were and what they did. The rest of the people buried in the church, their history was known. We may not find out what happened to all the remains, but it was more than likely they were scattered over a 30 square yard area I had been working on.

The situation was a mess. I have to admit, it wasn't funny, but did have a humorous side to it. Especially when people came in to visit and look at the old headstones, they sometime said they didn't want to walk over graves and were careful not to. But I hadn't the heart to tell them when they walked the area at the southeast outside the church, they could not help but walk over the remains of people taken from within the church proper.

The second area of the structure I investigated was on the southside, and after removing earth from the width of the structure west to east to a depth of about 12 inches below the descending pyramid-like bricks, I came across the residue of a brick and flagstone floor that people had broken away to accommodate more graves. The graves in the area to the south were in what would have been the inside of the structure; just how far to the south the structure would have extended was anyone's guess. But the arch to the east with the independent wall in front of it was the actual back of the building and this was confirmed when I found another brick arch about 15 feet away that was in line with the arch behind the independent wall that blocked off the exit from the tunnel.

It was impossible to look at each side of the arch because to the east of it was another large headstone, placed hard up against the arch and the grave was on ground that would have been on the outside of the building and the inscription on the headstone faced the church. Because back then in death, people believed if when the second coming arrived it would come with the sunrise from the east. Many a date had been predicted for this major event and it must have been a great disappointment to those people when it didn't in their lifetime. So, I was confident that the grave that went with this headstone was on the outside of the structure. The occupant of the grave was a man called Thomas Benham who died aged 55 in 1828. Also, further along to the south of the Benham grave was a wide void enough for another three graves but without headstones or the residue of grave mounds.

The next headstone however was in line with the Benham headstone and was the resting place of John Prowting who died on 21st July aged 35 in 1832. After his death, his wife Elizabeth née Purdue married again to a man also called John, John Vear who unfortunately died as well on 23rd June aged 55 in 1855 and Elizabeth Vear/Prowting née Perdue buried the two men side by side.

The two Johns' headstone had been neatly fixed within the brick and flagstone floor, so they too were buried outside the structure on the east side of the arch. This arch was more than likely to have been fashioned around a window or external doorway of the original building and had been used as a buttress to support the headstone. The arch was intact and showed no signs of decay that would have caused it to give up the ghost, so to speak. Like everything else, I had found there was a mystery surrounding it. I was confident that the two arches that were in line were both part of the east side of the structure and that everything on the westside of them was the floor area of whatever the building was that had the tunnel beneath it.

There were about a dozen graves within the floor area, some had headstones and the ones that didn't would just have what was left of the grave mounds. These mounds were hidden because of the soil that had been thrown on the top of them; the other graves within the floor area would have been cut into the floor but because they had no headstone you couldn't tell where they were. However, finding more of the floor, the two Johns' headstone had been secured proving there was a good-sized building on the site.

To find out how far south the building extended would have to wait because if I worked in grids one grave at a time, it would take some time to reach two more graves with headstones one row back from the two Johns' graves. But these headstones would have to be cleaned to find out who rested there, and I wanted to see if the headstones were secured with material from the floor. Consequently, things were moving well, I had found what I thought was the east wall having already found the northeast L-shaped wall. The next thing to do was to investigate the west side of the structure that faced the church, I had already found what looked to be the entrance to the tunnel that measured some 30 inches high and 24 inches wide.

This entrance was accessed by two steps that descended from the brick and flagstone floor of the building. In fact, the width of the steps only being 24 inches wide meant the steps could have been covered by a wider flagstone that hid the fact there was an exit from the building and was more likely to be a priest hole hidden under the floor. I couldn't be sure if the brick and flagstone floor abutted the churches east wall because there was a line of graves with headstones about six feet from the church. This was where Chrissy Rumbold and I removed the old path that ran over these graves and the ground in this area had also been raised.

So, the only real chance of finding out if the structure and the church were once linked would be to find the end wall to the south that ran east to west and abutted the church. Once that was found, the size of the building could be established. If it was just one structure with a secret tunnel that ran beneath it then I wanted to find out if the tunnel's floor ran beyond the independent wall to the east. If it did, then the legend of there being a tunnel that ran to the east would be true. But the only way to find out would be to dig at the southeast corner of the structure. We couldn't look at the northeast corner because A.N.Other's remains were there.

So, another investigation to dig down at the southeast corner of the structure was approved by the General. What with one thing and another, it had taken me six months to reach this stage. The plan was when I had dug down on the southeast corner of the structure to the floor level, which I hoped ran from the tunnel and would indicate the tunnel ran further east, Adrian Abbott would come and take photos of what I had found so far.

In the six months, both he and Shannon had been busy and had found more information regarding members of the Hersent and Pope families. But as for information regarding Thomas Pope and his demise there was nothing more than what had been in the newspaper in 1879 about Thomas Pope and his impressive coffin. However, a copy of the will of William Oysell written in 1410, found inside a book in the Muniment room, was available. The archivist at Winchester College told Adrian he could have a copy. It was written in Latin that would need translating. While Adrian couldn't do that, he knew a man that could. At last, I was to learn something new about William Oysell other than the snippets that were banded around from, for all I knew, uninformed sources.

When the will arrived from the College it was fascinating but threw up as many questions as it answered. The will was a copy drafted in 1523 and attached to it was a copy of the real one. The documents had yellowed with age as one would expect, however the time it had spent inside the book had preserved it. I have written it as it was written back in 1410, when many of the words were spelt differently, as in the first line back then Oysell was spelt Hoysell and the translation from Latin went something like this: "In the name of God A Men. I William Hoysell Chaplin at Durley, the first day of August in the year of the Lord 1410, sick of the body yet sane of mind, make my will in this manner. In the first place, I bequeath my soul to God and the blessed Mary and all the Saints and my body to be buried in the Chapel of the Holy

Cross of Durley. Item, I bequeath to the work of the Chaple aforesaid one Cow. Item to the light of the Holy Cross aforesaid 40 pence. To the Church of St Swithun's Winchester, 3 shillings and 6 pence. Item to the rector of Upham 6 shillings and 8 pence. Item I bequeath to the celebration of mass for my soul and souls of all the faithful deceased XXX masses in one day. Item I bequeath to the Chaplin of Mer'wyl (Marwell Hampshire) 1 Cow. Item I bequeath to Galfride Colton 1 horse. Item to Agnes Colton 1 cow. To each of my godchildren, 1 bushel of barley. Item to Thomas Porteref 1 gown. Item to servant Esabelle cloth for one gown with hood. Item to William Martyn 1 inventory. The residue of all the goods not bequeathed as above I bequeath to my wife that she orders and disposes of for my soul and the souls of the faithful deceased. Item I ordain and constitute executors of this before testament, last will of me faithfully to discharge by William Martyn and my wife above said. Given the day and years above said."

William Oysell was the chaplain at Durley and went to some lengths to secure his place within the chapel after his death. Also, his legacy to the church of St Swithun's of three shillings and sixpence was interesting, as a young ecclesiastic he could have trained there and records of his time at St Swithun's would be in the archives at the Cathedral in Winchester. Also, the fact William Oysell had a wife meant he wasn't ordained, but as I found out chaplains of schools, colleges, hospitals and the military to name a few didn't have to be ordained but what would be interesting was how he found his way to become the chaplain at Durley. If he was at St Swithun's where many ecclesiastics trained, I would have to find more information about the man, but it may not be easy because all I had is what he bequeathed to others in his will. There didn't seem to be a record of his family archives, as I found in the research I did regarding the Reverend Thomas Scard MA.

Meanwhile back at the churchyard early in January 2021, it was bitterly cold, and the low mist took until midday to clear. Large black crows were my only companions. They looked on from the top of the huge headstones as I dug out the southeast corner of the structure. The earth was loose and the deeper I dug it became clear the soil was imported. From the rough chiselled stone and brickwork at the end of the 18-inch left side wall of the structure, it became quite obvious that at some stage the tunnel did run further to the east. Then as I reached the depth of two feet, I found several rusted coffin handles – there was nothing to indicate they were at one time attached to a coffin in the area I was digging. I had found no residue of a timber coffin at all, and the handles were too close to the independent wall that blocked the arch. If there had been a coffin where I was digging, the handles would have been on each side of a coffin facing east to west, but these handles were all in a line against the independent wall.

As I dug one more spit of my spade, I came across another skull and some de-articulated human remains; this time they were adult remains. When we had found A.N.Other, its skull was much smaller than the one I had just discovered, and there were a few other bones with this one. It was also too close to the independent wall for it to have ever been in a coffin, only being two feet under the ground, so this soil I had dug out was infill and this indicated to me that the tunnel did run further to the east and at some stage had been cut away or had fallen in on itself then filled in with soil from another place.

So, what I did was to use some wide boards we keep for placing over newly dug graves at night to protect the public and wild animals who may wander in. Then I placed earth each side of the remains and placed the timber across the area that made a sort of coffin over the human remains. I then recorded what I had found and how many coffin handles were there. I put them in a bag and placed them on top of the boards that covered the remains and began to backfill the hole, but then I stopped and, while smoking a cigar, thought about taking the top three lines of bricks off the top of the independent wall.

My thinking was if I placed a rod down against the inside of the independent wall, I could work out how deep the floor was. I also thought about getting a better look at the coffin lid with what was thought to have the name Mears written on it. There was also the possibility I could see what was left of the Thomas Pope coffin with the fabric marks that had been fixed with brass nails. I thought about all these things and thought I would sleep on it because I was that close to having questions answered and I would never have the opportunity again. Not that I wanted to know for knowing's sake. It was I needed to know for Thomas Pope and William Oysell's sake and find out as much as I could. They were, let's not forget, around before the Reformation and were of the Catholic faith.

So post the Reformation King Henry VIII doctrine is what the likes of the Reverend Richard Ferguson followed, so he and the clergy of his day would not think twice about destroying the coffins of Catholics, any more than the rectors at Durley post the Reformation neglected many a Methodist grave and left them to the elements and become lost in the woods.

So, I didn't think about not having a look for long; and by the time I had finished the cigar, I worked out how I would do it. By taking the top three courses of bricks out from left to right to halfway across the independent wall, there would be enough room to look in on some lost history. All the photos I had were quite gruesome to look at, so how I would react to seeing what lay behind the independent wall, I couldn't say. If I thought about it for too long, then I wouldn't attempt to look in and the thought of it made me shiver, and I was scared, but then I was when I took out the bricks to drop the camera in at the west side of the tunnel structure. I was not going to wait now, I had made my mind up to look inside because it was quite possible it could be my one and only chance. I didn't want to make a meal of it either, all I would do was look. There would be no moving of bones, skulls or the residue of coffins, the photos of the fleur-de-lis emblem was clear enough in the photos we had. The only thing I was prepared to look at, if it were possible, would be the steel name plate that was covered in dust that Adrian thought said Mears. And while I was stood there, I also thought about taking bricks out of the side of the chest grave, to see what was in there and if the story of the probation officers' visit was true. I thought it was because I had seen the man and he was clear about the bones. Also, Adrian's friend had put right things that were damaged in the church and the history of the churchyard being damaged at the same time was talked about.

So, it was a spur of the moment thing. I had no time to ask the General, because I made up my mind to do it right then. What I did was take three bricks out of the west end side of the chest grave just above the bricks I had taken out when we dropped the camera into the tunnel, given Adrian and others thought the stone lid on top of the chest grave came from another place, i.e. where the vestry is now. The bones were taken from another chest grave in that area and a new chest grave built on top of the tunnel structure then the stone lid was put back in place in 1879. If there was nothing in the way of bones inside, it could prove the chest grave was broken into and the bones taken away as the probation officer told me. The chest grave did look as if it had been repaired in more recent times; so, was I trying to convince myself? Not at all. I believe there were no bones inside and I was right, there was not one bone, just broken bricks and mortar. And the thing that proved the story was right was on one of the spades full of earth and bricks I pulled out from inside the chest grave – a ring pull drinks can!

They were not around till the mid-70s when the church was broken into and the probation officer took bones from the churchyard early one Sunday morning. So the person that made good the chest grave in the 70s may be had his lunch and put the empty drink can with all the residue of bricks inside the chest grave before placing the stone on top of the chest grave that was first built in 1879. Finding that ring pull can was another fine moment because up till then the story of the probation officer was far-fetched, according to others. But I had seen the man and believed everything he said and, more importantly, it was more information for the General. That evening I called the General and told him I had looked inside the chest grave on the spur of the moment and there was nothing but soil and rubble and one ring pull drinks can indicating that the probation officers' story was correct. I also asked for permission to look inside the tunnel by removing bricks from the independent wall just to look inside. The General gave me the go-ahead so I emailed Adrian to tell him what I proposed and what time I would be doing it and if he could come and take photos for the record.

Chapter 24
Pope, Mears, Woodlock and Oysell

When the day came to look inside the tunnel, it was a bitterly cold and frosty morning. I dressed for the occasion, wellington boots with my thermal jeans tucked into them and two chunky jumpers given to me by ladies from the village who made sure I would always be warm in the winter months. Gifted gloves from another to keep my hands warm, a scarf covered my face and my eyes peered out from the gap between it, and the brim of my hat and with one extra jumper around my shoulders for good measure.

I was ready to look into the tunnel. I still shivered, not from the cold but the apprehension of what I was about to do and what I may find behind the independent wall, separated only by the wall from the modern world I lived in, and the other side from a time forgotten, that something spiritual had drawn me to. I wondered if the spirits of who lay behind the independent wall were as apprehensive as I was.

But it was too late to think about that now, the only sound in the churchyard to begin with that morning was the scratching sound on the brick. The noise of course came from the saw I used to cut through the hard mortar joints of the independent brick wall. These joints were much harder than when I raked out the soft lime mortar between the bricks I removed from the structure below, to allow the camera to be dropped in. The harder mortar indicated the independent wall had been built in more recent times because the mortar mix contained a greater volume of cement and meant the end of each brick needed a gently tap with a hammer and bolster to become detached from the course below. It took me 20 minutes to remove enough bricks to make an opening that looked like a dark cave.

When Adrian arrived, he too was dressed to keep out the cold and worked quickly to set up his camera to the right of the opening looking west. Then, rubbing his hands, he declared that I should be the one to look in first because I had found the tunnel. So, I switched on my flashlight, knelt down and leaned forward into the tunnel, and as I shone the light on the area just behind the wall, I found myself looking at what I had seen in one of the photographs. The neat pile of de-articulated bones, and just beneath them was a person's skull, and to the right laid the side of what I believed to be part of Thomas Pope's impressive coffin.

You could see quite clearly the stain and print left from the rotted fabric that once decorated the side of his oaken coffin. Some of the brass nails were still in place and I could see the holes left from the ones that had gone. There was a coffin handle well rusted but still partly attached to the side of the deep coffin, and I was sure what I was looking at were the remains of Thomas Pope. As I looked over the wall at this pitiful sight, all I could say was "My God, Thomas I am so sorry, what have they done to you, my friend?" As I moved the light around the remains that were so old and were a yellowy/brown colour in places, I found myself leaning right over the wall shining the light to look at his remains from different angles. His skull was side on as if at rest and I could see one of his eye sockets that, even without an eyeball in place, felt like he was looking straight at me. I thought the day before I would be too scared to look, but as I did, I felt connected and glad I had bothered after all.

I looked around the rest of the tunnel with the flashlight and there were at least four other skulls scattered around, and the only way to describe them was they all looked so very lonely. That may sound a daft thing to say but they did, another pile of de-articulated bones to the right of what I was sure were Thomas Pope's remains. These could have been the de-articulated remains of William Oysell, but I didn't think they were, because I didn't get the feeling I had when I looked at the remains, I thought to be Thomas Pope's. They had to be someone's of course, but I just couldn't connect spiritually, they were what they were – just a pile of very old bones.

Part of the steel coffin lid that Adrian thought said Mears was close to the wall in front of me and I stood back to allow Adrian to take photos. As he did so, I pondered on what I had seen and was convinced I had found Thomas Pope's remains. But who was he, I may never find out is what I felt spiritually because maybe I was only meant to find him and there was nothing in the church's burial, baptisms or marriage records to say he lived in Durley. There was no doubting he was special in life to some people to have been buried in such an impressive coffin, so now he would be regarded as special in death now I knew where he was. He had been "Too long in exile" as Van Morrison would sing.

When Adrian finished taking photos, we talked about what we had seen. We didn't say how it made us feel and we still haven't, but when you see something like that and the expression on your face cannot be seen by another living soul... Well for me anyway, I just momentarily fell apart, silently letting my feelings go inside that dark tunnel away from everything and everyone. It was a natural reaction to what I was looking at, something I will never forget and so glad I found what I had been drawn to in the first place. I was glad for Adrian, he had searched for so long and was rewarded for his efforts with the satisfaction and knowledge it gave him and sometimes that's enough for anyone.

We decided to take out and photograph the dusty steel name plate that was once fixed to a coffin; it was close to the wall surrounded by blue broken bits of coffin. Using a long-handled pair of grippers, I took the item out and, once cleaned, looked in good condition. It was black and rusted in places and looked like the Mears family crest. The old English inscription was in gold and simply said in bold lettering across the top "Richard Mears". Beneath that, in large fancy artwork, it said "Died", followed underneath by the date of his demise "March 27th 1861" and stated "Aged 85 Years" when he departed this earth. As it turned out, when Adrian had a quick look at his records, Richard Mears was the father of Thomas and George Mears who lay to the right of where we were standing in the first grave north of the chest grave.

Later Adrian discovered that Richard Mears was married to Elizabeth Mears née Prowting, and she was the daughter of Robert and Mary Prowting née May and they were another set of my Nan's grandparents. Robert being the father of Grandfather David, Susan Matilda's Father David, who married Peter Houghton's widow Sarah. You couldn't make it up could you folks!

So, I was related to Richard Mears by marriage according to Adrian, who photographed the Mears' coat of arms for his records and also took one of me with it. We then placed the Mears family crest back inside the tunnel. I could just see the steel plate with the emblem of the fleur-de-lis on it, but it was further back in the tunnel and while we had a good photo of it anyway it was still a mystery how it got in the tunnel in the first place. If it came from within the church, was there a French person buried in there too?

We each took one last look around the inside of the tunnel, turned out the flashlight and said good day to the history that lay behind the independent wall. I then put back the brickwork as I had found it and blocked off the tunnel once more. As I did so I thought if the Richard Mears coat of arms was in the tunnel he must have been buried in the church as well and taken out with the others. His widow Elizabeth died aged 90, a year before the work was carried out in the church. If she had been alive and Ferguson wanted to dig Richard Mears up, I am sure there would have been opposition from her. After all, he had only been dead for 18 years, but Elizabeth Mears died the year before work started on the church. Richard and Elizabeth's children, apart from one, were all dead as well. So that gave the Reverend Richard Ferguson and co. a free run with no one to stop them in their crime against humanity.

What we found out about Richard and Elizabeth Mears was straightforward enough, and Adrian worked out who was who in the Mears clan in no time at all. We also thought that Richard Mears could have been reburied in the chest grave above the tunnel, his remains would have been fully articulated, his coffin too would have been in good condition. But having found nothing in the chest grave, what did happen to Richard Mears!

I also wondered if the clergy of the day would have needed an ecclesiastical faculty before removing Richard Mears from within the church given the short length of time he had been dead. So, from not knowing anything about Richard Mears before finding his family crest, there was plenty of information to pass on to people researching the Mears family.

I also decided I could never look for anything more regarding Thomas Pope, because I had found what I was supposed to find. When I saw his remains it was like I had been spiritually awakened to the fact that enough was enough, and that one glance at his deep eye socket was like being spoken to. Not told off, but more of a plea to leave well alone.

Before that, I had looked many times to try and find out who he was. The nearest I came was when I found a marriage record of a John Pope from Fareham in Hampshire. The son of a wealthy brewer, or maltster as it was called back then, John Pope married a woman called Mary Mears from Durley. He was 27 and she was 26; they were married at the Holy Trinity Church in the grounds of Winchester Cathedral. So maybe that's why I couldn't find a marriage in the records at Durley. Mary's father was Mr John Mears and there is a John Mears buried to the southeast at the front of the church. All the dates matched. I had thought from the start that Thomas Pope wasn't an adult after reading about his coffin. I thought this because of the way it had been decorated in such a special way, maybe by his grieving parents or because there was some special reason he and his coffin should be remembered. But I set aside all I found because that's what I felt was the right thing to do, and after seeing what was left of him, I knew I had done the right thing.

I concentrated my efforts on finding more about William Oysell. In his will he confirmed what he left to others but nothing about the man or how he became the chaplain at Durley. No information explained why he had such a high-profile coffin within the church proper. Once again, I would spend my evening researching whilst by day look after the churchyard. If I had time in the afternoons, I would work around the tunnel area, and after looking into the tunnel finding the Mears family crest and confirming the fleur-de-lis emblem was on what looked like a steel plate, progress was finally being made. The tunnel ran further to the east and the only external wall that needed to be found was the one to the south, that ran east to west and could have abutted the church.

It had been easy finding the L-shaped wall to the northwest and the long wall facing east with the arches and headstones as a guide, and if the wall to the south was found it would definitely be a major find. One of the two other headstones to the south once cleaned revealed it pre-dated John Prowting's, John Vear's and Thomas Benham's headstones by 91, 114 and 87 years respectively. So, if this headstone that was in memory of another Mears, by the way spelt Meeres, if it had been secured in the floor of the structure then it made the structure even older. I can't say older than was thought because no one had any idea of the structure's age.

I had talked to the General about what he wanted to do regarding archaeology in the area of the tunnel and the old brick and flagstone floor and, as always, he was honest with his answer saying he was still looking into things and was in communication with the archdeacon. The General was as keen as anyone who had become interested in the project; and to be honest I was lucky he trusted me to get on with things that were in the best interest of the churchyard. And I trusted him to do the right thing when the time came regarding archaeologists. For myself, well we needed them but couldn't afford them. It was frustrating, and the longer the General took, the more I could do by way of making the area look presentable. We had so many visitors who came to look around the tunnel as well as other areas that the General and I had worked on improving.

He looked after the War Grave Commission and MOD graves and was keen to make sure every military person lost in the wars was honoured for their ultimate sacrifice. He arranged with the rector and his co/churchwarden, Mrs Jane Chamberlain, to have an outside service during the lockdown to mark Remembrance Day. The service included a Scottish piper who played for the church congregation who followed the rector to the graves, pausing while the General placed poppies on each of the war graves. This man is so well organised and well-liked by the villagers as his father before him was, and as the under sexton, well the General was coming along quite nicely thank you. Still a lot to pick up from the maestro of course!

It would take me until the middle of 2022 to conclude everything and after eight years of hard work and research I could finally see an end to things in what had been quite an adventure. I had gone as far as I could in respect of finding out what the structure was that would be ongoing, and now we needed professional help with that because I was reluctant to touch anything I wasn't sure of. The removal of the earth from on top of the graves at the southeast would also be ongoing, as for the ways and methods used in the construction of both the church and the tunnel structure, I understood enough about that to keep looking for new things. I had researched interesting work by learned people published by the Hampshire Field and Archaeology Society, that told us a lot, in their opinion, about this curious out-of-the-way place called the Church of the Holy Cross at Durley. Also, how individual settlements had grown in the area and that the church had never been part of a nucleated population. These settlers moved to Durley to work the lands 'held' by wealthy families such as the Hersent family, who had business interests in Southampton. These lands and tenements they held were the property of the Crown, leased to them by the Bishop of Winchester on very long terms – as much as 160 years – and more for the benefit of hospitals, universities, colleges and monasteries.

So, when the newspaper report from 1879 said the Hersent family name was now obsolete in the village, it could have been because there was no one left who wished to lease the lands held on the same favourable terms as their ancestors. If the remainder of the lease could not be leased with a vacant possession, then the lands would go back to the bishop until they were leased again. With the lands not being held by a reputable family whilst a workforce occupied the tenements, then the Crown wouldn't want the lands vacant for too long. Many of these families over the years played a big part in church life and in the community, doing enough to be thought worthy of being buried within the church proper. By looking deep into the records of the lands held in Durley by important wealthy families, some of them were linked by marriage which gave them an even bigger say on what went on in the village. Because each of the major families had people who had chosen an ecclesiastical life as rectors, this gave them a greater say on all church matters. Among the tenants of the Crown at Durley was the Woodlock family.

The Woodlocks were holding a considerable amount of land in the 14th century, and in 1348 John, son of William Woodlock, was the rector of Upham cum Durley for one year and the lands they held were possibly near to the same estate which were in the hands of Sir Peter Philpot. Remember it was John Philpot, his son, the former Revd Archdeacon of Winchester, who became a martyr for his religious beliefs. He was seized in 1555 and burnt at the stake at Smithfield in London. After kissing the timber that was to burn him he prayed: "I will pay my Vowes in thee O Smithfield."

It was the Philpot family that owned the old cottage that once stood at the west end of the churchyard at Durley, and a record of that was part of Gwen Houghton's historical records she passed on to the History Society. What Gwen found back then may not have meant a lot at the time, but know I was finding out such a lot meant Gwen's part of this jigsaw became important long after her demise. So, the Rev Archdeacon John Philpot would have been familiar with Durley church and its history. Like many other wealthy and important families that held lands at Durley, including the Heathcote family from Hursley in Hampshire, many of their number were clergymen. But you will not find any Heathcotes buried in Durley churchyard; the Heathcotes had their own neo-classical mausoleum built in the churchyard at Hursley by Sir Thomas Heathcote 2nd Baronet of Hursley in Hampshire. He considered the family vault under the church at Hursley no longer adequate so when the new mausoleum was completed, Sir Thomas Heathcote 2nd Baronet had 38 coffins of earlier members of the family removed into the new mausoleum.

As well as the Heathcote, Hersent, Philpot and Woodlock families all having held land at Durley, there was one other interesting family – Mr and Mrs George Bolney. They also held lands at Durley, and they were early residents of the manor of Leckford Abbess as it was once known. Owned by the Abbey of St Mary Winchester, originally the possession of the Crown, the manor had been granted by King Edred in 947 to a mass priest named Edulf on the understanding that on the King's death half the land went to the Abbey.

Down the years, Leckford changed hands many times until ending up as a private estate purchased by John Spedan Lewis of Oxford Street London in 1929. He was described as a visionary retailer with extensive knowledge of botany, entomology and aquatic life who later founded the John Lewis Partnership according to the history of the Leckford Estate. So what attracted these wealthy people to Durley in the first place and did they know the history of the chapel? Who built it and why in such an out-of-the-way place? What we have to remember is most of these families were Catholics, George Bonley and others were described as being 'papists'. Now a papist was an abusive term used to describe someone who outwardly conformed to the protestant way, but inwardly were devoted to the Pope and the Catholic Church.

To discover more about the Church of The Holy Cross at Durley and the lands held that would benefit it and other ecclesiastical places, I had to go way back to find and follow the names of people linked to the settlements, the chapel and each other. The names and dates would be from differing timelines, but they could all be linked one way or another, and the main reason for the research was to see if it was possible to find out who was involved in the original construction of the chapel and tunnel structure.

Finding William Oysell's will was fine, but I believe if I were to dig deeper there could be more information. William Oysell's will once translated was superficial, just an ordinary will and lacked depth; but then when it was written he wouldn't have thought that one day his remains would be dug up and removed from his final resting place. The will would make an interesting discussion for people attending a monthly historical gathering most definitely. But the next day, how many people would want to find out why William Oysell left money to St Swithun's? What his connection with Marwell was? Who was his wife, and the other people mentioned in the will he bequeathed things to?

The fact is, I wanted to know and thought by following the names of people, not only in William Oysell's will but the people that held lands in Durley, may well lead to something interesting. If it turned out to be a waste of time then so be it, nothing ventured nothing gained. The first name I researched was Woodlock, and as previously stated, John, son of William Woodlock, was listed as a rector of Upham cum Durley in 1348. His name was among a list inside Durley church of rectors from 1304 to 2012 put together in loving memory of local person Mr Thomas Jury. Another important Woodlock I found was Bishop Henry Woodlock of Marwell Woodlock, the name of his family's estate in Hampshire. He was prior of St Swithun's, 1295–1305, a Benedictine monastery St Swithun's provided clergy to the Cathedral of Winchester, and Henry Woodlock became the Bishop of Winchester in 1305 following in the footsteps of Swithun himself, who was Bishop of Winchester from 852 till 862.

In correspondence as Bishop of Winchester, Henry Woodlock called himself Father Henricus. Some of the information I found relating to Bishop Henry Woodlock was in another interesting paper called 'Marwell Woodlock; The Creation of the Manor and its Descent, 1300–1920' by Mr Stan W. J. Waight. What I was able to find about Henry Woodlock in that paper and other documents held in various places was a great help to me and would be to anyone researching the Woodlock clan.

But before I talk about Henry Woodlock himself, remember I said we should follow the names. We have both him Henry Woodlock of Marwell Woodlock, the place of his birth who was Bishop of Winchester and former prior of St Swithun's. Also, William Oysell chaplain at Durley who left a sum of money to the Priory of St Swithun's, and one cow to the chaplain at Marwell in his will. Now the two men were born too far apart to have known each other, but William Oysell would have known about Bishop Henry Woodlock; they were linked by their faith. St Swithun's and may be John, the son of William Woodlock Rector of Upham cum Durley in 1348 nearer the time of William Oysell,

The link would be stronger if William Woodlock, father of John, was a relation of Bishop Henry of Marwell Woodlock. Anyway, when Henry Woodlock became Bishop of Winchester in 1305, he granted freehold lands to the world and its wife as well as many of his kinsman and why not, nothing wrong with a few acts of family patronage. And if the money came in from the rents for the benefit of the schools, colleges, monasteries and rectors, etc. and of course pleased his king, then all well and good. Pleasing a king, whoever he was, any bishop whoever they were had a job on their hands. The bishop also granted lands like the ones in Durley to wealthy friends as well as relations and by doing so controlled many manors and villages. Nothing wrong with that either; he granted lands to the great and the good. The great and the good hired tenant farmers, and the tenant farmers employed local labour from the settlements that had grown into a village community.

The bishop ran the show; much of the lands were grants to the church anyway in the first place by one king or another. The article I read did say that Henry Woodlock Bishop of Winchester and the Woodlock family during the rise of Marwell Woodlock showed a high degree of nepotism and a disregard of legislation relating to land tenure. They were also granted lands during the creation of Marwell Woodlock by the previous Bishops of Winchester John de Pontissara from Pontoise in Seine-et-oise in France. He was Bishop of Winchester between 1282 and 1305 during the creation of Marwell Woodlock and while Henry Woodlock was still the prior at St Swithun's. The information regarding the disregard of land tenure was taken from 17th-century transcripts held in the archives of Corpus Christi College in Oxford taken from so-called Twyne Transcrips, 484 years after Henry Woodlock had served his term as the Bishop of Winchester. So he bent the rules a little during his 11 years as the Bishop of Winchester and by doing so kept harmony among the many people who held and worked the lands Henry Woodlock presided over.

Being in charge of any big organisation which being the Bishop of Winchester was, it seems Henry had his enemies, which is not surprising if he was granting lands to kinsman, friends, and by doing so controlled vast areas with like-minded people that would keep him in a position of power. In 1311, seven years into his term as Bishop of Winchester, Henry felt it necessary to petition King Edward XI for help. The nature of his request in the record I found said: "The Bishop of Winchester states that he is being wrongly slandered in the court of Rome through the hatred and envy of malevolent persons. And requests the King's letter recommending him to the Pope's Chamberlain and to the other Cardinals and asking them not to hear or expedite those wishes to harass him."

When Henry Woodlock was made Bishop of Winchester, Pope Clement V was the head of the Catholic church and Henry III was king. Pope Clement V, originally named Bertrand De.Got, was born in France in 1260 and served as Pope from 1305 to 1314. To some he was best remembered, along with King Philip of France, for suppressing the order of the Knights Templar and allowing the execution of the Grand Master Jacques De Moley on charges of heresy, satanism and sacrilege.

Many of Knights Templar members were nobleman who were burned at the stake and much of the treasures they acquired were never found, leading to many historical legends down the years. King Philip of France also banished the wandering Jews from France in 1306 they had already been banished from England in 1290 where they had gone in the 11th century after the Norman Conquest. King Philip of France thought the Jews a liability; they had their material usefulness but were never accepted in either country and were treated shamefully by both kings. Henry Woodlock served three kings as Bishop of Winchester. When he was first appointed, King Henry III was on the throne, a weakling king easily led by people with a grudge against the bishop. Henry himself got on the wrong side of the King by helping one of his own metropolitan friends who was himself out of favour with the King.

The King let Bishop Henry Woodlock know this displeased him greatly by confiscating all the bishop's assets. But not long after this action, King Henry III died and was succeeded by King Edward I. He ordered all Bishop Henry's assets be returned. These kings were a fickle lot weren't they folks! King Edward I, himself, was unpredictable. Dubbed Longshanks because of his height of six-foot two, he had an uncompromising attitude towards his nobility and his brutal treatment of the Welsh and the Scots was legendary. He had also expelled all the Jews from the Kingdom of England in the late 12th century. Jews were not allowed to own land or pass on money to relations after death – all their wealth was taken in taxes by the Crown. They could work on the land or earn a living as tradesmen and from a population of around 3,000 Jews, many were arrested, imprisoned or hanged. They were blamed for many crimes persecuted and finally banished from England by Edward I, and Longshanks' genocide towards the Jews was complete. Their expulsion lasted until 1657 when it was formally overturned by Oliver Cromwell.

It's said that Longshanks also fathered 22 bastard children, was a clever politician but an utterly temperamental king. King Edward died on 1st of July 1307 aged 68, whilst being carried north just to oversee another brutal campaign against the Scots who rejoiced at the news of his passing. Longshanks was succeeded by his son King Edward II.

He was a different kettle of fish altogether and it was common knowledge he enjoyed the company of both men and women but, he was the king so he could shaft whoever he wished. Even though homosexuality was condemned by the Catholic church, legend has it that Edward II was brutally murdered at Berkley Castle on 21st of September 1327 by being held down and having a red-hot poker inserted into his anus. My word, Lucy Worsley never mentioned that and she's a real clever clogs where kings and queens are concerned! I'm not sure I believe that account of his murder; it was no job for an inexperienced poker inserter, methinks.

Anyway, not surprisingly it's said the King's screams could be heard for miles. This cruel torture was devised as a punishment for his presumed sexual acts with other men. So, Bishop Henry Woodlock, it seems, had a cross section of 'We three Kings' to contend with during his time as Bishop of Winchester. The first one was a weakling, the second a bully, and the third habitually swung both ways. I did find the record of what happened regarding the bishop's petition to King Edward II; it was regarding the use of the Crown's land at the Manor of Merdon. I think the complaint was brought by the Reverend of Merdon against Bishop Woodlock. The issue, it seems, was festering for some time before the crown got involved. Henry Woodlock argued that the lands were used while the manor was vacant and that Nicholas Woodlock, who was the steward and bailiff at the Manor of Merdon, had kept the wheels turning till the estate was leased again.

Nicholas Woodlock was an older relation of Bishop Henry's who had also been, or was still at the time, sub prior of St Swithun's. So, Henry Woodlock seemed to have all his bases covered and went on to finish his term as the Bishop of Winchester. There was another record of a Walter Woodlock being granted a free pardon for using the Crown's demesne land without paying for it. Demesne land was part of a manor not granted to a freehold tenant but retained by a manorial lord for his own use and occupied by his villeins. Villeins were a low hereditary class of slave attached to a lord who would provide safety and protection from outside threats. His villeins, peasants and serfs provided the labour to run the manor in return for fixed dues in kind, money and service.

So, Walter Woodlock must have been working land that had been granted to him by a nod and a wink from Bishop Henry Woodlock because a licence in Walter's name was given to enclose woodland and fell the trees. However, it couldn't have been that bad because he was pardoned, and after Bishop Henry Woodlock died on the 29th of June 1316, Walter Woodlock remained in favour with Bishop Henry's successor John of Sandale.

John of Sandale was a Gascon Medieval Lord High Treasurer, Lord Chancellor as well as being Bishop of Winchester. Sandale inherited the manor of Wheatly within Long Sandale, Yorkshire. He also held the manor of Great Coates, Lincolnshire, and Walter Woodlock became John Sandale's deputy keeper of his parks and bailiff of four of his manors. It seems the Woodlocks had always been on favourable terms with whoever was Bishop of Winchester, having been granted lands by previous bishops while Henry Woodlock was still prior at St Swithun's. So, there were a few fiddles to keep the wheels turning, looking after so much land for the Crown must have been hard work for Bishop Henry Woodlock. But granting so much land and tenements to kinsman meant there were plenty of records relating to what they held.

The records were old and hard to read until getting used to the wording and name variations. The contents of each record were set out the same, stating what land and tenements were involved, so all I had to do was look at the name at the top of each document and after looking at a few I soon got the hang of things. The documents showed what lands were held by an individual in the county of Hampshire, and the Woodlock name showed up many times and it was quite obvious that the late Bishop Henry Woodlock had gathered in and looked after as many of his relations as possible. He was responsible for some 50 manors in Hampshire for the Crown and ten others in Berkshire, Buckinghamshire, Oxfordshire, Surrey, Somerset and Wiltshire. His own family's Marwell Woodlock Estates included 235 acres of land held by 17 copyholders. But a major part of the estate was represented by over 700 acres of demesne lands. In addition, over 50 acres in Owslebury and other outlying Hampshire lands in nearby Brambridge, Hensting, Baybridge and Upham were all held by copyhold and were all individually enclosed. If you remember, it was in Hensting where John Boyes rented Henstings Farm from Lady Mildmay; and under the rules of the manor he lost "His Little Home", as Lord Palmerston had put it in his patronising letter in support of John Boyes to Home Secretary Lord Melbourne. As I looked through the list of people who rented farms and copyholds, other recognisable names from the 18th century emerged. As well as John Boyes, there was Walter Long Esq. Remember him? Well, he was on a list and was the tenant of ten different holdings that were occupied by nine copyholders. By custom of the manor, the tenant of the copyholds might be held for the term of three lives, with the additional provision that the widow of husbands who had died were entitled to widows' estate. I think this meant the widow of the tenant of the lands received five of the copyholds' rents from the occupiers of the copyholds, including elements in kind such as livestock, hens, a cockerel, cows, etc. Which was the case regarding Walter Long – his widow, Alice Long, became the tenant of the owners of the lands that in 1800 belonged to Corpus Christi College in Oxford who had purchased the Marwell Woodlock Estate around 1520.

So, Alice Long became the tenant of the copyholds and part of the demesne lands including the hall. These records indicated that the hall was Marwell Hall next door to the Marwell Woodlock Estate. Marwell Hall in time became the home of King Henry VIII's brother-in-law, so the record stated the King had persuaded Corpus Christi College to give the hall to Henry

Seymore when the King was courting his sister Jane Seymour. Legend has it that a private ceremony of that 'eternal bonding' between the two took place at the hall before the public ceremony.

The amount of Woodlock names I could follow was interesting. Even though they came from different timelines, they were all related in some way or another. One of the biggest problems I found was that most of the lands or manors mentioned were all to the north of Durley church and the tunnel structure.

It was clear that Corpus Christi College at Oxford owned much of the lands and along with Winchester College they seemed to have the whole of the county of Hampshire and some beyond pretty much under their umbrella, so to speak. My problem was I was looking too much into the history of the Woodlocks; it was all very interesting but keeping me from the primary task of business which was to try and find out who built Durley church and the tunnel structure.

So, I turned my attention to the Doomsday Book and Saxon Charters. Rather drastic one may think, but many medieval village churches were recorded in the Doomsday Book, however our Durley wasn't. There was a Durley in Wiltshire and in the hundred of Redbridge southwest of Southampton on the edge of the New Forest. I looked at the British History Online website and tapped in Durley and the earliest mention of our Durley, was in a grant of land to the Abbey of New Minster by Edward the Elder in AD 900. Well, that took us right back in time, nearly 400 years before Durley even had a church, chapel, tunnel structure or anything else on the small original site upon the hill. Now Edward the Elder was the son of Alfred the Great, King of the West Saxons from AD 871 to AD 886 and King of the Anglo Saxons from AD 886 to AD 899. Not only was Alfred a fine warrior who walloped the Great Heathen Army from across the seas, but he was also a man of vision. A hereditary trait down through the generations you know, like father like son, like grandfather like grandson, like great-grandfather like great-grandson, and that's how far I went back to the time of King Egbert the great-grandfather of Edward, the elder and King of the Wessex Saxons from AD 802 until he died in AD 839. In his kingdom, there was a priest ordained by Helmstan, the then Bishop of Winchester, after which this priest's reputation grew, and on hearing of the priest and impressed by the utterings, King Egbert appointed the priest as tutor to his own son Aethelwulf. The priest's name was Swithun who went on to become the Bishop of Winchester appointed by his former pupil Aethelwulf, who had succeeded his father Egbert as King of the Wessex Saxons in AD 839.

Swithun or Swithin wasn't made a saint for donkey's years after his death in 863. He was then canonised in 1093 and became St Swithun. His story is worth reading if you like a good yarn about miracles and strange happenings which of course I do. However, it's the influence he installed in others and the reputation he built up among the kings of the Wessex Saxons we have to follow. There are differences of opinions of course among the bow-tied and wide-frocked historians who browbeat each other and insist their version of the same story is the one to run with, when in reality they can only surmise. Some historians read and alter things to fit in with their version of events, whereas others read and wait for history to unfold but sometimes, as in this case, I will refer to Swithun now as St Swithun because we are not following all of the story up to the time he was canonised long after he was dead. Because that's who he became and his was one of the names to follow. In his new office as Bishop of Winchester, St Swithun became well known for his devotion to religious practices and his duties to all both rich and poor, whether it be temporal or spiritual matters, he regarded all earthly life sacred.

He was wise, trusted and at his request King Aethelwulf gave a tenth of his royal lands to the church. St Swithun was also instrumental in the building of new churches or overseeing the restoration of old ones. As was St Wilfred from a much earlier time, he was involved in so many of the early churches constructed throughout Hampshire and West Sussex. These two sainted monks had a big influence on their respective Saxon kings. In education too, St Wilfred's teachings to the Jutes and Meonwara people of the Meon Valley in Hampshire was well documented, as was St Swithun's teachings to King Egbert, and King Aethelwulf much of his teachings were handed down father to son.

The next in line who would be king of the Wessex Saxons was the late King Egbert's grandson Alfred the Great. Born in AD 849, he was nine years old when his father King Aethelwulf passed away in AD 858, and was 14 years old when St Swithun died in AD 863. The king and the bishop would have had a great influence on Alfred during his formative years, having spent so much time at court with his parents, and what little education he received then was from his mother Osburh and other tutors. But Alfred didn't learn to read English until he was older and learnt Latin instead from a bishop from Wales called Asser. Asser taught Alfred to read and write in Latin and was by all accounts one of Alfred's favourite teachers.

Alfred became king of the Wessex Saxon's when he was 23 and as well as being a great leader of men, he thought to learn was just as important and he started a curriculum of education since he lamented his own lack of education as a child. One of his achievements was his programme to educate not only himself but his people. Noblemen's sons attended a school at court, Alfred recruited teachers and scholars to come to Wessex from England and the continent. King Alfred the Great's reputation as a man of vision was further enhanced when one day while in the woods, maybe hiding from the Danes, he came upon a swineherder, an older man who impressed the King with his knowledge of life. This man was Denewulph or Denewulf, most records refer to him as Denewulf so we will stick with that. Anyway, Alfred recognised the potential in this person so sponsored his education, and in time made him Bishop of Winchester.

Denewulf served as bishop from AD 879, till AD 909, quite a promotion from a swineherder to a bishop. But he was King Alfred's bishop first and foremost, and the King was no fool, and while Denewulf got on with his bishop-ing, King Alfred continued with his desire to educate his people. He founded Athelney Abbey in Somerset, believed to be an enlargement of a monastery already on the site that became a religious house for monks of the order of St Benedict. King Alfred brought monks from France to populate the abbey and the King was instrumental in the creation of other religious houses for both monks and nuns alike. He was also involved with creation of Shaftesbury Abbey in AD 808 at Dorset and installed his daughter Aethelgifu as its abbess. Shaftesbury Abbey became one of the richest abbeys in England, second only to the wealth of Syon Abbey founded by King Henry V.

Shaftesbury Abbey survived for many years till it was dissolved in 1539, ordered by Thomas Cromwell, minister to King Henry VIII. It was obvious looking back as we can it was Shaftesbury's riches that Henry the VIII was after. Wealth built up over the years by Catholic monks and all these religious houses – monasteries and convents alike – were plundered for their riches to keep King Henry VIII's war chest full. So this is where you can see the story unfold as to who was the better king, whose side are you taking?

Well, King Alfred the Great or King Henry VIII, but not just yet as it's time to pop back and see King Alfred the Great for a while because he was busy working on other projects. He had Sumond Grimbold, a learned priest and monk of St Bertin at St Omer in Flanders, to assist him in this work. Grimbold arrived in AD 893, but it was not till the last year of King Alfred the Great's life that he told Grimbold about his intention to create a monastery at his Royal Borough of Winchester in the open churchyard immediately to the north of the cathedral. Alfred lived long enough to purchase the land from the Bishop of Winchester and his canons.

The bishop, of course, was the swineherder Alfred sponsored and who became his friend and ultimately his Bishop of Winchester, Denewulf, So from the vision of King Egbert and his appointment of St Swithun to teach his son the future king of the Wessex Saxons, Aethelwulf. Aethelwulf's wise move to make St Swithun bishop of Winchester, and the influence the King and the bishop had on the young Alfred who, when King of the Wessex and Anglo Saxons, followed in his forefathers' footsteps. By bringing to the team, already historically assembled Denewulf, Grimbold and others. To hand down all of their knowledge to King Alfred the Great's son, Edward the Elder.

Chapter 25 Final Opinion

After the death of Alfred, the Great on 26th October AD 899, Edward the Elder became King of the Anglo Saxons. He had to see off one of his cousins who also had claim to the throne according to the history books, but we won't go into that because Edward's our next name to follow. Eight months after the death of his father, Edward the Elder's coronation took place on 8th June AD 900, at Kingston on Thames at an important Saxon ceremonial site on the boundary of the two ancient kingdoms of Wessex and Mercia. For clarification, Kingston means 'King's farm' or 'estate' in Saxon lingo.

As King, Edward, as the history books tell us, was much inferior to his father in the cultivation of letters, but incomparably more glorious in the power of his rule. From reading about him, he seemed to have all of his forefather's attributes for the organisation of the people around him and the excellent sense to use all their collective knowledge and skills. Of course, he also had the positive information regarding St Swithun, what he did and stood for and how his great-grandfather Egbert had seen the good in the man and used it to the advantage of all. Edward's grandfather Aethelwulf had been educated by St Swithun, so handed down positive information to Edward's own father, Alfred the Great, who himself had found, educated and then made the former swineherder Denewulf his Bishop of Winchester. Alfred also brought Grimbald the learned priest and monk over from Flanders. He too eventually became a saint. Alfred also invited other scholars to his court for their linguistic and compositional ability to assist him in his literary pursuits.

So Edward the Elder would have known St Grimbald and Denewulf, as well as the history of St Swithun. With the help of St Grimbald, Denewulf and others, Edward in accordance with his father's wishes, founded the Abbey of New Minster. St Grimbald had already accepted the appointment as abbot to the yet unbuilt monastery when asked by Alfred the Great before he died. While St Grimbald had been instrumental in the creation of the Abbey of New Minster and its monastery with Edward, sadly St Grimbald died on 8th July AD 901 at around the aged of 81.

The monastery was consecrated in AD 903. Edward endowed the monastery with considerable possessions, including the grants of over 100 hides of land in Hampshire and Dorset. A hide were areas of land approximately 30 modern acres and considered sufficient to support a family. Edward's grant listed the hides each village held that could be divided up such as in Micheldever, nine hides x 30 = 270 acres that tax would be paid on to benefit the Abbey of New

Minster overseen by Denwulf, the Bishop of Winchester.

The village of Stratton held three and a half hides, Burton eight and a half, Popham ten, Woodmancote ten, Candover ten, Cranbourne four, Drayton-Juxta-Nunneton four (juxta means near or close for reference). Swarraton held three, Barton Stacy three, Northington six, Norton-Juxta-Selbourne three, Slastede one and a half, Tatchbury one and a half, Abbotsanne 15, Colingbourne 50, Chisledon in Wiltshire held 40. And then last on the list from the charter made by Edward the Elder it simply said, "And, Land at Durley," no mention of how many hides had been granted for the benefit of the Abbey of New Minster. The other thing you have to remember is these lands once held were for as long as anyone was around who wanted to work them, and if the land at Durley was held directly by the Abbey that could be for all time.

I think they could be moved by a Bishop from one particular hundred to another, but I think it would still be for the benefit of the Abbey. So could it be that this out-of-the-way place was built under the supervision of the monks as another place where they could further their work? Old survey maps of the churchyard shown in yards, reveal that the site was very small, the original boundary to the north was just 15 yards from the back of the church and the front elevation to the southwest is to this day narrower than that. The whole site is at a strange angle that slopes from north to south, and there are records of opinions by different eminent people published in the Hampshire Field Club and Archaeological Society who thought there could have been a churchyard on the site before a church was built.

It was, they said, only conjecture based on incomplete information, something I was endeavouring to complete by digging deeper than they were prepared to do, it seems. Strange, only doing half the job, if they were going to dig at least go the whole hog! But then it probably didn't mean as much to them as it does to me, spiritually that is. When researching so far back in time, one can only announce what seems to be reasonably true if there's nothing factual or without any reasonable doubt. Then people surmise, afraid to stick their neck out for fear of losing face, maybe. I'm not sure the same researchers further on, in the same research paper, came to another conclusion that the site wouldn't have been used to grow crops because the land took longer to warm on a daily and yearly basis. So that would give credence to their other opinion that a churchyard could have been on the site before the church.

What we do know is that the settlers gathered on the site in the religious observance of the Sabbath. The day when the Lord rested from all he created, and monks would care for the settlers' religious and spiritual needs. While the site was at an out-of-the-way place, it was perfect to have monks look after themselves while at the same time be involved with creating something by way of a structure. Or the restructuring of a building already on the site, which is what I think, because close to the site there's still a clear water river running just to the north so plenty of water to hand for personal use as well as construction. At the bottom of the church lane, the main river that ran through the Meon Valley would have been in full use and how the large stones would have been transported to the site in the first place.

Stone the Saxons shipped over from the Isle of Wight, were used to build the original old churches. There are maps showing the areas where the stone was taken from on the Island, as well as maps showing what areas the stones were used to build the churches on the mainland. Without these maps, I wouldn't entertain the notion that the stones were used in the Meon Valley, but the main structure, i.e. the large cornerstones that can be seen, are the same as other churches in the Meon Valley. Nearly all of them have wonderful, knapped flint work between these large stones that form the corners of the churches as well as around windows and doors.

The only difference is at Durley church the outside walls look such a mess, and because the old original building has been added too and altered so much over the years. Pebble dashing over the alterations was seen as a cheap way out. Originally the old, knapped flint would have been weather-pointed, set neatly against the protruding stones on each corner of the building and around the doors and windows making the stonework stand out. By going over old work that way, what's loose, in time, will fall off, as some of it has in places. There were available tradespeople who work with flint but it's a question of money and Durley church is last on the list as far as the powers that be are concerned. So that's why you have to look and see what's been so poorly done, compare it with other churches to see how it should look if someone had come up with the cash that is. But, we are where we are, and left with matters of opinions as to how it once looked.

I think whatever building was on the site to begin with was turned into first a chapel then a church and originally overseen by Benedictine monks from various abbeys. There were plenty, St Swithun's alone had over 70 Benedictine monks. They were hard-working, clever people; they would have used the free labour available. In medieval times, the abbeys could offer them food, beer, clothing and a floor to sleep on if needed. Working for the monks was one step up from being a slave. I hate to say it, but I think it's true, the difference being the monks prayed for you and meant it. Teamwork in the construction of a halfway house if you like, used on route by people travelling and concealing their true identity; wishing to observe what's going on elsewhere, they travelled incognito, maybe on their way to and from France. Or fleeing an unreasonable king, perhaps to hide relics from the plunderers of the abbeys that became so rich over time. It is something to think about. Let's not forget St Wilfred and St Swithun were known for their skills in building and the reconstruction of churches so these skills would have been passed on to different generations of monks who in turn would pass on the skills of self-alliance.

If Edward the Elder's charter hadn't said right at the end "And Land at

Durley", I wouldn't consider the possibility of what I believe to be true. I will as always try and find some sort of proof to back up my theory. Many of the villages mentioned in Edward's charter had ancient Saxon-influenced churches that in time were replaced by new ones built on the same site using some of the stone from the old churches built in medieval times. Back then it would have been the likes of St Wilfred and St Swithun who had a hand in their creation, a fact well-documented in records relating to both men and why I think their teachings to the monks and others in their respective timelines will eventually bring more information to light. Not further back, because from King Egbert through to his great-grandson Edward the Elder, there are enough clues in what's already been found that, once put together, will enhance the chance of finding out who was behind the construction of Durley church. The clues are not obvious at the moment, but I am confident they will be all in good time.

Some of the people needed to make the story fit, if there is one, have already been mentioned. But there will be more, you can be sure of that; they just need piecing together if and when they are found. There were also more charters to look at. I felt there had to be more information because the church didn't build itself. What I did find was information with reference to the Abbey of New Minster when later it became further enriched with treasures when King Cnut and his wife Emma of Normandy became great benefactors to the minster. Not just with the gift of land, of which there was much, but by the gift of "A Legendary Gold and Silver Cross Richly adorned with precious stones", There were also relics among the gifts received by the monastery that in time became the target of greedy people, keen to steal and enrich themselves with these wonderful gifts. Rich too were Shaftesbury Abbey and Athelney Abbey in Somerset, all creations of the Saxon kings from three generations of visionary men and associates.

Time moved on at the Abbey of New Minster. Denewulf, the former Illiterate swineherder and loyal friend to Alfred the Great, was the Bishop of Winchester during the Abbey's creation and died in AD 908. There was little information regarding the man's age, not that I could find anyway, and the person I think was a credit to his father and grandfathers was Edward the Elder. His reign as king of the Anglo Saxons ended when he died aged 50 in AD 924 of wounds gained after putting down a Mercian and Welsh revolt. He was laid to rest at the Abbey of New Minster at Winchester in the county of Hampshire.

It had been interesting reading about the Saxon kings from the time of Egbert through to Edward the Elder, but it was time to move on and after researching more records I eventually found another reference to the Marwell Woodlocks. This time in the area southwest of Durley church, about a mile as the crow flies over farmland and just beyond what was believed to be the area of a lost Saxon settlement. The talk of a lost settlement called East Horton to the southeast of the church had come up in many conversations, but it was only now after finding the tunnel structure. The obvious signs that the 14th-century additions to the church at Durley were built over the top of what would have been a long narrower building on the site and why I think it was turned into a religious venue. I couldn't prove it, but I could show people what I found and they could make their own minds up.

Anyway, the information regarding the Woodlocks was in relation to a place called Allington Manor. Allington, in the Doomsday Book of 1086, was called "Alditona". It was recorded as a settlement in the hundred of Mansbridge in the county of Hampshire. The manor was held by a man named William Alis, and had a recorded population of 11 villagers, six smallholdings, ten slaves as well as land resources of 67 acres of meadow, 20 acres of woodland, two water mills and "One Church". William Alis, after the conquest, held the land directly from the King and was tenant-in-chief in 1086. The king was William the Conqueror or 'William the Bastard' as he was also known because he was one. His reputation for brutality was feared after defeating a rebellion led by his own cousin. William the Conqueror ordered that the hands and feet of the defeated rebels should be cut off as punishment. So he could indeed be considered a right bastard!

William the Conqueror was responsible for the Doomsday Book and William Alis, like all tenants-in-chiefs at the time, would have signed an oath swearing allegiance to the King. The oath was called "The Oath of Surum" which is Salisbury today. William the Conqueror wanted to know what land he would gain tax from and sent out official government inspectors for information from the courts. Once the King had established the worth of his kingdom, he didn't hang around for long and from 1086 he spent the rest of his life engaged in his favourite pastimes of hunting and eating. He died in 1087, injured by the pommel of his saddle. At his funeral it was reported that the monarch's stomach exploded, prompting the priest to hurry through the funeral rites and that was the end of him.

Meanwhile, back at Alington Manor there was a record of one of the mills being owned or held by a Woodlock, indicating areas of the manor had been granted to the Woodlock family well before Henry Woodlock became Bishop of Winchester or the prior at St Swithuns. But then in the charter by Edward the Elder, the land at Allington was granted to another William Alis in 1204. He must have been a relation of the first William Alis and had taken on the land maybe on new terms. The land was granted to him by Godfrey-De-Lucy (sometimes spelt Luci). We need to remember this important man as he served for 15 years as the Bishop of Winchester after administration rolls at Exeter, Lincoln, London and Salisbury. He was also a Royal Justice and another bishop that fell out of favour with a king. From losing favour he lost his lands for a while, but then regained them after a spell on the naughty step.

Anyway, the lands at Allington Manor came with pannage rights given to the Austin Canons at the Priory of St Denys in Southampton, Hampshire.

Pannage rights is the practice of releasing livestock into the forest to feed and roam freely. The descendants of William Alis continued to hold the land with his son Roger Alis recorded as the holder in 1223. His son Thomas Alis, grandson of William Alis, held the manor until he died in 1304 without male issue. His widow retained a life interest and remained at the manor, the lands were left to their two daughters, Isabella who married a Robert-Le-Helyon and Margaret who married William-Le-Rolleston.

The sisters each inherited a portion of the manor known as a moiety. In law, a moiety title is the ownership of part of a property. The word derives from the French 'moitie' meaning 'half'. Two years after Margaret inherited her moiety in 1306, she sold it to Richard and Margaret Woodlock. They held the moiety until Richard died and Margaret continued to hold the moiety until she died, at which time it passed to their son John Woodlock and his wife Agnes. They owned the moiety in 1379 and passed it on to their daughter who was in possession of it by 1410. As it turned out, the daughter of John and Agnes Woodlock was Jahana, she had married twice, and her first husband was William Oysell the chaplain of Durley church.

So the link between William Oysell and the Marwell Woodlocks was clear; he was related to them by marriage. I knew by following the names I would eventually find something, and I was right! I had to look way back in history to find a link between the Marwell Woodlocks, St Swithun and William Oysell. However, the one thing that puzzled me was if William Oysell and wife Jahana née Woodlock lived at Allington Manor, why was he the chaplain at Durley when Allington Manor was recorded in the Doomsday survey as having a church in 1086? After all, if you married a nice lady who happened to own part of a manor with its own church why would you be the chaplain at Durley?

The only way that would make any sense would be if Durley church was part of Allington Manor. When the first William Alis was tenant-in-chief at Allington with two mills and a church, that was in 1086 which would make Durley church, or the original structure, very old indeed. But we will never know, all I can say is the nearest Medieval church to Allington other than that of Durley is St Mary's Church at South Stonham, built in 1204. The old buildings linked to the water mills along the river are still there; water mills were situated along the riverbanks in many villages, they were an important part of rural life and used for many things. However, what church the 1204 charter referred to is something I will have to research; it can stay on the back burner for now until another clue is found to add to it.

The church mentioned in 1086 couldn't be St Marys at South Stonham, that wasn't built for another 118 years. So is the original structure and tunnel at Durley what the Doomsday survey of 1086 refers to? The other thing I discovered was after William Oysell died, Jahana's half of the manor was given to the steward at Winchester College, John Fromond, who took on and held the moiety until he died in 1420. His wife retained a lifetime interest, and the lands became the property of Winchester College. For me, some things were as clear as mud with nothing to get your teeth into; there had to be something else so I kept looking, not way back but in the timeline of William Oysell's will, give or take a year either side. And eventually I found information that would help bring a conclusion to much of what I thought may be true, even without any solid evidence to confirm I was right. There were enough clues to make sense of it all, at least to me anyway.

Once again, I started by looking at British History Online for more information about William Oysell, and after a few 'Your search yielded no results', somehow I ended up on another website called the 'History of Parliament'. This led to 'The British Political and Social Local History' website where a record of William Oysell was supposed to be in the personal biography of a man called Edmund Picard of Winchester in Hampshire. By reading the whole text, I found some other information, relevant to the research, that I would never have found without these links.

Edmund Picard was a politician and former Mayor of Winchester who had worked his way up in local politics, holding posts such as constable, bailiff, and was often required to serve as a trustee of local property that came into the Corporation's possession. Edmund Picard owned land and property in and around Winchester, some of which was by way of a second marriage to a wealthy widow. He was a skinner by trade and a member of the Worshipful Skinner's Company of London. London in the 10th and 12th centuries was the world's major centre during the evolution of the fur and skin trade, in and around the area at the mouth of the River Walbrook. Then in the 13th century, the skinners first appear in the records as owning tenements in the Walbrook area, associated with the Parish Church of St John Walbrook.

The Earl of Cornwall owned the Copped Hall, which occupied much of the site of today's hall, and he granted the hall to the skinners in 1295. The skinners' formal beginning came in 1327, when Edward III granted the Worshipful Skinners of London the right to elect "Good and Trusted Men" to oversee the quality of the furs sold in the city and elsewhere. Then in 1393 the Worshipful Skinners of London paid £60 for a royal licence to form a fraternity dedicated to "The Most Holy Body and Blood of Christ" aka "Corpus Christi" which was empowered to elect a master and four wardens to wear a livery – "A Distinctive Design of Clothing" – and to hold land in perpetuity.

They formed an organisation of fraternal orders, traditionally for men associated together for various religious or secular aims. The same as Freemasons, Odd Fellows and gentlemen's clubs, they were by invitation only and gave protection through the ecclesiastical courts. The Skinners Company holds a Corpus Christi service at St James, Garlick Hythe close to the Skinners Hall. The church dates from the 11th century and was rebuilt after the great fire of London in 1666, and again after being bombed in the Second World

War. In the Middle Ages, the church was adjacent to the quayside, convenient for trading with northern Spain. Also, pilgrims would depart from this quay on their pilgrimages to the Cathedral of Santiago in the northwest of Spain.

The Skinners Company controlled the English fur trade until the 18th century, but in the 13th century, Edmund Picard had worked his way up in the political world and became a merchant and was also a member of the Worshipful Company of Mercers, for merchants who exported wool and imported fine cloth fabrics of superior quality like velvet, silk and other special fabrics. The Worshipful Company of Mercers' motto was "Honour Deo", Latin for 'Honour God'. So, both the Worshipful Skinners Company and the Worshipful Company of Mercers, of which Edmund Picard seemed to have been a member of both, had a strong connection within the church.

Edward Picard was appointed royal 'Alnager'. This was a Royal officer who examined cloth and affixed a seal in guaranty of its quality or measure. He also shared in the running of the fulling mill at Priors Barton in Hampshire, vital for the cloth and fur trade. The mill was one of many situated on the banks of the River Itchen that ran south to the port of Southampton.

The River Itchen, formally known as the River Alre, ran from an old Saxon settlement at Old Alresford in Hampshire, belonging to the church at Winchester. It was after the Bishop of Winchester, Godfrey-De-Lucy (remember him!) well he established a long-term programme that produced a new community on the banks of the River Alre called New Alresford, along which the mills were built and to keep the canal navigable. The bishop partially dammed the river with a weir and dug drainage channels from surrounding marshes to create a reservoir. This kept the mills in business and as the owner or holder of the land the weir was built on, Bishop Godfrey-De-Lucy kept a tight control on both the mills and the river that was used by merchants to and from the port of Southampton.

It was interesting that the Bishop of Winchester, in order to control the river and the mills, would grant lands to his chosen men like William Alis at Alington Manor. It was one of the things that made me sit up and take notice, because if the bishop controlled the river that the people who worked the fulling mills relied on for their living, working for the merchants who used the river back and forth from the main port of Southampton to export goods and import fine fabrics as well as spices from far off trading places, then the Bishop of Winchester was a powerful and clever man.

I was beginning to realise Bishop Henry Woodlock was too, his keenness to grant land to kinsman was no coincidence. The two men used the same tactic of placing their people in certain places even though they were Bishops of Winchester 116 years apart. Could it be a fraternity, a brotherhood of bishops associated together with others for various religious or secular aims? My thoughts of fraternities were further enhanced when I read that Edmund Picard had dealings regarding certain ruinous properties with the Cathedral

Prior of St Swithun's and took on these properties at a reduced rent and passed them on again as landlord.

Then in 1410 Edmund Picard acted for a gentleman in the purchase of a moiety at the Manor of Allington and that gentleman he helped with the perchance of the moiety was William Oysell. Fraternal brother? Well, who knows, but the obvious question is why William Oysell would purchase part of a moiety at Allington Manor when his wife, Jahana, already held it and as her husband he would too. But as we know, Jahana's moiety was only held, eventually it would return to whence it came so why would William Oysell be concerned if, after his demise, Jahana married again. The use of the moiety passed to the new husband who would have known the moiety's future would eventually become the Bishop of Winchester's responsibility again. So it seems William Oysell purchased a moiety of the moiety, i.e. part of the moiety, not all of it.

But, which bit, was it part of Jahana's moiety or part of Isabella-Le-Helyon née Alis' half of the Manor. Remember, it was Isabella's sister Margaret-Le-Rolleston née Alis who sold her moiety to Richard Woodlock in 1306, which is how it ended up being held by Jahana Oysell née Woodlock having been passed down through the generations via Richard Woodlock. So was it Jahana or Isabella Le-Helyon née Alis who sold part of their moiety in 1410 and what was so special about the particular area in question?

If it was the land Durley church was built on, there must have been a good reason for it to remain in the ownership of a particular individual, who could then grant it to whoever they wished in the knowledge it would never fall into the wrong hands. If the church did hold some ancient secret and the knowledge of that had been handed down through the generations within a fraternity of like-minded people, the fact William Oysell, a chaplain with connections with St Swithun's, could call on the services of a powerful man like Edmund Picard who dealt with property matters for the Cathedral Priory of St Swithuns was not a coincidence. More a causal connection within a fraternity was more likely between the two men, and the very fact William Oysell was buried in Durley church could well be that he owned the land it was built on as many a lord of a manor had done for centuries.

So what do we have to work with? (1) There were four Saxon Kings that had the vision to learn, teach and construct wonderful religious buildings that would in time become places for the most famous philosophers in the science of the ancient academic subject of theology. These beautiful building would soon be enriched with incredible treasures given freely by people from all walks of life who prayed together, for each other in the name of the Divine Lord. (2) There were Benedictine monks from all over the globe who learnt the ways of St Swithun, to pass onto those who wished to follow their brother monks and keep the secrets entrusted to them by time honoured silence. (3) We have leaders of men, the bishops, such as Bishop Henry Woodlock, who as the Prior of St Swithun, would know all the secrets it held. He would know who to trust as not all the bishops could be. From the time of Bishop Denewulf's demise in AD 909, there had been 29 bishops of Winchester before Bishop Henry Woodlock in 1305.

Over a period of 396 years, some of the bishops were only in office for a short time, some died while in office, most were well connected, clever and intelligent men and reading about each of the bishops from information available, the first 100 years' worth of learned gentlemen followed not only St Swithun's desire to learn and teach but the wish to build new things. That would in time also be gifted with artefacts of great wealth to be looked after by brother monks. It could be a goblet made of gold, a painting or, in the case of St Swithun, his actual remains kept hidden in a silver casket that became a magnet for pilgrims to pay their respects at the shrine of a great man. A legend long after his demise, and in that first 100 years of various bishops, priors and monks who venerated not only St Swithun but the four Saxon kings who created those wonderful buildings that housed these sacred treasures, and in the first 100 years post-St Swithun, fraternities of bishops, monks and laypeople emerged not granted by a royal king because they in time would become a big problem along with an untrustworthy bishop, like the high-borne Frenchman Bishop Henry-De-Blois, brother of King Stephen.

They were the grandsons of William the Conqueror, and it's alleged that Henry-De-Blois, two years prior to retiring to his estate in France after 29 years as Bishop of Winchester the richest Holy See in England, had been sending precious treasures to France, stolen from various religious houses. 'The See' refers to the area of a bishop's ecclesiastical jurisdiction. Henry-De-Blois couldn't be trusted; he was instrumental in his brother Stephen being recognised as King in 1135, after the death of King Henry I, who had nominated his daughter Matilda to be his successor. But the council, considering a woman unfit to rule, sided with Henry-De-Blois and offered the throne to his brother, Stephen-De-Blois.

That gave Henry-De-Blois even more power to his elbow. The council made a big mistake by not offering the throne to Matilda who, after setting out her plan of action in Normandy, invaded England and fought for nine years against her cousin in a bloody civil war in which Henry-De-Blois changed sides twice. First he left Stephen and joined Matilda because she was winning but after conflict with her, he changed side again and backed his brother, only for them to lose to Matilda's superior tactics. Stephen was captured and the Clerical Council, which Henry-De-Blois must have been a part of when Matilda had been rejected, now proclaimed her "Lady of the English". But after entering London, Matilda made large cash demands that provoked the powers that be to expel her before a coronation could take place.

On Stephen's release, Matilda suffered defeats and fled back to Normandy which was controlled by her second husband, Geoffrey of Anjou. While

Matilda's efforts failed, she did lay the foundations for successful claims by descendants of her family, the first being her son, King Henry II, who must have found it difficult having his second cousin in office as Bishop of Winchester still occupying the richest see in England. As well as being the richest man in England, referred to as a king without a crown, he also had several castles built illegally, including one for himself and his brother King Stephen during his reign. These castles were all built while there was widespread devastation as a result of the destructive war. One of the first things King Henry II did in a bid to establish some authority over his second cousin and the barons, who had also jumped on the free property bandwagon same as Henry De Blois and built castles on land they didn't own, was to order all the castles to be slighted, each and every one of them pulled down, no matter how grand. Then the King had a falling out with his Archbishop Thomas Becket and ordered Henry-De-Blois to preside over the trial. But Henry-De-Blois secretly supported Thomas Becket's family before and after the trial. After Thomas Becket's assassination, when he was brutally murdered at Canterbury Cathedral on the orders of the King who was slowly getting to grips with mess that was left after civil war. it seems Henry-De-Blois lived a charmed life, but you wouldn't trust him. However he did preform one task that seems out of character when he founded the Hospital of St Cross at Winchester in 1132, known as the 'Alms-house of Noble Poverty', making it the oldest almshouse in England, but it would be others who looked after the almshouse that was under the care of the Knights of St John and the noble order of poverty flourished.

Henry-De-Blois was a very clever man, at least in his own mind, and there was hostility between De-Blois and fellow Frenchman St Bernard of Clairvaux, founder and abbot of the Abbey of Clairvaux. St Bernard was one of the most influential churchmen of his time and he blocked moves by Henry-De-Blois to become the Archbishop of Canterbury because he was untrustworthy.

St Bernard, born of Burgundian landowning aristocracy, had a deep respect for mercy, justice and loyal affection for all others; faith and morals were also taken seriously. The Pope himself relied on St Bernard's opinions regarding important matters. St Bernard of Clairvaux was also the patron of the Knights Templar and they were held to no one's authority except the Pope's. Bishop Henry-De -Blois had upset too many powerful people to have held a more important position; he was not only a greedy bishop but a lucky one too and continued in his quest to become even richer than he already was He wanted the gold and silver cross that King Cnut and his wife had gifted to the Abbey of New Minster, which by then had moved with the prior and monks from New Minster Abbey, to a new home with more accommodation. The site was on the north side of the city walls known as Hyde Mead and from then on, the important Benedictine house would be called Hyde Abbey.

The old site of New Minster Abbey had been given back to King Henry I, who gave the site to the Cathedral Church of St Swithun. The monks at Hyde Abbey were granted another King's Charter and among the new regulations was that a joint procession of the monks of St Swithun and Hyde Abbey would be held each year. The first one was when their new home was ready for occupation in 1110/11 when the monks of New Minster Abbey carried with them to the Abbey of Hyde in slow procession their sacred relics – the Great Gold and Silver Cross of Cnut's Benefaction, together with the illustrious remains of King Alfred the Great, his wife Ealhswith, and their son Edward the Elder. The new Abbey only lasted for 30 years when the city was fired in 1141 during the fierce civil war. The Abbey of Hyde perished in the conflagration.

Then for several years there was continuous strife between the monks of Hyde Abbey and the high borne and imperious Bishop Henry-De-Blois. By him, say the Hyde annalists, was the Great Cross of Cnut burnt alluding to its loss in the great fire, when the bishop directed fire balls to be thrown from his property at Wolvesey into that area of the city adjoining the abbey. Bishop Henry-De-Blois endeavoured to persuade the Pope to convert the ancient see of Winchester and make him archbishop, and for Hyde Abbey to be the centre of one of his Suffragan bishoprics.

But his scheme failed with the help of St Bernard of Clairvaux, and a new abbot for Hyde Abbey called Selid was elected by the Pope in 1151. For 17 years of Selid's Abbacy, the continuous suits against Bishop Henry-De-Blois for the return of Hyde Abbey's property, was at last decided in favour of Hyde. Amongst other acts of restitution, Bishop Henry-De-Blois presented to the Abbey of Hyde as skilful a reproduction of King Cnut's gold and silver cross as the art of the day could fashion. Parts of the abbey were rebuilt but the work was gradual and not started till 1182. Abbot Selid died in 1171, the same year as Bishop Henry-De-Blois and there were two vacancies, one for an abbot of Hyde Abbey, and another for a bishop of Winchester. So, what happened to King Cnut's damaged gold and silver cross, I wonder?

It could be a fraternity of priors, monks, loyal brothers and like-minded people moved the cross and kept the secret of it and other hidden treasures. The cross became the symbol by which the fraternity was dedicated, then from 1171 to 1174 the position of Bishop of Winchester remained vacant until Richard of Toclive aka Ilchester became the bishop. He was a medieval English statesman and a high-ranking member of the clergy who was loyal to King Henry II. He rewarded the bishop by granting him a mill at Ilchester situated on the River Yeo five miles north of Yeovil in the West Country. It seemed Richard of Ilchester had brought back some form of normality to the position of Bishop of Winchester, he gave endowments to the St Cross Hospital at Winchester and allowed it to double the number of poor who needed food. The place became a more relaxed Almshouse of Noble Poverty. Richard of Ilchester, Bishop of Winchester, said, "When there is a General Interdict in the land, having closed the doors and shut out the excommunicated and interdicted you, may then celebrate divine service with a supressed voice and no bells ringing, you may also receive Clerks, or Laymen fleeing from the secular power. Freshly and absolutely and retain them in your college without contradiction from anyone." The almshouse took in people who needed to get away; they could seek sanctuary within a church but only for 40 days. Then they had to leave England for good or face death and it would be a network of people whose service was required to help, the clerks and laymen fleeing from both a religious and secular power under the banner of a particular cross.

It could be the white eight-pointed cross on a black background, the symbol of the Knights of St John, worn on the robes of those first brother Knights at the Hospital in Jerusalem. St John's Cross is also the international symbol of St John's Ambulance, emblazoned on the sides of ambulances and on the uniforms of its highly trained volunteers and remained unaltered through the centuries as the enduring emblem of humanitarian care. Of its charities that dates back almost 1,000 years, St Peter's Church and the farmland around it at Woodmancote in West Sussex in about 1228 was given to the Knights Templar and in 1312 it passed to the Knights of St John. Both organisations joined by their respective humanitarian aims, the Knights Templar's cross is red on a white background, displayed on armour and shields. So, neither of those crosses could be used on a banner for everyone connected to this network of escape. Fraternities of like-minded people working with St Bernard and his people in France, he could call on the Templars as their patron and friend of the Pope, all these people on each side of the Channel may have worked together and their muse could have been King Cnut's lost gold and silver cross.

Henry-De-Blois didn't have it and I believe most of the Benedictine monks didn't know where it was but knew it was safe. With a little more digging, I will offer an opinion, and by looking at every piece of information available I wouldn't say it's easy to work out. But if presented with the facts, then individual opinions can be reached. Richard of Ilchester was the Bishop of Winchester for 15 years and died while still in office on 22nd December 1188. Richard's successor in 1189 was Godfrey De Lucy, another mill-owning, intelligent Bishop of Winchester who also served for 15 years and continued Richard of Ilchester's normality of the position of bishop.

Calm water continued to flow not only on the river system Godfrey De Lucy created but within the fraternities of like-minded people, and with the passing of each year their secrets remained that of legends. From 1204 until 1238, Peter de la Roches became the Bishop of Winchester. There were five more bishops from 1238 until 1305 when Bishop Henry Woodlock took over and we have covered his interesting period. The other bishops leading up to the time of the Reformation were much the same, but one I found interesting was in the history of Bishop Richard Fox. He served for 29 years as the Bishop of Winchester. Fox's crowning glory was his foundation of Corpus Christi College Oxford which he, with others, established in 1515–1516 and which he was roundly praised by humanist, Desiderius Erasmus.

I read that originally Fox intended the foundation to be an Oxford house for the monks of St Swithun Winchester but Bishop Fox was dissuaded by his colleague Bishop Oldham, who foretold the "Fall of the Monks". So, I wondered what Bishop Oldham meant, was he referring to the Reformation of 1534? If so, that didn't happen for another 19 years. When, according to a Professor George W. Bernard in a document he wrote after the event, nearly 900 religious houses, about 260 for monks, 300 for regular canons, 142 nunneries and 183 friaries, some 12,000 people, 4,000 monks, 3,000 canons, 3,000 friars and 2,000 nuns would be affected. So, if Bishop Oldham had foreseen what was going to happen, who else did? And if anyone did, would they have moved precious items from these religious houses, some of which had suffered enough in the civil wars up until 1515?

You wouldn't have to be that much of a visionary to predict something much bigger would come along in the future, and if any of the 12,000 monks, canons, friars and nuns took precious items to hide away so they could start again from a position of strength post the Reformation, you could see the logic in that. I doubt very much they would sit on their hands and watch it happen. It could be Bishop Oldham had given Bishop Fox good solid advice that not only he but many other like-minded people within all manner of fraternities were preparing for a victory in the knowledge that most of the important artefacts had already been moved.

Henry VIII and his band of renegades may have had no idea what was in those religious houses, it was only when the King needed funds for his continued war efforts that Thomas Cromwell put into action a plan to take what the church had been collecting for many years. He was instrumental in the plundering of these religious houses and the melting down of precious treasures that were the gifts of time and irreplaceable. Henry VIII probably did think that the church had been sitting on their hands, when in reality they had been marking time. Because when Bishop Oldham told Bishop Fox about the "Fall of the Monks", the church had 19 years before the Reformation happened, and there were other conflicts. The network of compatible comrades had been quietly working within fraternities, both monastic charitable foundations and secular societies, who could rely on people such as the Catholic leaders of the richest establishment in the world by the time of the "Fall of the Monks".

Pope Clement was at odds with King Henry VIII anyway, there was also St Bernard of Clairvaux, a powerful clergyman of his day, as well as patron of the Knights Templar made up of brave noblemen who had formed the templars foundation and were also well placed throughout the globe. I kept reading the sentence that said Bishop Fox had been dissuaded by Bishop Oldham who foretold the " Fall of the Monks" and I couldn't find anything online that was linked to any other story about it. I had been reading about bishops till I was blue in the face; they just seemed a repetition of good bishop, bad king, and vice versa so when I looked at Bishop Fox's history it needed something like Bishop Oldham's dissuasion remark to reboot my enthusiasm.

From a quick look at Bishop Oldham's CV, I found he helped Bishop Fox in the creation of Corpus Christi. He held many posts in his rise to becoming the Bishop of Exeter, one of them being Chancellor to the Household of Lady Margaret Beaufort, the grandmother of King Henry VIII. Bishop Oldham's information to Bishop Fox regarding the "Fall of Monks" was not so much as a visionary, more of receiving inside information from someone in the know. Apparently, Lady Margaret Beaufort was instrumental in Bishop Oldham becoming the Bishop of Exeter so maybe Lady Beaufort said something regarding the "Fall of the Monks", or the bishop may have overheard someone talking who should have been more careful because walls do have ears. Bishop Oldham became the Chancellor of Lady Margaret Beaufort estate in 1492, 23 years before he told Bishop Fox about the "Fall of the Monks", and only when Bishop Fox informed him of his intention to have Corpus Christi as an Oxford House for the Monks of St Swithun, Winchester.

There was also something else in Bishop Fox's historical information about the crown of his career being the foundation of Corpus Christi in 1515. Which reminded me of the Worshipful Company of Skinners' fraternity's dedication to Corpus Christi and it being the most Holy Body and Blood of Christ. I had read about church dedications, and how during their consecration the building would be named in honour of its patron, martyr or one of the many saints. That made me think to what honour was Durley church dedicated to. There were several examples I found online. (1) "Describing the 'Solemnity' a formal dignified ceremony of the dedication or anniversary of one's own church." Well that wouldn't necessarily apply to Durley, you can't have an anniversary if you have no idea how and when the building came about. (2) "The Solemnity of the title or founder of a Religious Institute." Well it was part of a religious institute as a Catholic chapel, but there was nothing in the title linking the chapel to a founder. (3) "The Solemnity of the Title of one's own Church, The Mystery or Saint to Which it is Dedicated." Well that was interesting, there was a saint linked to the Mother Church St Mary's at Upham while the chapel was part of Upham cum Durley, but when it became a church in its own right in 1852, then Cappela Santa Croce became the Chiesa Santa Croce, but there was a mystery as to why the original building was where it was.

The real mystery is what cross 'Le Cappela' or the 'Le Chiesa' was dedicated to. It couldn't be named after St Cross Hospital Winchester, that cross was connected to the Knights of St John's Cross of Jerusalem. Nor was it the Red Cross of the Knights Templar, it could be the wooden cross that would have been on the site when the settlers came to the churchyard on a Sunday. I would have gone with that, it was a Cappela then 'Le Cappela Santa Croce', however that would be a disappointing end to a story that still had a way to go, spiritually that is. Because it didn't feel right it couldn't end with finding an old wooden cross, not after so many things that had fallen into place. It could be what I was looking for was what the old wooden cross represented, and in my reflective moments I thought it was or could be 'Le Cappela Santa Croce'. Or King Cnut's missing gold and silver cross, there was a real mystery surrounding what happened to that.

Undisputed was the existence of a cross given to the Abbey of New Minster in 1041, and it was still in possession of the monks in 1109 when they moved to Hyde Abbey. Then in 1141 part of Hyde Abbey was burnt down and the analysts of Hyde Abbey said the cross was lost and for 19 years Abbot Selid fought to get back artefacts taken by Bishop Henry-De-Blois. Just for a moment I thought I had got Henry-De-Blois all wrong and the treasures he sent to his estate in France was to keep them safe. But the thought didn't last long when I remembered he fired parts of Hyde Abbey, and if he had moved things for safekeeping, he would have told Abbot Selid. Instead he caused the man grief in his attempts to get other artefacts back from Henry-De-Blois.

The reproduction of the gold and silver cross was for effect only, guilt that he had fired the abbey causing the sacred cross to be lost. However, what if the cross had already been moved by people, whoever they were? They would have known the cross wouldn't be safe at Hyde Abbey, the place was in ruins. It could be the cross spent some time at St Swithun's before being hidden forever taken to a safe place. An out-of-the-way place or maybe the gold and silver cross, once rich with precious stones, was lost for all time.

My research so far had taken me from June till October 2021, most of which was done in the evenings and weekends. At the churchyard it was still very busy, the weather had not been kind; it was too hot one week and another week it rained and what with COVID restrictions it was a job to keep up with what you could do and what you could not. The General and his PCC, along with many people who helped in the church, worked hard all summer long, keeping the church open at weekends for the villagers and whoever wanted to come and reflect on life and the situation the world faced.

Remembrance week that year was very special. The General and his team had the church looking wonderful, everyone involved was a credit to the village. There were funerals during the lockdown, it was not an easy situation for the relatives or Gregg the rector because of the number of people allowed to attend and the powers that be couldn't allow a service inside the church. Gregg blessed each coffin outside the west door; it was the best he could do at the time. Then Gregg and the General asked for permission from the archdeacon for the coffins to be taken in the church and turned round and come out again, receiving a blessing from Gregg on the hoof, so to speak. It was a difficult time for everyone concerned. During my time as sexton I had helped the gravediggers Chris and his son Patrick with burials, and it was never easy given I had got to know many of the people whose grave I would then look after. I also got to know about the people who were already resting in the churchyard, from the relations who came to tend their graves.

You could say I knew a lot of people who were all spiritual friends of mine and all important to the history of the village. I had missed one or two families that came every year from faraway places they had moved to, but the lockdown put pay to their visits. One lady came each summer when Somerset, her team, played Hampshire at cricket. She would visit the grave of her mother who happened to be another Houghton whose father was a man called William (Champion) Houghton, a brother of Shoemaker Bob. It was said that Champion was a fine cricketer for the village in his day; there was a picture of Champion in John Bosworth's book working at his allotment. I also had photos of Champion and his wife Mary Houghton née Goater that were among many photos that John Bosworth didn't use, part of the historic records left by Gwen Houghton. I am not sure how long Champion and Mary had been married but they died within one week of each other and rest next to each other in grave 281. William died on 6th January 1915 aged 87, and Mary passed away on 12th January 1915, she was 85 years old. The lady from Somerset told me her mother said Mary died of a broken heart. They both rest in the churchyard and their headstone is right in line with Hampshire's cricket ground that can be seen from up on the hill.

Next to William and Mary, grave number 279, are two of their grandchildren who rest next to each other. Nellie Mable, beloved daughter of William and Ellen Houghton née Cook. She died on 8th October 1909 aged 18. I also have a wonderful photo of Nellie; she was a beautiful young woman. Next to Nellie Mable is her beloved brother George W Houghton, son of William and Ellen Houghton née Cook. He died on 18th March 1913 aged 28. The lady from Somerset helped with the identification of the graves. However, one I had not found before the lockdown but did during it and will show the lady when she returns was the grave of her own grandfather, and son of William (Champion) and Mary née Goater – the father of Nellie Mable and George W Houghton, and that is the legend of Durley, William (Slocks) Houghton.

Now if you have relations buried at Durley, chances are they would have passed on a story about 'Slocks', so called because his boots were two sizes too big without laces so he would slock along. The front of his boots was filled with straw to keep his feet warm while working in the cold as a wood-hoop maker. Slocks also had a dog that was kept on a very long piece of string and if you saw the dog come around the corner, Slocks wouldn't be far behind. Slocks never changed his clocks, preferring to keep one time all the year round. There is a photo in John Bosworth's book of Slocks dressed for work. He has a beard and in another photo given to me by various relations of his, as he got older his beard got longer and greyer as the years progressed.

Chrissy Rumbold's mother, Nellie Rumbold, had a fine photo of Slocks at an advanced age; it truly is a great picture. There are photos of him with the dog, as well as with his loyal wife, Ellen Houghton née Cook. Durley man,

Stewart Collins, told me that each Good Friday, Slocks Houghton would take his small cart and pick up all the chicken manure kept by Stewart's father for Slocks for his allotment. Slocks would load the cart; it took about seven runs through the day and each time Slocks got to the Farmer's Home pub, which was about halfway between Mr Collins' farm and the allotment, he would go in to quench his thirst. Not once or twice but each time he passed by the pub and by late afternoon Slocks was more than half-cut! William (Slocks) Houghton is a legend in Durley folk history. He died aged 77 on 25th June 1934. He actually died while having an attack of the hiccups. Ellen, his widow, died the following June 1935 aged 75. They rest in a nice big double kerbstone grave, number 406. They were proper Durley people.

At the end of the summer 2021, a gentleman and his wife turned up one morning. He had been working on his family tree during the lockdown when the travel restrictions were in place. He had been adopted at birth and came to the churchyard to find his birthmother's grave. He had some information about his mother, so that was a start. I gave him several email addresses for information and suggested to him it would be a good idea to have a DNA test. I gave him other bits of information and, after looking around the church, the couple left knowing a little more than when they had arrived. Then about two months after, I noticed two other people standing next to the same grave as the previous couple. I had seen the lady in the churchyard before. She lived and worked in Botswana; she was born in Durley but moved to London when she left school to start work in the jewellery industry. I was not sure if I should say anything to her about the gentleman who came in, but I did, and she told me her aunts had said there was another child but that's all the info she had and she had also had a DNA test and matched with the gentleman that had been in before.

And they were meeting that day for the very first time at the grave of their mother. It was a great day for them. It was a busy day in the churchyard, lots of people came that day; it's not often I get to see the full circle of a story, but it makes everything I do worthwhile. I also met a family whose mother's ashes were to go in the grave of her parents. A new headstone was ordered for all the names to go on, and in a conversation with one of the daughters of the deceased lady she told me about her grandfather who was the first occupant of the double grave, and how in the World War Two D-Day landings, he was one of two men called the 'Secret Carpenters'. They had carved the map for the D Day landings out of wood; they were kept under house arrest for several weeks for their own safety. Then after the D-Day landings were over, the men were let back out into civvy street, only to be arrested because the men, as part-time soldiers, had not helped after the bombing raids. Their problem was when asked where they had been, they couldn't say because they had signed the Official Secrets Act. All they could do was to give a name and number and were released as soon as a call was made to the powers that be.

It was one of many stories I felt privileged to have been told and was proud that we had another war hero in the churchyard. The wooden map is still around today at the Southwick Estate in Hampshire. Also, the rector who took the service that day was from Soberton Church in Hampshire, and we had a long conversation about the tunnel structure, because one had been found at his church. They had a retired archaeologist as a member of their church, and he sorted the whole business of protocol regarding what to do with their tunnel. It had been used way back by smugglers who could at that time take flat-bottomed boats upriver from the coast through the Meon Valley. On one occasion, one member of the clergy would not conform with King Henry VIII's wishes and after being hidden in the tunnel made his escape in a muck cart. The history of these happenings is well documented and by talking with the rector it helped a great deal in what we could do with what we had at Durley. It also helped in a way regarding my theory of escapes, fraternities and the hiding of artefacts could indeed be a reality. But I needed more evidence if that was possible. Many things I had researched regarding the tunnel structure and the area of an original building on the site was proof enough to me that something more would turn up. After going way back in history as far as King Egbert, I felt anything was possible.

Meanwhile, back with the research, I set out to find a record of the land transaction between William Oysell and whoever it was he bought the moiety from. I wasn't at all sure how to go about that and had to research before I could research, if you get my drift. But then none of this research had been easy, and while I waited for information on that, I took a look at the Saxon Charters and landscape evolution in the South-Central Hampshire Basin, another fine document presented by the Hampshire Field Club and Archaeological Society. This document covered the land boundaries of the historic manors of North and South Stoneham, Bishopstoke and Durley. The document's author was Mr Christopher K. Currie, and what interested me was the pioneering work carried out by a Mr Grundy in 1924 regarding those boundaries that were all covered by charters. There was also a charter for East Horton without boundaries that was identified in their study as the lost Saxon settlement that I thought the original structure at Durley could have been linked with.

There were no boundaries to the southwest to separate East Horton from Durley and the land opposite the church looking south extended way down over many fields till you reached the main road that ran all the way to Winchester. Mr Currie's re-examination of Mr Grundy's work seemed to have verified my assumptions that the original ecclesiastical structure on the site could be part of the lost Saxon settlement. Further on in the work carried out by Mr Grundy he had identified that the AD 900 charter of boundaries set out by Edward the Elder for the benefit of the Abbey of New Minster were not the same as the boundaries in the AD 960 charter between the boundaries of North and South Stoneham, Bishopstoke and Durley where the three manors adjoin. Mr Currie points out that another gentleman's opinion more recently, Mr Brooks in 1982, suggested that the AD 960 charter may be an 11th-century forgery. He does not however seem to doubt the authenticity of the content of the charter as he considers it was made to justify the administration of a disparate group of estates in a single unit of 100 hides. Mr Brooks then continues interestingly, that an additional part of Durley opposite the church roughly conversant with the area known in medieval times as East Horton and the lost Saxon settlement granted to the Abbey of New Minster was the subject of a later dispute between the monks of St Swithun's Priory and the Bishop of Winchester, Henry-De-Blois. It's that man again! Then Mr Currie makes reference to another gentleman's opinion, a Mr Goodman (1927) who said how this land came to be disputed is not known. But it suggests that the motive for the original forgery may stem from a dispute between the Bishop of Winchester and New Minster in the 10th century.

Well, any dispute in the 10th century couldn't have involved Henry-De-Blois because he didn't become Bishop of Winchester until 1129. There were six bishops of Winchester in the 10th century, but I could only find two of interest who overstepped the mark – Bishop Stigand 1047. He first appears in historical records as Royal Chaplain to King Cnut of England, he of the gold and silver cross. King Cnut reigned from 1016 to 1035. Bishop Stigand served six successive kings; however, he was not popular with everyone and was excommunicated for his pluralism in holding sees or bishoprics of Winchester and Canterbury concurrently and received a reward in exchange for services rendered and a retainer for future services. This went against Stigand and he was deposed in 1070, had all of his estates and personal wealth confiscated by William the Conqueror, and was imprisoned at Winchester where he died without regaining his liberty and buried at the Abbey of New Minster, so greed put pay to him.

The only other bishop of interest was a man called Walkelin, Bishop of Winchester 1070–1100. He was the first Norman bishop of noble birth and was related to William the Conqueror whom he served as Royal Chaplain before the Norman Conquest. A former canon at Rouen Cathedral and cousin of Henry-De-Blois, Walkelin installed his brother Simeon as prior of Winchester and influenced Simeon becoming Abbot of Ely in 1082 where he began the New Ely Abbey. Walkelin himself was a great cathedral builder and replaced the old Saxon church at Winchester with a New Cathedral Church in the grounds of what is now Winchester Cathedral. The king of the day, King William I, granted Walkelin half a hide of land on the Isle of Wight with licence to search and excavate stone for his new church.

The King also granted Walkelin as much timber his carpenters could take in four days and nights for the building of his new Winchester Cathedral Church and scaffolding from the forest of Hempage Wood on the old Arlesford road in Hampshire. The bishop put together a troop of carpenters and within the time given cut the whole woods and took all the timber back to Winchester. Soon after, the King passed by Hempage and cried out in shock, "Am I Bewiched or have I taken leave of my senses? Had I not once a most delectable wood upon this spot?" And he became violently enraged and summoned the bishop who, at the King's feet, humbly begged to resign his post and merely requested that he might retain the royal friendship and chaplaincy.

The King was appeased only observing, "I was as much too Liberal in my grant as you were too greedy in availing yourself of it." The bishop kept his head on his shoulders and completed the Cathedral Church in 1093. In July that year, the fifteenth St Swithun's day 1093, in the presence of nearly all the bishops and abbots of England, the monks of St Swithun moved from the old Anglo Saxon church to the new Cathedral Church with great rejoicing and glory, and took from the old church to the new one "All the Treasures of St Swithun" with all honour.

The next day, the bishops' men began to demolish the old Anglo Saxon church which was completed within one year except for one porticus in the area of the great altar (a porticus is a small room that may function as chapels or burial places). Then one year after the demolition had taken place, more artefacts were dug up in the area beneath the great altar by the monks and taken to the new Cathedral Church and reunited with the monks of St Swithun.

Bishop Walkelin died 3rd January 1098, and while he and Bishop Stigand seemed to have got themselves in a pickle of sorts, I don't think they anywhere near as bad as Bishop Henry-De-Blois. Two things I found by looking into the two bishops' historical information, more so in Bishop Walkelin's, was clarification that stone was brought from the Isle of Wight for the construction of churches in and around the Meon Valley. It seems it was a Saxon tradition. Having found it, why look anywhere else. The other thing was the discovery of more buried artefacts in the old Saxon church at Winchester could have been what the dispute was about in the 10th century between Bishop Walkelin and St Swithun. It's understandable when you think about it, he must have been really peeved off with the monks of St Swithun, after all he sent men to the Isle of Wight to bring all the stone for the new church. His carpenters cut down the King's forest at Hempage Wood, which could have cost the bishop his head. Then after a wonderful opening of the monks' new Cathedral Church attended by all in sundry. Then one year later more artefacts are found and taken to the new church.

So, the fact was neither side trusted the other, the monks looked upon the artefacts as sacred having been given to the old Saxon church, the original home of St Swithun. As far as they were concerned, those hidden artefacts went with them; the artefacts could have been worthless but to them, they were sacred. I think that proved it was a common thing and maybe what happened to the gold and silver cross along with other artefacts given to the Abbey of New Minster when that was first built by Edward the Elder.

Those artefacts were taken by the monks to their new home at Hyde Abbey on the outskirts of the city where they stayed until Hyde Abbey was destroyed in the civil war and fired by Bishop Henry-De-Blois. I think all the treasures at the old Saxon church were so special, the fact the monks waited one year before moving them was clear it was planned, that way those treasures had been protected down the years, information passed on by one trusted person to another within a fraternity of like-minded people.

The two disputes with St Swithuns must have been with Bishop Walkelin in the 10th century, and Bishop Henry-De-Blois in the 11th century and let's not forget the two men just happened to be cousins. So, the removal of the artefacts would have been part of their family history, how the monks fooled Bishop Wakelin in the 10th century, and how in the 11th century Bishop Henry-De-Blois got his own back by stealing many artefacts to take back to France. But that's just my opinion and there will be others.

Back to Mr Grundy (1924), his work during his archaeological investigation of the boundaries around Durley highlighted in black on the location map with each marker numbered (1) to (16), the boundary markers were trees, the river, stiles, hollows and mounds, as well as old tree stumps next to well-worn tracks. He walked near enough to each marker shown on the maps of the AD 900 charter bounds comparing it with the AD 960 charter boundaries but when he gets to marker number (4), the boundary diverts >>> north into what is the area of the church and churchyard to marker number (5) and then it diverts back <<< westward to marker number (6) moving the area of the church and churchyard so it looks as if they are in East Horton to the south which of course was the area of the lost Saxon settlement which the original building on the site was probably part of all along.

In Mr Grundy's notes and he had seen the two charter maps says, "At least one of Durley's boundary markers indicates without question that the AD 960 boundary marker number (5) has been moved >>> to the north "Of tham stocce de westan burnam on thone grenan weg". From the stump on the west side of the green way, the "Stocce and Grenan Weg" are two of the markers on the AD 900 charter bound map. That were changed sometime in the 11th century clearly there was a forgery and given the records of the chapel not being a religious venue till early in the 13th century the structure on the site could have been part of the lost Saxon settlement.

The fact I had found from my desk-based archaeological investigation so much information made me appreciate the historic work Mr Grundy had done in 1924. Also, by finding his work that led me to look at more records of bishops Stigand and Walkelin had indirectly solved the mystery surrounding William Oysell's moiety because as well as the black outline of the bounds of Durley, South and North Stoneham and Bishopstoke, it also highlighted the vast areas in between each of the manors with no boundaries and that included East Horton and Allington. They had no boundaries because they were not manors in their own right but sub manors and part of the 100 hides that were lost in the 11th-century forgery, along with the area of Durley's church and churchyard.

It could be that William Oysell's moiety was the area that included the churchyard, so the reason he had such a high-profile stone coffin inside the church was because he could have owned or held it in perpetuity. As a chaplain with links with the Marwell Woodlocks and St Swithun's, it could be that Durley church was the end product of the first building on the site that the monks of the Abbey of the New Minster had created.

I also believe that the chapel then the church could have been dedicated to King Cnut's gold and silver cross. The Church of the Holy Cross and it and other artefacts could have been buried within the church near to the altar as the artefacts were in the old Saxon church and were removed one year after that church was demolished. I also think that Thomas Pope's impressive coffin, draped in fine silks and fabrics fixed with brass nails and secured with lock and key with a viewing point each side at the head of the coffin, was not just for him. But artefacts a Hidden Reality from the past hidden in a vault or room under the floor of the first chapel and somehow accessed to view the sacred artefacts. Brass turns an oaken coffin to the colour of blue and so too does gold, not only from the artefacts but from the gold-lined fabrics and golden nails that could have secured the fabric to the oaken coffin. The residue, which I have seen close up just a foot away from bones, were a strange colour, the like of nothing I have ever seen before, a rich yellow and dark black from the passage of time.

Thomas Pope's coffin was not opened by accident. As the newspaper article reported, whoever disturbed Thomas Pope and others from their slumber, they knew what they were looking for. Not one local village person would have moved human remains from the sacred church, that would never happen and there was no reason on earth to pull down all the ceilings or remove all the plaster from the walls. I have read all of the architects' instructions and the bills of quantitates for each trade along with the price for each job delivered by Mr Heath the builder. The main projects were the creation of a new boiler room under the new vestry which indicates that the room under the vestry was already there in some form or other. Also, when I found the tunnel structure and gently tapped to see how far the thick side tunnel wall extended, our local plumber, who was working down in the boiler room some 25 metres away under the vestry in line with the tunnel structure, could hear the tap, tap, tapping through the east wall.

The south wall in the boiler room is under and close to the area of the altar above, so it could be the graves inside of the church close to the altar could have been in an existing vault or room accessed by the removal of flagstones situated in the floor near to or even under the altar. Members of Droxford Church in Hampshire, Meon Valley, found one such vault under the floor of their church similar to the hidden tunnel at Soberton Church, also in the Meon Valley. This gave credence to the fact there were many secret hideouts within the Meon Valley. Also the creation of the Durley vestry only required two new walls to be built, one facing north and tied into the left west facing wall that was part of the 14th century addition to the church. The other east-facing wall, including the external vestry door, was tied into the old wall of the original building on the site dating way back to medieval times. So if there was an existing vault or room under the altar and somehow linked to the tunnel structure, it wouldn't have been discovered until the work was carried out by the rector Richard Ferguson and co. when they dug up the floor around the area of the altar. The room or vault couldn't have been known about when the 14th-century extension to the chapel was carried out, if it was then the secret stayed safe until Ferguson and co. came along. You see, from what I can make out, the conflict between the monks of St Swithun in the 10th century with Bishop Walkelin was simple – they kept him out of the loop, so to speak, regarding more treasures buried at the old Saxon church.

The 11th-century conflict with Bishop Henry-De-Blois was because the man was a high-borne greedy so and so who had no respect for anything. So that's why when you have friendly bishops in power, like Bishop Richard De Toclive, Bishop Godfrey De Lucy and others through to Bishop Henry Woodlock of Marwell Woodlock, things could run smoothly. There was a dispute in 1282 between Bishop John De Pontissara and the monks of St Swithun's, I'm not sure what this was about but it was soon dealt with because the prior of St Swithun's at the time of the dispute was Henry Woodlock of Marwell Woodlock. What better way to sort any more problems out of any kind relating to keeping Durley and its secrets safe, than to appoint Henry Woodlock as the Bishop of Winchester when Bishop John-De-Pontissara died. Which is what happened and Henry Woodlock became, I think, the first prior since St Swithun himself to hold both positions.

You could say that fraternities moved in mysterious ways, and for as long as there were friendly bishops in tune with the fraternities and their hidden secrets then everything was fine. However, as the keepers of these secrets became older and eventually died, their secrets became legends and the treasures were left unprotected and at the mercy of circumstance and that's what could have happened at Durley's Church of the Holy Cross. Because in 1853 when the chapel became a church in its own right, Durley church along with its former Mother Church St Mary's at Upham, were to be placed in the hands of the Bishop of Lichfield, the Reverend Mr George Augustus Selwyn, politician and former Bishop of New Zealand and Malaysia. It caused more friction between the monks of St Swithun and the new Bishop of Winchester; the disputes were hereditary. The monks wanted Durley to be for the benefit of St Swithun's, after all if my theory was right and their brother monks from the past had been instrumental in the creation of Durley's Cappela Santa Cruse and over the years placed various artefacts that still lay within, the only way they could protect those secret treasures from the past would be to give up their right to Durley, concerned maybe that the Bishop may have wondered what they were hiding. But as it turned out, their saving grace came in the form of the docile-natured dreamer, the Reverend Thomas Scard MA. Remember him? Well he became the rector at Durley in 1855, and served for 24 years in which time he managed to rip off Abraham Edwards, and others who bankrupted him. He had the likes of Mr William Gunner and Mr Hash Stairs, both prominent figures in the village breathing down his neck to be paid. He also forgot or couldn't be bothered, if truth be told, to record many burials, who the people were, and where they were resting.

So, what better protection could the fraternities of like-minded people enjoy knowing that their secrets were safe while the Church of the Holy Cross was in the hands of such a fool. Mind you, if Thomas Scard had known what hidden treasures were right under his nose, every time he gave a sermon he would have had his coachman and servant, my great-uncle Frederick, digging for Britain. But then Thomas Scard did leave Uncle Frederick 19 guineas in his will who then high tailed it out of Durley to manage the Ship inn Public House at Crowborough in East Sussex. So you never know. So everything was going along smoothly but then Thomas Scard MA messed things up when he just up and died and that was the beginning of the end for the fraternities of priors, monks and like-minded people because the Bishop of Lichfield George Augustus Selwyn lumbered Durley with the Rector Richard Ferguson MA in 1879 who in 12 years disrupted and destroyed, with others, the village of Durley's Church of the Holy Cross.

Then in 1890, three years after suffering at the hands of Ferguson and co., the Church of the Holy Cross was taken away from the Bishop of Lichfield and transferred to the Lord Chancellor's office. I am not sure how long it stayed in the safe hands of the Chancellor. In 1891, the Rector Richard Ferguson MA was replaced by the Reverend Mr Edward George Mowbray MA Oxon. He served for two years and handed over to the Reverend Mr John Jenkyns MA Oxon, and through to the 19th century more intelligent and respectful men of the cloth ran the Church of the Holy Cross and that trend continues today. Now in the safe hands of the Reverend Mr Gregg Richard Mensingh BSc Hons and he along with many people led by Major General Balfour, Under Sexton, look after the village Church of The Holy Cross.

We will never know if the cross represents King Cnut's gold and silver cross or what other treasures once graced the church hidden away from those who mean harm. But the church still stands in that out-of-the-way place. It knows the truth. I am not sure how I found the tunnel structure or any of the graves at the lost west end area of the churchyard and Richard Hickley's headstone broken and hidden in two different places. I think things were mapped out long ago when my brother and I drove with our Uncle George Wilber through

Durley on a Sunday, and I would look over the fields at the church. But whatever it was that kept drawing me back must have been the spirits from the past asking for help to put things right, and I think I have done that. It's been a long eight and half years.

Would I do it all again? I really couldn't say. The normal work of a sexton was fine and finding the tunnel structure and what looked to be an original brick and flagstone floor was amazing. So was finding the old roof timbers inside the church that the 14th-century additions to the church were built over the top of the old roof. The research for everything was also interesting; it helped to try and tell the story and when one piece of evidence enhanced another that helped to form an opinion, it just may not be everyone's. But I stand by mine, sorting the discarded human remains just thrown over graves to the southeast of the structure affected me badly. The shock of it frightened me, in fact I couldn't understand how anyone could do such a thing.

What we found inside the tunnel was as shocking, however I knew the remains next to the residue of decorated coffin were that of Thomas Pope. I was drawn to him anyway, a connection that can't be explained so I wouldn't even try. As for looking back to the former Saxon Kings, that too was fascinating and led me to where I am now. And that's the end of a story that just happened as it's been put down in words.

I have worked from one timeline to another and hope that's not been too confusing but that's how I found each bit of information. What led me to it, well that was a combination of belief there was something to find and a desire to find it in research of history. As for the task I took on from the start, well that's best summed up if I say, "We each find something in life we can't give up everything for, but if we are spiritually drawn to it you will give up everything. Thy Will Be Done."

Acknowledgements

I would like here to acknowledge the work of everyone at Tricorn Books. More personally, my thanks to Dan Bernard and Gail Baird for their encouragement, guidance, and patience.

Thanks too to my virtual secretary Rachel Barbi at team (B), to my family, friends, and colleagues who provided comments help with ideas, and general support.

Thanks to Gary, my brother, sister June and our uncle Ramon Gingel for their collective memories of our ancestors.

I would like to thank Adrian and Shannon Abbott for their work with historical investigations, and Adrian's work with me in search for what, at the time, was just historic hearsay.

My thanks to all the visitors from the village and other far-off places for their gift of time to me; it was invaluable.

I must mention the collective personal written accounts of the local history of the late Miss Gwen Houghton and Mrs Vera (Pat) Cox; following their lead was encouraging, and so too was the advice given to me by my late friend and musical director, Mrs Catherine Mc Clerg. These three ladies helped me long after their demise.

The foundation and inspiration for this work began many years ago, and I have my parents to thank for that, and it is to them I dedicate this book. My father, Leonard Charles Prowting and my mother, Inez Thelma Hazalean Prowting, née Gingel.